Praise for *Stand a Little Out of My Sun*

"An elegant…compelling multigenerational drama…the text is entertaining and vibrant, rich with details of Greek American culture, '50s and '60s Chicago."
—*Kirkus Reviews*

Kirkus Reviews - featured in the June 2021 edition…One of the *Top Indie Summer Reads.*

Winner - *National Indie Excellence Awards 2021*: Category: General Fiction

"This uplifting 1950s coming-of-age saga demonstrates how courage, compassion, and faith can overcome emotional adversity. Visual artist, Voss's moving debut novel portrays an immigrant family's struggles and triumphs with the same warmth and emotional depth that resonate in her paintings. This intergenerational story spans eras and locations, but it transitions between them with smooth clarity."
— *BookLife Review & Publisher's Weekly Magazine*

"In her debut novel, Greek-American Author, Angelyn Christy Voss, draws on her experiences growing up in an immigrant family on Chicago's Southeast side. Set in the 1950s, cultures and generations collide in a story of love, betrayal, loss, community, redemption, and the true meaning of family."
— Maria Karamitsos, author, publisher, editor of the *Windy City Greek*

"The author paints a vivid picture of the East Side, with its vibrant, colorful neighborhoods, and passionate voices of familiar characters."
—Antigone Polite, Greek Chicagoan, pharmacist

"The setting is so well realized in Angelyn Voss's riveting novel that I now feel familiar with the East Side of Chicago during the 1950s. The reader is immediately drawn into the joys and tragedy of an amazing immigrant Greek family. The first generation, while clinging to their old ways, teaches a moving lesson of forgiveness and understanding."
—Margaret J. Anderson, book club member, author, *Searching for Shona, From a Place Far Away,* and *In the Keep of Time*

"The author's flowing prose awakens all the senses and immerses the reader in time and place, making her characters come alive and win the reader's heart."

—Nancy Chesnutt Matsumoto, poet, middle school teacher

"*Stand a Little Out of My Sun* is a beautifully gripping story told in a style reminiscent of, *A Tree Grows in Brooklyn*. The characters jumped out of the pages and into my heart. This novel made me laugh out loud, cry tears of grief, cry tears of joy, and ultimately shared the hope of redemption and forgiveness. The beauty of the author's words transported me into a time and place beyond my imagination. The sights, smells, and feelings allowed me to become a part of the world she shared in her novel. It was an unexpected delight to read this book that touched me so deeply."

—Janell Stevens, writer, book club member

"I cheered for the characters from beginning to the end."

—Patti Kimberly, teacher and avid reader

"This powerful, touching tale challenges the reader to imagine forgiveness under the most impossible circumstances. It's the best novel I've read this year."

—Pat Eshleman, Clinical Research Director, RN

The **Timberline Review**, a publication of *Willamette Writers* in the Pacific Northwest has featured an excerpt of *Stand a Little Out of My Sun* in their Spring/Summer issue.

Stand a Little Out of My Sun

Angelyn Christy Voss

Angelyn Christy Voss

Nature's Light Press
Corvallis OR

Nature's Light Press
Corvallis OR 97333
www.NaturesLightPress.com
www.angelynchristyvoss.com

ISBN 978-1-7347260-0-8 print book
ISBN 978-1-7347260-1-5 ebook

Cover Illustration – Angelyn Christy Voss, artist
Cover & Interior Design – Anita Jones, Another Jones Graphics

This book is a work of fiction. All characters and events portrayed in this novel are products of the author's imagination or are used fictitiously.

Publisher's Cataloging-In-Publication Data
(Prepared by The Donohue Group, Inc.)

Names: Voss, Angelyn Christy, author.
Title: Stand a little out of my sun / Angelyn Christy Voss.
Description: Corvallis, OR : Nature's Light Press, [2020]
Identifiers: ISBN 9781734726008 (print) | ISBN 9781734726015 (ebook)
Subjects: LCSH: Greek-Americans--Family relationships--Fiction. | Brothers
    and sisters--Fiction. | Family-owned business enterprises--Illinois--
    Chicago--Fiction. | Chicago (Ill.)--History--20th century--Fiction. |
    LCGFT: Historical fiction.
Classification: LCC PS3622.O83 S73 2020 (print) | LCC PS3622.O83
    (ebook) | DDC 813/.6--dc23

Printed in the United States of America

Dedication

This book is dedicated to all teachers. There is no greater calling than to help a young mind grow.

For George – husband, encourager, and best friend

And a special dedication to Paul, Jenny, Hannah, Ellen, Tim, Scott, Megan, Abby, Kate, Benjamin, and Elizabeth

List of Characters

Sophie and Niko
Siblings
Yiayia Sophia and Papou George
Grandparents

Christina – Ma
Sophie and Niko's Mother
Tom – Pa
Sophie and Niko's Father
Anna, Alexander, and Demetri
Christina's Siblings
Mildred and Maisie
Tom's Mother and Sister Respectively

Elena and Vasilios Giannakopoulos Ioannou
Yiayia Sophia's Parents
Alexandria, Andrew, Angeline, and Theodore
Yiayia Sophia's Siblings

Cousin George and Cousin Angie
Sophie and Niko's Cousins

Thea Stefania
Sophie and Niko's Aunt
Thea Toula
*Yiayia Sophia's Cousin. Sophie, Niko and Cousins call her, Thea
(out of respect)*
Theo Taki
Yiayia Sophia's Cousin. Tom's shifty business sidekick

Noops
Niko's Best Friend
Vitto
Neighborhood Bad Guy
John Bernaski
East Side Police Sergeant
Johnny
Young neighbor of Christina's family, later Poulos family member

Bernetha Jones
Christina's childhood friend
Beth Goldman and Mary McCorley
Christina's Army friends at Langley Field, Va.
Colonel James Reynolds
Pilot in the Royal Air Force

Emerson and Jim
Sympathetic prison workers
Margaret Edwards
Sophie's friend in Oregon
Sam Tucker and Johnny Tucker
Sinister characters
Peggy
Sophie's college roommate
George Littlefox
Sophie's love

Contents

Stand a Little Out of My Sun

1981

*S*ophie had arranged her life to set aside painful memories of her little brother, but something switched on like an unwanted light when she knelt down in front of her new student. *What is it about this boy's face?* With a broad smile he said, "Ah be Henry! Yes ah is! Henry *B.* Jackson," nodding once to punctuate the importance of his name. Her heart faltered, and for a moment, space seemed to tilt. That's what Noops used to say! "Ah be Noops! Yes ah is!" And that brought back memories of her brother, Niko, and his friend Noops Potter.

Sophie steadied herself and took his small hand. "Hello, Henry."

She muddled her way through the day, like a distant figure with the classroom in the foreground. The children sat at her feet, faces eager and scared. Sophie smiled and said things a kindergarten teacher says to calm and guide them, but she found herself staring at Henry, his wide eyes, and his spindly legs sticking out of too-big shorts. She clutched the small medallion that hung from a chain around her neck, and rubbed her thumb over and over its familiar contours.

During recess, she watched and listened as the children invited Henry to play, but they couldn't understand most of what he said. *Was Henry sent to me? I need to help him and figure out what he's saying.*

Enough years had gone by for her to regard the events that led to her family's undoing with a semblance of peace, but this encounter with Henry brought it all back. Sophie's resolve could not shelter her from raw memories.

The flinty smell of steel and motor oil in the garage, the way Niko's eyes got the same hard flash as their father's, his torn black shirt—it all came back and split her heart down the middle. Sophie had known something was wrong when he looked down and wouldn't meet her eyes, but she couldn't pry a thing out of him. Instead, he unloaded his secrets on Noops. Most people couldn't follow what Noops said, so words stayed safe within his innocence.

PART ONE

1

The Elephant Talked
and the Boy Understood

Nothing is ever lost to us as long as we remember it.
— L.M. Montgomery, *The Story Girl*

1956

*I*n the humid heat waves on that sizzling June day in 1956 when the air swelled and the tar bubbled on the sealed cracks in the streets, twelve-year-old Sophie, her little brother, and their grandparents went to Brookfield Zoo.

The kids left their grandparents fanning themselves on a bench under a shady elm and ran down the gravelly footpath to the Pachyderm House. They kicked up gray dust as the gravel crunched under their feet. When they slid to a stop, Sophie lifted her chin and sniffed the elephant air. It smelled heavy, like honey, and musty dirt.

Niko stared at the elephant closest to them. The elephant stared back with its penetrating brown eye. Niko cocked his head sideways and then hummed a strange low tone in his throat. He took two steps back and lobbed his peanut bag into the enclosure. It landed on the rocky edge of the barrier moat. Sophie stood a minute, balancing on one foot, then the other, ready to admonish Niko, but she waited. The elephant lumbered over to the bag of peanuts. It stopped, eyed the children with calm indifference, and blew the red-and-white-striped bag to the side with a huff. Niko gripped the railing and leaped up stiff-armed to get a better look. The elephant swept the peanuts into a neat pile with its trunk's delicate fingerlike protrusion, and managed to lift every last one into its mouth.

"Wow," said Niko, grinning like the cleverest monkey in the tree. "Did ya see that, Sophie?"

"I did, but Niko…"

"She told me to throw my peanuts to her, so I did!" He jumped down from the railing and snapped his suspenders.

"How did she tell you?"

"Gee whiz, Sophie. Didn't ya hear her?" he asked. "She rumbled deep down in her throat and told me to."

Sophie sized him up and believed him. Sometimes she wondered if his imagination answered for him, but she knew her eight-year-old brother felt things instinctively, as if he had an advantage over most living creatures. His tousled curls, the color of brown shoe polish, sprouted every which way from under his Cubs baseball cap. She tore her eyes away from him, and for a moment, time crumpled in on itself.

Thinking of the fight at the breakfast table that very morning made Sophie shudder and dig her nails into her palms. Her Pa slammed his hand on the table because his toast was burnt around the edges. Ma yelled. He flung the toast at her and Niko started crying. Sophie screamed, "Stop!" Pa narrowed his smoldering eyes at her and Ma fluttered her hands. Niko bolted out the back door.

Mostly it was stupid stuff that set them off, like the toast, or forgetting to drag the stinkin' garbage barrel out to the street for pickup, or Pa calling Ma names like "ignorant Greek."

Sophie was determined to wear a calm face for Niko, but all that stuffed-inside anger hurt her chest, as if it could crack her ribs. She looked back at the elephant and watched it sway in contentment on thick padded feet and half-moon toenails. Tenderness for the elephant surged in Sophie as it flapped its speckled ears.

Niko slid down the metal railing on both forearms and followed the elephant along as it joined her companions.

The atmosphere changed when they heard a man holler, "Hey, you kids!"

Sophie and Niko whirled around and saw a zookeeper storming towards them. They caught a second wind of swearing, and Niko inched backwards into Sophie. She put her hands on his shoulders.

The zookeeper planted himself in front of the kids and eyed them as if they were criminals. Sophie stared. His brown hat looked like a cop's hat minus the checkerboard part above the bill. The pockets of his khaki trousers bulged.

"Doncha read the signs?" he said. "No-feeding-the-animals."

Sophie's eyes grew sharp and she crossed her arms hard against her chest. Niko took one step forward, stretched out his arms, and said, "But Mr. Zoo-man, she *asked* me for the peanuts."

Something about the way Niko said that, with uttermost sincerity, seemed to poke holes in the zookeeper's resolve. A faint line appeared on his forehead when he raised his eyebrows and smiled. He rocked back on his heels and said, "Well, young man, she may have told you, but make sure you don't do it again."

Niko bobbed his head in agreement while crossing his fingers behind his back. "Uh…I'll remember," he said with a dimpled smile.

"Okay, good," said the man. "Now run along."

The kids turned on their heels and started walking towards their grandparents. Sophie gave her brother a swift looking-over. "You're some smooth talker." He snapped his suspender and gave her a sly grin.

He leaned towards Sophie, like temptation being the most delicious item on the menu, and said, "Hey, Sophie, let's ask Yiayia and Papou to buy us another bag of peanuts."

"You're pushing your luck, Niko." But for a long, wonderful moment, she visualized both of them throwing bags of peanuts to every elephant in the enclosure.

Niko picked up a round pebble and pitched it at a nearby tree. Sprinting after it he called back, "Well, it *would* be fun!"

Their grandparents hadn't moved an inch from the shade of the sprawling elm. Sophie felt a whispery rustle of breeze in the tree when they got closer.

"Here you are, *pethia*!" said Yiayia, unscrewing the lid of a thermos. Sweat glistened like tiny beads on her forehead. "Did you see the elephants?"

"Yep," said Niko. "One ate some of my peanuts."

"Well," said Sophie, grinning sideways. "One ate a lot of his peanuts."

Yiayia's eyes crinkled at the corners behind thick-lensed glasses. "*Bravo*, Niko." She pulled some paper cups out of a bag on the bench and poured icy lemonade for all of them. "Squeezed the lemons this morning. This will cool you off."

"Ooo," said Papou, waving his straw Panama hat in front of his face. "It's one of those hot dog days."

Yiayia dropped her chin and looked over her glasses. "You mean dog-hot days, Pa."

"Okay, Ma, dog-hot," he exclaimed, slapping his knee.

Sophie regarded Papou. His snow-white moustache and eyebrows looked striking against his dark olive skin. He had a circlet of thick, wavy hair, and when he walked, his noble carriage and the size of his frame bespoke a proud Spartan heritage. Besides his sparkling eyes and good humor there was something else. The physical effect of his kindness made Sophie want to be near him.

When they finished their lemonade, Yiayia stood up and discreetly ruffled the hem of her flowered dress to fan her sweaty legs. She pointed into the distance and said, "Look at those faraway clouds. I smell rain coming."

"Time to go, kids," said Papou. "We gotta get to the store and help Thea Stefania get ready for flippin' the Monday hamburgers."

"What are we doing next Sunday?" asked Sophie.

Papou pushed the brim of his hat up and smiled. "We need be in the store so's Thea Stefania can visit her ailin' ma in Kankakee. But in two weeks, the surprise with cousins."

"Oh boy!" said Niko as he danced a little jig. "I can't wait!"

"Tell us, Papou!" said Sophie.

His smiling gaze traveled from one to the other. He stroked his moustache and said, "You's see!"

"Let's walk by the monkeys on the way out to the car," said Yiayia. "That baby orangutan makes me laugh with its stick-up orange hair."

"Can I sit up front with you and Papou?" Sophie asked.

"Hey, no fair, Sophie!" said Niko.

Sophie grabbed his wrist to slow him down. She whispered close to his ear, "Do ya want to go home?"

He glared at her and said, "NO, but you're squeezin' my arm!"

She let go of him and said, "I didn't mean to, Niko. You can have the whole back seat to yourself and play with your cars."

Niko gave her a cockeyed smile and said, "Oh. Okay."

They climbed into the car and Sophie snuggled between her plump grandparents. Sophie breathed in their smell. Papou smelled like spent cigars; Yiayia, a mixture of lemons with earthy sweat. She watched a ladybug creep along the gridded roadways on a Chicago city map resting on the dashboard. The ladybug stopped, fluttered its beetle wings, and rubbed its hind legs together. It went into a strange tailspin and smacked into the windshield. Sophie coaxed it into her hand and let it fly out the passenger window.

The hot air folded in waves over the roadway, and distant buildings quavered in the blistering heat. Sophie tugged on the hem of her pedal pushers and opened the Nancy Drew book on her lap. The words blurred together and her head buzzed.

Sophie glanced away from her book, trying to fight down the jitters. She took a slow breath and whispered, "Yiayia, uh...I've been thinking. Can Niko and I live with you and Papou?" She looked over at her grandmother with large, tired-looking eyes. She tried not to sound whiny. "Please can we?"

Yiayia raised her eyebrows and her glasses slipped down. She turned to face her granddaughter. "Why do you ask to live with us?" For a couple of seconds there was nothing but road noise and a heavy, painful silence. "Is there something wrong at home?"

Sophie's ears reddened and she could feel her pulse quicken. She sat up straight and starched. Her eyes darted back to the book. "No, but I…I just think it would be nice," she said. "Besides, our cousins are always at your place. We could play, clean the apartment, and help you in the kitchen."

"Your Ma and Pa would miss having you home with them."

"No, they wouldn't! They could see us anytime! I know it would work!"

"Sophie, you would tell me if something were bad for you and Niko, right?"

Sophie hesitated. "I…I would," she said, looking down at her sweaty palms. But how could she tell Yiayia about the vile way her parents fought—her Pa's drinking? He hated the Greek family like they were something beneath him, and that put a gnawing sting inside her heart. She swallowed hard and a lump in her throat burned.

Yiayia Sophia tilted her granddaughter's chin with her fingertips and met her eyes. "Don't you's be afraid to talk to me about anything."

"Okay."

Sophie noticed the lines around Yiayia's eyes deepen.

Yiayia Sophia spread her hands over Sophie's. "When I was a young bird, my ma told me I was like a loaf of bread," she said. "The crust is golden, the insides delicious. To make bread, the right ingredients are measured into a bowl, stirred with a strong wooden spoon, and then kneaded into a ball. The dough is covered with cloth and kept warm. It rises proud but gets punched down. It goes in a pan and wants to rise again. How will it come out of the oven, I ask you? Sophie, you are becoming a nice loaf of bread. I know, I see."

She turned to face Sophie and smoothed back her dark chestnut hair. "You have the eyes of Byzantium."

Sophie reached up and turned the rearview mirror towards her face. She studied her brown, dark-rimmed eyes. "What does that mean?" she asked.

"Fire in your eyes."

Sophie sat up and kissed her grandmother's cheek.

Yiayia returned the kiss on the palm of her hand and turned to stare out the window at a passing Greyhound bus—the stretched-out dog running along the shiny corrugated siding. The rumbling tires filled her ears. A forlorn-looking woman on the bus sat with her forehead pressed against the window. Yiayia's hand went to her chest, seeing that hangdog look, just like Sophie's Pa. She breathed in deep.

"In the mountains of Tripoli, in the Peloponnese, my family picked the olives for food and oil. My ma, your Great-Yiayia Elena, hung olive branches over the front door of our little stone house for *Theos* (God) to protect it. I was just seven years old when my family sailed on the big ship to America. Ma brought an olive branch to put over our door in Chicago.

"I will tell you the legend of wise Athena. She gave the people of Greece a great gift: the first olive tree. Before the Golden Age of Greece, the Persian Army set Athens on fire. The people came back to their ruined, scorched-up city and saw that Athena's olive tree had already grown a sturdy new branch. They raised their fists and built their city back up, even better than before. Sophie, you're strong like the olive branch and the bread. Remember who you are, Spartan from the Poulos side, and my people from Tripoli. With *Theos*'s help, we never give up."

The car went through a short lit-up tunnel. The light made a mirror out of the window glass, and Sophie could see their mingled images. She hugged her arms to her chest.

"A long time before you were born, Papou came to America with his family when he was sixteen years old and started working at the steel mill when he was seventeen. He shoveled the coke into furnaces through the clouds of smoke and metal dust. When we married, he'd come home dragging, stiff-haired, gray-faced, with black soot so deep in his ears he couldn't scrub it out. I ironed clothes for people, he shoveled the coke, and we scraped together money to open the little wooden hamburger shack on the corner of 106th and Ewing. Now look…East Side Hamburgers! A brick store with a soda fountain!"

Yiayia bent forward and looked around Sophie to see the effect of her words on her husband's face. He smiled. She clasped her hands on her ample belly.

Sophie pulled on a thread from the bottom edge of her sleeveless blue-and-white-striped blouse and leaned into her grandmother. "I like your stories, Yiayia."

"Ptew, PTEW!" Yiayia pretended to spit on her fingers as a finishing touch to her words. "Now the evil *mati* won't get you."

They lapsed into silence and listened to Greek Hour on the radio.

When they got to the Southeast Side, their car jolted to a stop at the flashing crossing gates in front of the Ewing Avenue Bridge spanning the Calumet River.

Papou turned to his wife. "Uh-oh," he whispered.

Niko rocked from side to side and made a muffled sound through his hands. He tried to be brave, but he fell down onto the backseat floor and scrunched into a ball. He clamped his hands over his ears and moaned, "Papou! Why does it hafta open now?"

"Because the boats," said Papou in a soothing voice. "Look out the side window, Niko! A proud little tugboat push a big freighter ship! Coal, coke, iron ore, and limestone to make the steel."

Niko rose up slow and easy. He peeked out the side through little slits between his fingers and saw huge storage silos along the river. A mountain of coarse salt rose up almost as high as the silos to help melt the ice-coated streets and sidewalks on winter days. The red-white-and-black tugboat puffed and nudged the ship along. The freighter blew its throaty horn.

"I like boats, but I *hate* the bridge!" He hunkered back down on the floor and clapped his hands over his ears in anticipation of the thunderous noise to come.

The street on the bridge split in half, and each side lifted one hundred feet into the sky. Heavy vibrations rattled the car. Sophie blinked her eyes at the massive wall of road rising up before them.

"A pony truss bascule bridge, kids," said Papou. "Is good."

Sophie turned to Papou and smiled, knowing how much he loved bridges. He named the type of every bridge they crossed over in Chicago.

"Niko," said Papou. "Someday, you look."

A small, subdued voice said, "I don't think so."

"Is okay."

The boats chugged past, and the two halves of the bridge folded back together. Niko popped up and wrapped his arms across Papou's chest.

In the darkening sky, Sophie saw the flaming smokestacks of the steel mills light up the night on the East Side. Republic and U.S. Steel's open-hearth furnaces—the low, somber hum of all machines working, churning, never ceasing, hung in the air. Silhouettes of grain elevators and factory smokestacks stood like guards over the Chicago landscape. Each stack gave birth to its own cloud of acrid, metallic smoke, which plumed up high into the sky and enveloped their corner of the city. Ash and grit from the factories and mills dusted the roofs, windowsills, and sidewalks like a sooty veil.

Today, there was peace for Sophie, but the anguish, calmed when she was with her relatives, would come back at home with the fighting. It felt like the choking air from the smokestacks seeped straight into the cracks of her home.

But as they neared home, a whisper of hope came over her. There was something about her parents when brief moments of peace rained down, like they had never fought hard or fierce. She walked in on them one evening while they danced lightly in their stocking feet around the kitchen table to "Singin' in the Rain" on the radio. She had smiled a happy, bashful smile and wondered, *Why can't it just stay this way? Maybe they won't fight tonight.*

⁓

Heat built up in the night sky, and the earlier clouds gave way to a crackling thunderstorm. Sophie woke up with a start, drenched in sweat. She rubbed her eyelids with stiff fingertips, raised herself up on her elbow, and turned to look at her bedside clock. The glowing hands on her Baby Ben alarm clock read 11:55. Rain belted sideways against her bedroom window. She got up, looked out at the drowned sky, and watched the wind whip the tree branches in her backyard.

The streetlight's glow made the sheets of rain look silvery. Sophie huddled down on her knees and opened the window a couple of inches. A spray of rain misted her face.

Just then, she heard house-rattling pounding on the back screen door. Her father's voice rose above the storm. "Damn it, Christina! Get your butt down here and unlock this door!"

Sophie shivered and twisted a chunk of her hair. She turned and stared at the crack of dim light underneath the door. *Jerk. He better not wake Niko up.* There was nothing to separate the rooms in their house but the thinnest of plaster walls.

Real easy, she tiptoed to her bedroom door and cracked it open. She saw Ma poised at the top of the stairs in her blue cotton nightgown, gripping the stair railing with both hands, rocking back and forth. Sophie waited until Ma got all the way down the stairs and then sneaked down after her. The plank steps groaned while she crept, and she could hear her own uneven breathing. She tiptoed down the hallway and peeked around the corner to see Pa stumble though the door, clutching his beat-up leather suitcase. She bit her bottom lip hard.

"Well, look who's here, soaked to the gills and smellin' like a goddamn tavern," mocked Ma. "You and Jack Daniels!" She threw her head back and laughed.

"Get outta my way, woman!" shouted Tom as he pushed past her. He smacked his hip hard against the sideboard and swore blue sparks into the dim light.

Sophie backed up the stairs quickly, with anger working its way up her neck. With a trembling hand she cracked Niko's door open and could hear rain gushing through a downspout outside his window. Mercifully, he was sound asleep. She closed his door, went into the bathroom, and yanked a towel off its hook. She kneeled down in front of Niko's room, rolled the towel lengthwise and shoved it under the door. *Stay asleep.*

Her parents kept going at it. Rage seized in her chest. It built in Sophie like a flash and felt plain dangerous. She ran downstairs, burst into the kitchen, and screamed, "Stop it, you damn idiots!"

Tom jerked around. His lips pursed white with rage. "What did you say?" he snarled.

"I…I said you're idiots!" Her heart thumped like a locomotive. "You're gonna wake Niko up! Have you seen his hands? He's biting his fingernails bloody because of you two!"

Tom stormed across the kitchen and slammed Sophie against the wall. He raised the back of his hand to slap her. She flinched sideways. Christina drew in a sharp breath. Tom stopped short.

Deliverance? Sophie didn't care. She clenched her jaw, narrowed her eyes, and turned back to face him.

He dropped his voice down. "You…you keep your goddamn mouth shut and remember our business stays here!"

"Don't ya tell your grandparents!" pleaded Christina.

Something like a roar filled Sophie's head. Dizzy. She bore her eyes into Christina's with disgust, then turned on her heel and stormed up the stairs.

In bed, she clamped the pillow over her head and choked on her tears. Sophie spent the rest of the night in a fitful sleep.

2
Spark Plugs

We can easily forgive a child who is afraid of the dark;
the real tragedy of life is when men are afraid of the light.

— Plato

The next morning, Niko peeked around the corner of their detached garage, clutching his toy gyroscope. His father was lying on a rolling wooden pallet under a jacked-up Buick. His work boots and the turned-up cuffs of his blue overalls were all that stuck out. Niko heard the metal clatter of tools.

Sophie walked behind Niko and tapped him on the shoulder. He whipped around and met her eyes.

"You scared me!" he whispered.

She took his hand and pulled him around the corner of the garage. In a low voice, she said, "I wouldn't go in there if I were you."

"How come?"

"Niko…you know how Pa is. He can be a jerk, and he'll go crazy if you bug him. He came home late last night and…" Her voice trailed off.

"And what?"

"And…nothing! Just stay away from him."

"I *won't* bug him! I just want to watch! Pa knows everything about cars and electricity and stuff. He's smart!"

Her deep-seeing eyes rested on him. "I wouldn't if I were you."

"Gee whiz, Sophie, it'll be okay!"

Sophie gave him a long, steady look that radiated waves of disapproval. "Just leave if he gets mean."

Niko rolled his eyes, turned, and walked away.

"Pa? Hey, Pa?" asked Niko in a small voice. "Can I, um, watch you? I promise not to bother you." No answer. "Pa, can you hear me?"

His father slammed the floor with the heel of his boot. "Why aren't you playing with your friends?" he asked in a gruff voice from under the car.

"Um, because I want to see what you're doin' with the cars. I like cars. Maybe I can help you."

Tom grunted.

Niko shifted from foot to foot, feeling erased. He stopped moving and studied a gold ribbon of sunlight on the cement floor for a minute. A squadron of little black ants moving up a wooden leg of the workbench caught his eye. He spun the little silver wheel of his gyroscope with his finger and waited.

"Pa. I'm almost nine years old. I can do anything you tell me to do."

Tom slid out from under the car. His face and hands were smudged with grease. He pushed round safety goggles to his forehead. Niko felt pinned to the wall by his father's cold blue eyes. His heart sank.

"Sit over there on that stool and keep your mouth shut while I'm working on this engine. I got a business to run."

Niko sprang up to his feet. "I will, Pa!" He climbed up on a tall wooden stool and sat with his hands clasped on his lap. He took a quick breath. "Pa, just ask me to get ya anything and I can do it!"

Tom gave the back tire of the car a firm kick, swore something unintelligible, and got back under the car. Niko didn't move, and after a minute Tom muttered, "You sit there and I'll think about it. Say one more word or touch anything, you're outta here."

Niko cast his eyes sideways for a moment and bit the inside of his cheek. He got off the stool and scooted it to the worktable. A Banner's Tavern ashtray with stubbed-out cigarettes sat to the side. He wrinkled his nose. All the crumpled cigarette butts were the same size, angled in the same direction.

Tools were arranged neatly on the table. *Motor's Auto Repair Manual*, tattered and frayed around the edges, rested against the wall. Little stuff like screws, nuts, bolts, and nails were in labeled wooden drawers. Electrical cables in wound-up bundles dangled from nails on the wall. Wrenches hung in precision from smallest to biggest on a pegboard.

He rested his elbows on the scratched wooden table and propped his chin with both hands. Three-dimensional pencil drawings of car parts and black-and-white photos of airplanes were tacked all over the wall. He leaned forward and studied the intricate drawings. Niko's lips moved, but his "wow" was inaudible. In one photo he saw both parents dressed in their soldier's uniforms standing next to a big silver plane with a sideways tail that looked like a dog's bone. Pa had an arm draped over Ma's shoulder. A small hand-printed quote next to the photos caught Niko's eye.

The skies are painted with unnumbered sparks. They are all fire, and every one doth shine. Julius Caesar, Shakespeare.

He held his gaze around the words and read them again.

The pleasant smell of flinty steel, tires, and grease filled his head. For a solid hour, Niko watched his Pa's quick, purposeful movements. His rapt attention to detail and sure, steady hands under the hood of the car were captivating.

Pa got into the driver's seat, started the engine, and backed the car a few feet out of the garage. A cloud of blue oily smoke billowed into the air. Within a few minutes, the radiator cap began to wobble and steam started to whoosh out. He switched off the engine and unscrewed the cap with the tips of his fingers, jerking his hand away to escape the hot burst of steam. A hollow bubbling sound came out. With swift movements he reached into the back of his overalls for a small wrench and tightened the clamps on the radiator hoses. Sweat began to bead under his eyes and on his nose. He wiped his forehead with the back of his hand.

Niko looked up smiling at the crisscross rafters of the garage, and it seemed to him the whole canopy of heaven.

Tom stole a quick glance at Niko looking up. His eyes warmed. "Hey, Niko," he said in an easy way. "Aren't you tired of sitting there?"

"Nope. I like to watch." He drew his knees up and hugged them with his arms, making a shelf for his chin to rest on.

A half hour later, Sophie walked into the garage with an air of detached interest. Niko jiggled on his stool and gave her a grin. A shaft of sunlight lit the back of her head and shined golden on her hair.

She stood there a moment staring at him. Niko saw her brows knit together.

Tom looked up from the Buick's engine and said, "Hey, Sophie. What've you been up to?"

His question startled her, as if nothing had happened the night before. Her simmering, defiant eyes bore into him. "Why do *you* want to know?"

Tom raked his hand through his sweaty hair. "Because, I like to know what you're up to." His voice sounded like a cold wind.

She crossed her arms and looked sideways at him. "Yiayia needed me at the store."

"Figures," he said.

She let out a slow breath through her pursed lips. "Niko, Ma wants you to help shell peas."

"Time for you to go," said Pa.

"Can I watch you tomorrow?"

He smiled. "We'll see."

⟶

The next morning, Niko tiptoed into the garage from the open side door. The headlights of the Buick hung down on the front fender like popped-out eyeballs. Tom straddled a short wooden stool and was fiddling with the wires. He wore a light blue T-shirt and brown work pants held up by brown suspenders that crisscrossed on his back. A greasy rag hung out of his back pocket.

"Pa?"

Tom jerked his head up and his eyes shot holes into Niko. "Hey! Knock before you come in!"

Niko recoiled and said, "But, the door...oh...okay."

Tom swept his hand over to the side and said, "Learn the names of all those tools on the workbench. When you have them memorized, leave. Say one word and you're gone. Understand?"

"Yes, sir."

"I'll test you on the names of the tools tomorrow."

Niko clambered onto the tall stool and counted nineteen tools neatly lined up, with cut-up paper labels under each. The even writing on the labels looked crisp. His eyebrows came together, and his body went rigid. *I gotta learn them,* he whispered to himself.

He silently read the labels: ratchet, flex-head ratchet, sockets, regular pliers, angled needle-nose pliers, spark plug pliers, spark plug spacers, vise grip, breaker bar, extension bar, hammers, rubber mallet, ball-pein hammer. Screwdrivers: torx, stubbed, heavy-duty flathead. Wire lock-picking tool. Pry bar, and extension bar.

Niko heard a tap-tap sound on the window and looked up. A little sparrow sat on the sill and tapped away. Niko smiled. The sparrow cocked its head at the boy and took off.

He picked up each tool with care and felt its weight in his hands. He traced the shape with his finger and said its name in his head, over and over, forwards and backwards. Eyes closed, he felt the tools and mouthed their names without a sound. He turned the labels over and double-checked himself.

After an hour of studying, he slumped down and buried his head in the crook of his elbow. Within the minute he felt the light around him change. He looked up. The streaming sunlight was blocked by a shadow. He shivered, feeling Pa's eyes bore into his back. He clenched his teeth, turned slowly, and met Tom's eyes.

"Pa! Can't you see I'm trying to learn!" Niko said with force, punctuating each word. "Stand a little out of my sun!" Tom's eyes widened. He stepped aside and turned away.

Niko jumped off the stool, slipped out of the garage, and raced down Ewing Avenue, past the modest bungalows to the business area. Sparse blades of grass and weeds grew in the cracks of the sidewalks. Tiny anthills of fine, scratched-up dirt sprouted from the cracks. He zigzagged over them, being sure not to crush any.

He slowed to a walk. The buildings reminded Niko of an ever-changing carnival. Gene's wooden newsstand looked like a giant green cardboard box with a reach-through flap. The *Chicago Tribune*, *Sun-Times*, and *Daily Herald* were stacked high in their wire racks on the sidewalk. He skirted around a metal placard advertising S&H green stamps in front of Robnett's Hardware Store. He heard the cash register ping inside. People moved slowly and flicked flies in the sweltering shade of the storefronts.

Several bars had opened their doors to the hot afternoon, and the familiar smell of stale beer, cigarettes, and men's sweat filled his nostrils. A stinky old man lay sleeping on one of the scarred benches, with a newspaper spread open across his face. His withered hands looked like white chalk.

A giant jar filled to the brim with dill pickles caught Niko's eye in the window of Kornblatt's Deli. He stopped and poked his head into the open doorway to get a better look at the waist-high jar. The inside of the store smelled like toast and weenies.

"Hey, Niko!" yelled Mr. Kornblatt from behind the bread case. "Want a pickle? Only a nickel!" Mr. Kornblatt's roguish dark eyes gleamed, and his teeth peeked through his bushy moustache.

"Naw, I don't like 'em, but that's the biggest pickle jar I ever saw!" he said.

"You bet! Biggest one ever! Those pickles will fly out the door. You'll see. Hey, say hi to your grandparents for me!"

"Yeah, I will," he said, waving. "Bye, Mr. Kornblatt!"

Niko ran to the three-storied redbrick fire station and looked up. The fancy trimming on the top of Station 74 looked like the curved turret of a castle.

He walked to the corner of Ewing and Avenue N, touched a telephone pole streaked with black creosote, circled the block, and started to run back home. The sunbaked sidewalk felt hot under his sneakers. He leaped over a square of cement glittered with shards of broken glass.

His breath came fast and his legs burned when he rounded the last corner. He plopped down on the grass next to the red fire hydrant and pressed his shoe against the bolted base. The dry grass felt prickly on his bare legs. Niko lay back and studied the delicate leaves of the tree in his small front yard. He pulled the frayed string from his gyroscope out of his pocket and wove it over and around three fingers. His breathing came easier.

Niko sat up straight when a black Buick with flashy chrome fenders motored down the street and turned into his driveway. A hefty red-faced man wearing a wrinkled black Sunday suit got out of the car. The suit didn't fit him very well and his pockets bulged. A big gold watch-chain hanging out of his coat pocket glinted in the sun. The man strutted over to Pa like one of those little bantam roosters Niko had seen at a fruit stand in the country, only this guy was big. Pa said, "Vitto," and shook his hand, but Niko could see his back stiffen. The rooster-man poked his smoking cigar in the direction of the car sitting halfway out of the garage.

A ragged feeling caught hold inside his chest. *Vitto! He's the bad guy Yiayia said to run away from! What's Pa doing with him?*

Vitto raised his voice. "Taki said you was the man for these jobs, so ya better not make a liar outta him." Tom stepped back, gave him a serious nod, and mumbled something. Vitto punched his fist into the palm of his other hand. Darkness entered Niko's chest, and for a few frightening seconds he wondered if the man would hit Pa. Niko stood up, balled his fists, and stared at the man until he got back in his car. Vitto turned his black eyes to Niko and scowled. He flicked his cigar ashes out the window.

When Niko walked back into the garage, he kept his eyes fixed on the cement floor and made his way back to the workbench. He scrunched down on his knees atop the stool, mixed the labels up, and arranged them in a random line. He matched the tool to the label, whispering in his head, and started over again.

After dinner, Niko went back into the garage and worked on his matching game again. This time, he shouted the tools' names at the top of his lungs. He grinned. *I'm ready!*

3
Inside the Trunk

The life of a marionette has grown very tiresome to me and
I want to become a boy, no matter how hard it is.
— Carlo Collodi, *The Adventures of Pinocchio*

The ticking clock felt like a pleasant companion when Niko opened his eyes that next morning. The sun streamed through the window, warm and happy. He bounced out of bed, got dressed, and ran down the stairs to the kitchen. Christina wore a flowered housedress and stood barefoot at the stove, prodding slices of bacon with a fork in the high-sided cast-iron skillet. Sizzling bacon filled his nostrils, and he smiled. The kitchen always seemed like the center of the house to him.

"Hey, Ma! Hey, Sophie!"

Sophie glanced up and said, "Hey, Niko." She twirled a pencil in her hand and went back to reading the comics.

Christina turned and smiled. Tendrils of wavy dark hair spilled out of her loosely crafted bun. "Good morning, sunshine!" she said. "You're up early!"

"Pa needs my help in the garage!"

"You sit down and eat your breakfast first."

"Ma! Can't ya see I'm in a hurry? I'll be back in a few minutes."

"A few minutes will turn into an hour. Eat your breakfast."

He sighed.

Held captive by his Ma, Niko sank down in the chrome-legged chair next to Sophie. Christina coaxed batter from a bowl into the waffle iron with a rubber spatula. She pulled down the lid and set the timer. Niko squirmed in his chair. He lifted his eyes to the ceiling and recited the tools' names in his head until Christina served him. Sophie gave him a sideways glance. He bolted breakfast and shouted, "Done!" He scooted his chair backwards and ran to the back door.

"Why are you in such an all-fired hurry?" Christina asked.

"I got man's work to do, Ma!"

Christina smiled and said, "Bring your dishes to the sink first."

Sophie's lips were tightly compressed when she looked up from the comics.

Niko dumped his plates into the sink and ran out. He rounded the corner of the house and tapped lightly on the side garage door.

"Who is it?"

"It's me, Pa. Can I come in?"

"You just wait!"

Niko heard metal and glass clanking. A minute went by. Tom finally unlocked the door. He stood in a sleeveless white T-shirt and blue ticking overalls. A hazy circle of cigarette smoke hung by the rafters. Niko got a whiff of beer, just like in Banner's Tavern.

"Hey, Pa."

Tom looked down at Niko's worn blue tennis shoes and tangled shoelaces. One sock pulled up, the other drooped over the shoe. He folded his tanned arms across his chest and said, "Are ya ready to tell me the names of the tools without the labels?"

"Ready, Pa." Sweat started to gather at the edges of Niko's hair. He walked over to the workbench and lifted each plier slowly and deliberately. "Angled needle-nose pliers, spark plug pliers, regular pliers."

The side of Tom's mouth twitched in an imperceptible smile. "Good. You got the pliers. Go on."

Niko went on with increased eagerness and picked up his pace as he lifted each tool. He grinned proudly, knowing he got every one right.

Tom put his hand on Niko's shoulder and gave a quick laugh. "I'll keep laying out tools until you know every one in the garage. If ya do good and stay quiet, I might let you help me."

"Ya won't be sorry, Pa. I'm grown up now."

"Humph."

Niko sat down on his stool and watched his father lift a boxy thing from the engine. It dripped with black oil. Tom put it on a rag and started picking it apart, piece by piece.

Niko sat patient, quiet. Within the hour, he felt a change in the air. The garage window went dim and he heard a distant clap of loud, metallic thunder. He looked up at the window and saw the sky broil with dark clouds. Tom worked, unmoved. Niko walked to the side door. Big drops of rain splattered onto the sidewalk. Soon, rain spilled out of the sky, like thousands of water buckets emptying. Sophie's voice rang out above the deluge.

"Niko! Come in the house!"

"Time to go," said Tom.

"Do I have to, Pa?"

Tom flashed his eyes at him. Niko turned and waited at the doorway. In a few minutes, the rain slowed to a steady patter. He dashed to the back door and stopped in his tracks. A scrawny black-and-white cat sat tucked under the eaves in the middle of the doorway. The tip of one of its ears had a bloody, jagged tear. Its fur was crusted and matted with filth. The cat sat there, looking at Niko. It stood up, stretched, and rubbed against his bare leg. Warm splashes of rain fell on both of them.

"Hey, cat," said Niko. He reached down to pet its soggy head. The cat pushed and turned his head into Niko's hand to get his good ear scratched. He picked up the cat and carried it over the threshold into the kitchen. Something delicious, like a buttery chocolate smell, filled the kitchen. Sophie was bending over the open oven, poking at some tin cake pans with a toothpick. A glow of light from the oven shined on her face. Her ponytail was tied back with a thin blue ribbon, and her sandaled feet were brown from the sun.

"Ma! Sophie! Look what I found!"

Sophie turned. Her eyes softened. "Oh, Niko. Where did you find it?"

"Just sitting at the back door!"

She walked over and scratched under the cat's chin. Niko felt a steady purr vibrate in its chest. "Poor thing," Sophie said. "Look at its icky ear. It's so skinny and dirty."

"Where's Ma?" he asked.

"Gone to help Yiayia at the store," she said. "It looks like it's starving. I'll open a can of tuna."

"Maybe we can keep him."

"How do you know it's a boy without looking?"

"I can just tell," he said. "He's a special cat." Sophie watched, admiring Niko because of the way he hugged the filthy cat close to his face. He was always like that. There was the way he talked to the elephant, watched but never stepped on worms or hills of ants, and brought stunned birds back to life. He moved in a tender way with genuine love of all creatures.

The cat plowed through the can of tuna. It purred loudly between gulps. The kids laughed.

"Let's give him a bath," said Sophie. "He stinks."

They carried him upstairs, filled the tub with six inches of warm water, and gently lowered him in. The cat didn't flinch.

Sophie's eyes widened. "I can't believe this cat!"

He sat with a nonchalant expression in the middle of the tub and licked the pads of his front paw. His green eyes looked luminous as they washed him, slow and easy, with warm water and a bar of Ivory soap.

"He likes water!" said Niko. "Listen to 'im purring. I told ya he's a special cat."

The water turned gray, and fleas floated like sprinkles of pepper on the surface. "Yuck!" said Sophie. "Let's hold him down in the water so they drown." Sophie studied his ragged ear and scooped water onto it without touching. "I better put something on his poor ear."

She opened the mirrored door of the medicine cabinet and took out some iodine and a brown bottle of hydrogen peroxide. She studied both bottles in her hands. "I think I'll use this peroxide stuff. It doesn't sting as much." She unscrewed the brown bottle and tipped it upside down on a cotton ball. When she dabbed the cat's ear, the liquid fizzed on the raw part. Sophie winced. The cat gave a chattering meow and shook his head.

They drained the dirty water, rinsed him under the faucet, and wrapped him up like a newborn baby in an old towel. Sophie held him close to her chest and petted the purring cat on his head. Her ponytail hung over her shoulder onto its back. The cat licked her hand with its sandpapery tongue.

"He *is* an amazing cat, Niko."

"Yeah, like the King of Cats!"

"Let's take him on the roof," said Sophie. "The rain stopped."

They climbed out her bedroom window onto the slanting roof. The air smelled fresh to Sophie, and the sandy brown shingles felt warm in the sun. Steam rose up and enveloped the three of them. They unwrapped the cat and took turns cradling him. He slept peacefully in their arms. They picked out some rogue fleas with their fingernails and flicked them in the air.

Niko held a flea close to his eyes and studied it. "It's got strong hopper-legs."

"Look, Niko," said Sophie. "Pinch it between your fingernails like this." She pinched a flea and they heard a tiny crackling sound.

Niko cringed and said, "Naw." He held his hand aloft and the flea sprang up like a miniature acrobat. "Bye-bye, you bloodsucker!"

After a while the cat's fur fluffed out. He looked clean and handsome.

"Look," laughed Sophie. "He's all dressed up in his black-and-white tuxedo."

"Do ya think Ma and Pa will let us keep 'im?"

"I'm thinking Ma will," she said.

They sat with lightness, rehearsing how to ask. When satisfied, Sophie turned and met her brother's happy eyes. "Niko, is Pa treating you okay?"

The smile vanished from his face and his brows knitted together. "I wish you'd shut up and stop buggin' me a zillion times."

Sophie looked at him long and hard. She saw that hard flash in his eyes like Pa's. "What's with 'shut up'? You've never said that to me before."

"What's wrong with 'shut up'?"

"It's not nice, that's what."

Niko lifted his shoulders to his ears. "Yeah, well, Pa says it all the time. He's teaching me all about tools and cars. Pa's smarter than anyone, even smarter than Papou."

"Pa doesn't seem so smart to me, the way he treats everyone and hates our relatives." Her hand tightened around his. "If he treats you mean, get away and tell me."

Niko pulled his hand away and shoved it into his back pants pocket. "He's not gonna treat me bad! Stop sayin' stuff like that about him. Doncha know how good he is at stuff?" His eyes rested on her long and hard. "Hey, why'd you call me in?"

"Because."

⁓

Christina took pity on the skinny little cat and let the kids keep him. The kids agreed on the name, Teddy. Tom ignored the cat and regarded him as a probable troublemaker.

By the end of the week, Niko learned the names of every tool and piece of equipment in the garage. Tom shook his head in wonder. He started giving Niko brusque orders to fetch things and do small jobs. His son kept quiet.

Niko never tired of watching his Pa work. His rangy, muscular body was charged with purpose and energy. He felt proud of his smart, handsome father. His head was dizzy with joy, and his heart swelled.

Whenever the cat wandered into the garage, Tom would stomp his foot and shout, "Get out!" Teddy would stand his ground and scrutinize Tom with a steady, unflustered gaze. He couldn't meet the cat's eyes. "Get your damn cat outta here!"

All the boy would need to say was "Go, Teddy," and the cat would blink good-naturedly and, like vapor, disappear.

———

Tom noticed his son's nimble fingers and capable hands. Niko had the ability to concentrate and complete any tedious task asked of him. An ever-watchful, clever boy, he remembered everything. He only had to be shown how to do things once.

The following week, Tom showed him how to clean built-up carbon off spark plugs with a small wire brush. Tom occasionally sneaked a glance at Niko and smiled to himself. His tousled curls cascaded to just above his eyebrows, and his sneakered feet wrapped around the stool legs. Niko wore blue denim overalls with a rag hanging out of his back pocket, just like his father.

"Look, Pa, these plugs are as good as new, doncha think?"

"Humph."

"Pa, can I set the gap on spark plugs too?" he asked. "Just tell me what numbers to put together on the spacers and I can do it!"

Tom placed a spark plug in the palm of Niko's hand. "Spark plugs on different types of engines have varying spark distances," he told Niko. "Do you see the distance between the center and side electrodes?"

Niko mustered a grown-up voice and said, "I do, Pa."

"When the gap is set just right, the perfect symphony of piston, cylinder, gas, air, and spark makes the engine run."

"Wow, Pa," said Niko dreamily. "It's like magic."

Tom showed him how to run the metal spacers through the gap. "You want the gauge to go through fairly easily, just catching the electrodes as it passes. I'll write the numbers down for the space on different spark plugs and you go ahead," Tom said. "Now, don't talk unless I talk to you. I'm busy."

Niko squared his shoulders and said, "Okay."

He became Tom's quiet, adept assistant. Tom taught him how to change fuel filters and thermostats and to clean engines with solvents. Niko's heart quickened if he noticed his Pa glancing in his direction.

Tom watched him with frank admiration, and a warm smile flitted over his face. *Damn, that kid is smart.*

Niko washed and waxed the repaired cars till they gleamed.

"How am I doin', Pa?" Niko asked.

"You're doin' good, kid."

Niko glowed with the meager attention but knew not to bother his Pa with anything besides cars.

The next day, the early morning sun spattered corn-yellow on the sidewalk between the house and garage. Niko stepped inside the open side door wearing baggy navy blue shorts, a white T-shirt, and his Cubs baseball hat. "Hey, Pa," he whispered. "It's eight o'clock on the dot."

Tom looked up from the engine of the black Buick sedan. He reached for the set of keys on the pegboard against the wall. "Here," he said. "Catch." Niko caught the keys in midair. "I want you to vacuum and wipe down the inside of this trunk while I work on the carburetor."

"I'll do it, Pa!"

The heavy trunk lid popped open when Niko turned the key, but it took some muscle to lift. He pulled the vacuum cleaner away from the wall and stepped on the power button. As the motor went up the scale to a steady whine, he dragged the gray hose along with him into the cavernous trunk. The inside had a rank, musty smell. Niko wrinkled his nose. He crouched down on his bare knees and started running the brush attachment into a dark corner. The carpet felt prickly. When he crawled to the other corner, he felt something sticky on his knee. He climbed out of the trunk and inspected a splotch of what looked like crusty red paint. Bending over, he swiped it with his finger and brought it up to his nose. A sweet metallic scent filled his nostrils. It wasn't paint. He felt a wave of nausea and turned off the vacuum.

He drew in a deep breath and said, "Pa, I kneeled on something icky in the trunk. Look. Do you think it's blood?"

Tom snapped his head up and looked at his son around the open hood. His heart gave a start when he saw Niko's knee. "It's nothin'," he said harshly. He walked around the car and slammed the trunk shut. "Paint. That's all it is. Wash it off and get busy polishing the chrome." His steely glare told Niko to drop it.

Niko pulled on the neck of his striped T-shirt and walked out of the garage. After washing off his knee with the garden hose, he pulled the bill of his baseball hat down low and shuffled back into the garage. He reached for a polishing cloth on a shelf and started rubbing a door handle with quick, jerky movements.

"Damn it, Niko," said Tom. "You're nosy and ignorant, just like your relatives."

Niko flinched. "No, I'm not! I don't think they're nosy and ignorate, Pa."

"Well, big britches, you don't know much. Keep hangin' around those relatives and you'll get soft in the head just like them."

"But, Pa, I…I like them. Papou's funny, and he knows the names of every bridge in the whole city."

"That doesn't make for smart. Now, shut up and do your work."

Niko swallowed hard and felt prickles run down his back.

The next day, Niko rummaged through the garbage barrel and found a used-up spark plug. He shoved it into his pants pocket and walked over to Noops's house. He gave Noops the spark plug and they made engine sounds together.

The difference between the boys seemed a contradiction, but Niko couldn't resist his friend's gentle simplicity and playful nature. Noops basked in Niko's pure acceptance and friendship.

To an uninformed observer on the streets, it was a peculiar sight to see these two boys walk down the sidewalks together with a white hen named Blackie. The boys took turns holding Blackie under the wings of their arms most places they went.

Noops had found the skinny hen standing in the middle of jagged chunks of coal in a bin behind Piggly Wiggly one frigid November day. She was completely black, from the top of her comb down to her chicken legs. The hen must have lived on coal and whatever bugs she could scrounge. She had blinked twice at Noops with a diminutive amber eye when he lifted the lid of the bin.

He brought his hand to his cheek, grinned with enchantment, and whispered, "Ah...ah be Noops. Who's-you?" She gave him a frail "cluck" and that was all it took to cement their unusual dedication to each other.

When Noops spoke, his tongue twirled around like an appendage suspended on a loose hinge. "Ah be guh, ah is," Noops mumbled, with his cock-eyed grin and quick head nod. Those were some of the few coherent words Sophie ever heard him utter when kindly folks asked him, "How ya be?"

Newt Potter hadn't always walked like a wobbly toy and talked funny. As a perfect, robust baby he was affectionately known as New Potato. Pretty soon New Potato became Noops and that name stuck. He helped his Papa deliver coal into cellars around their mill town neighborhood on the East Side. The blackened coal bucket proudly swung between Noops's sooty hands while his Papa shoveled the fuel into a wheelbarrow from his rusty pickup.

Noops and his Papa lived for baseball. In the morning, before deliveries, they dove straight into the newspaper's sports page and talked over box scores. In the summer they played catch until the lightning bugs danced their lights into the dark of night. If they weren't playing catch, the two took in local games or were found huddled around the radio listening to the Cubs or Sox.

Noops wore his oversized, scuffed leather mitt to every game. One sultry July evening when he was just eight, Noops and his Papa sat high on the rickety wooden bleachers in left field at the neighboring Hegewisch community baseball park.

"Crack!" The batter hit a towering pop fly directly towards them. Noops and his friend Joey Kowalski scrambled up to the top bleacher with their baseball gloves at the same time. The boys danced on their toes, yelling, "I got it, I got it!" As the arching ball came down, Joey leaped in front of Noops, elbowing him in the face. He snagged the ball in the very top edge of his glove. Noops lost his balance. His father dove to reach him, but it was too late. He fell backwards, arms windmilling to somehow slow the inevitable.

"Noooo!" screamed his Papa. The crowd collectively froze and then gasped as Noops landed smack on his back on the unforgiving dirt with an ungodly thud. His skinny brown legs lay at an odd angle, and thick blood oozed out of his ear. Joey looked down at Noops. The ball fell out of his glove onto the dirt below. He turned away and vomited.

A month later, when night faded, and the lights around the Hegewisch baseball field winked out, Mr. Potter could be seen sitting on the top bleacher, tossing a baseball into Noops's glove over and over again. It took a long time for Mr. and Mrs. Potter to believe their boy would never be the same. They did their best to make sure Joey Kowalski didn't feel the blame. What happened to Noops became legend on the East Side.

Niko could tell Noops anything.

4
Hum Like a Bee

Be like the bird that pausing in her flight awhile on boughs
too slight feels them give way beneath her and yet sings
knowing that she hath wings.
— Victor Hugo

The night before the surprise trip with her cousins, Sophie went into the bathroom and drew water high into the tub. Teddy the Cat trotted in with her and curled up on the multicolored rag rug next to the tub. "Hey, Teddy," she said. She climbed in, plugged her nose, and slid underwater. With eyes wide open in the warm silence, she watched her hair floating like a circular blanket around her. She turned over, sank back down in the water, and studied the back of her hands through the dappled light. Her thoughts drifted while suspended in the weightless calm, but when she turned to sit up, heaviness filled her chest as she thought of the attention Niko was getting from Pa. She lay back in the tub and stared blurry-eyed at the fine cracks in the plaster ceiling, wondering how she could keep him away from Pa.

"Teddy, Pa's just using him with all this car stuff, and Niko's picking up bad things." Teddy meowed. She lathered her hair with green Woolworths shampoo, plunged back down in the water, and shook her head. It was easier to think about how much she loved road trips with her crazy cousins.

Their lives seemed more carefree than hers and Niko's. A familiar, bitter thought stung. *Was it because both parents in every other family were Greek?*

She slipped a hand behind her neck, picturing how all of them would pile into their grandparents' yellow Oldsmobile sedan, with its torpedo-like fenders and sleek rocket hood ornament. She always raced to be the first one to scramble up to the narrow, carpeted window shelf above the back seat of the car, where there was room to stretch out. The rest of the cousins crammed in, legs tangled all over each other's laps. Cousin George always had his fists half-cocked, waiting to be ambushed on all sides as they elbowed and pushed.

Niko couldn't keep up with Sophie as they ran and walked the twelve blocks to their grandparents' place the next morning. He skirted a small construction site on the sidewalk and yelled, "Hey, Sophie! Wait up!"

She laughed and ran faster. The streetlight was with her, and she darted across 106th. The flashing *Don't Walk* sign stopped Niko.

"Hey, no fair," he yelled through cupped hands.

Sophie rounded the corner past Pasquale's Pizzeria and then came to a stop. She backed up a few steps and looked through the sidewalk-level window. Pete Pasquale was twirling pizza dough high up in the air, like a circus performer spinning plates on sticks. Sophie waved. A broad smile crinkled his face, and his bushy eyebrows curled towards his dark eyes. He was a thin man who wore a full-length white apron, a floppy chef's hat, and a red bow tie when making pizza. The pungent aroma of pizza and handmade sausage made her hungry.

Pete rented the corner of her grandparents' brown brick apartment building on 106th and Avenue L for his take-out pizza business. The shop's entry was a half-stairway down from the sidewalk. A black wrought iron handrail bolted to the bricks guided customers down to the darkened landing. A cut-open cardboard box sat in front of the door as a welcome mat.

Niko caught up and bumped Sophie's shoulder. They waved to Pete and ran around to the front of the building. The three-story apartment building

was boxy looking, with the inset doorway in the middle. A curved orna-
mental cornice made of cement dignified the porch. Rows of double-hung
wooden windows lined up across the front. Shades, colorful curtains, and
venetian blinds suggested the warmth of life behind each window.

Sophie pushed through the heavy front door of the apartment building.
A bell tinkled and the top of the door grazed the hanging chain from the
hallway light. Sunlight pierced though the side windows onto the dizzying
pattern of little white hexagonal tiles. She caught a whiff of furniture polish
from somewhere. Sophie took two steps at a time up the groaning, flow-
er-carpeted stairs to the second story.

Niko burst through the apartment door after her. The venetian blinds
scattered the late morning sun into slats of shadow and light on the small
Grecian urns and mini-statues in the living room. Papou looked out from
behind his newspaper. He was sitting with Cousins George and Angie at the
dining room table covered in yellow oilcloth. He raised his eyebrows and
his glasses slipped down. "Here you are, kids," he said. "We started lunch
without you." His smile conveyed a gentle apology.

Steaming bowls of avgolemono soup and small bottles of Coca-Cola
waited for them.

Both cousins said, "Hey." Cousin George pulled a comb out of his back
pocket and ran its teeth back and forth along the edge of the table. Yiayia
walked in from the kitchen with a plate stacked high with bread.

"Put the comb away, George," she said. "*Catsa hamou,* Sophie, Niko. We
have a big day. Eat."

Sophie took a swig of Coke, dipped a thick slice of crusty bread in olive
oil, and savored the frothy egg-lemon soup. They ate the same meal every
Sunday.

She was just sopping up the remnants of rice and chicken at the bottom
of her bowl with a chunk of bread when Papou announced, "Kids, we going
to the Field Museum!"

The children cheered.

"Can Noops come?" asked Niko.

"Not this time, Niko," he said. "We pick up Thea Toula on the way!"

Papou's idea for this road trip seemed like a good thing to the kids until he mentioned Thea Toula.

"Damn," Niko mouthed in barely a whisper, but Sophie heard. She looked at him in surprise and felt heat rise in her face.

The table became so still that the mantel clock's tick-tock seemed deafening. Sophie wondered if her all-too-readable face would give her away, but she clamped her mouth shut. Cousin George said something inaudible. Sophie's eyes flickered at George. She shook her head, warning him to silence.

"Papou!" complained George, holding his arms outstretched. "There's no room!"

"George!" said Yiayia. Sophie smiled. Yiayia could fill a room just by saying one word.

In the thick silence, George bit down on his cheek. Sophie heard a crazy fly tap itself over and over against a windowpane.

"Thea's family and she going," boomed Papou. "Is no more talk."

George let out a heavy sigh.

Sophie turned and studied him. It was a curiosity to her how eleven-year-old Cousin George didn't look like anyone in the family. His stick-out ears, clear blue-green eyes, and smattering of connected freckles fascinated Sophie. He wore shorts in the winter and habitually twisted his tawny-colored hair that spilled over his forehead.

George snapped chewing gum with his front teeth. No one could do it like him. He'd take a wad of Black Jack gum, circle it stringy on his forefinger, and then smash it on his grinning teeth, pretending they got knocked out. His laugh was quick and cheerful.

Sophie couldn't believe how Cousin George zoomed through his days in perpetual motion.

"No fly is ever land on that boy," Papou would say.

His craziness and bold-as-brass statements were an inspiration to Sophie; besides, she liked that they were linked in the "different" department. Everyone else in the family had big bones and sturdy-looking bodies, but she was an aberration. She was long and leggy like a young foal and bean-pole thin.

When they finished eating, Sophie, Niko, and the cousins bolted from the table and tumbled down the apartment building's steps to the car. Sophie skidded to a stop by wrapping her arm around a fat streetlight pole in front of the car. She looked down and couldn't resist making faces at her reflection in the big chrome bumper Papou had just polished to a mirror finish.

"*Ella tho!* Hurry up, Sophie!" pleaded Niko, tugging at his sister's hand. "We gotta get the shelf first! Thea Toula's coming!" He yanked her by the hand to the driver's side in the street just as Papou unlocked the back door. Sophie pushed in first and leaped up onto the shelf. She saw a slow grin spread across Niko's face. George punched Sophie on the arm. She propped her chin on the palm of her hand with an impudent air, wrinkled her nose, and stuck her tongue out at him. George scrunched his face in a menacing scowl and got in the front seat with Yiayia and Papou. Niko and Angie settled into the temporarily roomy back seat.

Niko knew his sister would tuck him like a spoon next to her string-skinny body on the shelf after a while. When the car got moving Sophie lay down on her stomach, pressed one ear hard on the window shelf, and plugged the other one with a finger. She heard the fat whitewall tires hum their tune on the road. Her voice vibrated with the spinning tires—a soft vibrato over the metal grate on the bridges and a thicker "ba bump, ba bump" over concrete highways. Finally, she reached down and pulled Niko up with her and wrapped an arm around his small waist. It was a tight fit. He felt safely cocooned.

"Niko, let's you and me pretend we're flying away," whispered Sophie close to his ear.

"Where can we fly to?"

"Magic places."

Niko smiled.

Sophie imagined the two of them having wings to get away when things fell apart at home. She hated when her parents simmered in stony silence and cringed when they yelled and threw stuff. Both raised their clenched fists in mock threats but stopped short of slugging it out.

Things had gotten bad a couple of nights before. Sophie and Niko had escaped by hunkering down in the corner of the basement by the cement sink. Sophie pulled a thin, stained ticking mattress around them to make a small cave. Their bodies sank deep within the space. Niko leaned into her side and tucked his head under her chin. She pressed the palms of her hands against his ears to drown out the misery. But she heard.

"Hum, Niko. Hum like a bee. It's like magic. You can't hear nothin' except your own humming."

He hummed and her breath felt warm on his face.

The car slowed.

Papou pulled up to Toula's small-shingled row house in Hammond and honked the horn twice. "Kids, move over and make room for Thea," he said. The kids collectively groaned.

The family waited and waited. Cousin George fidgeted in his seat. "When the hell is she comin'?" he said. "She's takin' forever!"

Papou raised his eyebrows and said nothing for a moment. He looked in the rearview mirror. "Sophie, get Thea Toula." In his nonnegotiable voice, he added, "George, get out of the car. I talk. You listen."

George's shoulders rose up to his ears. He slunk out of the car.

Sophie got out after George and stared at Thea Toula's shacky-looking house. Chunks of the sandy siding, like fake multicolored bricks, were buckled and peeling away here and there. Rain-rotted shingles drooped over the eaves.

The small front yards of the adjoining houses had their own personalities. Some yards were dotted with planters and filled in with small cinnamon-colored lava rock or crushed white rock. Some were scrubby and covered with weeds. Others looked raw, with patches of bare dirt and a smattering of bushes.

The fact that Thea Toula's lawn stood out in sharp contrast fascinated Sophie. It had lush rectangular carpets of green grass on either side of the short walkway to her house. Two times a day, she hand-watered her patches of lawn with an industrial-looking hose and sprayer. She loved everything that grew in God's earth, except for weeds. If she found a mere blade of crabgrass, or a thistly weed, it was war. She'd pounce down and dig it out with a vengeance. If it left a hole, she'd fill it with soil, replant the grass, and place heavy-duty wire mesh over the spot long enough so the birds wouldn't peck at the seeds.

The red plastic geraniums that lined both sides of her narrow cement walkway seemed a contradiction to Sophie, but she figured Thea made a treaty with herself and settled for the delicate balance of real and fake.

Sophie stepped up the sagging front steps and knocked on the screen door. It clattered with her knock.

A singsong voice rang out, "Come in!"

Sophie walked in and startled when the spring-loaded door slammed behind her.

"Who is it?"

"It's Sophie!"

"I'm almost ready, *koukla!* Get yourself something to eat and make yourself comfortable."

Sophie straightened her sleeveless plaid blouse and walked into the closet-sized kitchen to get a glass of water. *Nothing has changed.* The pink-and-gray linoleum floor tiles were cracked in places and worn thin in front of the sink. Clay pots of African violets lined the windowsill. She reached up to an open shelf for a glass. A pink rubber sprayer was attached to the end of the faucet.

Next to the sink sat an old gas oven with two top burners that exploded in high flames whenever Thea Toula lit them with a wood match. The knobs and handle on the oven face reminded Sophie of a frowning old man. Instead of an electric refrigerator, she had an icebox, with a big hunk of sawdust-covered ice in a high-sided metal tray. A rusted drip pan sat underneath. The centerpiece of the living area was a chipped white enamel kitchen table covered with scrubbed oilcloth.

Sophie walked over to the prayer corner in the tiny living room and, out of habit, crossed herself. It was wallpapered in soft pink rosebuds and winding green vines. A smattering of icons hung on the east wall—the direction of the rising sun. Sophie studied her favorite icon of *Theotokos* holding baby Jesus, with his cheek resting gently against hers. Golden halos shimmered around their all-seeing, noble faces. She ran her finger around their halos. The finish was rubbed off the sides of the icon, maybe where Thea's thumbs had held it. Tucked behind some of the icons were little rectangles of paper with handwriting on them, a small blue feather, and dried-up remnants of Easter: brown carnations and slender palms fashioned into crosses.

Sophie leaned forward to read the tiny writing on the papers. She saw they were prayers. One read, *Miss Fanny's hands, twisted up with the arthritis. Joey Sauer's cloudy blind eyes.* Then, *Baby Jimmy's little burnt tongue after licking the conk hair straightener off the floor at the salon.* Another, *Help me meet a nice man.* A string of small Christmas lights encircled all the icons. Sophie hugged her arms to her chest and smiled.

The living room lamp, with its narrow, yellowed lampshade, looked like a rocket ship ready to launch from its metal tripod base. She breathed in the bittersweet scent of burnt-up charcoal laced with frankincense from a brass censer next to the lamp. It all had the appearance of a miniature flea market, and yet it looked and smelled like a sanctuary to Sophie.

She pulled her hair back and sank down on the plastic-covered burgundy couch. A thoughtful sadness came over her, and she sighed. A red Radio Flyer wagon holding two cardboard boxes sat in the opposite corner. Thea Toula didn't have a car, so she wheeled her groceries from the Hi-Lo store in her wagon. Papou said she barely earned enough to feed a chicken as a part-time manicurist and hairdresser at the Hair Castle Beauty Salon, so the family paid her extra to cut her nieces' and nephews' hair.

5
Toula

If life were predictable it would cease to be life,
and be without flavor.
— Eleanor Roosevelt

There were secret tragedies in Thea Toula's life, and Yiayia had told Sophie never to mention them. She inched back on the couch and rested her elbows on her knees, thinking about the last Fourth of July. The family had gathered on Thea's back patio for a lamb barbeque before the fireworks show at Soldier Field. Thea was in the kitchen washing the dinner dishes, with Sophie drying and Cousin Angie putting away, when she plunged her hands into the soapsuds and started crying. Sophie tucked in her lower lip and stared at her. Tears dropped into the soapsuds. Eight-year-old Cousin Angie gave her a sideways glance and took a couple of steps back. At the same time the teapot started whistling on the stove. Sophie had reached around Thea to turn off the flame.

Between sobs, Thea announced in a rather loud way, "Did you know I was jilted!"

Sophie saw a flame in her cheeks. Thea Toula lifted her soapy hands out of the water and covered her face with a dishtowel. She stood rooted to the spot, so worked up that her hands trembled. Sophie touched her arm.

Thea Toula let the towel drop and turned to look into her eyes. "I was young and beautiful in my satin wedding gown. The wedding crowns sat on

··40··

a pillow at the church altar, the priest in his golden robe; the crowd waited, and he didn't come. Why, I ask you? I was pretty. He was a fireman."

"I'm sorry, Thea," said Sophie. Cousin Angie backed out of the kitchen.

Toula put her hands to her cheeks and started hiccupping. "Oh, my *kouklas*, I shouldn't have said. I made you's sad. You's kids are my happiness."

"It's okay, Thea," said Sophie. She saw a shiny film come into her eyes—the beginning of tears.

"I gotta put it out of my mind one of these days, if I'm going to go on."

Sophie leaned on the arm of the couch as sadness clutched her chest. There was something else. A couple of years before, when Sophie was ten, she had overheard her Ma and Yiayia talking in the kitchen with their voices dipped down. Thea Toula was going to have a baby with that fireman, but she had a miscarriage after she was left waiting at the altar. Sophie walked in on them and asked what a miscarriage was. Yiayia told her about Thea losing her baby. She made Sophie swear to secrecy. Sophie remembered how her heart squeezed up thinking about Thea, but at the same time, a grown-up feeling came over her. Yiayia trusted her.

"*Poe, poe.* It broke her heart. My poor cousin," Yiayia had said. "The doctor told her she would never have a baby after that. Something went wrong. She cried so bad and tore at her clothes. I was sure she was going crazy. I brought her home with me, sang to her, hugged her in my arms. After eating nothing for weeks, she dove headfirst into food. It didn't take long for her to plump out. She cooked for us, made trays and trays of baklava, and stacked the refrigerator with so much food, we started feeding the neighbors.

"Sometimes, she sat on the wooden steps of our fire escape outside the kitchen door humming to herself and smoothing her apron. Then came the daily rearranging and dusting of every little knickknack in our apartment. She'd lift them with gentle fingers, wipe them carefully with a soft damp cloth, and arrange them in thoughtful ways. Sometimes I'd see her kiss pictures of you's kids. With time, she started to act like a regular person. We laughed during meals, and she became interested in the family again, especially her baby nieces and nephews. When she started going to church with us, we knew she was better. Six months later, when she was well enough to go back to her house, she tried crazy diets to get her figure back. I think she's given up. Guess I don't blame her."

Sophie asked what Papou did when Thea lived with them.

"I got real mad at Papou because he had a bad opinion of her when he heard she was having a baby," she said. "But when he saw how she suffered such humiliation, I told him that he was a fine one to talk. I reminded him about the time he bought the cooking grill for the store from some gangsters, after getting a tip about a good deal from my no-good cousin Taki. Those hooligans roughed up a poor Italian man who ran the hot dog stand down the street from Wrigley Field. We found out later the man owed money to the wrong people, so they took everything away from him and locked him up in a warehouse overnight to scare him. Then, they sold his cooking supplies. Lucky they didn't kill him.

"This is what I said: 'Pa, you bought stolen stuff under the table. Let that be a lesson for both of us.' Who doesn't make a mistake, I ask you?"

Thea Toula's story cemented Sophie's love for her.

"Sophie!" Thea Toula sang out. "Go out to the car. I'll be right there!"

"It's okay, Thea. I'll wait."

"No, *koukla*. I have a little surprise for you's."

Sophie walked back to the car. Niko and Cousins George and Angie were sitting on the curb, flinging rocks across the street. A ratty collie dog with an aged-white face rested on the grass with the kids like it was storing up energy just by watching them.

Yiayia leaned out the car window. "Is everything alright, honey?"

"Yeah. Thea says she has a surprise for us."

"Is she comin' yet?" said Cousin George, pulling on his ear. "How long do we hafta wait?"

As if on cue, Toula cracked her front door open, peeked out, and daintily waved her white-gloved hand at the carload. She turned and grabbed her purse and a box tied up with string. Toula awkwardly backed her sizeable bottom out the door. Sophie grinned as her pink pleated skirt billowed like a circus tent. Toula turned her key in the bolt and ambled to the car in shoes that looked painfully tight for her pudgy feet. She tugged at a nylon stocking that bunched at her ankle.

"Pa," Yiayia whispered. "Toula's changed her hair color."

"She change more than hair," said Papou.

The carload went momentarily silent in a spell of open-mouthed staring. Toula had colored her hair fiery magenta and had heavily penciled arched eyebrows. She wore ruby-red lipstick, which seemed to creep marginally beyond her lips.

"She looks like a cartoon in the funny papers," said Cousin George.

"*Stamata*, George! Shh!" admonished Yiayia.

"George, you respect!" said Papou.

"Ooo," Toula crooned while gaping through the car windows. "How's my *kouklitses*? Wait till you's see what I made!"

Niko leaned into Sophie and whispered, "She scares me."

"Toula," said Papou. "The grass look good."

Her lips moved silently for a moment. She stood taller and said, "*Efkharisto*, George."

The car rocked and groaned on its springs when Toula settled into half of the back seat. Cheap perfume seemed to fill every particle of air in the car. Each kid gave her an obligatory kiss and quickly piled onto each other's laps.

Sophie studied her with fascination as she got into the car. After getting accustomed to Thea's enormous girth and looking past her gaudy makeup, Sophie liked her kindhearted smile and cheerful voice. Her dark brown eyes had a fresh sparkle. She knew Thea Toula also had a particular penchant for all children. Her raucous laugh slid up and down the musical scales.

Niko backed away because, Sophie knew, he was scared of Thea's gigantic bosom. Sophie could hardly breathe when Thea hugged her into her "pillows," as the kids called them. She wore tight undergarments that drew them up to lofty heights and made her rear end bubble out alarmingly. Sophie had seen how folks would step aside and stare when she lumbered down sidewalks. It made her angry to hear them whisper and laugh behind Thea's back.

Toula leaned over and kissed unsuspecting George. The red lipstick left a circular smooch on his cheek.

Niko laughed and sang, "You got lipstick, George!"

Cousin George furiously wiped his cheek with his hand and said, "Hey, Sophie, it's my turn for the shelf."

So began the tumultuous change as each kid vied for a better spot in the car. Sophie nudged Niko. He slithered from the back window shelf and folded his body small and close to the door opposite Thea. He started picking at a knotted snarl of shoelaces on his right shoe.

"Hey, no fair, Niko," whined Cousin Angie. "You had the shelf. I get the window."

She shoved Niko next to Toula, who lifted him onto her immense lap. His head touched the fabric ceiling of the car. Thea squeezed him in a crushing embrace. Niko's eyes widened.

"My little Niko," she exclaimed, jiggling him to and fro on her lap. "You's so cute!"

Niko said in a whisper voice, "You're nosy and ignorate, Thea Toula." Thea stopped mid-jiggle and gasped.

Sophie heard and seethed under her breath, "Niko! That's *so* mean and not true! You say you're sorry to Thea."

He leaned into Sophie's ear and whispered, "But that's what Pa said."

"He's wrong! Now say you're sorry."

Niko swallowed hard and said, "I'm sorry, Thea."

Thea Toula wiped a tear away with her finger. She turned him on her lap and looked him in the eye. "Niko, remember who loves you's. I forgive."

He buried his face in his hands and through his fingers said, "Okay."

Sophie looked at her brother, then out the window.

In a perfectly orchestrated move, George dove into the back seat and noisily clambered onto the shelf as Sophie climbed into the front seat between Yiayia and Papou.

Only one kid at a time could wedge in between them, as they were a plump pair. The front seat kid got to spin the radio knobs.

Sophie bounced on the seat. Her heart always swelled proud sitting up there with them.

Peace disappeared with Cousin George in the back. He pretended to smoke a rolled-up gum wrapper, then a spectacular, throat-rattling burp thundered out of him, and pretty soon cousins started gulping air to out-burp one another.

"George pinched me, Papou!" yelled Cousin Angie.

Thea Toula waggled her finger at them. "Now, now, children. You's behave."

"Don't have to," whispered George.

Cousin Angie pulled on his sleeve.

"What?" Papou thundered. He slammed the big steering wheel with his fist. "You listen to your Thea!"

Toula tugged on one of her rhinestone earrings and gave a weak smile. She tucked in one side of her lower lip, knowing once again her admonitions had no effect.

Yiayia turned slowly, lowered her glasses, and said, "George?"

The kids quickly looked down and elbowed one another in the ribs. A slow burn flushed onto Cousin George's cheeks and ears. His body stiffened as he meditated upon his crimes. Sophie clapped a hand over her mouth to keep from laughing.

"Does Papou need to pull over?" Yiayia asked in an ominous voice.

"No, Yiayia," they chimed in unison.

"George?"

"No, ma'am."

Sophie glanced sideways at Yiayia, and their eyes met. Amusement poured out of her face like she was lit from within. Thick white hair, tucked and wrapped in a roll around her head, sprang wispy on her face and neck.

Thea Toula lifted Niko onto Angie's lap. She yanked on the hem of her skirt to straighten its pleats and said, "Are you's ready for a little treat, my *kouklas*?"

"Yeah, Thea!" they chimed. The kids knew they were in for a treat, as Thea's desserts almost made up for every inconvenience she imposed.

Toula reached for the cardboard box, untied the string, pulled off the lid, and took out a stack of paper napkins from a stiff white envelope. She unwrapped neatly folded wax paper to reveal *kourabiethes* butter cookies coated with a thick layer of powdered sugar. Toula daintily placed a cookie in the center of a napkin and began passing them around. Soon, the sugar exploded like snow throughout the back seat. It speckled the fabric ceiling of the car and the kids started sneezing.

Sophie smiled, thinking about the differences between two of her "take on road trips" theas. Thea Stefania took up very little space in the back seat. Toula was undeniably larger than life. Sophie absolutely loved going anywhere with her grandparents, cousins, and an occasional thea or theo. Everything about the family captivated her senses and occupied her thoughts in happy ways. Their noisy, untamed antics were funny; besides, it was a respite just to get away from the misery at home.

Sophie startled as Yiayia kicked off her shoes. "*Poe, poe*, Pa, so good to take these tight *paputsias* off," she said. She used her suitcase-sized purse as a footrest.

Sophie shook off her troubling thoughts and marveled at Yiayia's purse. It was full of treasures to amuse her grandchildren: mazes with tiny metal balls, yo-yos, a bearded and moustached guy called Wooly Willie, a Slinky, comic books, coloring books and crayons. She fed them along the way with fruit, nuts, saltine crackers, and sesame seed and honey bars.

If Sophie and her cousins were especially good, she'd reward them with hard, chewy, or chocolate candy, Chiclets, or Doublemint gum.

Today, the kids became stickier and grimier with each mile.

There were the emergency supplies: toilet paper, extra underpants, tweezers, Vaseline for dry lips, Band-Aids, iodine, and Vicks in a blue glass jar.

Sophie and her cousins made sure they stifled their sneezes and swallowed their coughs; otherwise, Yiayia would shout, "*Yasou!*" and pull out that Vicks jar, unscrew the lid, and smear pungent menthol under their noses and on their chests.

"*Poe, poe*, just listen to that nose! A little potion of Vicks fixes everything."

The adventures at the Field Museum had been nonstop. The museum was filled with taxidermic animals, but that day there were two live rhesus macaque monkeys in a giant cage by the entry. Thea Toula reached through the bars to feed one of them a kernel of popcorn, but it ripped off the middle finger of her white glove. She screamed bloody murder. Cousin Angie's hair got entwined in the crank of a penny-smashing machine, and Cousin George got a severe talking-to by a guard for ducking under the ropes to touch the bones of a triceratops. A little girl in the bathroom line asked Thea Toula why she had a moustache. Toula cried for a solid fifteen minutes. Niko took her hand.

Papou took back roads on the way home. Sophie settled into sleepy contentment in the front seat. Thea Toula snored open-mouthed in the back seat, and the children used her cushiony body to nap on.

Papou pulled over to a Sinclair gas station and said, "Everybody out. Is time to fill up the gas tank and use the *banyo*."

As the kids and Thea Toula spilled out of the car, Yiayia Sophia took her granddaughter's hand and said, "Come, Sophie. Let's use the *banyo* first and go for a little walk."

They walked slowly to the crest of a small grassy hill. Yiayia stopped under the rustling shade of a giant elm tree. She reached into the bodice of her dress and pulled out a white lace hankie to dab the beads of sweat from her brow.

She turned to Sophie and asked, "Does that low-down Taki hang around your Pa?"

Sophie nodded her head and felt her stomach turn just thinking of him.

"It's like something unraveled in my cousin years ago. His own pa got him into bad business. My poor aunt...but that's not your worry."

"I can't stand him, Yiayia." Her voice felt strained. "I…I hate him."

"I understand, *pethie mou*. Papou and I will see what we can do. There are ways of doing things you don't need to worry about. But Sophie, you're old enough to understand some things. Papou and I expected a lot outta your Ma when she was your age. She was the oldest and we were strict. Too strict. Papou wouldn't bend and it hurt your Ma. The last time I heard my Christina laugh was before your christening day."

"Ma doesn't laugh," Sophie said, shaking her head. "She has sad eyes."

"I know, honey. But I'll tell you, your Ma and Pa love you kids. No sadness is your fault. It's important you and Niko know that. You are the sun, the moon, and the sky," she said softly, like pearls slipping off a string. Yiayia cupped her granddaughter's cheeks with her warm hands and kissed her forehead. Sophie smiled into her eyes, bent over, and scooped up a small rock. She fingered its roughness, rolled it over in her hand, and looked down the hill.

Niko waved with two arms and hollered, "Come on, Sophie and Yiayia! Papou says it's time to go!"

Sophie tucked the rock into the pocket of her pedal pushers and walked down the hill hand in hand with Yiayia. They all got into the car and found their places of comfort after adjusting to Toula's formidable girth.

Papou exclaimed, "Push down them locks on da doors good, I tell you. We don't want you's kids fallin' out like Cousin George almost did when he was five. Remember, George?"

"Yeah," drawled George with a sly grin.

"I want to tell it!" said Sophie, laughing.

Niko jumped up and down in his seat and said, "Tell it, Sophie!"

"I was six years old when the back door flipped open across the Calumet Bridge. Cousin Angie was lying on the window shelf. Cousin Angelo, George, and I were sitting in the back seat. George popped the lock up and started messing with the door handle. I yelled at him to stop, but the back door flipped open halfway across the bridge. I screamed like crazy because I thought he fell out. When Papou stomped on the brakes, we flew forward and smacked into Yiayia and Papou. Cars all around us zigzagged sideways, and tires squealed. It's like the tires of our car skipped sideways across the road before we came to a stop. I looked over and saw George dangling on the window crank from the tool loop of his overalls. He gave me the most wicked, bloody smile, and I could see that his front tooth was dangling."

She turned to him. "I swear, George, your pants saved your life, and the freckles on your face sort of danced with happiness. Yiayia jumped out of the car to unhook you and then she screamed, '*What were you doing?*' And you said, 'Uh… just trying to stand on my head.' You weren't one bit upset about your smashed-in front tooth or the craziness you caused."

"Yeah! It was fun!" said George.

Papou smacked the steering wheel and laughed. "You's like a skyrocket, George. Lucky landing."

It got quiet in the car. Sophie sat back, drew her legs up, and rested her chin on her knees. The tires were singing their tune, and Papou turned the radio on. A man's silky voice doing a commercial for Camel cigarettes came on. Sophie smiled and considered her family. It was a happiness to be dissolved into something whole and good.

6

Elena Giannakopoulos Ioannou

The plow turned over a strip of sod on top of the seed corn.
But the corn would fight its way up through the matted roots,
and there would be a cornfield.

— Laura Ingalls Wilder, *Little House on the Prairie*

1901

*E*lena shielded her eyes with one hand; the other rested on her swollen belly as the tangerine sun slowly descended into the cobalt sea. She kicked off her leather-strapped sandals and felt the wood of the stalwart pier with her toes, its grooves and earthy texture. She watched and waited until the bright, full moon rose and sailed high overhead. The twinkling lights of the freighter ship faded into the night. All that was left was the moon and the endless swath of stars.

Will I ever see him again? He's the kindest man Theos ever blew breath into and a good papa to our children. Tears spilled down her finely formed, sun-browned face. She panted ahead in worry but moments later bit her lip in resolve. Her hand reached into the vapor of the night.

The olive orchards lay open before Elena in the poor, mountainous village of Tripoli. The Giannakopoulos family was known for their sturdy hand-knit olive nets and their skill in harvesting and pruning the trees. Most of the graceful, billowing trees around their village were hundreds of years old. She and her family spread the tightly woven nets in a circular swath around the gnarly, deep-rooted tree trunks to catch the ripe olives. The work was hard. The slender silver-green leaves were sharp and leathery to the touch. The family hand-plucked the olives in a gentle milking motion from the elegant branches. The olives poured down onto the nets.

The older children helped, and everyone kept an eye on the babies. Elena's mother had a tranquil, clean beauty. Her steel-gray hair gathered in a wispy knot at the back of her head, but her back and shoulders were bent from endless pruning, picking, hauling water, and slaving for orchard owners on the dry, rocky land.

"Go to America," she said. "We're stuck between living and not living. Leave this poverty and give your children a chance."

Four months passed before the first letter from Elena's husband came to her little stone house. She heard the quick flutter of morning birds, the quiet thudding of a donkey's hooves, and the shouts of her children. The bearded postman with his short-billed gray cap handed her the letter from America with an air of reverence. The children circled, watching her every move.

Her trembling fingers peeled open the flap of the envelope, and a photo of her husband slid out. She held the picture at arm's length for all to see. They stared with wonder at the image of proud Vasilios standing in front of a brick building, wearing overalls, a heavy-looking tool belt around his waist. His arms folded, bulging biceps below his rolled-up sleeves. Tears came to Elena, and her joy looked nearly like sorrow.

She turned the photo over and read, *Vasilios Ioannou, July, 1901.* She handed the picture to her eldest, Alexandria, and said, "Watch the children. I'm going down to the stream to read the letter by myself."

My dearest Elena,

I close my eyes and see you. Sunlight flashing on your hair, smooth skin like the inside of the seashell. Do you see me from far away? Nothing can separate us. You and I are not common in our love. We are like the bricks I hold in my hands every day. Strong.

Our children like olive branches. I want to hold our new baby in my arms. Is it a boy or girl? Please write soon and tell me. I pray for you all the time.

My brother, Theodore, bought a camera called Kodak Brownie for one American dollar, so I will send more photographs to you.

I live in the middle of downtown Chicago with Theodore and Cousin Andrew in a tiny apartment on the fifth floor of a tall brick building that soars up where the birds fly. It's by the corner of Lake and Wabash Streets. They call the area The Loop because of a streetcar that loops around the city. We are right by a beautiful lake called Michigan. It looks like the sea at home.

Theodore, Andrew, and I cook together and laugh about all the different things here.

We stumble in our English.

It seems the sky is made of iron and forever growls like thunder. I look out the window and see train tracks built above the street on giant steel beams. Everyone calls it the "L," for elevated. Big steam engines pull train cars behind them. Heavy trains go by and I feel the rumble and roar of the wheels turning on the tracks. Steel on steel, screeching. People climb down steep stairs and go about their work. Below, horses pull rattling wagons and trolleys jangle their bells. It's noisy and crowded, but so much is happening. It's exciting!

The summer air feels thick and sticky, but the breeze from the lake helps. I swim to cool off. Everyone says that snow and cold will come in the winter. I can't believe it.

Let me tell you some funny things. They eat sausages in long buns called hot dogs, and play a game called baseball. People hit a ball with a fat wood stick and run around in a circle stepping on bags of sand. I hear about the White Sox and Cubs teams. They play baseball in Chicago. It seems like everyone chews gum here. It's different from the mastic gum at home. Here, it's sweet. They blow little bubbles and snap the gum in their mouths, especially when playing baseball. I like the gum called Wrigley's Doublemint, and the licorice-flavored Black Jack. We have electric lights and people ride up and down inside some of the buildings in boxes pulled by big cables.

My boss calls me "Master Bill" because I can lay perfect bricks, paint, and build with wood. He says I can swing a hammer better than anyone! I make good money! $3.50 every day for ten hours of work! Soon, you and the children will be proud to live in America.

Please take care of yourself. Write to me. Kiss the children. I love you, Vasilios

After two years, Vasilios sent enough money for Elena and the children—Alexandria, Andrew, Sophia, Angeline, and Theodore—to sail across the ocean to join him in New York City. As he purchased a train ticket from Chicago to New York, they prepared to take their journey across the world in the hold of an immense Cunard steamship.

Elena and the children stood on the wharf in a long line with other steerage passengers. She held in her hand the cheapest tickets. There was no escape from the scorching Greek sun. Sweat trickled down their faces and necks. Their earthly belongings were carried in roped packs on their backs and in large hand-woven baskets with goat-leather handles. Elena marveled at the array of Greek dialects and other languages, mixed into a jumble of long and clipped vowels. The world already seemed bigger and noisy with many languages.

They were separated half the length of the ship from wealthy passengers who were escorted onto the upper decks and clothed in their finest. Europeans were beautifully dressed in silks and linens, Middle Eastern men and women were robed in jewel-colored tunics adorned with intricately embroidered golden and silver threads. Elena's eyes widened as they all streamed up the gangplank. Servants had loaded their steamer trunks and large baggage into staterooms before they had even boarded. Errand boys and maids scurried around, carrying smaller luggage, canvas dress boxes, and round hatboxes. The children had attendants holding their hands.

Elena gazed down at her children, stretched her arms over them like a mother hen, and felt proud that they carried their own weight.

The family of six inched closer and closer to the looming ship. Streaks of rust ran down the sides of the white smokestacks, around rivets, and under portholes—metal weathered by ravages of the sea. The ship was lashed securely to iron moorings on the dock with heavy ropes. The straining ropes bristled with broken twines. Elena was swept forward by the outpouring of her husband's confidence yet pulled back by uncertainty of the voyage and the strange new life ahead.

Theodore leaned against Elena's legs and started whining. As she lifted his sturdy little body upon her hip, she craned her neck forward and saw that each steerage passenger was issued a tin pan and cup, utensils, a soup-bowl-sized hand basin, and a dark blue canvas-covered mattress filled with wood shavings and mapped with stains.

"*Oxi efkharisto.* I don't want the mattresses," Elena said with her palm held up. "We have our own bed rolls."

She nodded with self-satisfaction as she saw tiny bugs crawling all over the mattresses. She'd rub wine vinegar over her children to keep the bugs away.

"I'm scared, Mama," said Sophia.

"That's the biggest boat I ever saw!" said Angeline.

"Look! It's a good, strong boat, made of steel. We're together and Papa's waiting. We're in *Theos*'s hand." Elena crossed herself with three fingers joined like a cloverleaf. "We'll be fine." Her bright, assured eyes, which shone over them, belied her anxious heart. Her pulse quickened and she felt hot breath trickle out of her. She clenched a fist and sucked in a slow lungful of resolve.

The families struggled in clumps up the steep gangplank and then climbed down a nearly vertical metal staircase. The sunlight dribbled down like sparkles through the metal and then gave way to the yellowish glare of light bulbs in metal cages.

At the first landing, a large open hatch with a ladder disappeared even further. The children recoiled. A thickset Spanish laborer in a striped shirt and black dungarees stepped over to Elena's side. He took off his fisherman's cap with respect and tucked it into his back pocket. His face was ruggedly formed and his calm, dark eyes set deep. He leaned forward and offered her a hand.

"Señora, por favor, permítame ayudarle a usted."

Elena looked into his dark eyes, smiled, and said, *"Efkharisto."*

He looked down at the children and said cheerfully, *"Buenos días, niños. ¡Me llamo Pedro!"*

Their eyes widened with bewilderment.

Pedro ruffled his thick brown hair, smiled softly, and said, *"Está bien, niños, no se preocupen. Estoy aquí."* He deftly offered his hand to each of them as they took their first step down.

The treads of the ladder were narrow, and each of them walked sideways to get a better foothold.

"¡Buen viaje! ¡Vayan con Dios!" Pedro called down reassuringly. Elena turned and smiled at him.

Down, down, into the dimly lit bowels of the ship, below the water line, with no advantage of portholes.

The stale air and close quarters felt claustrophobic. The floor was strewn with a thick layer of sawdust. Dust charged the air as they shuffled about. There were only five toilets and sinks for seventy-five people. Families formed into clusters and were given narrow metal bunks.

Five-year-old Sophia clutched her misshapen muslin doll to her chest. She gazed into its wide embroidered eyes and crescent-moon smile and whispered, "Don't be scared, Antonia. I'll take care of you."

"Mama, may we go upstairs now?" asked nine-year-old Andrew with a quavering voice. "It stinks down here."

She gazed into his wide sky-colored eyes and answered, "We'll visit upstairs soon."

She draped blankets on the narrow, stacked bunk beds for privacy. The family settled in. The ship's massive engines vibrated to life and rumbled deeply as it moved away from the dock. A big hooting whistle blew every five seconds, and a slight waft of cool air came through the vents by the low ceiling. Little Theodore clapped his hands and laughed. They climbed back up into the open air and waved farewell to their country.

"Look! Look, Mama!" yelled Andrew, pointing down through the rails to the clear turquoise water. "The dolphins are following us!"

"Oh, *Theos*, such good fortune!" exclaimed Elena. "The dolphins even wish us well. Look, they smile!" She solemnly pressed her hand against her chest and patted the necklace hidden under her blue muslin dress. She ran her fingers around its thin brown leather strap, and pulled out the small golden medallion. A Greek key design encircled the dignified profile of helmeted Athena, the goddess of wisdom, giver of the olive tree. She turned the medallion over slowly and peered into the eyes of a wise owl on the other side. Elena touched it to her lips, wrapped her fist around it, and uttered under her breath, *Theos, give me strength.*

She bent over at the waist and lifted Theodore. She nuzzled her face into his warm neck and said, "Look, *pethaki mou*. Remember the white rocks and blue, blue sky of Greece."

Angeline tugged on her skirt, "Mama, will we come back someday?" she asked.

Elena felt a hot pang. She touched her daughter's soft, dimpled cheek and said, "I think so, *pethia mou*, but just wait until you see America! Papa says it's magical!"

The children made friends and played games on their beds. They rumpled their blankets and pretended sawdust chips were donkeys galloping over hills and valleys.

Every day, the family climbed up to the open lower decks to run and gaze across the infinite ocean. The fresh salt air filled their nostrils and cleared their heads. They danced happy jigs in the open air. Elena fashioned a slender padded rope around Theodore's waist and shoulders in case the unpredictable two-year-old got too close to the railing. Kindly passengers on the upper decks sent bowls of leftover food down below to help feed the children in the steerage compartment.

Six days into the two-week voyage, the morning sky broiled with black clouds. The wind howled, the rain sheeted, and the ship groaned as it pitched and rolled in every direction. Seasickness swept over the entire ship but was relentless in the steerage compartment. The heavy air reeked of vomit. They lay on their mattresses and rode the storm holding onto metal bedposts bolted to the walls. Elena braced her body and clung onto the three little ones. Her muscles quivered.

Please help us, Theos, she prayed frantically as the ship shuddered and lunged forward.

When she could no longer manage to hold onto them, she laid Theodore, Angeline, and Sophia side by side, like little toy soldiers, on top of one of the beds. She tucked a thick blanket around them and tied a rope securely onto the bed frame in crisscross fashion over the top of them.

"Mama!" shouted Sophia over the ship's deafening protests. "I...I think we're going to die!"

"*Theos*'s hand will stop the wind," said Elena. She could barely hold her own head up. Blood pounded in her ears. The children were thirsty. She tipped water into their mouths from an earthen jug.

In the middle of the night, while nodding off fitfully, they heard a loud crash and shrieking. A bunk had yanked free from the wall, scraped across the floor, and smashed into another bunk on the opposite side.

The lights came on and several men stumbled across the pitching floor to hang onto the wayward bunk. No one was harmed except for seventeen-year-old Pavlos. He was traveling alone to meet his uncle in New York. He lay moaning, facedown on his mattress.

Stephan, an older, bearded man, said in a soothing voice, "Let's see what we have."

He slowly turned the boy onto his back. Pavlos let out a piercing scream. Several onlookers gasped as his right shoulder was sticking out at an ungodly angle. Blood streamed from a jagged gash above his eye.

Stephan gripped the bed and covered Pavlos's shoulder with a blanket. "We know just what to do, Pavlos." The men quickly wired the bunk to the beds against the wall.

Using all the force of her will, Elena staggered over to the boy. Prickles ran down her arms when she saw him.

"Help me," he cried.

She put pressure on his brow with the hem of her skirt until the bleeding stopped. Stephan rummaged for a clean strip of linen. He and Elena wrapped it around Pavlos's head.

She stroked his good arm and shouted, "Pavlos, your shoulder is in the wrong place. I can put it back, but you must be a brave boy. I did this for my brother when he fell out of an olive tree. Here, bite down on this cloth and turn your eyes away. It will hurt, but the pain will get better fast," she assured. "Do you believe me?"

"I…think so," he cried. "But hurry!"

"Stephan!" Elena yelled over the ship's groaning. "Wrap your arms around my waist and hold me tight." Stephan nodded and held her with strong arms. She braced her foot on the bed frame, gripped Pavlos's wrist, and pulled downwards slow and steady with all her strength. Pavlos let out a gut-wrenching scream as his shoulder slid back into place.

"Oh," cried Pavlos, surprised how relieved and loose his body suddenly felt. He sighed heavily and mumbled, "Oh! Oh…that's better."

"Now, we need to keep this arm still." She tore a bedsheet into strips with the help of Stephan, and wrapped his bent arm firmly across his chest. "You're a brave boy."

Stephan helped Elena to her bunk, and she sank into the mattress, white-faced and rattled to her core.

After two days, the seas calmed. Passengers streamed up the ladders and marveled at the tranquil sea, so recently fierce. The ship chugged across the Atlantic under fair skies.

Excitement rippled through the upper deck as passengers leaned over the railings, pointing to the thin strip of land in the distance. The ship's throaty steam whistle gave out a series of long blasts, harkening their arrival.

Soon, shouts from the hatch above filled the compartment.

"The Statue! The Statue!"

The ship's immense engines shuddered to a deafening roar and slowed. Everyone in steerage flooded the upper decks to see. Pavlos sidled up to the family and took a collapsible brass telescope out of his duffel. He tucked it between his knees and pulled it open with his good hand.

"Let me see! Let me see, Pavlos!" shouted Andrew, dancing with excitement. Pavlos grinned and handed him the telescope. "Oh, Mama," said Andrew with a voice lowered in reverence. "Look! Look at her pointy crown. She's holding a book."

"She's green, Mama!" said Sophia as she sat her doll, Antonia, on the railing for a better view.

Elena's heart swelled when she saw the great crowned lady with her torch proudly held high. Sophia leaned against her mother's side. Elena's brow furrowed with worry when she glanced down at her daughter. Sophia had become covered with raised itchy spots the day before.

Stout little tugboats with bright red smokestacks nudged the ocean liner skillfully against the moorings. The ship gave a final bellowing blast of its horn and the shipload cheered wildly.

Before walking down the steep gangplank, the immigrants were issued a copy of the ship's manifest and a tailor's T-shaped pin. They were instructed to pin the manifest on their clothing. Elena gathered her children close to her sides. They stepped onto the wharf with their belongings looped through their arms and strapped on their backs. Uniformed officials separated the passengers into long lines to await ferries that would transport them to Ellis Island for processing.

Elena and her children gaped at the city skyline. It seemed alive with billowing smokestacks, and too many buildings to count. The windows reflected the bright sun as sparkling jewels in the distance.

After a long wait, the family walked up the short gangplank of the ferry and scrambled to the front railing. They leaned forward and watched the prow of the ferry cut through the inky water.

"Look, Mama!" said Angeline. "The Statue's getting bigger and bigger!"

"She's welcoming us, children!" said Elena.

The throng of immigrants filed into an enormous brick building, eyeing the magnificent structure with curiosity. Inside, brilliant natural light poured through the vaulted arched windows onto the shiny floor, casting a warm glow on every wall. The children's eyes were round with wonder.

The new arrivals were herded and separated into long lines once again, according to their country of origin. They were informed that first, intake officers would scrutinize their paperwork, and then doctors would give each of them a physical examination.

Elena bent down eye level with Sophia and instructed in a firm voice, "Stay behind me and don't make a single sound. Do you understand?"

Sophia's body shuddered and her face burned. She hugged Antonia hard. "Yes, Mama," she whispered.

Elena looked at her children and said, "All of you. Be on your very best behavior. Don't say a word unless you are spoken to."

"Yes, Mama," they chimed in together.

Elena Giannakopoulos Ioannou, eyes weary with dark circles, gathered her children close under the wings of her arms and stood trembling. She made a desperate attempt to appear nonchalant. *What will they think of Sophia? Maybe they won't notice her.* She clutched the immigration papers in her hand. A line of uniformed men and women sat at a long wooden table to receive the newcomers. A customs officer with a neatly cropped moustache nodded and then beckoned to Elena. She urged her children to move towards him. He extended his hand to receive the papers. She noticed a small American flag sewn onto his breast pocket.

"I-o-ann-ou. Hmm. Does that name have an English meaning?" the officer asked a translator sitting next to him.

"Ioannou. It means son of John."

"Ah, that's easy. Now, your last name is Johnson!" he said with an encouraging smile. He stamped their papers with a flourish and sent the family to join others in line to receive their physical examinations.

Elena joined the line with a sense of dread welling up in her throat. The children began to fidget.

"Mama," said Andrew. "They sound funny when they talk."

Elena raised her brows and gave them all a stern look. Andrew clamped a hand over his mouth. The others stood wide-eyed.

As they were ushered into a partitioned area, a doctor and nurse instantly gazed down at Sophia, who peeked around her mother's skirt. The doctor turned to the nurse and prefaced his words with a throaty "ahem." He looked at Elena and spoke in a somber voice. "Your child looks sick. We need to examine her."

Elena shook her head and said, "*Then milo Anglika.*"

The doctor nodded to a uniformed officer who, in turn, summoned a translator. As the doctor stepped towards Sophia, she backed away, clutching Antonia to her chest with both hands, and vehemently shook her head from side to side. He and the nurse grabbed Sophia by either hand. Antonia tumbled to the cold cement floor.

Sophia struggled to pull away and collapsed, screaming, "Mama! Antonia! *Mi tous afisis na me paroun apo sena!* (Don't let them take me from you!)"

"I don't understand!" Elena shouted. "Why do you need to take her? Can't you look at her here?" She sank to her knees. Bewildered tears filled her eyes. She reached over and scooped Antonia up in her arms.

The translator helped Elena stand and said, "Be patient. Wait. They need to make sure she's alright."

"Will they bring her back?"

"Yes, yes. Try not to worry."

She held the smiling doll to her breast and buried her face in its brown yarn hair. Sophia was gone just ten minutes and ran back to her mother's outstretched arms. She pressed fully into her mother. Elena kissed and kissed her daughter's hot face.

"Your daughter has a whopping case of chicken pox," said the doctor. As his words were translated, his eyes softened as he looked at the handsome children. "It's too late to quarantine her. Most likely, all of your children will come down with chicken pox, but it will go away." He examined the rest of them and was satisfied.

"Now go," he smiled with a sweep of his hand, "and be well."

The worry in Elena's chest loosened. She gratefully crossed herself and said, "*Theos na fila.*"

Just outside the immigration building, Vasilios stood on his toes scanning the faces of people streaming out the exit doors towards the boat dock. His fingers gripped the heavy-gauge wire fence separating sponsors from immigrants. People walked in various forms of happiness, distress, and confusion. He watched them, heart wrenched, remembering, blood pounding in his ears, breath caught in his throat. Then he saw them, clumped together, awkward, hauling possessions. Kids bigger! Little Theodore! When their eyes met, Elena dropped everything on the ground and ran to him. The day's brilliant light revealed every aspect of her beauty and goodness.

The Johnson family changed their name back to Ioannou and fell in love with their life in Chicago. It took Elena time to adjust to Chicago's finicky weather. It swayed from frigid cold to soaking hot and everywhere in between.

They rented a small brick cottage by Greektown and stayed tight within their family, church, and community of immigrants. Elena found friendship with other émigrés at Jane Addams' Hull House on Halstead Street. They became like sisters and blessed the teachers that taught them how to count American money, shop, sew with treadle sewing machines, light gas stoves without blowing them up, and do laundry in washtubs, instead of streams like at home. Elena hung up clothes to dry on the clotheslines in the back alley of their house. In winter, the lines traveled back and forth close to the ceiling in the basement.

Vasilios brought home the biggest American flag he could find, and flew it on the Fourth of July. He said, "We can be anything in America!"

Music filled their home. Vasilios found a scarred-up wreck of an upright piano someone had thrown away in a downtown alley. It had been rained on, the wood was warped and scratched, keys were missing, and it had no lid, but Vasilios said, "The big cast-iron harp is solid. Perfect! The bones are good."

He and his brother Theodore borrowed a truck from work and hauled it home. It took Vasilios over a year to understand the workings of the piano, how to fix it. He took the heavy harp out and studied the insides of other upright pianos with a magnifying glass. He'd sing the parts of the piano to his children.

"Pin block, hitch pins, web, stress bars, and caaaaaapo d'astro!"

The children begged him, "Sing, Baba, sing!" His big baritone voice could go down deep and deeper. He clapped his hands and his foot thumped rhythm on the floorboards. The children laughed and laughed. His voice rang out in the morning and when the sun went down.

"Music fills the heart with gladness," he said.

He restrung the piano, made a new lid, and replaced most of the keys and pads. The walnut wood shined like brand-new. Always the proud centerpiece of the home.

7

The Lone Ranger

A fiery horse with the speed of light, a cloud of dust
and a hearty "Hi-Yo Silver"—The Lone Ranger!

1956

*S*ophie and Niko couldn't stand Theo Taki. He was Yiayia's first cousin, but he made the kids call him the elevated "Theo" instead of "Cousin." Taki carried his worn, striped leather-handled suitcase wherever he went and slinked about like a rat sniffing for a tidbit of garbage. His beady eyes darted around and never rested for long on any one thing. He had an oily, raspy voice. His face was the color of a dirty rag. Black varnished hair, slick with Brylcreem, made him appear like a skinny cartoon evildoer.

Taki showed up in their garage on a regular basis and talked to Tom about "this deal or that." He had always told the kids to get lost, as if he was hiding something, but since Niko had become Tom's helper in the garage for the summer, Taki figured he had listening privileges that Sophie didn't.

Ma's cooking filled the house with delicious smells one Saturday evening. It always made Sophie feel good inside. The only person that surpassed Christina's natural abilities in the kitchen was Yiayia. *Kota reganata* – chicken baked for hours in lemon juice with oregano and olive oil. Greek-style green beans simmered in sweet-smelling tomato sauce in a big blackened pot on the stove.

Sophie stood barefoot on the cool kitchen floor in her cut-off jeans and yellow short-sleeved blouse. She hummed while slicing cucumbers for the salad. Christina looked over and said, "Sophie, call everyone in from the garage. Dinner's ready."

She laid the knife down. "Do I have to, Ma?"

Christina waved her hand in the air and said, "Yes, go."

"I hope you're not having Taki for dinner."

"He's family, and you should call him Theo."

The blood ran hot in Sophie's head. "Why should I? He's not even my uncle, and besides, me and Niko *hate* him. Even Yiayia told me to stay away from Taki because he's got the *diavolos* in him."

"I know, Sophie. I'm not crazy about him either, but like I said, he's family."

Sophie jerked the refrigerator door open for no reason, and her brown eyes flashed dark at her Ma. "He would drown our cat if he had a chance," she said. "I can't believe you let Niko be near him. What does Pa do with him anyway?"

Christina lowered the wooden spoon and stared at Sophie straight-faced. "Niko's not alone with him, and he helps bring car business to your Pa. We need the money. Just go."

Sophie set her jaw and slammed the refrigerator door shut. She walked in the side garage door and found Niko perched quietly on his stool. Tom was working under the hood of a shiny black Lincoln. Taki was just finishing his conversation in Greek with a young man by the open garage door. She saw that the man didn't wear American clothes. His cream-colored shirt had embroidery on the points of the collar, and his khaki trousers hung baggy. A thin, neatly knotted white rope cinched his pants at the waist.

The man looked over at Sophie and tipped his short-billed black cap. His skin was dark, and a bright smile gleamed through his closely cropped beard and moustache. Sophie smiled and walked over to shake his hand.

"*Ti kanies,*" he said in a shy voice.

"*Kala,*" said Sophie. "*Poselene?*"

"*Me lene, Kostas.*"

"*Me lene, Sophie. Hero poli.*"

Kostas gave a slight bow and turned to leave. "*Kronia Polla. Adio.*"

"*Adio,*" she said.

Sophie walked to the front side of the car and fiddled with a bolt on the worktable.

"Pa, who's that man? He seems nice."

"Ask your Theo," Tom said with a look of annoyance.

Sophie turned to Taki with a contemptuous stare. There was a smell of stale whiskey about him. Even his loathsome movements made her feel sick.

"Yeah, Kostas," said Taki. "He's just a stupid DP, don't ya know!"

"What's a DP?" she asked.

"Don't ya know? He's a Displaced Person." Taki smiled a freakish, yellow-toothed grin under his twisted moustache. "It's someone who don't know nothin' about bein' here—don't even know English. Someone who just got off the boat and is an ignoramus." Theo flicked his cigarette ashes at her feet. "Yeah, only been here a week and moochin' off relatives." Sophie felt her lip curling. She balled her hands into fists.

Now it was even more glaring to Sophie how much Theo Taki looked like a snake and talked like one, if a snake could talk. Theo sneered out of the corner of his mouth and found reasons to make fun of everyone.

Sophie took a bold step towards Taki and said, "Theo, didn't all of our older family come from Greece? Didn't you? Are they all DPs too?" She walked off smiling, but said over her shoulder, "Oh, Ma says to come in for dinner."

Taki seethed "smart-ass" under his breath.

The children bowed their heads and Christina gave thanks to God for the food. Tom stared ahead. Niko sat between Taki and Sophie. The dishes were passed around, and Taki piled food on his plate. He snorted and slouched leisurely to eat his dinner. Sophie leaned forward and eyed him with disgust.

Taki caught her all-too-legible look and grunted. She put her hand on Niko's shoulder and stared at Taki in defiance. Something about her penetrating, earnest eyes made him sniff and look away. Oblivious to the exchange, Niko scooted his fork along the pattern on the oilcloth covering the table. Taki smirked. He leaned close to Niko and whispered, *"Garage rat."*

Niko turned to Taki and scowled. He cupped his mouth to Taki's ear and whispered, *"Vitto."* Taki's face blanched, and he put his fork down. His hand wandered to the back of his neck.

Tom wolfed down his dinner and drained the last of his coffee, knowing cousins were on their way over. Sophie decided Pa could do just about anything except connect with people.

"Let's go, Taki," he said.

"Yeah, you go ahead," said Taki. "I'm not finished."

"Finish and come out," snapped Tom. Taki winced.

Niko jumped up. "Can I turn the radio on, Pa? It's time for the Lone Ranger!"

"No, damn it! Don't you ever touch that radio. You could get zapped! I'll turn it on."

Tom had built the radio from scratch. It was an odd electrical contraption with exposed glass tubes, coursing wires, weird dials, and colorful resistors to control the flow of current. To Sophie, the conglomeration looked like a miniature city on top of its three-inch-tall metal box.

The radio sat tucked in the corner of the kitchen counter. Tom ducked under the cupboard and flipped the toggle switch. The glass tubes glowed from dim to bright orange within fifteen seconds. Sophie sat mesmerized by the intricate filament springs held up by Y-shaped wires inside the tubes. The radio crackled to life. Tom turned the black dial to WGN Chicago and then walked out.

The kids sat around the kitchen table and listened to the Lone Ranger and his faithful friend, Tonto, bring justice to the American West. Sophie saw that Niko's face had a look of undisturbed serenity. He clutched his white plastic horse with its black saddle. It looked like the Lone Ranger's horse, Silver.

Sophie stared out the window and listened.

On summer evenings while Yiayia Sophia did the accounting for the apartment and store, Papou visited with friends. She always kept a firm grip on their finances. She dipped her pen in a blue bottle of ink and wrote in a big leather-bound ledger. With the window open, Yiayia Sophia breathed in the aroma from hundreds of East Side kitchens.

Papou George dragged three faded green metal chairs out on the sidewalk in front the apartment by Pasquale's Pizza. He talked for hours with Pete Pasquale and their neighbor, Mr. Simonian, while twirling and flipping his *komboloi* worry beads with one hand. Mr. Simonian looked like a bushy-browed, sleepy old toad. All three suspendered old men passed their time freely offering authority on most subjects of the neighborhood and the world. Papou smoked his brown stogie down to an inch-long stub and stuck it on a toothpick to finish inhaling the last pungent bit.

Yiayia called out the window to see if they needed anything and would invariably say, "George, those stinky cigars aren't good for you!" He'd shrug and keep smoking.

Niko liked to play with his small metal cars and pea-green plastic army guys on the sidewalk where the men congregated. Any bits of cellophane, cigarette butts, cardboard, or bottle caps found on the sidewalks became obstacles for his cars or bunkers for his little soldiers. He found friends in the alley.

Everyone kept an eye on each other's kids, but one sultry evening when the lightning bugs lit up, Niko went missing. Sophie had been helping Yiayia roll phyllo dough on the kitchen table with a long wooden dowel.

"You know, honey, I haven't seen Niko all day, and now the sun's going down," said Yiayia. "He always pops in. Call your Ma. He's probably home, but I'll go poke around and ask neighbors."

I'll bet he rode his bike too far with that Jake kid, thought Sophie.

She dialed her home phone—no answer. She ran down the fire escape stairs in the back of the apartment and headed around the block looking for him in the alleyways. As she rounded the corner of the building, Papou called out, "Hey, slow down, Sophie, where you's going?"

"Have you seen Niko, Papou?" Sophie asked.

"No. I haven't seen him. Go run to home. We look down streets."

Sophie ran the twelve blocks to her house. The spring-loaded front screen door slammed loudly behind her. She stopped and bent over, resting her hands on her knees to catch her breath. The blood pounded in her ears. "Hello? Anyone home?" She ran through the house and found Ma in their backyard pulling dry clothes from the clothesline. Teddy the Cat was curled up by the wicker basket of folded clothes. Wind out of nowhere snapped a sheet.

"Ma, where's Niko?" she asked. "Is he in the garage with Pa?"

"No, your Pa's not here. I thought he was with you." She rubbed her chin. "Go back to the apartment. I'll look around the school and baseball field and meet you there if I don't find him."

"Okay," said Sophie. Teddy scampered behind Sophie as she ran back down the street. Another sudden gust of wind raked the trash in the gutter as she ran. An uneasy feeling settled in her stomach.

She found Yiayia scurrying along 106th Street by the Hi-Lo store. Sophie knew neighbors were asking questions and searching the alleyways. The alarm had been sent out throughout the neighborhood by her grandparents. Just as birds know where to go when a storm is brewing, the neighbors would join hands and mobilize when there was trouble on their streets.

Sophie ran down to Thea Stefania's on 105th, but he wasn't there. There was one place she hadn't looked. The basement in her grandparents' apartment building. She wove through the alleyways, calling for Niko. When she rounded the corner of the apartment, she saw Teddy sitting nonchalantly on the front stoop.

"How'd you get here?"

The cat stared at her and ran his tongue over his white whiskers. He rubbed against her bare leg. She opened the front door.

The air inside seemed hazy, slanted with light from the side windows. Sophie paused at the top of the basement stairs as the cat ran down ahead of her. She flipped on every light switch she could find and crept down the groaning stairs. Fear coursed through her limbs like electricity as she thought about their neighbor, Mr. Brown. She and Niko had seen Mr. Brown's dead body in Apartment Number One, down by the basement, when Mrs. Brown had screamed for help the year before.

Most things in the basement didn't bother Sophie when she was with Yiayia, running clothes back and forth through the rubber rollers on the wringer washing machine on laundry day, but she hated being down there alone. It was a dark place in spite of the narrow shafts of light streaming through three small windows by the ceiling. A naked light bulb hung down from a rafter on a crinkled brown wire. The gigantic, rattling furnace looked like an octopus, with arms waving up to the low ceiling. A drain in the middle of the gray cement floor funneled away dirty water from the washtubs with loud swirling, slurping sounds. When she was small, Sophie thought it would suck her down too. White rope clotheslines held up with long wooden sticks looked like spiderwebs crisscrossing between heavy wooden beams.

"Niko, Niko, are you down here?" No sound. She came to the lowest landing. The floor was tiled in little white hexagons with splotches of dark green insets. Teddy paced in front of the scuffed-up wooden door. She turned the big brass doorknob, pushed the heavy door open, and stepped over the threshold.

Sophie searched for the light bulb's chain with her hand. It brushed her fingertips and she jerked down on it. The swinging light cast sharp shadows throughout. The dank air was still and she could hear her own breathing. Her eyes scoured every corner. The cat slinked to a wood-slat closet door where the mops and cleaning supplies were stored. He meowed low in his chest.

"Niko!" she called. A whimpering sound came from inside the closet. "Niko! Are you in there?"

"Sophie, help! Let me out!"

She flipped the wooden lever up and threw the door open. Teddy rushed in.

"Oh…Sophie! Teddy!" Niko said in a choked whisper.

As her eyes adjusted to the darkness of the closet, she saw the small form of her brother crouched in a corner under a shelf clutching some old towels and rags. Teddy sat at his feet.

"Niko, what's happened to you?"

"I…"

Sophie got down on her knees and pulled Niko onto her lap. His striped T-shirt was torn by the neck and wet with tears. His forearm and one side of his cheek had little bruises. She rocked and rocked him on the cold cement floor, holding tight. He shivered in a released spasm of pent-up fear. Niko buried his face into her shoulder, squeezed her arm, and sobbed, "I was scared no one would find me, and I could hear a big rat and dead Mr. Brown kicking the rat till it squealed."

"Mr. Brown is dead and gone," she said. "I'm here now, you're okay. Who put you in here? Was it that neighborhood toughie, Jake?"

"I, no, it wasn't him." Niko let out a muffled groan. "I…I can't tell."

"What happened to your fingernails? Why are they bloody?" she asked. "Niko, if somebody hurt you, I gotta know! Tell me."

"I bit my nails, but I can't tell!"

"Why?" asked Sophie. "Niko, something awful is happening and you have to tell me."

"It will get worse for me and be bad for you, too."

"I don't care. Who did this to you?"

"Promise you won't tell?" Niko pleaded. "You gotta keep it a secret!" He clasped his hands together and lowered his eyes. His thick black lashes glistened with tears.

"Come on, Niko. I promise," she said. "Now tell me."

"Cross your heart first."

Sophie crossed her heart and spit in her hand for good measure.

"It, it was that snake, Theo Taki! I can't tell you why! Don't make me!"

"That jerk! I shoulda known." She smoothed down Niko's disheveled hair with soft strokes. "He hurt you. What did he do?"

"He caught me playing with my little cars in the alley and dragged me through the back basement door."

"Why?" she asked. "What did you ever do to him?"

"I told ya!" he yelled. "I can't tell!"

"Alright. I'll help you clean up at the laundry sink and we'll just say you were playing and accidently fell. Let's hurry and get outta here."

As they walked up the stairs, Christina met them halfway. She sucked in her breath when she saw Niko.

"Niko! What happened to you?"

"I…it's okay, Ma. I was playing with my cars on the landing for a long time, but then I fell backwards down the stairs." His face turned red as the lie buzzed around his head like a disturbing fly.

"Oh, *Theos*, be more careful!" Christina cried as she hugged him close.

"I…I will, Ma."

Niko remembered what Papou had told him a while back. "Is a man's job to protect the womens," he said. "You's younger than Sophie, but you's can both look out for each other."

Niko later told Sophie that he had broken Taki's good watch while winding it up too tight.

"What were ya doin' with his watch?" asked Sophie.

"I found it on the workbench 'cause he…he left it there." Niko's mouth twitched.

"Breaking a watch is no reason to hurt and scare you that bad, Niko," she said. "I'm gonna tell Ma."

"No, no, don't tell Ma! If Taki finds out, he'll do something even worse!"

"But Niko, he's dangerous."

"I know he's stupid and crazy. But I'll stay away from him for sure."

Sophie bent down eye level to Niko and put her hand on his shoulder. "Don't ya ever, ever get close to him again…promise? When he comes in the garage, leave! If I find out that he messes around with you in any way, I'll tell. I don't care what he says."

"Okay, okay," said Niko, pulling his eyes away from her gaze. He nodded and crossed his heart with two stiff fingers. "I promise."

The next day Sophie saw Niko walking down the sidewalk on Avenue L with Noops, who had his pet chicken, Blackie, tucked under his arm. She turned and studied Niko, talking and wildly gesturing at Noops. *What is he saying?* she wondered. She shook her head and thought, *Probably just boy stuff. Maybe I could try and get something out of Noops. But how?*

8

Noops

My poor heart is sentimental
Not made of wood
I got it bad and that ain't good.

— Duke Ellington

Sunday, July 8, was a day for the record books. It hit 92 at eight o'clock in the morning, 90 percent humidity, with the promise of reaching a blistering 104 before noon. When the Chicago air got wicked hot and thick, like soup, people flocked to the Lake.

Niko's friend Noops came along whenever the family went to the beach.

Papou pulled up to Noops's tan brick bungalow on Ewing Avenue with the carload. He honked once. The venetian blinds parted, and within seconds Noops burst out the front door. His blue-and-red Cubs T-shirt hung baggy on his skinny frame. He was puny for a twelve-year-old. Bottle caps bulged in the pockets of his plaid swim trunks. Everyone in the car knew they would get a bottle cap as a present.

"Hey, Noops!" Niko yelled out of the back-seat window.

"Ahhh!" exclaimed Noops, waving an arm over his head. As he ambled down the walkway with his rhythmic limp and loose-hinged arms, Sophie noticed that his rich chocolate-colored skin made his toothy grin even brighter. She couldn't help staring at him. His broad smile and awkward movements radiated over his body, perhaps peculiar to onlookers, but beautiful to her.

"That boy is always happy," said Yiayia. Sophie smiled.

Cheerful Noops brought a sense of purity to those around him, as if the sun shimmered on him perpetually. To move took some measured courage on his part, as he'd be unsure if his legs could get him where he wanted to go or his hands to connect with things he intended to touch.

Kids made fun of Noops at school and mimicked his awkward gait, but he would grin and wave good-naturedly at his tormentors, humiliating them with his innocence. The Poulos family, the neighbors, and Noops's parents did their best to surround him with protection. The cruelty seemed to pass right over his head—that is, until this day.

Niko flung open the car door and Noops scrunched into the back seat next to him. Niko helped him take the bottle caps out of his pockets and pass them around. The kids sat skin to skin in their bathing suits. Rivulets of sweat mingled. Every window was cranked open in the blasting heat. When the car picked up speed, the stifling wind whipped through in all directions. The heat shimmered on the road, making the air look wavy. Sophie was sure they'd roast alive if they didn't hurry to the beach.

Papou repeatedly tried to smooth over the few long white hairs on top of his head, but they seemed to blow straight up.

"Pa, stop messing with your hair and just wear your hat," said Yiayia Sophia. He plopped on his straw fedora with its wide ribbon band.

He flashed his eyes in the rearview mirror and said, "Did you's hear about Antnee Cirelli's boy who tumble out the car door, break both elbows, crack his head like an egg and is never same since? He don't talk right. He don't walk right."

"Enough, Pa!" Yiayia Sophia admonished. She whispered, "What are you thinking? You're scaring the kids, and Noops is in the car!"

He winced and crossed himself. "*Theos* help me." He lowered his eyes at his wife and confided, "Ya know, Ma—a little scarin' is no bad thing, but I didn't choose the right time to say."

Papou became quiet for a while, and then he started singing songs offkey between chewing on his unlit stogie. As they got closer to the Calumet Park beach he gunned the engine at a stoplight just to hear its big V-8 engine roar.

"Step on it, Papou!" yelled Cousin George.

Exhaust billowed out the back as the car exploded into action on a green light. Just then, a red Chevy Bel Air raced around their car and almost clipped the front fender.

Papou lay on the horn, shook his fist, and yelled out the window, "You idjet! Whatta ya think you doin'?" Yiayia bit the knuckle of her thumb.

"Pa, let it go," she said in a strong voice.

He reached inside his breast pocket and pulled out an oversized hand-kerchief to mop the back of his neck. "I tell you, Ma, they all idjets on the road."

"Honestly, Pa, you're gonna give yourself a stroke when you carry on like that!" she said with her hand propped on his shoulder. "Do you think yellin' at them is gonna make them better drivers?"

"They could use a lesson or three!"

Sophie knew that whenever Papou got hopped up, Yiayia could reel him in like a wriggling fish on a stout line. Sophie couldn't help but feel the difference between them and her parents when they disagreed. It took some yelling back and forth with her grandparents, but all the while, it worked into something good.

"Why don't you tell a joke to the kids," Yiayia said.

He shook his head and said, "Okay, *pethia*, what did a strawbedie say to da otha strawbedie?"

"We give up, Papou," shouted the kids in unison.

"My brotha is in a jam!" he guffawed, hitting the enormous steering wheel with the palm of his hand. Good-natured Papou George got the grandkids laughing with his thick Greek accent and attempts at jokes. Papou thought himself so funny that it made the kids laugh all the harder.

Yiayia cranked the radio dial onto Greek Hour. The kids rolled their eyes and bumped each other a smile when their grandparents sang and cried with the music. When the live news reports from Greece came on, the kids weren't allowed to say a word. Their grandparents lived for the news from commentator Giorgos Kapetanakis. His voice kept thousands of Chicago

Greeks connected to the old country. A short excerpt of the liturgy from the Assumption Church in Hegewisch was repeated after the news. With each chant of *kyrie eleison*, Yiayia made sure everyone crossed themselves.

Calumet Park beaches were closest to the steel mills and loaded with dead fish. Sophie and the kids would bat the white-bellied "floaters" away while swimming.

Theo Stephan, who worked at Republic Steel, said, "Yeah, they dump da wasted mercury right into that lake. I tell you, just don't swallow the water, kids," affirming his words with an upward jerk of his head and a tongue click. "Then you be okay."

When the kids tumbled out of the car, Niko stood by Noops's side. He took him by the hand and led him around the maze of colorful beach towels towards the water. Noops lifted his chin to the smell of fish and hot sand. The pair turned heads, as it was uncommon to see a colored boy holding hands with a white boy. Some grumblings caught Niko's ears. He frowned.

Without warning, Noops's hand jerked away. Niko whipped around and saw his friend flat on his back on the hard, wet sand. His arms and legs flailed like a turtle turned over on its shell. A look of terror crossed Noops's face and he panted, "Ah, ah, ah!"

"Ah, ah, ah!" mimicked a muscly teenage boy with a contorted smirk on his face. He kicked Noops hard in the ribs. Noops gasped and grabbed his side. "What are you? Some kind of nigger-freak?"

Just as Niko raised both fists to defend his friend, Sophie hurtled into the boy from behind, knocking him face first in the sand. With movements so swift they seemed a blur, Cousin George quickly turned him over, straddled his chest, and bloodied the boy's nose with a quick, fierce punch. He jerked the boy to his feet by his wrist and shouted with unleashed fury, "You damn coward! Now, say you're sorry!"

The boy reeled back, covered his bloody face with both hands, and sputtered a feeble "uh…sorry."

"That's not good enough," George seethed. He grabbed the boy's thick arm and spun him around to face Noops. "Tell *him* you're sorry!"

Noops recoiled and whimpered.

"I'm…I'm sorry," the boy said with a shaky voice.

George gave the boy a hard shove and said, "Now, get outta here."

The boy wheeled around and stumbled away with his gang of thugs. The close-by sunbathers looked on silently, but with surprising approval for Sophie and George.

Niko sat down on the sand beside Noops. He pulled him by the arm to a sitting position. "I'm here, Noops."

Noops choked tears. He wiped his streaming nose with the back of his hand. Niko grabbed a towel and wiped his face. He brushed sand out of his close-cropped, wiry hair and asked, "Are you okay?" Noops rubbed his side, looked up, and opened his mouth to say something, but shut it again.

Niko patted him quietly and began to build a small sandcastle for him in the wet sand. With two fingers, he scraped an oblong channel around the castle. He filled the channel with lake water to make a moat. Noops stared and then traced a finger along in the water. Niko tapped Noops on the shoulder to get his attention. He stretched his tongue out and touched the end of his nose. Noops tried to copy him, and they shook with laughter.

"Look," said Niko, reaching his finger to the sky. Noops squinted up and watched a gull fly in lazy circles. It flew down and skimmed the glimmering water.

After a while, they walked into the cool waters of Lake Michigan. Noops glided effortlessly. The water buoyed his movements. Noops and Niko giggled and splashed happily.

Cousin George bumped Sophie on the shoulder and said, "Hey, Sophie, look at 'em." With a stiff hand Sophie shielded the sun from her eyes to watch. She smiled.

Sophie sat in the front between her grandparents on the way home. When the rest of the family and Noops settled in the car, Sophie bounced on the seat and said, "Yiayia, tell us the story about how you married Papou."

"I've told that story so many times. Aren't you kids tired of it?"

"No!" the children shouted.

"We want to hear it again," Sophie said.

"Come on, Yiayia!" said Niko. "Again!"

She sighed and studied her husband's profile. His face had not ignored the passage of time but recorded it with lines, furrows, and scars that told their own story. He turned and met her warm hazel eyes with a smile. His big, thick hand enfolded hers.

"Okay, kids." She tucked her unruly hair tighter. "I tell you, this hair used to be dark, dark brown—like chocolate."

"*Omorfos*," said Papou George. Yiayia smiled.

"I was just eighteen years old and thought my Pa, your Great-Papou Vasilios, would choose Theo Stephan, the oldest. But I knew he wouldn't be the good husband for me. He was thirty years old! Too old! He smelled like mothballs and had a big bushy moustache that curled around his mouth. He bragged that he could eat five hard-boiled eggs at once. One Easter dinner, after midnight mass, I saw him showing off his egg-eating in the Hegewisch church hall. He peeled the red eggshells into a messy pile, lined the eggs up on the table, and ate them in a minute! His cheeks looked like balloons, and eggs dribbled out of his mouth."

"Eew," the kids said in unison.

"Now you know, kids, Theo Stephan is a good man, and we respect, but I didn't want him. I couldn't say anything. I shivered inside, knowing I had to obey my parents."

Cousin George stamped his foot and said, "I wouldn't do it."

"It wasn't my decision, George. I had to respect."

"Well, I'd run away."

Yiayia continued, "Ever since I was thirteen years old, I had my eye on the youngest Poulos boy, your Papou."

Papou George tapped the steering wheel lightly and said, "I watch you too. We was shy and didn't talk."

"Papou stood tall and straight, like a proud, handsome soldier. He had kind eyes and dark wavy hair."

Papou George patted his head and said, "The hair is gone, Ma."

Yiayia gave a full-bosomed laugh. "The night of the formal engagement, that April evening, I couldn't come out of my bedroom. I stared out my window and saw the moon hung full in the sky like a bright white ball. My hands shook like two leaves blowing in the wind. I went into the bathroom and ran the water cold and iced my hot, shaky hands to still them. It didn't work.

"Your Great-Yiayia Elena called from the bottom of the stairs, 'Sophia! *Ella cato!*'

"I smoothed my blue satin dress and squeezed my hands together to steady them. I walked slowly down the stairs. I didn't look up. I couldn't breathe."

"'Ah, my Sophia,' said my baba, your Great-Papou Vasilios. 'Here is your future husband.'

"I looked up, and who should be standing there with a bashful smile but your Papou and his parents! I blinked and blinked my eyes. I couldn't believe it!"

"My Baba clapped his hands and said, '*Tha matheta na agapetheta. O Theos na sas evlog me pola pethia stin zoi sou sas eleouclathia, Kronia Polla.* (You will learn to love one another. May God bless and grace you with many children around your table like olive branches. May you have many years!)"

Papou smiled. "We made a match, like two birds in a nest."

"It's a good story, Yiayia," said Sophie. She ran her fingertips along Yiayia's arm and smiled, thinking how her grandparents laughed loud and even fought loud while walking down the street holding hands.

It had grown quiet in the back seat. Sophie turned around and saw Niko and Noops leaning into one another, sound asleep. Cousin George put his finger to his lips and smiled.

9
Piggly Wiggly

*But all these were only dreams, in reality there was
only one thing left to do—to get away as quickly
as possible, not to stay another hour in this place.*

— Anton Chekhov, *An Upheaval*

Tom and Christina's craziness drove the kids out of their basement refuge a couple of evenings later. Sophie heard a deafening crash and glass shattering. The membranes of her ears seemed to separate. Ma screamed, "You don't care about anybody except yourself! Our poor kids, all we do is fight!"

A deadly silence followed for a couple of minutes. Sophie felt a blanket of darkness wrap itself around their house.

She grabbed Niko's hand and said, "Let's get outta here."

They burst out the basement door and ran to the end of their block. The cat loped after them. Niko stopped, lifted Teddy into his arms, and hugged him close to his chest. The cat's spread-apart paws kneaded the fringe on Niko's brown-and-white-plaid cowboy shirt. The kids stared at one another with dull eyes, but Sophie wasn't about to let her brother unravel. With a thin voice she said, "Come on, Niko, let's catch lightning bugs!"

Niko's breath quickened. "My friend Jake says if you take a lightning bug's light-butt off you can stick it on your finger like a shiny ring."

"That's mean, Niko," said Sophie.

"Yeah, I know," he said. "I'd never pull its light-butt off. The poor lightning bug would be hurt and die, but it's kinda amazing though, doncha think?"

"Yeah, I suppose," said Sophie.

Niko set the cat down and said, "Stay here, Teddy." The cat turned two times and sat at his boy's feet.

Sophie showed him how to cup a bug in his hands and peek through till it lit up. In the long twilight that evening, they watched the swallows sweep through the neighborhood and disappear into their places of nighttime rest. The wind stirred and darkness descended. The streetlights popped on up and down the street. Chain-link fences between some houses glistened under the lights. Sophie put her brother's hand in hers and pulled him close in a tight hug. He looked up at her, heavy-lidded, smiled, and then snapped his fingers.

"You stay here, Niko," said Sophie. "I'm gonna listen and see what's going on."

Niko shoved his hands in his pockets, arched his shoulders up to his ears, and said, "Okay." He flopped to the ground and put Teddy in his lap.

Sophie ran back and crept slowly to the house to get within earshot. The neighborhood rested, except for their house. Dim lights burned from deep within, but Tom and Christina's voices continued to rage.

"Are you drinking in front of him?" yelled her Ma.

"How dare you question me!" he slung back. "I'm teaching him. The kid's got some brains, not like the stupid people in your family!"

A wild, hot feeling flooded Sophie's arms and made her want to throw something. She heard the rush of blood in her ears and began to feel sweat gathering on her forehead. Her eyes narrowed in a sharp sideways glance. She turned away and took her time walking back to Niko. The full meaning of the evening's events hit her, and she began to cry.

Sophie wiped her eyes before Niko saw her and said, "Come on, Niko. I know a fun place to go."

Niko heard her voice quaver.

"I hate them," said Niko. "Why don't we go to Yiayia's?"

"Because we can't!" she said with an edge in her voice.

"Gee whiz, Sophie, how come?"

"Because we don't...never mind, I just said so," she said brusquely. "Now, don't ask me anymore."

His shoulders drooped a little. Sophie could always catch his mood by the way he stood. She pulled her thick hair back and said quietly, "We'll go see Yiayia tomorrow."

"Promise?"

"I promise."

She grabbed his hand and they streaked wildly down a couple of blocks. Niko pulled at her hand to slow down. "Sophie! What are ya doin'? You're running too fast!" he panted. They heard a cat meow behind them. Niko skidded to a stop and turned around.

"Uh-oh. Teddy followed us."

The cat caught up and rubbed up against his pants leg. Niko's face crinkled up in a smile as he squatted eye level with the cat. "Hey, Teddy. You need go back." Teddy sat down, licked his front paw, and gazed into Niko's eyes for a few seconds. "Go home." The cat stood, hesitant, and then disappeared into the shadows.

"Good boy," said Niko. "Hey, Sophie, where we going?"

"You'll see."

They took off running again. Sophie led him around the corner onto Avenue O and stopped in front of Piggly Wiggly. The modest brick grocery store had a painted plywood marquee of a smiling pink pig wearing a soda fountain cap cocked to the side. The store's lights glowed onto the sidewalk. Circles of squashed dried-up gum dotted the cement.

"Come on, Sophie! Let's climb the Piggly Wiggly tree!"

"You can, Niko, I don't want to."

Niko climbed atop the bulging trunk of a solitary elm tree growing through the sidewalk. The tree squeezed bravely through its small patch of earth, roots lifting the sidewalk at jagged angles. Niko stepped up onto one of the thick roots and wrapped his arms around the wide trunk, not saying a thing. He pressed his cheek against the coarse bark. A rogue nighttime sparrow skittered on a slender branch above his head. He looked up and pulled on a thin suspender holding up his baggy khaki pants. Sophie heard his breath come easier from the run.

"Come on, Niko," said Sophie. "Get down and let's go in."

Niko blinked out of his momentary reverie and said, "Can you buy me some gum, Sophie?"

"We'll see."

Inside, the store smelled like baking bread, and the speckled linoleum floor gleamed under the humming fluorescent lights. Niko slid his brown oxford shoes across the floor like an ice skater.

Mr. Cusimano waved from behind a checkout stand. "Miss Sophie and Mr. Niko!" he exclaimed. "Howsa you's kids?"

Niko shoved a hand in his pants pocket and gave a sideways grin. "Okay."

Mr. Cusimano walked over to them, touched his white paper cap with a slim finger, bowed deeply with a flourish, and said, "Welcome to Piggly Wiggly!"

Niko eyed his starchy blue-and-white uniform, with Piggly Wiggly pig patches sewn on both sleeves of his deep-pocketed jacket. When Mr. Cusimano smiled, Niko studied the tiny silver hooks fastened to the outside of his four front teeth. Mr. Cusimano saw him staring. His cap magically levitated an inch above his head.

Niko's eyes bugged out. "How'd ya do that?"

Mr. Cusimano winked. Niko clapped his hands as his attention amounted to polite fascination.

"Hold out your hands," Mr. Cusimano said. He thrust his hand into his pocket and pulled out Bazooka Bubble Gum for each.

"Thanks, Mr. Cusimano!" they said.

Niko tore open the wrapper and stuffed the thick chunk of soft pink gum in his mouth. He unfolded the waxy Bazooka Joe comic strip. "When I grow up," Niko said with bulging cheeks, "I wanna work in the Bazooka factory. Then I could chew all the gum I want!"

"Good idea, buddy!" said Mr. Cusimano, smiling.

Sophie took Niko by the hand and walked down an aisle. She looked over her shoulder and grinned at Mr. Cusimano.

"Hey, Sophie. Do ya think I could get silver on my teeth someday?"

She smiled down at him. "Hmm, maybe."

Sophie found an abandoned shopping cart, and Niko climbed into its wide basket.

"Now sit down low and hang on!" she said.

She pushed him down empty aisles and careened around corners until he got his belly laugh going.

They ditched the cart and cruised the candy and little toy aisles hand in hand.

"Hey, Niko," said Sophie. "What's Pa doing with you in the garage besides teaching you about cars?"

Niko lifted his shoulders up to his ears. "I already told you! Just showin' me stuff and…"

"And what?"

"He…"

Just then, Noops and his Pa came around the aisle. Niko ran and touched Noops's arm. "Hey," he said.

Noops turned, threw his arms out, and whooped.

They turned to the racks of toys and started playing with a Chinese finger trap. Noops squeezed one in his hand. Niko took it and stuck his fingers in on either side of the woven tube and tried to pull them out. His fingers got stuck and they laughed.

Sophie said, "Hi, Mr. Potter."

Mr. Potter touched the bill of his cap with one finger and said, "It's always nice to see you two." He walked over to his son and took his hand. "Come on, Noops. We need eggs, and Ma's waiting. Say goodbye to your friend."

"Bah, Niko."

"Bye, Noops."

Niko pulled Sophie to the butcher counter to stare at the lake trout lying on their sides in crushed ice. Their mushy, staring eyes fascinated him. He drew a finger along the slimy grain of a trout's scales and then lifted the edge of its curved gill to see the bloody-looking insides.

"Niko, you were gonna tell me what else Pa's doing with you."

"Nothin', Sophie! I told ya. Just car stuff!"

An unhinged weariness came over Sophie. Her eyes dropped down to the varicolored speckles on the linoleum floor, and for a fleeting moment she felt lightheaded. *I will protect him. No one else will.* She stroked Niko's soft head. He smiled and snapped one of his suspenders with his thumb.

10
Slim Jim

Piglet was so excited at the idea of being
useful that he forgot to be frightened anymore.
— A.A. Milne, *Winnie-the-Pooh*

Sophie lifted the heavy lid of the deep freezer in the back of the store. The frosty air mingled with the day's pent-up heat and billowed cool vapor onto her face. She leaned into the freezer, breathed deep, and rested her hands on the big round tubs of ice cream. She cupped her cheeks with her hands and sighed a happy sigh of relief. That afternoon she had helped her grandparents by sweeping the floor, filling napkin dispensers, and topping off ketchup bottles and salt and peppershakers. The industrial-sized fan blew hot air around like crazy but did little to cool the store.

Before walking home, she climbed up the two rickety wooden steps to use the closet-sized bathroom by the back office. The tiny-screened bathroom window close to the ceiling was open a few inches, and Sophie heard what sounded like Taki's whiny voice. Movements so quiet, she closed the lid of the toilet, climbed on top, and looked out into the narrow alleyway. She caught a whiff of cigar smoke and saw that Taki was talking to the most feared thug on the East Side, Vitto Biducci. His bull-thick neck, fleshy pig-eyed face, and enormous scarred hands scared her.

"You's never be sorry with this guy," assured Taki. "He's all brains. He was a radar guy in da war and can fix cars and do any electricity stuff you want. I tell you, he's one of them geniuses, that guy is." She saw Taki spit a silvery stream on the ground for emphasis.

A tremble traveled down her arms when she heard the words, and the air went raw around her. *Pa. He's talking about Pa!*

"Da boss don't care how ya do it, just get those places fixed up like we tol' ya. Got it?" Vitto poked his forefinger into Taki's hollow chest so hard that he stumbled backwards. Taki sniveled and clasped his chest but quickly recovered.

"Da cars is good," said Vitto. "Keep it goin' like you do and you'll get your cash. You do good and more jobs come your way."

Sophie peeled her eyes away and shuddered. She stepped down from the toilet and sat on its lid. As hot as it was, she got a chill and rubbed her bare arms over and over. Her eyes flickered from the toilet plunger in the corner to her open palms. She shook her head and whispered, *I'm telling.*

She'd seen Vitto walking the streets, coming out of the bars, or cruising the neighborhood in his flashy black Buick. His rumpled, greasy-looking black suit and a stained white shirt with a skinny black leather tie seemed to be his uniform. He wore thick-soled lace-up black boots, and kids at school said he kicked in doors and hobbled anyone that got in his way. They also said he hid a gun and knobby brass knuckles in his bulging pockets. He acted like the East Side was his.

Yiayia and Papou told the kids if they ever saw him coming their way, go the opposite direction and don't even look at him. "His crazy eyes burn holes," said Papou.

The thing Sophie didn't know was that Vitto had met Taki while running whiskey and favors for the cops at the South Chicago Station on 89th and Exchange Avenue. Taki was an idiot, but Vitto knew he would do anything to turn a buck. He also had connections within the Greek community. Tom was a gold mine of electronics and automotive brains, but the guy had his weaknesses. Vitto could smell Tom's greed. He would make sure Taki met his end of any bargain they had made.

Vitto was a gritty scrounger who was trusted to dig out information and set up jobs. He and his boys also handled the car end of the family business.

Taki found Tom in the garage the next day.

"Yeah, that kid of yours is doin' good, Tom, but you better make sure he keeps his flap shut," threatened Taki. "I seen him talkin' to that idiot Noops all the time. Then I seen 'im showin' a Slim Jim to that fool kid Jake, in the alleyway. I made sure he wouldn't do something like that again."

"What do ya mean, you-made-sure?" Tom asked with narrowed eyes.

Taki nervously pulled at the brim of his sweat-stained hat and scratched the back of his head. "I just gave 'im a talkin' to, that's all. Whatta ya think I am?"

Tom stepped closer to Taki, eyed him, and grabbed up a wad of his ratty shirtfront. "That better be all you do."

Taki swallowed nervously and shook his head. "Ya don't need to worry 'bout me doin' nothin' to 'im. Ya can trust me."

"Good," said Tom as he let go of him. Taki looked significantly subdued. "Niko will do anything I ask. He's just the help I need right now. Go figure—a kid."

"Yeah, so what if he's a snot-nose kid. He's got them good kinda hands. But can he keep his mouth shut?"

"Yeah, he worships me," Tom said. Softness crept into his eyes. "He'll do what I say."

Taki figured Niko would be perfect for night jobs. A few weeks earlier, he had convinced Tom to teach Niko how to use a Slim Jim to get into locked cars. Stiffer than a tape measure, the thin, flexible metal strip could be wheedled between the uppermost part of a closed car window and its rubber gasket. Once slid in, it could be angled down, and a forked hook on the end, like a rigid snake's tongue, could pull a door lock up. Niko practiced over and over on cars in the garage until he could open a locked door faster than Tom.

Tom taught him to pick locks. Twelve picks of varying sizes were held together by a strong wire with the ends twisted together. His young ears became trained to hear the right sounds of clicks to crack a lock open. Niko, with his small fingers, had a delicate touch.

———

"You're ready, Niko," said Tom in a monotone voice.

Niko grinned with pride. "Do ya think so, Pa? What do I gotta do?"

"You'll see," said Tom. "Tonight, make sure you remember to wear your Mickey Mouse watch to bed, ya hear?" said Tom. "We're gonna help our family."

"Okay!" exclaimed Niko, standing up straight. He knew his Pa had good ideas because he was smarter than anybody.

After Christina went to sleep that Thursday night, Tom quietly got Niko out of bed at one in the morning and sneaked out of the back door into the garage. He had made sure the door hinges were well oiled so they wouldn't creak. From a cupboard in the garage, Tom pulled out a change of clothes for Niko: sneakers, thin pants, a shabby zip-up jacket, and a cap. They were all black.

"Keep these gloves on all the time. Don't take em' off. Ya hear me?" Tom whispered harshly while shaking his finger in Niko's face. The thin black cotton gloves fit snug.

"Do I gotta, Pa? They're kinda tight."

"Do what I tell ya," he snapped. "No complaints."

"Oh, okay."

"Pa," said Niko quietly. "I…I gotta pee."

"Just wait till we get outside!"

Niko danced a little jig to hold it in.

Tom synchronized their watches and headed out with a couple of small flashlights, suitcases, and the beat-up leather briefcase.

"Ready to have some fun?" Tom whispered.

With his hands clasped together, Niko jumped up with joy and whispered back, "Yeah, Pa! Let's go!"

"If ya do good, I got two surprises for you."

They started at Avenue M and 106th and headed north.

"Now go," said Tom. Niko turned and peed in the bushes.

They walked past Noops's house. Niko knew how dreamy things floated around in Noops's head, how he liked to peel the cork out of bottle caps and make funny noises, but in the quietness and dark of the night the two front windows and brown door of his friend's house somehow looked sad. There was no flicker of light anywhere in the house. Niko sighed a long sigh and turned away.

Tom and Niko stayed together for the first hour and a half. For a brief time, Tom held his son's hand. Niko was so happy he felt as though a balloon were swelling inside him.

Tom whispered out of the corner of his mouth, "We're goin' for the nicer, newer cars. Guys like us are smart."

Niko got the hang of it. A lucky find was a wallet with thirty-two dollars tucked inside, under some papers in a glove box. Tom smiled. Niko could hardly remember the last time he saw his Pa smile.

"Hey, Pa!" Niko exclaimed in a whisper as he danced alongside. "We're pickin' the good cars!"

"Okay, here's the first surprise. We're gonna split up."

"What?" Niko asked incredulously. "I, I don't get to stay with you?"

"If ya do good, I got a Baby Ruth for you in my pocket. That'll be your second surprise. Meet me at exactly four, right here," instructed Tom. "Got it? Make sure you look under the seats and the glove boxes. People are stupid."

"Please, can't I stay with you?" Niko pleaded, wide-eyed.

"Nope, we can go faster if we split up. Besides, this is real man's work," Tom said. "You're a man, ain't ya?"

"Yeah, Pa, but..." Niko whispered quietly while looking down at his gloved hands.

"Remember, meet me at four and try not to use your flashlight until you're in the car. Point it down. Oh yeah, don't forget to dodge the streetlights. If ya see a car or a cop, hide fast. Pretend you're like a creepin' cat lookin' for a mouse. Got it?"

"Yeah, Pa. Like a creepin' cat."

Niko sucked in his breath as they walked in opposite directions. His heart hammered in his chest. He crossed his fingers.

"Creep like Teddy," Niko whispered through his teeth.

He walked down a block and a backyard dog started yapping. Niko jumped and sprinted fast on his toes. The rubber on his sneakers gave him good traction on the sidewalk. Just as he slowed down, the street was suddenly illuminated with the beams of car lights turning the corner towards him. He dove behind a big dark green mailbox, panting. The car crept by slowly, and its tires made a low gravelly rumble. The puddles of light ran over the road like ripples.

A peculiar hollow feeling came over Niko, as if he were being watched. He got up off his knees and ran again.

Looking in every direction, Niko skidded on the loose gravel into a nearby alleyway and dove behind a rusty oil drum stinking of garbage. Sitting on his haunches, he leaned against a brick building and took off his sweaty cap. He felt his own teeth chatter and couldn't stop them. Telephone and electrical wires draped low between creosote-coated poles along the narrow alley. The gravel at his feet was littered with broken glass.

Every night noise he heard was magnified threefold. A delicate scratching sound from above startled him. Niko aimed his flashlight up into the glinting, beady eyes of a huge gray rat perched on the rim of the metal drum. It looked ready to spring on Niko.

Niko flicked his flashlight off, grabbed the handle of his suitcase, and dashed down the alleyway into the next block. He felt the eyes of the rat on him.

He saw two nice cars parked on the same side of the block. He tried the Buick first and lifted its lock with the Slim Jim in seconds. His hands felt all around. "Nothing," he whispered. All he got in the Olds was one quarter and a stubbed-out cigarette under the driver's seat.

"Oh, Pa's gonna kill me." His heart quickened and he picked up his pace.

He rounded a corner and saw a gleaming dark blue Cadillac with enormous fenders parked by a curb under a street lamp. Its silver hood ornament was a horizontal, streamlined winged woman. Her raised face looked as if she were defying the wind, her tucked wings propelling her forward.

Pa told me not to be by lights, but I gotta try this car, Niko thought. He set his small suitcase down on the sidewalk and looked in every direction. There wasn't a soul in sight.

Carefully, Niko flipped the latches on his little suitcase, opened the lid, took out the Slim Jim, and started to coax it into the front passenger window. The rubber gasket was way too tight. He gave up and decided to pick the lock. Five minutes turned into ten. His fingers began to tremble.

"What's wrong with this lock?" Niko whispered under his breath.

After about five more minutes, Niko heard the familiar click. He hit his knee with excitement. Slowly, he depressed the button on the door handle with his thumb. With great care, Niko pulled the well-greased, heavy door open without a sound. The inside of the car had a familiar aroma of cigars.

He reached in, but the glove box was locked. Niko had never worked on one before. He sat on the edge of the seat and inserted the littlest picks into the key slot. The lock popped open easily. With his left hand, Niko pulled out a small black leather zippered case. After he unzipped its three sides, it fell open like a book. He aimed his flashlight on a couple of black-and-white photographs of two little girls in party dresses. The third picture had a smiling older couple holding the girls' hands between them.

Does a grandpa own this car? He thought about Yiayia and Papou and knew that if somebody broke into their car, it would be bad. Niko leaned his forehead on the flashlight and closed his eyes as a weary sadness crept over his body like a heavy cloak. He remained thus for a few seconds, then lifted his chin. He glanced at the photos again but tore his eyes away and flipped though some papers. Two fifty-dollar bills were tucked inside!

Niko jumped up from the seat and hit his head on the ceiling.

"Wow! Wait till Pa sees this!" he whooped loudly.

A few seconds later, a light flipped on and shined through a small window onto the skinny passageway aside the brick house. Niko stuffed the bills into his pants pocket and dropped the little leather case on the plush carpet. He left the car door open, grabbed his suitcase, and ran as fast as his legs could carry him.

"Hey, stop! Who's that?" a man's voice shouted from the doorway.

Niko rounded a corner and ran until the burning muscles in his legs wouldn't carry him any farther. Panting, bending with his gloved hands on his knees, he looked up and realized he had run all the way to the Ewing Avenue Bridge.

Niko faced his hated bridge and shouted, "I...I'm not scared of you!"

An ominous-looking mist was rising up like a floating veil above the murky river. He felt prickles course down his arms.

Under the haloed radiance of a street lamp, he pulled up his sleeve and looked at his watch. Mickey Mouse's hands pointed to three fifty!

"Oh no, I'll never make it back by four!" he groaned.

He leaned against the damp lamppost to rest a minute and then took off running back to the meeting place. Stopping to catch his breath every few blocks, Niko finally made it and stood exactly at the agreed spot. He looked at his watch; it was twenty minutes after four! He spun around but couldn't see his Pa anywhere.

"Damn it, Niko!" Tom seethed through his teeth. "Get over here!" Niko looked behind him and saw his Pa crouched behind a bush. He walked to him with his eyes fixed on the sidewalk. Tom leaped up and slapped his son across the side of his head. Niko fell off the curb into the street.

Tom picked him up by the scruff of his jacket and raised his hand to hit him again.

Niko flinched sideways and begged, "No, Pa! Don't hit me again! I done real good like you told me!"

"What do ya mean, you done good? You're late!" Tom spat. "What a fool I was. I thought you were ready!"

With tears streaming down his face and a drop of blood trickling out from his ear, Niko reached into his back pocket and pulled out the two fifty-dollar bills. Tom's eyes lit up. He grabbed the money and held the bills under his flashlight. He raised his eyes to Niko's face and stopped breathing.

A tiny trail of blood streaked down his neck and his face glistened with tears. With slow movements, Tom reached up and wiped the blood away with his gloved fingertips.

"Okay," said Tom with a catch in his voice. "You done good awright. Let's hurry and get back before daybreak."

Niko choked back tears and wiped his face with his hands. He trudged behind his father in silence but then became racked with quiet chest-heaving sobs.

Tom shivered upon hearing Niko's soft sobs, and he bit his bottom lip. He stopped, turned, and put his hand on his son's shoulder. "Niko, I…I'm sorry I hit you. I've never done that before. I don't know why…"

Niko put his hand up to his ear and stood silently. What had built up inside became eased and his breathing relaxed. Tom took his hand and they walked on in the stillness of the night.

When they got back into the garage, Tom gave Niko his pajamas and tucked away his clothes. He avoided his son's eyes.

"This is our secret, Niko. When you get up, don't ya act all tired."

"Okay, Pa," whispered Niko. He turned and walked to the side door, shoelaces trailing.

"Oh yeah, here's your candy bar," said Tom. Niko stopped and turned. Tom tossed the Baby Ruth and Niko caught it midair. "Put some ice on that ear."

Niko nodded. "You'll see, Pa. I'll look at my watch next time."

He tiptoed up the stairs and lay awake until dawn's light began to seep into the day. His body felt unwell with something indescribable, something that couldn't be relieved. He wrapped his arms around himself, rocked back and forth, and finally fell into a fitful sleep.

⁓

"What happened to your ear, Niko?" asked Christina the next morning as he came into the kitchen. Sophie had been sitting at the breakfast table, drawing a picture of the kitchen stove in her sketchpad. She put her pencil down and eyed Niko quizzically. He threw her a look she couldn't read.

Christina walked over to take a closer look. Niko quickly put his hand up to hide his ear.

"Let me see," said Christina as she pulled his hand down gently. She and Sophie gasped upon seeing his swollen, purple ear. "Niko, how on earth did you get this bruise?" Christina asked. "I didn't see it last night when you went to bed."

"I…I was tossing a baseball and in, I mean in bed, and I missed so I went to grab it, but fell off my bed and hit my ear on the corner of the dresser."

Christina looked him in the eyes. "Is that what happened, Niko?"

"Yeah, Ma, I told you!" Niko yelled.

Sophie pressed her hands into her hips. "I bet Pa hit you!" Niko's face reddened.

"Sophie!" said Christina sharply. "You know that can't be true. He wouldn't hurt Niko."

"Oh yeah?" she spat. "I'll bet he would!"

"No!" Niko shouted, backing away from them. "Pa…he, he would never hit me!"

Christina cupped his chin with her hands. She took him in her arms and hugged him close. Tears welled up in his eyes and he swallowed hard. "I wish you had shown me your ear last night. We could have put ice on it."

"Yeah, I shoulda, Ma," said Niko. He pulled away from her and headed towards the back door. "Gotta go, Ma. Noops is waiting for me."

"Sit down right now and eat some breakfast."

With a dour expression, Niko tucked his hands in his pockets and sat down slowly. When finished, Niko burst out the door. Sophie turned to Christina and said, "Ma, something's goin' on. I heard Taki talk about Pa's car business to that gangster guy, Vitto." Christina's eyes widened. Sophie saw her mouth set suspicious and firm.

"You let me deal with this, Sophie."

The day's heat was unbearable, and the prospect of working at the store in the afternoon made Christina weary. Up in her bedroom, she glanced at the round alarm clock, supported by its three tiny legs on the nightstand, and slipped on her pink Sophia's Hamburgers work uniform, with black piping around the short sleeves and collar. She tied a starched white apron around her waist and flipped the switch of the oscillating fan on her dresser. She unbuttoned the bodice of her uniform, propped an elbow on the dresser, and cupped her chin with one hand. It felt good to feel the wind. It blew her thick hair back, and her eyes watered, streaking across her temples. Her thoughts whirled dizzily in her head like the blades of the fan.

A breathless feeling crept into her chest, and she balled her hand against her leg. *O Theos, please help me know what's going on with Niko. With Tom.*

She closed her eyes to the thought and saw the day ahead: the store's slamming screen door, the mounds of onions, the sizzling grill in need of constant scraping, the long counter with its salts, peppers, napkin dispensers, red-topped stools, and foot rail. The dime jukebox with records stacked up like black pancakes, ready to swing out onto the spinning turntable. The wall decorated with a rectangular poster of the Parthenon, edged with the Greek key pattern; a winking boy holding a bottle of Coca-Cola on a round red sign; the menu printed on a black chalkboard. Mopping the length of the counter with bleach cloths, and the spreading fan of armpit sweat staining her uniform.

Christina shook herself and gazed out the window. She looked down at the three kids tossing a ball back and forth over the clothesline. A soft smile crept across her face. Sophie's thin, coltish legs, and Niko trying to make farting sounds with his hand under his armpit. Noops laughed and tried to drop-kick the ball but fell before his foot connected. He rolled on his back and laughed harder. Sophie reached to help him up but lost her balance and fell to the ground in a heap. Christina couldn't hear them over the droning fan but watched happiness flow between them.

She hadn't seen Tom all day and decided to leave the house an hour before her shift to search the neighborhood. The kids could manage by themselves for a while.

"God, it's hot," she said under her breath as she made her way to the business area. The soup-thick, still air felt suffocating. She walked to the shady side of 105th Street and waved her hand through a cloud of gnats swarming her face. She stopped and leaned against the warm metal of a streetlight pole in front of the Ewing Department Store. A couple of dark-haired boys she didn't recognize sat on the steps, drinking bottles of neon-orange Nehi pop. "Looks like you boys are staying cool."

The older of the two heaved a sigh. "Yeah, tryin' to."

She looked down the street and thought she saw Tom talking to a uniformed cop. Her heart gave a start. She sucked in her bottom lip, waited for a couple of cars to pass, and walked across the street. As she got closer, sure enough, it was Tom talking to Police Sergeant John Bernaski, in front of Ace Hardware. Tom's back was to her. He had a paper bag tucked under his arm and was gesturing and nodding to John. Christina walked up to them casually, going through a hasty mental pantomime of what she would say. John was wearing his long-sleeved blue cop shirt, navy pants, checkered cap, knotted tie, and heavy, shoulder-strapped gun belt. *How can he stand the heat?* Tom looked cooler in his khaki pants and a sleeveless ribbed T-shirt. A lock of dark hair curled down on his forehead.

John was the first to see her. He took off his cap and said, "Well, good day, Mrs. Peters. It's nice to see you." His graying dark hair was wet with sweat. She saw Tom's shoulders stiffen. He turned, shifted his feet, and then widened his eyes at her. He said nothing.

"It's nice to see you too, John," she said. "How are the kids?"

"Fine, fine." He hooked his thumbs in his belt and rocked back on his heels. "Well, I better be on my way. You two stay cool."

Christina gave a quick laugh and said, "We'll try."

When John was out of earshot, Christina turned to Tom and searched his eyes. "What was that about?"

"Just business." His voice cut crisp through the thick air. He flicked a fly off his arm.

"What kind of business?"

Tom rubbed the back of his neck, looked at her in a measured way, and then shoved his hand in his back pants pocket. "I'm helping the cops with some electronics. They know I'm good at it, and I have some connections they're interested in. Besides, it's good to make money on the side."

"It all sounds dangerous to me," she said.

He gave her a crooked smile. "I got it all under control." He eyed her fitted uniform and the sheen of sweat on her face. "Don't you need to be at the store?"

"I've got twenty minutes." She searched his eyes and said nothing for a moment. "I need to talk with you about Niko."

Tom shifted from foot to foot and cast his eyes aside for a second. "Yeah. What about?"

"He came downstairs this morning with an ugly bruise on his ear."

"What did he say?"

"He was tossing a baseball in bed and fell on his dresser trying to catch it."

"Yeah, you know kids."

"I've asked you before. Are you pressuring him? Sophie thinks you're hurting him."

His arm tightened against the paper bag. "Well, Sophie's wrong."

She looked straight in his eyes. "She also heard Taki talking to that nasty thug Vitto. You're fixing Mafia cars *and* helping the cops."

"So what?"

She took one step closer to him. "I'll tell you what. You're putting us in the middle of danger with all your schemes. For what? Money?"

"Yeah, you know we need the money, and I work on any car that needs fixing. What of it?" he said, shrugging. "It's business, and they pay me damn good. You're always naggin' how we don't have enough. Besides, maybe we can get out of this dump of a neighborhood."

"Are you crazy? I'm not leaving this neighborhood. Where are you coming off calling it a dump?"

"Just thinking of the future—for the kids."

"It's just fine here."

He breathed out of his pursed lips. "Yeah, for you."

She eyed him sideways. "Yeah, for me *and* the kids. We all like it here except you. I hate that we fight in front of them and you're always acting unhappy for no good reason." Her anger dropped away for a moment and she placed a hand on his chest. "What's happened to you, Tom? What's happened to us?"

"I dunno what you're getting at."

"Everything's changed. Don't you want better for us?"

"Can't you see?" he said. "I'm working for better."

She shook her head, renewed with venom. "Back to the money, Mr. casual 'its just business.' It seems like more's going out than coming in. What is it, Tom? Alcohol, gambling, giving money to thugs, working with the cops? Seems like you're involving Niko in your schemes." She grabbed his wrist. "You know Niko worships you. If…if you hurt him in any way, I'll…"

"You'll what?" he said. He took her hand and pulled her close. His eyebrows crinkled together in a hard frown. She pulled away. "Whatta ya think I am? I've told you, Christina, I'm teaching Niko all about car repair. He's smart and he's been a big help to me. That kid can set the gap on spark plugs and name just about every tool and car part in the garage. He's eating it all up."

"Does Niko have anything to do with this 'business,' as you call it?"

"Naw. He just helps me with the cars in the garage."

"That's all?" she asked.

"Trust me."

PART TWO

11
Christina

Don't ever take the fence down until you know why it was put up.
~ Robert Frost

1938

"Christina!" Pa yelled down the hallway. "Get your brother dressed!"

Her father's voice roared in her ears. She stood paralyzed for a moment, not even moving her eyelids. She debated whether to swallow her thoughts or say them.

She turned to face him and said in a quiet voice, "All I am is a dumb slave in this family."

"What did you say?" he hissed.

Christina scowled at her father and stretched out her hands. "I feel like a dumb slave! All I do is take care of my brothers and sister, clean, iron, cook, and work at the store! I'm sixteen now! Why can't I have a little freedom like other girls?" she pleaded. "I'm not allowed do anything. You won't even let me think for myself! This is America, not the old country!" Christina looked down with a contrite face and bit the side of her lip, not believing the boldness of her words.

Her father marched down the hall and pinned her to the wall with a glare. He shook both fists in her face and shouted, "Do like I tell you! Is your job to look after your brothers and sister. Ma and I no want no trouble for you! Someday you say *efkharisto* to your Ma and Pa. You see!"

Christina's face went hot. Her jaw tightened. It was as if something in her chest turned inside out and a bitter seed began to grow.

George and Sophia Poulos had raised Christina, the first of their four kids, with great love but extreme strictness, as many immigrants did, so afraid were they of losing control of their children in this new land filled with possibilities but fraught with temptations.

From the time she could lift a plate from the table, Christina helped her hard-working parents. At East Side Hamburgers she waitressed, cooked, wiped down tables and counters with bleach cloths, mopped floors, and took care of the grease on the griddle and the french fry baskets. The smell of onions and grease permeated her clothing, her hair. The work never ended.

"May I take your order?" she'd ask customers—and answer with "Yes, ma'am. Yes, sir."

"Such a nice girl," they'd say. "George and Sophia must be proud."

Her smile froze upon hearing what a good daughter she was. Sometimes imagining not doing what she was told made her head dizzy with temptation.

The large, hot griddle spit and sizzled with rows of hot dogs, Polish sausages, and hamburger patties, and mounds of browning onions. Christina was skillful with the long-handled spatula: scraping, flipping, scooting onions close to the meat so the flavors mingled. The buns darkened toasty on the grill, and she deftly tossed thin squares of cheese like yellow blankets over the hamburgers.

Christina could make three milkshakes at once. She reached deep into the sliding glass–topped freezer case and scooped ice cream into large stainless steel tumblers. Without measuring, she knew how much milk and flavoring to use. She hooked the tumblers onto the big green Hamilton Beach mixers. They whirled the contents smooth. The thick shakes were coaxed out of their tumblers into soda glasses with a long spoon and then topped with whipped cream, sprinkles, cherries, and a straw.

At age fourteen, Christina's brother Demetri did his part. His muscles grew strong and his shoulders broad from lifting and moving supplies in the store. In the summer he wore sleeveless white T-shirts and kept a comb in his back jeans pocket. He walked with a swagger.

One evening, while Christina was mopping the floors in the store with a giant rag mop and a soapy bucket of Spic and Span, Demetri burst through the front door. He slid clear across the wet floor on his slick-bottomed sneakers. He did a jig and gave her a cocky smile.

"You jerk! Look what you did with your filthy shoes!" Christina yelled, a hand propped on her hip. "Get over here and mop up this mess!"

"Nope, that's girls' work!" He flexed his arm muscles in her face. "Check these biceps, Sis!"

She punched his shoulder and rolled her eyes to the ceiling. "You think you're somethin'—well guess what, hotshot, you're not!"

He whipped the comb out of his jeans pocket, ran it through his wavy brown hair, and winked at her.

"I'm gonna puke," Christina said, clutching her stomach.

—

It was Christina's duty to make sure her siblings were fed if Sophia was at the store. "Hurry up or we'll all be late for school!" she'd yell. "Breakfast is ready!"

Her brother Alexander needed help from everyone. Crippled from a raging case of spinal meningitis when he was just two years old, the only reason he lived was because of the sturdiness of his body before sickness engulfed him.

Every morning he'd swing his withered legs over the side of the bed and wait. "Hurry, I gotta pee!" he'd shout, pounding his fists on the pile of sheets and blankets. One morning he rocked the bed back and forth so hard, the nightstand tipped over and his steel alarm clock shattered to pieces on the hardwood floor. His shadowed eyes took on a fearful expression. "What if they don't come?" he muttered, holding his crotch. "I'll pee all over myself!"

Everybody but little Anna helped him dress and buckle the leather straps of his cumbersome leg braces. Once up, he'd clunk about awkward and slow. Sweat streaked his face with exertion. If they ran late, Christina and Demetri hooked arms on either side of Alexander and sped him down the sidewalk to school. Sometimes they'd make Alexander laugh until he cried. Anna galloped behind.

—

By age seventeen, Christina worked almost as hard as Sophia when she wasn't at school.

"Honey, you know we couldn't make it without your help," said Sophia one Saturday morning as she opened the store's three door locks with her bundle of keys. A friendly bell tinkled as she pushed on the door. She turned, looked into Christina's face, and cupped her chin with one hand. The lines around her eyes deepened. "You're our strong girl. See how business grows? It's because we're all working together, that's why. We got the respect."

"Oh, Ma, I don't mind the work so much, I just want to go out with my friends once in a while. Their parents let them! Can't you understand?" she asked. She plunged her hands deep into her coat pockets and pressed in the sides of her thighs.

The pain in Christina's voice made Sophia cringe. She reached over and drew her daughter into a hard hug. "I love you as high as the stars," she said. Her eyes scanned her daughter's face thoughtfully. "Humph. Tell you what. I'll talk with your Pa and see if we can give you a little time."

Christina smiled and said, "Oh, thank you, Ma!"

That night, in the privacy of their bedroom, Sophia unpinned her long hair and slipped a freshly ironed cotton nightgown over her generous frame. The soft glow of the red prayer lamp filled the room. She faced the East and rested her eyes on an icon of Theoktokos cradling baby Jesus in her arms. A worn rag doll with a barely recognizable face rested on the dresser below the icon. Sophia smiled and whispered, "Antonia." She crossed her arms over her chest with fingertips hooked over her shoulders and prayed. She gazed up to the ceiling, did the sign of the cross, and slowly turned to her husband. He sat on the edge of the bed.

"George. I want to talk to you about Christina."

"What is it?"

"Do you see her?" she said. "Christina is blossoming. She's like a flower, a young woman—already seventeen years old! I've been thinking…and you need to hear me out. She needs a little freedom. I see a girl frustrated. We ask so much of her."

George looked at her and pounded his fist on the nightstand. "I say NO!"

"Look, George, she's growing. I say let her go to movies, maybe a school dance, and spend more time with girlfriends. That's what I think." Sophia locked eyes with her husband and placed her hands on his shoulders. "George, she's our first, and a good girl. You know she is. We couldn't make it without her help."

"Ah!" He slapped his leg and sat brooding for a moment. "This is what I say." George frowned, rubbed his chin with big, knotty fingers, and sighed deeply. "I say, okay—BUT, no dances, and no asking for more! You give a little string, and she want more and more."

Christina's eyes brightened when Ma told her the very next day in the kitchen. It seemed like the ceiling peeled open to the sky. But in time, George was right: the string felt too short. She took walks with her girlfriends, went to movies, and rode the crowded bus to the beach in the summer, but she couldn't go to school dances or anywhere with boys except in the company of her brother or male cousins.

"You go with Demetri," said Pa. "He take good care of you."

"I'm the only girl my age that tags along with her stupid brother!" she cried. "You think he wants me? Besides, I'm older than him!"

"You no argue and say a bad word about your brother, or you go no places!" Pa yelled. "Remember, I choose a nice boy for your husband. You no have to meet boys!"

Christina stormed out of the room, slammed her bedroom door, and fell on her bed in tears. She screamed into her pillow, "I hate him! I'll do what I want and he can't stop me!"

Before everyone went to bed, Christina opened the front door. Her mind spun with a plan to sneak out.

"Where are you going?" Ma asked, searching her daughter's face.

"Oh, just outside to look at the sky and cool off. It's sticky hot in here."

"Okay, honey," said Sophia as she flipped the toggle switch on the fan. "*Poe, poe*, it *is* hot."

Once outside, Christina picked up the wooden milk box from the front stoop and carefully set it down against the red brick wall directly beneath her window. Christina's plan caused her hands to tremble. She found herself looking down at a tiny ant struggling with a bread crumb on the sidewalk. She shook her head at the ant and walked in to kiss her parents goodnight.

"*Kali neekta, pethie mou,*" said Sophia.

"*Kali neekta,*" Christina said, with a slight quaver in her voice. George looked up at her.

An hour later, when she knew they were asleep, Christina buttoned her shirtwaist dress and slung the strap of her black patent leather purse over her shoulder. With great care, she unhooked the screen from her bedroom window. A piano plinking along softly down the street distracted her for a moment. She heard voices and ducked behind the white curtain. A young couple walked along the sidewalk across the street.

Oh, hurry up.

Just as they were almost out of sight, a blue sedan drove by. When it was all clear she sucked in her breath, hiked up her skirt, and started to climb out. She smacked her left knee loudly on the wooden window frame. "Ow," she said under her breath, and froze. She rubbed her knee and waited. Nothing.

Christina climbed out and dangled by her hands from the gritty windowsill until she could feel the milk box under one foot. It tipped on edge and nearly toppled over until she placed her other foot down to steady it. After regaining her balance, Christina stepped off slowly, by degrees, and put the box back in its spot. She raced down the sidewalk without looking back. Halfway down the block she cut through the rutted alleyway to 104th Street. The rusty oil barrels, lined up like the alley's sentinels, were overflowing with stinking garbage.

She kept running until two loud metal clangs made her skid to a gravelly stop. The streetlight cast its slanted incandescence on six-year-old Johnny

Paventy, pitching rocks at an emaciated cat across the street. The yowling cat made a beeline for the next block.

"Damn, he got away!" he said. Johnny's hand quickly sought the back of his neck. He turned to face Christina and eyed her with an air of speculation. "Hey, Christina, whatcha doin'?"

"Oh, ah, nothing," she said. "Well, actually, Ma wants me to check up on Mrs. O'Connell. Um, ya know, she slipped and fell at the Hi-Lo grocery store." *I'm so stupid. I didn't need to tell him that.*

"Oh yeah," Johnny said airily, pushing his filthy cap back off his forehead. "Mrs. O'Connell's nice. She gives me money, and I like her dog, Tippy." He squatted down and started picking at a bloody scab on his knee.

Christina's brow furrowed. He was a handsome little fellow under all the grime.

"Johnny, why are you out so late?" she asked. "You know my Ma would be very worried."

He looked at her cross-eyed like she was from another planet and said peevishly, "Can't ya see, I'm jes lookin' for stuff." He gazed down at the gravel, stiffened a little, and said quietly, "Don't ya worry your Ma."

"Where's your Pa?" she asked.

He shrugged quickly and said, "I dunno. Maybe Banners'."

Christina had never seen Johnny out so late at night. If her Ma and Pa knew, it would cement the deal they had made with his father, Rico Paventy, and the authorities. If he left Johnny alone one more time, they would take him in and raise him as their own. *How can I tell them?* I'm *not supposed to be out.*

Distracted from her mission, Christina stared at Johnny. His mother had died of tuberculosis the year before. She knew his drunken, foul-mouthed, argumentative father didn't give a rip what his little boy did. Johnny hung around the store like a ragged, starving dog, hoping for a scrap to eat. Christina and her Ma regularly gave him sacks of food. Johnny had become more and more part of the Poulos family.

12
Johnny

For Mercy has a human heart, Pity a human face...
— William Blake

"*Poe, poe*—poor thing," Sophia would say, shaking her head. "Liliana Paventy loved her little boy, but that fool husband made her work like a dog and drove her straight to her death from the TB. Can't hold down a job, struts around like a rooster, and drinks what little money he has at Banners'. Poor Johnny's covered with the bugs and smells like an outhouse—just a baby! Liliana must be wringin' her hands from heaven."

Sophia finally took matters into her own hands and started caring for him at the store, and that became the beginning of changes for Johnny. The first time she washed and cut his hair, it had been raining. Johnny was soaked through, shivering and bedraggled like a sinking little soul.

Sophia lifted his wet hair off his forehead to get a better look at him. "Come on, *pethaki mou*, let's get some dry clothes on you."

He reached up and brushed away a drop of water that seemed to linger in his eye. "Okay, Mrs. Poulos," he said.

She turned to Christina and said, "I put some grocery sacks filled with clothes and shoes the boys grew out of on the top shelf by the big cans of ketchup. Can you get them for me?"

"Sure," said Christina, with a twinge of sadness in her voice. Johnny smelled like mildew and stale urine.

Sophia took Johnny by the hand and led him to the bathroom at the back of the store. She yanked on the long chain of a naked light bulb fixture and sent it swinging from the high ceiling. Johnny watched it sway. The light bulb lit the old plaster walls with a buttery sheen. Johnny studied the long, ancient pipe that ran halfway up the wall from the back of the toilet to a water tank.

"How about I wash your hair while we're at it?" she said cheerfully.

He stepped from foot to foot and said, "Okay."

Sophia helped him peel off his thin jacket and dirty gray T-shirt. She cranked on the warm water and boosted him up onto a wooden Coca-Cola crate. She gently tipped his head over the deep concrete sink. Slowly, deliberately, she scrubbed his hair with special soap and then washed the dirt off of his neck and ears. Sophia wrapped his head with a clean towel and then bathed his slender upper body with a warm, soapy washcloth. He stood tranquilly with a soft smile and let her care for him. A silence fell between them. The fresh color of his young skin glowed with the dirt removed. Sophia's throat constricted while gazing at his forlorn eyes.

She unwrapped his head and then cocooned him snug in the towel. After lifting him off the crate, Sophia stood him in front of her.

"Humph," she said. "How 'bout I give your hair a nice trim?"

Johnny nodded and said, "Ma used to cut my hair." He smiled and stood tall.

She grabbed a pair of scissors from a high shelf and sat down on the toilet lid. Sophia brushed his long, unruly hair and then clipped it with the practiced hands of a maestro. Coils of chestnut hair fell to his toweled shoulders and onto the floor. When finished, Sophia parted and combed his hair neatly to the side.

"There," Sophia said, with a quick nod of her head. "Now, don't you look clean and handsome, Yanni!"

"What's 'Yanni'?" he asked.

"That's your Greek name."

Johnny climbed back up on the crate with Sophia's help and looked into the medicine cabinet mirror. "Hmm…Yanni." He tapped the top of his head and smiled at his reflection. Christina walked in and stood smiling, with her hand resting on a hip.

"Johnny!" said Christina, "Look at you—sooo handsome."

He blinked. "Thanks!" he said, boyish pride slipping into his voice.

"Yanni, you stay here with Christina," Sophia said. "I'll be right back."

She bunched up his filthy clothes and threw them away in the rusty trash barrel out back. She gave Johnny clean underwear, socks, shoes, a button-down flannel shirt, and navy blue corduroy pants.

"Now, take off your wet pants and socks and put these clothes on," she said. "I'll stand right outside the door. Come out when you're finished dressing."

In a little while, Johnny opened the door and peeked out. His wet socks were halfway pulled off. "Can't get 'em off," he said.

"Here, *pethaki mou*, let me help you."

She pulled off his socks and flung them in the corner. She bathed his chafed feet with a washcloth and toweled them dry.

Christina watched her Ma finish dressing him with purpose. Sophia wrapped her arms around him as if he were her own and whispered, "Yanni, always remember, you a good boy. A smart boy. Only the stars up in the sky are greater than you. *Theos* has his hand on you." Christina smiled; she had heard the same words when she was small.

Johnny lifted his chin and leaned into Sophia, somehow knowing a gentle kiss would be planted on his cheek.

"Now, Yanni, go right home and get out of this bad rain."

Looking down, he tugged at his ear, glanced sideways at the floor, and said a quiet "Okay."

Sophia huffed when Johnny walked out of the store. She marched past George over to the cash register and picked up a pencil absentmindedly. She twirled the pencil between her fingers, slammed it down loudly on the countertop, and knotted her hands tightly over her stomach. George looked up from the grill. His glasses had slipped a little, and he pushed them back up on his nose.

Sophia turned her gaze on him, tightened her jaw, and said, "George, I can't stand it anymore."

How well he knew this determined look of fury on her face. "What?" he asked, setting the spatula aside.

"Johnny needs a home, George," she said. "His good-for-nothing father doesn't give a damn about him." George saw she was shaking. "He's got nobody. No relatives. I tell you, that boy—he's gonna die on the streets if somebody doesn't take him in."

He looked her square in the face, drew in a deep breath, and said, "Let's pray and see what we can do."

13
The Dance

What matters most is how well you walk through the fire.
— Charles Bukowski

*C*hristina opened her purse and dug for some change. She bent down and turned Johnny's wrist over, placed the coins in his hand, and gently closed his fingers around them. He looked up grimly and said in a flat voice, "Do ya hafta go?"

Johnny's question was an appeal. Christina shuddered. "It's time for you to go home," she said quietly. She tore her eyes away from him, wheeled around, and said, "Bye, Johnny!"

He didn't answer but stood smiling at the coins.

Christina rounded the corner and tiptoed to a house with shingled siding—South Chicago style. It looked like fake, sandy brick, and all the adjoining houses had the same appearance—neat and snug. She saw the silhouette of her friend Lucy Coletti in the glow of her bedroom lamp. She tapped lightly on the screen and whispered, "Lucy, Lucy! It's me, Christina!"

The curtains parted quickly. "Christina, what are *you* doing here?" she said, loud and brash.

"Be quiet!" she whispered. "Remember when we talked about sneaking out?"

"Yeah, but…"

"Here's our chance!" said Christina. "Did you see the posters at school? There's a dance tonight that goes late. I'll bet it's still going."

Lucy's face went blank for a moment. "If my parents find out they'll kill me," she said.

"Are you goin' back on what you said?" Christina challenged.

Lucy rubbed her cheek thoughtfully, squared her shoulders, and whispered in a devious voice, "Okay, let's do it! They're all in bed. We gotta be real quiet."

Lucy slipped on a blouse and pleated skirt. She pulled out something from the bottom of her dresser drawer and shoved it deep into her purse. She unhooked the screen and climbed out the window. The two girls raced down the sidewalk until they were almost to the school. They slowed down.

Lucy turned and gave Christina a sly grin. "Look what I've got!" She rummaged in her purse and pulled out a half pack of Lucky Strikes. Her eyes blazed with excitement.

"What?" Christina said, shocked "Where did you get those?"

"From my Pa's cigarette carton," she said. "He never missed them."

Lucy tapped out a cigarette and gave it a confident pat with her forefinger. She put it cocky-like between her lips and plunged her hand back into her purse.

Just then a boy stepped out into the dim light of the school's open doorway and walked up to the girls. He flicked open his silver Zippo lighter and spun the flint wheel—smooth, with a *pfissst*.

"Hey, good-lookin', need a light?" The inch-long flame lit up Lucy's face.

"Sure," she crooned, leaning towards the flame. The end of the cigarette sizzled and then glowed as Lucy sucked in. She tucked her elbow into her waist and held the cigarette out from her hip like some movie star.

Christina looked incredulously at her friend. She whispered, "I didn't know you…"

Lucy gave her a devilish smile and held out her pack. "Here, have one."

"Who, me?"

"Why not?" Lucy challenged. "Who's watching you?"

Christina swallowed hard and pulled one slowly out of the pack. The boy lit up her cigarette and Christina drew in a puff. It scorched her throat, and she coughed a bitter, nasty taste.

"Hey, girl, first cigarette?" he asked.

"Yeah," Christina choked out.

He gave her a cockeyed smile. "Try another puff," he said. "It gets better." He ran a hand through his hair. "Steve's the name. What are your names?"

Lucy squinted at him. "Do you go to school here?" she asked. "I don't recognize you."

He flicked his cigarette to the side. "I go to George Washington in Hegewisch."

Lucy smiled and said, "Mmm, I'm Lucy, and this is my friend Christina."

"Let's go inside, girls." He looked over at Christina and said, "I've got a friend who would love to meet you."

They threw their cigarettes onto the sidewalk and crushed them under their shoes. Steve took Lucy's hand and led her into the building. Christina followed. Her pulse raced.

"There he is," Steve shouted over the music.

A reedy boy with a thick lock of blonde hair falling over one brow leaned against the wall. He wore a white T-shirt and jeans with the cuffs turned up. A pack of cigarettes was rolled up into one of his sleeves. Christina thought the bulge in his sleeve looked comical.

Steve grinned broadly. He took Christina by the elbow and stood her directly in front of his friend. "Jack, meet Christina."

Jack eyed her up and down.

"Hey, girl, how ya doin'?" he said casually.

Christina tugged at the skirt of her dress and glanced down with a shy grin. "Uh, I'm fine, thank you."

Jack smoothed his hair back, took Christina's sweaty hand, and said, "Come on, let's dance."

Christina backed away momentarily. She stood suspended, unmindful of her surroundings. The blood roared in her ears above the music. Jack smiled and guided her onto the crowded dance floor. He put his other hand to the small of her back and led her to Billie Holiday's "I'm Gonna Lock

My Heart." Her legs moved wooden-like at first, but after a few dances, she swayed in his arms—exhilarated.

They danced and talked in the darkened corners until the doors closed at eleven. Steve and Jack walked the girls home the long way, holding their hands.

As they approached 106th and Avenue L, Christina thought she recognized the bulky form of her father leaning against the building. He moved. Shadow became substance as the streetlamp lit the top of his fedora. She stood immobile and clutched her throat with one hand.

"Oh, God," she choked. "That's my Pa! I'm...I'm dead."

George stomped over to the group, grabbed Christina by the forearm, and dragged her a few feet towards their building. He yanked her around to face him and looked daggers at her, as if daring her to speak. Christina twisted her arm free. She ran up to their apartment, wiping the lipstick from her mouth with the back of her trembling hand.

The teens collectively backed away from George.

"Mr. Poulos, please!" pleaded Lucy. "It's not what you..."

He spat on the sidewalk and seethed, "You's! All of you's, GO!" They ran, and George wheeled around to the apartment.

Christina could hear her Pa stomping up the steps. He flung the door open with a frightening crash. The solid brass doorknob went straight through the plaster wall. He stormed over to Christina and gave her a stinging smack across the face. She spun, staggered to the opposite wall, and crumpled in a heap. Sophia ran into the room and gasped. It was the first and last time George ever raised his hand to his daughter.

Christina became more beautiful with each passing year. At age nineteen, she still wasn't allowed to wear lipstick on her full lips, date, or go off with her friends without permission. Loose-fitting cotton dresses hid her curvaceous figure. She shyly averted her eyes as men stared. But as much as Christina submitted to her father, the family—the streak of rebellion carved deeper within her heart.

14
Women's Auxiliary Army Corps (WAAC)

You must do the thing you think you cannot do.
~ Eleanor Roosevelt

After years of ambivalence to Nazi tyranny and sweeping threats of domination over Europe, America collectively woke up and plunged itself into World War II. Relatives in the villages and islands of Greece wrote to their families in America and begged for help.

Sophia clutched a tattered letter from her aunt in Tripoli and made sure everyone heard the words.

Dear Sophia and Family,

Please tell America to help us drive the Germans out! Thousands of our people all throughout Greece have died from starvation and punishments by the Nazis. They take our animals, food, homes, churches, and money. We have to do what they say or they shoot us with their guns. The soldiers pounded on our neighbor's door. When he wouldn't answer, they kicked the door open and shot him in the stomach. Please send money and American soldiers to help the Greek Resistance. They are fighting hard.

Give my love to the family, Thea Alexandria

At age eighteen, Demetri decided to join the Army. George and Sophia were worried but proud.

"Hey, Sis, promise you'll write to me?" he asked before boarding the South Shore train on his journey to boot camp in Oklahoma. He looked grown up with his military haircut.

"I promise, Demetri," she assured him with a hug. He hugged her back awkwardly. Christina's heart lurched. She smiled and found a semblance of consolation in his blundering, earnest affection. *He'll be back.*

"Please take care of yourself." She felt an urge to get on the train with him.

Demetri dipped his voice down so their parents wouldn't hear. "Sis, you gotta start doing what you want or you'll be stuck flippin' burgers forever."

Christina looked suddenly weary and gazed away from his face. "I know," she said in a quiet voice. She lifted and dropped her stiff shoulders.

"I love ya, Sis."

She grabbed him in a bear hug around his shoulders and said, "I love you too. Promise you'll be careful?"

"I…will," he said, low and soft. He looked away. His eyelashes were wet with tears.

Shortly after turning twenty-one, Christina started helping Sophia with the accounting and banking for the store. She made sure the orders of food and supplies matched the receipts. Sophia kept a meticulous ledger, but Christina did all the banking and helped her mother watch the budget.

On a misty April morning, Christina walked through the heavy brass door of the East Side Trust and Savings Bank clutching a green canvas pouch containing a cash deposit from the store. Next to the teller's gilded window she saw a small poster with the image of Uncle Sam pointing his finger straight at her. The words under him read, "Women Wanted in the Army." She ran her finger down to the small print underneath the blocky letters. *Must be 21 years old, at least five feet tall and 100 lbs. or more. Jobs include: communication specialists, mechanics, map analysts, file clerks, nurses, typists, equipment testers, motor pool drivers, and more.* Her finger hovered over the local recruiting station's address. She memorized it.

Just then, Christina felt a hand on her shoulder. She jumped slightly and whipped around to see her childhood friend Bernetha Jones smiling brightly at her.

"Oh, hi, Bernetha," sputtered Christina. She gathered herself and said, "I haven't seen you for so long." She took Bernetha's hand. "How are you? How's your family?"

"We all good. Whatta ya lookin' at that poster fo', girl? Are you thinkin' about joinin' up?"

"I'm just looking. Can you believe they want women in the Army?"

"Nuh-uh. Ah wouldn't go where mens folks be and the war and such."

"Well, I think things are changing."

Bernetha shook her head in wonder. "Mmm, mmm, you can say that again. It's the craziest thing. Lordy, ah wouldn't go and that's the truth."

After making the deposit, Christina gave Bernetha a hug, dashed out of the bank, and walked twelve blocks to 118th Street. She slowed, casually looked over both shoulders, and stopped in front of the recruiting station. Taped to the window she saw a large poster of a determined-looking woman wearing a polka-dot bandana knotted around her head and a blue work shirt with rolled-up sleeves. Christina felt the woman's confident, flashing dark eyes bore straight into hers. The woman's fist was raised and cocked in defiance. The top of the poster was emblazoned with bold words: "We Can Do It!"

Her heart skipped a beat. *Women! They really do want women in the Army*. She shook her head in amazement. For the next week, Christina could think of nothing else. She closed her eyes and saw the image of Uncle Sam pointing straight at her. Christina flexed her arm in front of the bathroom mirror. The bold woman on the poster looked like her. She wanted to help. She felt desperate to get away. *I could do this! They can't stop me!*

That next Monday morning, Christina lay in bed staring at the pattern of cracks on the ceiling. She drew the covers up around her neck until the sun dawned brighter through her curtains. The decision to enlist settled resolutely in her mind, but her eyes grew somber knowing her world would change if she were accepted.

Christina hurried to finish her shift at the store. George and Thea Stefania waited on customers. Anna was filling the napkin dispensers, and Johnny sat perched on a stool at the counter munching on a cheeseburger. Christina looked tenderly at her younger brother and sister. Johnny had finally became a Poulos and was already ten years old—the same age as Anna. His father, Rico Paventy, had skipped town and was never heard from again.

Sophia bent over the mop behind the ice-cream counter. The smell of sizzling hamburgers mixed with Clorox filled Christina's nostrils. She walked up to Sophia and swallowed hard.

"Ma, I've got some errands. Are you okay if I leave now?"

"Sure, honey. Go ahead. I'll see you at home for dinner then?"

"Yes."

Christina pulled her eyes from her Ma's stooped form and turned to walk out. She hesitated with her hand resting on the wooden door frame. She gave the door frame a meditative pat and turned back to gaze at Sophia. Strangely, time slowed as her Ma's purposeful movements stirred something deep inside Christina. She willed her eyes away, pushed the door open, and walked with hurried steps for blocks. Her breath came in quick bursts. After rounding the corner by the recruiting station, she stopped, stood in front of the poster, squared her shoulders, and walked in.

A sharp-looking, middle-aged woman in uniform sat behind a wooden desk stacked with papers. She looked up and asked, "May I help you?"

"Yes, I need, I mean, I'm interested in joining the Army."

"Well, you've certainly come to the right place," Lieutenant Willis replied with an inviting smile. Christina met her eyes and felt less timid. "Fill out these forms at the desk over there by the window. If the doctor is still here when you finish, he can do your physical examination."

"Uh, okay." Christina hesitated and then picked up a black fountain pen with a shaky hand. She walked over to the desk and started filling out a stack of forms all headed with the words "Women's Army Auxiliary Corps." She printed her full name, birth date, and address. When she came to the phone number, "Bayport one-one-three-one-six," she shuddered. A shadow crossed her face. *Their number. Am I doing the right thing?* She shivered the thought away, took a deep breath, and gathered a semblance of composure.

After passing the physical examination, Christina lifted her chin and answered questions with a measure of confidence that surprised her.

When everything was completed Lieutenant Willis stood up, saluted Christina, and said, "Well, young lady, welcome to the Women's Army Auxiliary Corps!" She handed her a big, official-looking brown envelope and said, "Here are your instructions. We'll see you back in two weeks. I wish you the best."

"Thank you!" said Christina with a grin. She walked out of the building and took long strides, feeling lighter than a feather.

While running the Hoover over the rugs in the apartment hallway, Christina rehearsed in whispers how she would tell her parents. At the back of the store, she wrote her words on a foot-long scroll of adding machine paper and shivered as her fear doubled. She spoke to the glowing streetlight through her screened bedroom window. After practicing for a solid week, she pulled herself together to confront them.

During dinner, she could hear her own panting.

"You're not eating much, Christina," said Sophia. "Are you okay?"

Christina folded her flowered cloth napkin carefully on the table, cleared her throat, and said in a rush, "I've joined the Army and I'll be stationed at Langley Field, Virginia." She could feel the blood leave her face.

"What?" George boomed. He stood up to his full height so quickly that his chair tipped backwards and crashed against the wall. "You can no go!" he shouted. "You a woman!"

Christina's first instinct was to bolt out of the room, but instead she sucked in a breath, stood up, and spread her hands firmly on the table. "I'm already signed up, Pa. They want women and I'm going," she said with eyes blazing. "I'm old enough and it's too late to stop me." She saw a flash of fear in her father's eyes. He looked away and mumbled something. She took a step toward him and said, "Pa, it will be okay. I can do this."

George closed his eyes and spoke through air that felt thick. "But we need you here with us! It's your job to be the oldest daughter. We can no do the store, Anna, Alexander, and Johnny without you!" He pursed his lips, frowned, and sat down hard in his chair. Silence seemed to ooze from the walls.

Christina regarded her Pa with unexpected compassion and fresh confidence. "You've got Thea Stefania, and Anna is growing up, Pa. Our country is at war, and I want to help, like Demetri."

George took his handkerchief out of his pants pocket and wiped his forehead. A strange sluggishness came over him. He heard the sudden velvet patter of rain on the kitchen window and said, "I can no stop you."

George and Sophia were astounded by her decision, but they didn't stand in the way. What could they say? Demetri was in the thick of it, fighting in France. Greece and all of Europe were suffering under Nazi oppression. Christina wanted to help—she wanted a change.

They drove their daughter downtown to Union Station to bid their final farewell. The three wept while standing on the platform by the train. Sophia wrapped strong arms around her daughter's slender shoulders and quietly hummed a few bars of a Greek song in her ear. She stopped as tears caught in her throat. It was an old lullaby she had sung to her children when they were small.

Sophia reached deep into her coat pocket, took her daughter's hand, and placed a golden chain and medallion in her palm. Sophia cupped her strong hands around Christina's and said, "Honey, take this Athena necklace. She and *Theos* will protect. I always save it just for you. This belonged to my Ma, Elena, and her Ma before. Wear it and know we always love you as high as the stars in the sky. Watch those stars at night and remember we see them with you too. I'll be praying for *Theos* to watch over you every day."

Christina held it against her chest and said, "*Efkharisto,* Ma."

"You be careful. Be good girl," said George with a quick nod. "Remember what we teach you. Remember who you are." He gazed deep into her eyes and managed to smile in a way that conveyed a quiet apology. In a husky voice he said, "Christina, I want to stop you but I won't."

Christina looked wide-eyed into her father's crinkled face. He rubbed his broad hand over his thick brows. His eyes filled with conflicted tears.

"*Se agapo,* Pa, I love you," Christina said through her own hot tears. She turned and stepped onto the steep metal steps of the train. The smell of grease and creosote from the railroad ties filled her nostrils.

"*Se agapo,*" said Pa quietly. "*Theos* be with you. I pray every day."

She found her seat by the window and watched her weary-looking parents lean into each other as the train slowly pulled away. Sophia looked small with her big coat, thick shoes, and oversized handbag. Christina wore a brave smile and waved a tentative goodbye. George blew his nose with his giant handkerchief and kept his eyes on the pavement. Christina leaned her forehead against the thick glass of the window. She lifted the medallion to her lips, kissed it, and rubbed her thumb over the raised contours of Athena. Slowly, she turned the medallion over to the wise owl and pressed it to her chest. Strange warmth surged from it like a tiny current of electricity.

Christina was proud to be stationed at Langley Field, Virginia, where the National Advisory Committee for Aeronautics, the predecessor to NASA, was located. The development of wartime radar took off during WWII. Langley's full-scale research wind tunnels influenced the development of retractable landing gear and faster, streamlined aircraft.

Christina jerked awake that first morning in the barracks as blinding light wrenched away the dark of night. As her hand shot up to shield her eyes from the glare, she realized the overhead lights had been flipped on. She blinked twice and gazed down through her parted fingers at the clock on her footlocker. It read four thirty. She pressed the starched sheets against her eyes.

"You've got thirty minutes to get showered and dressed and report on the field at attention!" shouted a woman.

Christina catapulted to her feet and started making her bed neat and tight, with squared-off corners. She watched the other women strip off their pajamas, gather uniforms, and rush off to the showers. She cast a sidelong glance at them and couldn't believe how brazen they were to walk buck naked in front of one another. Bravado she had felt the day before reversed to sudden frailty. Shy and sheltered, she was embarrassed to shower with the other women. She straggled behind to take her shower last.

Christina ran awkwardly to the field and tried to sneak to the back of the military formation. Drill Sergeant Harris elbowed and shoved his way through the ranks of women standing at attention. He barreled up to her and scowled. Veins like thin ropes bulged on his neck. He glanced down above her pocket to read her name. He stepped forward and stuck his menacing face a couple of inches away from hers.

"Poulos, you're late!" he shouted. "Explain yourself."

Christina's heart thundered in her chest and her face flushed red-hot. She blinked but didn't dare wipe the spit he sprayed on her face.

"I...um..."

"Hit the ground, Private Poulos!" shouted Sergeant Harris. "Twenty-five pushups!"

Some of the women averted their eyes and sucked in a breath of relief because they were spared; others stared and smirked.

As Christina's splayed arms began to quiver, the sergeant planted his heavy black boot on the small of her back and shoved her hard to the ground. Her face and the front of her uniform became smeared with mud in the dewy grass. She awkwardly started to stand up and he pushed her back down with his boot on her shoulder. Mud oozed into her mouth.

He swept his arm amongst the ranks and yelled with a booming voice, "Ladies, let this be a lesson to each of you! Pull anything like Poulos and you'll get worse!"

Christina staggered to her feet and wiped the mud from her mouth with the back of her hand. Sergeant Harris pointed his finger an inch from her face and spat, "Get cleaned up and find us in precisely twenty minutes or *you'll* get worse."

Furious to the core, her eyes blazed. Sensing her defiance, Sergeant Harris grabbed her by the shoulders. Christina shrugged his hands off, took a step back, and stood straight. She saluted and sputtered, "Yes, sir."

He narrowed his eyes and said, "That's better."

She ran to the barracks with hot tears streaking her mud-smeared face and made it back with three minutes to spare.

After hours of marching in the blistering sun, the wind started blowing about them and the sky became checkered with dark clouds. The pent-up sky gave way to a sudden cloudburst. Formation broke and the women ran back to the barracks.

As they slogged through the door, Christina felt an arm encircle her waist. She turned and gazed into the eyes of a stout girl with shiny black curls. "Hey, don't feel bad," said the girl. "He just used you as an example to scare the bejeezus outta all of us. Why, it could have happened to me just as well."

"Gee, thanks," said Christina with a grateful smile.

"My name is Beth Goldman. I'm a Bronx girl. Where are you from?"

Christina looked into Beth's open, friendly face. "I'm Christina Poulos. I'm from Chicago."

"Well, Christina Poulos, I think we're two peas in a pod: big-city girls in Virginia."

Beth's voice was something of a contradiction. It had a peculiarly appealing quality—a bit quick and gruff, yet reassuring. Her New York accent made Christina smile.

In spite of her awkwardness at being a world away from home, Christina gradually awakened to an incredible sense of freedom. After a couple of months, she didn't mind the discipline and wore her khaki uniform with pride. She caught her reflection in the window of the mess hall early one morning and saw a new self. Shoulders back, she wore a pillbox cap, with her dark wavy hair pulled away from her face by hidden black bobby pins.

Her crisp, long-sleeved shirt, sporting the insignia "Private First Class" on the upper sleeve, was tucked smoothly into her A-line skirt. It was a far cry from the flowered sack dresses she wore at home.

She carried herself with a new air. There was no doubt—Christina turned heads. Her natural beauty and guileless demeanor intrigued onlookers. She heard the comments and low whistles but wasn't about to act like the impetuous, brash women who threw themselves at anything in pants. She became fast friends with Beth from the Bronx and Mary McCorley from Kankakee, Illinois. They lived together in the same barracks.

Mary was willowy, with a thatch of curly auburn hair. "It's from my Irish grandma," she laughed. Her smooth skin looked just like fine porcelain china, her cheeks naturally rosy.

"Christina, we're Mutt and Jeff, light and dark." Mary's long limbs and purposeful walk made her appear boyish, but her smiling blue eyes gave a confiding, feminine expression. Her persuasive laugh had a lively intelligence to it. Her ways were easy and gentle.

Christina could say anything to her two friends. Beth Goldman reminded Christina of her Cousin Georgene at home. She chattered till there was no tomorrow and had the broadest smile and heartiest belly laugh. During off hours, the three of them walked arm in arm around the base. They could sing "Bugle Boy" in fast harmony and became the hit of their barracks. The girls taught Christina how to dance the jitterbug and laughed at her because she couldn't stop tapping her feet even when brushing her teeth!

Beth worked assembling radar units for fighter planes. Christina learned to type navigator logs for practice missions. Her fingers flew as she became a fast, accurate typist. Mary held a similar position, and they walked together every morning to a small brick building by the looming cargo aircraft hangars. The gray Royal typewriters tapped out a collective staccato hum, and the flung carriages rang their little bells.

Early one morning, after the girls settled into their work, a cadre of officers walked through the building. Christina sat up straighter and kept her eyes riveted on the log she was typing. A few minutes later, she became aware of someone standing behind her right shoulder. She smelled a waft of pipe tobacco.

"I am very pleased with your accuracy and speed, young lady," said an officer with a crisp British accent. Christina turned quickly and glanced up into the riveting gray eyes of a colonel. He said, "Keep it up."

Christina stood at attention and saluted. "Why...thank you, sir," she said, blushing. "How did you...?"

The Colonel tipped his hat, gave a slight smile, and walked off. He was a tall, distinguished gentleman with a natural, noble bearing. Christina's heart swelled.

Later that morning, while walking to the mess hall for lunch, Mary exclaimed in a burst, "God, Christina, do you know who that officer is?"

"No. Should I?"

"It's Colonel James Reynolds! He was a fighter pilot for the Royal Air Force in England and came to Langley to train American pilots. I heard what he said. Your hands *do* fly! I can hear how fast you fling the carriage on your typewriter." Mary vigorously bobbed in her chair for added endorsement. Christina grinned.

"It must be from making all of the milkshakes and hamburgers at my family's store!" she laughed, and sat up straighter.

"You better hurry up, girl!" yelled Beth through the window screen of the barracks. "The plane's waiting while you powder your nose!"

Christina threw the last of her belongings into her pea-green canvas duffel bag and burst out the double wooden doors. Beth had arranged for the three of them to stay with her family in New York City. New York! It was their first furlough and first flight on an airplane!

"Oh, God, I'm scared to death!" yelled Christina, walking across the hot tarmac to the C-47 Skytrain cargo/troop transport plane known as "the Gooney Bird." The thundering drone of its huge twin propeller engines was deafening. Christina clapped her hands over her ears. The rising rush of wind as she walked closer to the plane made her eyes water.

The three friends glanced nervously at each other. They were astonished to be the only girls boarding the plane.

"Hurry up, climb aboard!" shouted one of the soldiers, with gloved hands cupped around his mouth. He raised his brows and wondered how some women could look cool even on a hot day. Perhaps it was the breezy movement of their skirts.

"Ladies first!" he yelled.

The girls hiked their skirts to reach the first step. The men winked and elbowed one another. A soldier with "Peters" printed on his jacket gestured to Christina and said to the guys, "That one's mine." He walked over to her and said, "Here, let me help you up."

Christina felt a strong hand support her arm. Startled, she turned and stared into the piercing, almost luminescent blue eyes of a rangy, impossibly handsome man with smooth brown hair. He wore the crisp ironed khakis of a lieutenant and a brown leather bomber jacket with a radar insignia. They exchanged smiles. Christina stopped breathing and her heart seized inside her chest.

"These narrow steps are brutal," he said.

"Oh yes, thank you," said Christina, blushing. She leaned on him for support.

He tipped his hat and said, "I'm happy to be of service. Tom's the name; what's yours?"

"Christina. Christina Poulos."

"Well, Christina Poulos, you seem shaky. Is this your first time on an airplane?" Tom asked with amusement in his eyes.

"Yes. Yes it is."

"Sit by me and I'll take good care of you."

"Um, okay."

Tom pulled down the spring-loaded metal seat. "Here, let me help you with the seat belt." He positioned the wide seat straps over her shoulders and latched them together with the lap belt. His hands brushed hers and their eyes met for a second. Christina smiled and glanced down at the floor of the plane. His calm manner and friendly smile made her heart leap. Tom sat in the seat next to her. She studied his sun-browned hands. They were a bit callused, but his nails were clean and trimmed.

Beth and Mary were escorted in similar fashion. They caught each other's eyes and grinned.

When the engines roared to a deafening pitch, Tom gave her a reassuring smile and patted her hand.

15
Gee Whiz

I have loved the stars too fondly to be fearful of the night.
— Galileo

1956

A couple of evenings later, Sophie went looking for her brother. She hadn't seen him all day. The flutter of worry bore down on her again. She unlatched the front door and walked out on the porch. The gray painted wood under her bare feet felt warm from the day's heat. The darkening sky seemed desolate on the housetops, and she heard the distant barking of dogs. Shadows blurred into fuzzy obscurity.

A muffled sound like whimpering caught her ear. At the same time branches of the rose bush scratched the corner of the house when the wind stirred.

"Niko? Is that you?" She went down the steps and walked around the alley side of the house. The ground was littered with an empty Nehi bottle and newspapers. She found Niko scrunched on the ground and leaning against the rusty garbage barrel. His dirty baseball bat lay on the cinders next to him. "What are you doing out here?"

He brought his hands up to his face. "Nothing. Go away."

She pulled his hands down and saw that he had been crying. His face was streaked with dirt.

"What's wrong, Niko?"

"Nothing. I…I just fell down." His voice was flat, and he looked away.

"You keep saying 'nothing's wrong' all the time, but I'm not buyin' that. It's Pa and that jerk Taki, isn't it? They're doing something bad with you. You've been acting so weird lately. I'm not going anywhere till you tell me what's going on."

Niko jumped up and yanked on her hair.

"Ow! What ya do that for?"

He stomped on the cinders. "Gee whiz, I already told ya…I fell!"

She jammed her hand into the pocket of her shorts. "Come on, Niko, you can tell me anything!"

He waved her words away as if fanning mosquitoes. He looked down for a long time and dug a hole in the cinders with the toe of his shoe. "Leave me alone, Sophie. I told ya—I'm fine. Let's go in the house and play Monopoly or somethin'."

"I'm telling Ma."

"No! There's nothin' to tell."

They heard a rustle behind them. Teddy came around the corner with something bulging in his mouth. He lowered his head and dropped a gray fluffy ball at their feet. It moved.

Sophie squatted down to take a closer look. "What do you have there, Teddy?"

A little gray-and-tan sparrow shivered and puffed itself. It hopped sideways in a semi-stupor. Niko scooped it up in his hands and blew a breath of warmth on it. The bird unfurled its feathers and flew away. Teddy ran off.

"That was weird," said Sophie. "I can't believe he didn't kill the bird."

"Hey, Teddy, good job," shouted Niko after him. "You brought us a present." He turned his back on Sophie and ran into the house.

Niko stayed moody and silent the rest of the week. Sophie told Christina about her suspicions. "You should be more worried about how he's acting than me," said Sophie. "You're his Ma! I'm gonna tell Yiayia and Papou."

"No!" Christina winced and rubbed her temple with her fingers. "I don't want you to bother them."

"Are you afraid of what they'll think?"

"Sophie, I'm telling you, Niko's just growing up. You've gone through the same thing. I promise to look into it."

But Sophie became more and more troubled by her brother's peculiar behavior. Awkward smiles and vagueness seemed to define him, as if he were camouflaging some inner anguish. She knew something was wrong with him when he habitually looked down and wouldn't meet her eyes, but she couldn't pry a thing out of him. Confusion seemed to brew in Niko's mind. *Why can't Ma see?* She would see him waver from being a dull, sleepy-eyed boy who turned inside himself to a boisterous mischief-maker who gallivanted around the neighborhood—dabbling on the fringes of trouble.

Sophie and Niko played with their cousins and neighbors down the street and alleyways, but she didn't like how Niko looked up to twelve-year-old Jake. She knew Jake was a schemer. His mother had run off with the Pabst Blue Ribbon beer delivery guy, and his father had skipped town, leaving Jake to be raised by his Polish grandmother, who didn't speak a word of English.

Jake and Niko made their presence known in the neighborhood with flapping playing cards—held in place by spring-loaded clothespins—"motorizing" the spokes of their bike wheels. Jake dared Niko to ride outside his boundaries.

"I can ride my bike all the way to Hegewisch!" Jake bragged to Niko one sultry afternoon. "Do ya wanna come? I know the way, and there's a cool baseball card store there."

Niko's eyed him with suspicion. "I don't believe you—besides, it's too far away."

Jake lifted his chin haughtily and clucked his tongue. "Done it twice already."

"Does your Grandma know?" asked Niko.

Jake laughed. "The difference between you and me is I do what I want. My Grandma don't care. She trusts me."

Niko shifted his feet and looked up, marveling at Jake's boldness. "Well, okay," he said. "Let's go!"

"Now you're talkin'," said Jake.

Jake and Niko hopped on their bikes and rode four miles down busy Torrence Avenue, past the mills, and across snaking railroad tracks to Hegewisch. Niko kept looking over his shoulder the entire way. They made it back before dinnertime.

Papou George's friend Mr. Simonian thought he saw the boys in Hegewisch. Sophie was at her grandparents' when she heard Papou confront Niko on the fire escape right outside the kitchen's screen door. She heard Niko confess and promise never to go outside the boundaries again.

"You getting big, Niko, but not that big," said Papou. "Be careful who you's make for friends. A good friend won't push doing wrong things. So's you don't forget, I want you scrubbing the floor at the store with a brush and warm soapy water till it's all clean. We won't talk about this again."

"Okay, Papou."

To Sophie, Papou's words—few and strong—had a curious force, not worn out from constant use.

Later that week, Sophie saw Jake smoking with an older boy behind the bleachers at the baseball field. That same evening she peeked into Niko's cracked open bedroom door and saw him resting against the headboard of his bed, examining his collection of treasures in an El Producto cigar box. She said quietly, "Hey, Niko, can I talk to you a minute?"

He looked up and his eyes softened. "Yep," he said with a nod. He held something up between his thumb and forefinger. "Hey, Sophie, look at this ol' rusty spring I found in the alley. Do ya think it fell out of a car or something?"

She sat on his bed and examined it. "Yeah, maybe. Uh, Niko, I have something to ask you."

Niko glanced down at his cigar box.

"Has Jake ever given you a cigarette?" Niko fidgeted and his face reddened.

"Um, yeah," he said cautiously. "But if Ma or Papou caught me doin' that"—he stopped and sucked in a quick breath—"I'd be in BIG trouble."

"You'd tell me if he wanted you to do something you shouldn't, right?" she asked.

"All I do is ride bikes with him."

16
Mom-and-Pop Diners

Yaaa-HOO!

~ Papou

The following week brought cooler weather. Rain cleared the air and left a gray broth of steel mill grit in the street gutters.

During this interval of pleasant weather, Yiayia and Papou asked Christina and Thea Stefania to be in charge of the store so they could take the kids on a four-day road trip to the Henry Ford Museum in Detroit.

The family settled into the car, but instead of heading east, Papou drove north on Clark Street all the way to Wrigley Field and surprised the kids with tickets to a Cubs game. Most Southsiders were White Sox fans, but Yiayia and Papou had spent their first years as child immigrants in North Chicago and became dogged Cubs fans.

They spent the afternoon cheering the Cubs, eating hot dogs, and drinking pop. Sophie's favorite player was Mr. Sunshine, Ernie Banks.

On the long trip to Detroit, the kids talked baseball, read books, played jacks on the floor, and saddled up their little plastic horses to play cowboys and Indians on the seats. They leaned out the windows and let the air rush through their hair and fingers.

They zigzagged between mom-and-pop diners, with their flashing neon signs and Sophie's favorite: ten-cent square White Castle cheeseburgers with chocolate malts and fries. After gulping down their meals in the car, they tossed cups and bags out the windows onto the roadways. Sophie's greasy-faced brother and cousins jumped up on their knees and looked out the back window to watch the trash swirl and dance in the wind. "No throwin' things out the windows, kids," Papou scolded.

Detroit was all new territory to the kids. After their first day at the museum, Cousin George said, "They're crankin' out cars faster than poop."

"You learned *many* things there today," Yiayia said. "You's got to sit in Rosa Parks's bus. History turned upside down because she helped start better things for colored people. You's saw the car factory, Thomas Edison's light bulb lab, and the Wright Brothers' shop where they first thought about putting wings on a big bike to fly."

"Tomorrow we see the chair that Abraham Lincoln got shot dead," said Papou. "There's blood on it."

Yiayia lowered her head and looked above her glasses. "Pa," she huffed. "Sayin' too many things again." He pulled on the brim of his Panama hat and grinned.

That night, the family hunkered down at the Doze-Away Motel. The blinking, buzzing neon sign of the motel, with its string of *zzzzz*'s under the words, flashed through the thin window curtains into their room. Yiayia dug out a blanket from the car trunk and draped it over the curtain rod.

Sophie, Niko, and Cousin Angie slept side by side in a double bed, with Yiayia and Papou in the other bed. Cousin George bedded down on a fold-away cot in a corner of the room. Sleep washed over the family, and the grandparents snored softly.

The night's peace was shattered when something skittered between the legs of the three kids. Sophie and Angie shot out of bed screaming. Cousin George slammed his cot against the wall and jumped up with his fists raised. Yiayia flipped on the switch of the bedside lamp. Niko yanked down on the covers and shrieked. A two-inch-long brown cockroach with curved antennae shot off the edge of the bed onto the floor. Its legs clicked noisily over the tan linoleum. The four kids leaped over to their grandparents' bed and shrank down on their knees. Papou grabbed his shoe and chased the bug along the baseboard under the window. That cockroach gave him a chase. He slammed the heel of his shoe on the floor, over and over, but kept missing.

"Get it, Papou!" yelled George. "Squish the daylights outta it!"

Finally, Papou zeroed in on the brown tyrant and everyone heard a crackling sound. The cockroach flipped onto its back and clawed at the air. Papou smacked it two more times, and it finally lay dead at his bare feet. He raised himself to his full height and stood over the squished roach like a conqueror. The kids bounced up and down in bed and cheered. Their loud outcry prompted thundering wall banging and a "shut up" from the room next door.

"Way to kill that sucker, Papou!" said Cousin George, slapping his leg.

The kids jumped out of bed to examine the intruder's remains. Angie covered her eyes, Niko pretended to gag himself with his finger, and Sophie said, "Eeew," as she examined the squirted guts and dismembered legs.

"Did ya see it?" yelled Cousin George. "Ya'd think it was dead, but Papou had to whack it two more times to get the green and yellow guts to splatter out and the legs to stop wigglin'! The guts remind me of the green pickle Cousin Angelo puked in the car after riding the Tilt-a-Whirl at Riverview last summer. Then Niko hurled because of the stink."

"Stop it, George!" yelled Sophie.

George kept going. "Even after Yiayia and Papou cleaned it real good, it still stunk all the way home."

Yiayia gave George the no-nonsense look and he stopped. She wet a big wad of toilet paper under the bathroom faucet, wiped up the cockroach mess, and flushed it down the toilet. "Okay, kids, back to bed."

Cousin Angie started wailing. More wall banging came from the room next door.

"What, honey?" asked Yiayia.

"What if the cockroach has a friend or a family?"

"Let's look around," said Yiayia.

"What if they're in between the mattresses?"

"We'll look there too."

After searching every nook and cranny, they settled back down to bed.

It seemed to Sophie that they blinked their way from one surprise to another on that trip. Her grandparents not being perfect was one thing Sophie loved most about them. The biggest surprise was a new practice on the trip that didn't bode well for lessons against stealing. This latest behavior built upon the collections of salt and peppershakers Yiayia and Papou had in every room in their apartment—the sailboat shakers touching bow to bow on top of the toilet tank in the bathroom, the rooster and hen standing beak to beak on the kitchen table.

When Sophie was little, she played with the proud Greek soldier shaker standing with his pretty wife on her grandparents' lamp table in the living room. Dressed in their native costumes, they danced: he bowed, with the pom-poms on his pointy red shoes touching her slippers, and she curtseyed. When Sophie wasn't playing with them, they stood side by side, touching hands: he the pepper, she the salt.

On this trip, her grandparents' penchant for shakers, especially ones with restaurant logos emblazoned on them, manifested itself as petty theft. In the most unobtrusive way, Yiayia glanced around like a spy and slid the shakers into her open purse. Their glove box brimmed to overflowing.

"It's okay, kids, we don't steal nothin' else, and *Theos* knows how much we feed folks," explained Yiayia.

"We gonna give them away, but not the boots," said Papou.

Ceramic brown cowboy-boot shakers from the Spinnin' Lariat Restaurant in Detroit were their best find. Later, when Papou used them at the kitchen table with its flowered tablecloth, he'd whoop, "Yaaa-HOO!"

When the carload crossed the border into Indiana on the way home, they stopped at a fruit and vegetable stand in the country. Prickles of pure happiness ran down Sophie's arms as she burst out of the crowded car into the knee-deep grass. The grass tickled her bare legs, and its sweetness was strong in her nose. She twirled and fell down laughing. The restless clouds moved swiftly across the wide-open sky. Sparrows scattered the sun with their flitting wings, and the low-flying crows glided with their wingtips gently curved up. She watched the honeybees greedily buzz into wildflower blossoms. Sophie sighed, wishing she could feel this way forever. She felt a rhythm in the land; the fresh wind caressed the rippling grass and her upturned face. Her body fit into the soft stirrings of the earth.

She lay back, not wanting the day to end, not wanting to go home. Niko was himself away from Pa. He was his funny, happy self—not the moody boy he had become at home. Sometimes she wanted to crawl into Niko's skin, to feel what he felt.

Sophie shook off thoughts of her parents and turned her attention to her other relatives. She ran, feeling wild as the wind, over to Papou. He held a shiny purple eggplant in his hand, squeezing it slightly to test its readiness.

"Let me, Papou," said Sophie. "Let me pick the best ones!"

He smiled down at her and said, "*Nai, nai,* Yiayia is make *keftethes* tonight."

Yiayia had already filled a bag with apricots to make Sophie's favorite pastry dessert, *pasta flora.* In the garden alongside the stand, they picked mint and grape leaves from a sprawling grape arbor. At home, the fresh chopped mint would be rolled into garlicky fried *keftethes* meatballs, coated with thick tomato sauce, sweetened with red wine. The newest, most tender grape leaves, soaked in brine in the refrigerator, would be wrapped around rice-filled *dolmathes* meatballs.

17
Washing the Money

Every rascal is not a thief, but every thief is a rascal.
— Aristotle

*O*n the last Sunday in August, Sophie and her family drove northwest through Chicago to see Great-Yiayia Elena. This time, her Ma came along. They stopped along the way on a country road to pick dandelion and clover greens for Great-Yiayia.

Yiayia Sophia had a saying about the dandelions. "Look at the little field of yellow polka dots. The yellow flower is the sun, the wishing puffball is the moon, the seeds that fly away are the stars, and the greens are good and healthy to eat!"

Sophie stooped at the waist next to Papou and looked from side to side. Cousin Angie squatted next to them and piled pebbles on top of each other.

Sophie always got jumpy when they filled up their brown paper sacks on roadsides, as passersby often made stupid comments or gawked at them. She kept her head down. *Those dumb people don't know how good these greens are when Yiayia fixes them.* She closed her eyes and could see bunches of greens in a tall silver pot of salted water. After simmering the greens, Yiayia would drain them and pour on a stream of olive oil. As a finishing touch, she'd sprinkle sweet-smelling oregano and squeeze lemon juice on top.

They paused in their picking and looked up when they heard the loud roar of a souped-up car engine. The car fishtailed in the loose gravel, and the tires kicked up billows of dust onto the family. "Hey, look at the trashy greaseballs pickin' weeds!" shouted a boy from a car loaded with teenagers. Their laughter faded as they peeled down the road. Sophie stood up stiffly. She shielded her smoldering eyes with her hand. Her nostrils flared. Cousin George and Niko ran to the road, grabbed a handful of rocks, and pitched them at the car. Their wild throws missed by a long shot.

Cousin George spit on some bare ground and said, "That makes me madder than a pissant!"

"What's a greaseball?" asked Niko.

"Never you mind, Niko," said Yiayia, squeezing her hips angrily.

"He don't know nothin' about how good greens are! Pay no mind to those stupids; and boys, no rock throwing. It don't do any good to be a so-and-so like them."

Sophie leaned close to George and said, "I'm glad you and Niko threw those rocks."

"Yeah, Cousin," he nodded, spitting to the side. "We think alike."

They filled up their bags, got back in the car, and drove to the north side of Chicago. Before rounding the corner toward Great-Yiayia Elena's home, Papou pulled up to the crumbling curb in front of Kamberos's Grocery Store. Sophie got out of the car and stepped over the store's wooden threshold, concave from thousands of footsteps. Her eyes roved over the dotted pattern of small black-and-white tiles on the floor. She startled when the spring-loaded wooden screen door slammed behind them. Sophie's nostrils filled with the smell of kalamata olives and warm bread.

Mr. Kamberos, the portly grocer, turned, smiled broadly, and flung his arms wide. "*Yasou*, George and Sophia! *Yasou*, kids!" he said. He shook Papou George's hand and kissed Yiayia Sophia on her cheek. "What does Elena want today?"

"I know my Ma," said Yiayia, smiling. She filled her grocery basket with fragrant dried oregano, basil, feta cheese, and other Greek food.

Sophie surveyed the store and ran her hand along the smooth wooden counter by the cheese case. She bent close to the glass and eyed the labels on the *mizithra*, *kefaloterie*, and hard wedges of parmesan.

She took Niko's hand, listened to the Greek chatter, and breathed in deeply.

Elena lived on the first floor of a brick tenement building on South Halsted Street, near Greektown. Papou said Al Capone did some of his crime business on her street.

"Look out for da machine guns, kids!" he laughed. "Did ya hear how Capone's thugs pop one of his own guys off for spillin' the beans to cops about some washing money?"

"There you go, Pa!" said Yiayia. "It's laundered the money, not washed." Sophie covered her mouth and laughed quietly so Papou wouldn't hear her.

Papou knocked on the door and everyone waited. The wooden floor creaked and complained with their shifting weight outside Elena's door.

"Oh, *Theos*, I worry about her falling down like she did last winter," Yiayia muttered to herself, mopping sweat off her chest and the back of her neck with Papou's big white handkerchief. She knocked again, calling, "Ma! Open the door!"

Shuffling, slow clicking. Elena flipped open two brass locks and peeked through. Her eyes gleamed. She slid the chain and opened the door with a modest, close-mouthed grin. "*Ah! Ella tho. Ti kanies pethia mou?*" Her voice sounded soft like silk, not cracked with age.

"*Kala, kala,*" the family said in unison.

Elena sat down ceremoniously on her floral tapestry chair with its carved mahogany armrests and legs. Starting with Papou, Yiayia, then Sophie, each family member in turn kissed her with gentle reverence, as she was over ninety years old. Her satiny soft, wrinkled cheeks caved in slightly upon being kissed. She didn't like to wear her false teeth. Her liquid brown-black eyes smiled out from a weathered face etched by the sun in Greece.

Snowy hair, still sprinkled with black, pulled into a feathery bun. A small red-white-and-blue rhinestone American flag pinned to the collar of her black dress. Rayon hose, rolled up to a bit above the knees, looked just like doughnuts. Sophie saw that she had fashioned a knot in the back so they wouldn't fall down. Yiayia reached over and pulled the hem of her mother's black dress down over her knees.

Sophie lifted her chin, proud to hold the honored position in the family as the eldest great-grandchild. She leaned forward and gently touched Elena's papery, thin arm. Fine blue veins wove along the back of her ancient hand.

"Great-Yiayia, why is your forearm crooked?" Sophie asked. "What happened?"

"Ah," she said, gingerly tapping her arm with a gnarled finger. In Greek, she told Sophie about falling down the front stoop of her building. "Honey, I broke my arm. After resting, I pulled it straight and then wrapped it in a nice thick cotton cloth. I took a *Life* magazine, made a good splint, and wrapped it up with a string. I fixed it!" she exclaimed with a triumphant smile.

Sophie's eyes widened.

Elena turned in her chair to the round side table. She tenderly touched the gold frame of a proud picture of Great-Papou Vasilios. His gleaming, intelligent eyes smiled out. Sophie studied the picture. A handsome face— chin up, wavy black hair, full moustache, starched collar.

"*Ton agapouso poli, koukla.*" Her voice low, she studied Sophie's young features and said, "I wish the same for you."

Sophie sat down at Elena's feet and took her knobby hand. Stillness radiated between them.

"Yiayia," said Sophie, almost whispering. "Tell me about Greece—about coming to America. I've heard a little, but never from you."

Elena clasped her hands together and said, "Greece was poor. We lived in a little stone house with a garden and carried water in buckets from the stream. Our goats, Mati and Callista, gave us milk and cheese. We worked hard to pick the olives. The children helped. Uncles and cousins who had already emigrated to America wrote letters and said, 'Come. We are doing better in America!'"

Elena closed her eyes, sat back, and smiled dreamily. She nodded off, and Sophie went quiet.

"Yiayia," whispered Sophie, tucking a quilted coverlet around the old woman's thin legs. Elena felt a silky touch on her arm and heard the *pfissst* of a match being struck. Pleasant, smoky smell.

Stillness. Elena smiled. Her eyes opened to the glow of a candle on the side table. The flame flickered with a breath. She looked at Sophie with a faraway gaze.

"Saying goodbye to Papou Vasilios the day he sailed across the sea to America on that rusty freighter was the hardest thing I ever had to do. What if the sea swallowed him up? But he made it, and we managed to wait until he sent enough money for our passage."

Sophie held a stack of yellowed, ragged-edged letters in her lap. They were tied together with a worn blue ribbon. "I found these behind Great-Papou's picture."

"Ah, the letters," she said. Pride slipped into her voice. "I saved them. Your Yiayia asked me to find them for her to read. Vasilios wrote to me in Greece and I wrote back to him. Mail by ship took months to arrive. Two long years I waited for him to send enough money to bring us to America on the big steamship." She pressed a hand on her cheek and puffed a breath.

Screeches of laughter and Greek music spiraled to them from the radio in the kitchen. Delicious smells wafted. Cousins played games.

"Can I read a letter?" asked Sophie.

"It's all Greek. Can you read?"

"Remember, Great-Yiayia, I've been going to Greek School at Mrs. Geroulis's house, around the corner from the Hi-Lo store, almost every day after regular school since I was six years old."

Elena smiled. "Yes. I want to hear his voice through you."

Sophie could feel the pulse in her fingertips as she untied the ribbon and slid a letter out of its thin envelope. She unfolded the top flap and saw that a steady hand had written the letter with a fine blue fountain pen.

My dearest Elena,

A son! I'm so happy you are well. I worried. You named the baby Theodore, after my great-grandfather! He was a good man. His name means "Given by God." I lit a candle at church for him. Cousin Theodore thinks you named the baby after him, so he lifted five little glasses of ouzo to his namesake. He fell off his chair laughing and drunk. Please thank your mother for helping with the baby and children.

There are so many Greeks in Chicago! You and the children will be happy to make new friends. Pascha was an adventure for us. A family from church raised two lambs in their backyard near downtown. We roasted them right over a fire pit in the churchyard, just like home! We dyed the eggs red and cracked them end to end. A little girl named Anna won the good-luck egg game! We had a big feast!

I look out my window and see many smokestacks, buildings going up high into the sky, horses pulling wagons. Did I tell you there aren't any donkeys or goats in the city? Chicago is growing fast!

I'm saving all the money I can. We'll be together soon. I see the same moon you see. Look at the changing moon in the sky and know that I see it too. I'll keep lighting candles.

I love you. Kiss the children.

Vasilios

Sophie folded the letter and slipped it back in the envelope. Her eyes shined bright.

PART THREE

18

Tom

*Hope is the thing with feathers that perches in the soul,
and sings the tune without words, and never stops at all.*
— Emily Dickinson

1943

After the whirlwind trip to New York, Tom and Christina were insepa-
rable. On the first furlough day they had together, Tom drove Christina
outside the sprawling base in an open Jeep as fast as it could go, which was
about thirty-five miles an hour. He changed gears in smooth motion, dou-
ble-clutching to the cruising ratio, reveling in the engine's perfect pitch. The
sweet, fresh-mown grass in the Virginia countryside flooded his senses. The
wind played havoc with Christina's hair, her blue shirtwaist dress. She threw
her head back and laughed. He peeled his eyes off the road and glanced at
her smooth arms holding her skirt down in the wind. Her beauty was piercing and gentle, teasing, intolerant. The wild, shivering brilliance of her dark
eyes set him on fire, and a slight smile brushed his lips.

It seemed a luxury to give way to passion—to abandon persistent dissat-
isfaction. Tom had given up hope for the extraordinary happiness he read in
books and saw in others. With Christina, the traces of shame from his past
seemed to dissolve, and he reveled in it. He didn't need to drink.

For three weeks they spent most of their free time together. The epitome of a gentleman, Tom took his time and didn't rush her. When he dropped Christina off at her barracks, his lips lightly touched her cheek.

The following weeks were full for Tom. Trained in the secret advancement of radar to detect enemy aircraft, Tom impressed his superiors with his natural technical abilities. Langley made plans for him to lead a cadre of other technicians on a month-long mission to Canada. The two allies coordinated efforts to develop smaller rotating radar units for airplanes.

Late in the afternoon, the day before he left, Tom drove Christina to the seashore.

She wore a white button-down sleeveless shirt tied at the waist. Khaki pants fit snug around her middle. Tom veered off onto a gravelly side road to the sand. They hit ruts and bounced in their seats so hard, they fell into fits of laughter. He parked the Jeep by a large clump of tall reeds growing out of the sand and jumped out of the driver's seat. He grabbed a bag from behind her seat and took Christina's hand to help her out.

"What's in the bag?"

"Something from Georgia," he said. "You'll see."

They rolled up the cuffs of their pants and stuffed their shoes into Tom's small drawstring duffel. Through the reeds and small drifts, they walked hand and hand onto the hardened sand close to the edges of the shore. As the sun sank to the west, the sky turned a brilliant orange and illuminated the rim of the ocean. The tide rose, and the small waves rippled on and on over their feet.

Tom guided Christina towards the dunes. Their feet whispered on the soft sand. The full moon rose slowly, lit up the sky, and shined white on the breaking waves.

Tom stopped and pointed up to the sky with wonder in his voice. "Look at the blue moon, Christina."

"What is a blue moon?" she asked.

"It's when the moon is full two times in one month. It only happens every three years or so."

Christina shook her head. "Is there anything you don't know?"

Tom smiled at her and spread a green army blanket on the crest of a small wind-rippled dune. They sank down on the blanket and Christina wrapped her arms around her knees. Tom reached into the bag and pulled out two big peaches, heavy as croquet balls.

"So this is the surprise from Georgia!" said Christina. She took one from Tom, cupped it in her hands, and held it up like a prize in the moonlight. "This is the prettiest peach I've ever seen. The peaches we get back home are small." She bit into the fuzzy flesh and the ripe sweetness dribbled down her chin.

"Look at you!" Tom laughed. He leaned forward and wiped the juice off her chin with his white handkerchief. They ate the peaches down to the stony red seeds.

He wrapped his arm around Christina's waist and gently laid her down in one fluid movement. He pressed his length close to her. Christina buried her face into his neck and shivered with pleasure. He smelled clean, like pine needles and shaving lotion, with a faint whiff of something harsh, probably the cigarette smoke in the barracks. His masculine scent turned her inside out. As she moved to rest her head against his chest, a thousand thoughts raced through her mind.

"I'll miss you so much, Tom. I can't bear to be without you."

He leaned away from her, stared into her eyes, and kissed her mouth softly. She did not resist his kiss, his gentle hand against her cheek. Every particle of her body rushed with warmth and light.

He made himself pull away. "I'll be back before you know it," he said. "You're my girl. No lookin' at the other guys. Promise?"

Christina leaned back on his arm and saw that the night became absolute and tranquil, filled with grandeur above their heads. She gave him a reassuring smile and nestled in his arms. "I promise, Tom."

When he was gone, unfamiliar feelings surged through her and she yearned for Tom every waking moment. The way his shirt pulled across his chest; his hard, muscled arms. At night she lay restless in bed before sleep overcame her, imagining his eyes meeting hers when they talked, her body close to his. *If Ma and Pa find out I'm dating a non-Greek man, they'll kill me.* She shook the thought off. *It's my life, not theirs.*

She didn't hear from him. His work was top secret. The weeks crawled by, but Christina plunged herself into work with fervor and stayed busy with friends and activities on the base.

After getting out of the shower a few days before Tom was scheduled to return, she heard a booming voice through a propped-open window by the ceiling of the barracks' communal bathroom.

"Is there a girl named Christina Poulos in there?"

Beth was leaning over a sink curling her eyelashes in front of one of the steamy bathroom mirrors.

Christina grabbed her friend by the shoulders and squeezed. They looked at each other in the mirror. "Oh my God, Beth, that sounds like Tom!" she said. "He's not due back yet!"

Beth ran to the bunk area, parted the venetian blinds, and peeked out the window. She saw Tom leaning against a post with his arms crossed and cap cocked slightly over his forehead.

"Get yourself together, girl," said Beth, looking back over her shoulder. "Your honey's outside. I'll go out and hold him back! You better hurry or he might march right in to get you!"

"Oh, Beth! He's back!"

Christina fumbled with her many buttons, brushed out her hair, and smoothed on light red lipstick.

She turned to Beth and asked, "How do I look?"

"Smashing! Now get out there."

Christina burst out the door and ran into Tom's waiting arms. He grabbed Christina in a bear hug, lifted her off her feet, and swung her around. Christina threw her head back and laughed up at the sky. The fresh smell of her skin made Tom dizzy for an instant. He held her at arm's length to appraise her. He grinned, took off his cap, threw it up in the air, and embraced her again.

"I missed you something terrible," said Christina.

He ran his hands through her luscious, thick hair and traced the contour of her cheek with his fingers. "Oh, God, I missed you every waking moment …my beautiful Christina." He fixed his eyes on hers. She lowered her eyes and smiled one of those bashful smiles he loved. He lifted her chin, gazed deep into her eyes, and said, "I…I love you."

She pressed her hand to the side of his head. "I love you, Tom." He kissed her parted lips with abandon.

Several weeks later Tom received special permission from Colonel Reynolds to fly in a test run on a B-24 Liberator bomber.

"You're welcome to bring Christina along with you," said the Colonel with a wink.

Tom couldn't wait to tell her.

He ran into the mess hall and found her eating lunch with Mary. He grabbed Christina's metal tray, took her by the hand, and said, "Christina! I need to tell you something."

Mary grinned and said, "You two go ahead. I'll see you later, Christina."

Tom pulled her to a far table and sat down quickly.

"Tom, what is it? Is everything okay?"

"More than okay. You're not going to believe this, but Colonel Reynolds said I could fly a test run with him on a B-24!"

"That's wonderful!"

"But here's the best part! He said you can come along!"

"He did?" Christina gripped his hand. "I can't believe it! When?"

"Tomorrow morning!" he said, grinning ear to ear. Christina's heart skipped.

The day of the flight dawned glorious: the horizon pink, the sky crystalline blue. Christina clutched Tom's arm as they walked across the tarmac towards the plane.

"Look at this plane!" exclaimed Tom. "Four Pratt and Whitney radial piston engines, each with fourteen cylinders, a wing span of over a hundred feet, and a huge payload of bombs. It can fly farther than any other bomber, with a top speed of three hundred miles per hour. Check out the nose, tail, and belly gun turrets!"

Christina turned to Tom and grinned with amazement. He rubbed his palms together—his eyes were ablaze with excitement. "It's a huge plane!" she said with a shiver. "The tail looks like a giant dog bone lying on its side!"

Tom placed his leather jacket around her shoulders and drew her close to his side. She looked into his face and saw a peculiar brilliance in his deep blue eyes, as if he were summoning her to draw closer.

"It'll get cold up there," he said.

"I'm so…thank you."

Christina heard her own voice taper off. Her heart swelled, and she felt safe in his shadow. She turned, touched his cheek, and smiled. Tom brushed a tendril of hair from her forehead.

Colonel Reynolds, Captain Wood, the copilot, and six crew members stood by the narrow metal steps at the rear of the plane. Christina walked demurely towards the awaiting group of men. Admiring eyes turned in appreciation of her, envy of Tom. Her dark looks were striking. Tom gave a sideways grin and looked at her with pride.

Christina stood stiffly at attention and saluted the Colonel. He lifted his cap with a gentlemanly flourish and extended a hand to her. "Well, good morning, young lady. You're up bright and chipper. Are you ready to have a splendid adventure?"

Christina flashed a shy smile at the Colonel. "Oh, yes, thank you, sir." Everything about the Colonel was dignified. She noticed his confident, seamless movements.

She saluted Captain Wood. He took off his cap and looked at her mildly, amusement in his eyes. He said, "At ease, young lady. Here, let me help you climb aboard!" The touch of his sure hand and encouraging smile momentarily calmed Christina.

Climbing up the steep steps into the plane felt even more exhilarating than her trip to New York on the C-47. The forward gunner, Colonel Reynolds, and Captain Wood settled into their seats within the big windowed nose well squared off with steel struts. Christina eyed the unwieldy-looking controls. Tom and Christina sat side by side on small canvas-covered seats behind the cockpit. Tom squeezed her hand reassuringly.

The engines settled into a throbbing drone; the plane turned smoothly and taxied onto the runway. Christina sat up straighter, and her eyes lit up. The engines immediately revved to a higher, ear-splitting pitch. Christina bit the side of her cheek, clapped her hands over her ears, and pressed hard. She hummed to the same note as the engines and heard her voice vibrate in her head. Her nerves felt like strings being pulled more taut on some kind of screwing peg. The heavy bomber gained speed for a long distance before it finally lifted off the runway.

After the plane leveled off, Christina's pounding heart settled and she yielded into the adventure. She leaned into Tom and yelled, "Do you think it would be alright if I get up and explore the plane?"

"What?" Tom raised his eyebrows and gave her a skeptical look. "Are you sure? It's pretty bouncy."

Christina nodded enthusiastically. "Yes, I'm sure."

"You'll need to ask first," he said with a smile.

She leaned forward and shouted to Colonel Reynolds and Captain Wood, "Sirs! May I walk to the back of the plane?"

They looked at each other in surprise. The Colonel grinned and nodded.

Captain Wood turned to her and shouted over the din of the engines, "The catwalk is only nine inches wide. Be very careful and hold on tight!" Tom helped unhook her safety harness. He supported her elbow and steadied her onto the grated metal catwalk, which ran down the midsection of the plane to the tail.

Colonel Reynolds shouted over his right shoulder, "Hold on tight, young lady, and stay on the catwalk!"

Christina nodded. "I will."

Tom folded his arms and watched her with amusement. The large aircraft vibrated, bounced, and swayed enough for Christina to clutch onto the struts and whatever handhold she could find to keep upright. A wave of nausea overcame her. She swallowed hard, gritted her teeth, and shouted, "I will NOT get sick."

She clumsily made it to the rear of the plane and startled the tail gunner perched in his round, windowed turret. He raised his round goggles, looked up at her, and winked. She smiled and modestly pulled her skirt tight around her legs. Christina rose up on her toes to gaze out a thick rectangular window. Her heart swelled in awe of the infinite blue sky and checkerboard land below.

The gunner yelled up to her, "Pretty spectacular, huh?"

"Oh—yes. It's beautiful!"

Christina turned and cautiously walked back to the middle of the plane. Her stomach settled and she felt exhilarated. With her hand firmly holding onto a strut, she leaned over to look down into the plane's belly from one side of the catwalk, then the other. *I wonder what's down there?*

Christina craned her neck around to make sure no one was looking. She squatted down awkwardly, grasped the edge of the catwalk, and stepped onto the slippery belly of the plane. Christina smiled, smoothed her rumpled skirt, and took a few cautious steps forward. She glanced up and saw Captain Wood scrambling out of his seat in the cockpit. He gestured wildly at her with a look of panic on his face. She froze in her tracks. Tom and Captain Wood shouted, but she couldn't hear them. Christina leaned forward and cupped both ears.

"What?" she yelled. "I can't hear you!"

The drone of the engines was deafening. Tom ran down the catwalk and yelled, "You're standing on the bomb bay doors! They could roll open!"

Christina looked down in horror but couldn't budge. Tom gripped a handhold, reached down, and yelled, "Quick, give me your hand!" He grabbed her by the wrist and yanked her up onto the catwalk. Her legs buckled and she fell onto her knees. She cried out in pain as the jagged metal grating on the catwalk dug into her skin.

Christina struggled for breath and looked up. "Oh, Tom, I…I didn't know!"

Tom bent down and pressed his hand over one of her bleeding knees.

⁓

Tom was the most intelligent man Christina had ever met, and she knew he adored her. The shroud of expectation, of being pigeonholed and squeezed in by her family floated away. For the first time in her life, Christina felt free and alive. She could make her own choices, but she couldn't ease the family out of her worried thoughts.

"You don't know my parents, my family," she told Tom one evening as they walked down a narrow tree-lined path behind the barracks. Their shoes crunched on the gravel, and the air had the steamy, warm smell of wet grass and leaves. "They're so Greek, so old-country. They would never let me date and have always had plans to arrange my marriage to a Greek boy. If they knew I was dating a non-Greek, there would be hell to pay."

Tom raised his eyebrows. "That's ridiculous," he said. "They sound so backward. It's time you live your own life, and besides, you're in America, not the old country."

"I know. You're right," said Christina. "It's hard to explain. It would take a lot for them to come around."

She saw the flame of anger flash over his face. "Do you want them running your life forever?" he asked.

"No. I hate it."

He wrapped his arms around Christina's waist, pulled her close, and murmured in her ear, "Our love is all that matters, and…"

"Yes, but…"

Tom put his finger to her mouth. "No more discussion." He drew her hand to his lips and kissed her palm softly. Their eyes met, and her thoughts became less troubled.

"Tom, can I meet your mother on our next furlough?"

He dropped her hands. His eyes darkened. "Tennessee is too far."

"It won't take so long by train, and besides, we have a furlough coming up. It would be nice to meet your family and see the house you grew up in."

"It's just my Ma and sister," he said with an edge in his voice. "They live in the sticks."

Christina clasped his hand. "Tom, I don't care where they live. They're your family."

Tom pulled his hand away and grew quiet. The pulsing, lazy drone of a B-17 filled the night air. Tom searched the sky and spotted the blinking white wingtip lights and red taillight.

"I wonder who's flying tonight," he said.

Christina touched his arm. "Tom," she said. "Look at me. I want to meet your Ma and sister."

"You don't want to meet them," he said. He turned away from her, and she heard his breathing quicken.

"Why not?"

"Trust me," he said. "You're…you're too good." He looked away.

"Tom, don't you understand? I love you no matter what." Her voice was velvet. "I want to know all of you. It's important to see where—who you come from. It won't change anything between us."

Tom fixed his eyes on the fading silhouette of the plane and said, "It won't be pleasant."

19

A Blue Blowfly

For lack of wood the fire goes out, and where there is no whisperer,
contention quiets down.

— Proverbs 26:20

Mildred nodded tight-lipped, shook Christina's hand, and pecked Tom on the cheek. She was a worn-out, colorless woman with rigid shoulders, thin hair, and a bitter, stony face. A faded dress hung on her gaunt, angular body, and old stains of armpit sweat fanned out on her dress. Mildred took them into the kitchen with its dirty, peeled-up linoleum floor and showed them their side of the refrigerator. A whiff of mold mixed with the smell of rotten potatoes hit Christina's nose when the door opened.

"Y'all see this here side of the fridge?" she asked bluntly, pointing to an empty upper shelf.

"Yes," said Christina.

"Well, it's yours. Don't ya touch the other food."

Christina turned so Mildred couldn't see her roll her eyes at Tom. He glared at his mother and then looked dazed with shame. He stormed out of the kitchen and slammed the front door so hard, Christina jumped. She turned and felt Mildred's cold, judging eyes all over her face and body. At that moment, Christina's world went a dull gray.

"Ya treat him good, ya hear?" Mildred said with fake sugarcoating on her words, but her face had a pinched look as if she had just sucked on a lemon.

"Are y'all gettin' married? 'Cause if ya are, I don't want ya holdin' my smart boy back none. Ya hear?"

Christina's eyes darkened and she lifted her chin. "I don't plan to." She turned and walked out of the room. Mildred's eyes followed her with a contemptuous expression.

Late that afternoon, Christina came out of the bathroom and padded down the hallway in her slippers. She came to an abrupt halt when she saw Mildred in the living room resting her hands on the fireplace mantel. She backed around the corner, not wanting to face her. Christina watched as Mildred gazed up at a proud picture of Tom in his military dress uniform. Another picture of Tom as a young boy, cradling his violin, sat next to it. Mildred touched it with her fingertips and wiped her eyes with the back of her hand.

Her short-haired tabby cat rubbed against her leg.

"Whiskers," she said softly. "Come here."

Mildred bent over at the waist and picked him up. She drew him close to her chest, rubbed behind his ears, and buried her face in the striped fur on his back. Christina saw her breathe in deep, smelling his sweet cat scent. Mildred looked up and smiled at the ceiling. Christina squinted her eyes and shook her head in confusion.

That night Christina sneaked down the hall into Tom's room. He jerked up on one elbow and turned to her.

"What? Why are you here?" he asked.

"Tom," she whispered. "I want to be close to you." She cupped her body into his and slipped an arm around him. His body stiffened.

"What are you thinking?" Christina asked.

"Nothing," he said with a dry, detached voice. "Just...just leave me alone."

Christina turned away from him and sat on the edge of the bed. She gazed up at the ceiling. The bright moon peeked through the cracks of a yellowed pull-down shade and partially lit up the room. Tom's circumstances closed in on her. Her chest heaved and tears ran down her cheeks. She blinked and stared up at a single light bulb hanging precariously by a wire. She had a surprising sense of gratitude for her own family, sorrow for Tom. She got up slowly and left the room.

The next day, Mildred left the house with her rolling wire shopping cart to pick up a few things at the corner market. Tom was outside puttering in the garage, and Christina sat scrunched in the corner on an ancient brown, nubby sofa with a book—glad to be alone. The cat curled up by her side, and the words in her book muddled together. She pondered what to say to Tom, but instead, her eyes rested on the cat—the rise and fall of his flank as he breathed.

Christina gave a start at the sound of scraping and rattling on the front porch. The door flung open and rammed into the wall. A woman walked in and said in a brash voice, "Oh, y'all must be Tom's woman!" Christina stood up and stiffened into a cautious pose.

"I'm Christina."

"Well now, aren't you somethin'? I'm Maisie, Tom's sister."

Maisie wore a lot of makeup, greasy-looking tan stuff all over her face like a gaudy mask. Red lipstick on her thin lips streaked her two front teeth. Her thick feet crammed into too-tight high heels, with just her red-painted big toes sticking out of the holes in front.

Christina shook her hand and shivered. "Nice to meet you."

"Yeah, likewise I'm sure," Maisie said in a high-pitched, nasal voice. "So, ya got Tom to marry ya. Never expected that outta him."

Christina blushed. "We're not married."

Her eyebrows shot up. "Oh? Well, yeah…maybe you should keep it that way."

Christina took one step back and nervously smoothed her hair. "I'm not sure what you mean," she said.

"Well, ya know, my little brother, he ain't the marrying type."

Maisie put her pink clutch purse on the coffee table and turned back to Christina real slow. "I'm supposin' I oughta be nice to his girl then."

Her voice dipped down confidentially. "Come on with me. I gotta set y'all straight about my brother."

"I don't think I want to know," said Christina.

"Oh yes you do," nodded Maisie. "It's for your own good." She reveled filling her in, like some kind of gossip columnist.

Maisie grabbed Christina by the elbow, led her to the back porch, and shut the door. The wooden slats of the porch floor sagged under their weight. A blue blowfly whapped itself over and over against the window, fell to the floor, and spun around crazily. Maisie stomped on it.

"He's smart awright, but goes off in his own world—tinkerin', not talkin'. Sometimes acts cold as ice. Guess it's not all his fault."

"Tom's not cold with me," said Christina. Her head felt woozy, her chest tight.

Maisie pursed her lips and said, "Oh, y'all just wait. He can get that way an' his strangeness come outta nowhere. Sometimes he can spit in your eye for nothin'."

Maisie's seething drawl was so different from the way Tom talked. As her words poured out, her face suddenly changed from ugly and forbidding to sad-looking. Christina studied Maisie's eyes and her sagging posture.

"I'll tell y'all about this here family. Ma loved us best she could an' tried to keep our heads up, but her hands was tied in a knot with Paw. He was a loud, long-winded drunk, and that made Ma go from bein' crazy-angry to plumb dull-minded. That mean ol' coot beat the crap outta all of us and made Tom work like a slave stackin' bricks at the factory in town when he was only ten. He'd come home coughin' and covered head to toe in red brick dust. Poor kid. When he was stackin' bricks, me and Ma was workin' in the tobacco fields. Those fat green tobacco caterpillars were as big as my hand. Didn't matter how hard we worked—the little money we brought home was never enough." Maisie shook her head and looked at Christina with tired eyes.

"When Tom wasn't workin' or goin' to school, he'd stay away from home an' run aroun' the countryside like a wild weed. He'd find busted-up junk in other folks' trash and fix 'em up. Our neighbor, ol' Miss Jenny, feelin' sorry for us kids, gave us warm cookies an' a place to play. She made me a pretty rag doll an' Tom got her dead husband's violin with no strings or turny-things. She helped Tom fix it up, and then learnt him how to play. Paw wouldn't let 'im play in the house, so he just played it for Miss Jenny and the birds in the field. Miss Jenny was a good thing that happen to us. She talked proper-like, and helped us with schoolwork. I didn't care 'bout words and school like Tom did." She shook her head. "Nothin' matters now. Thank God Paw's six feet under."

Maisie went on to tell her that her Ma's own mother and wandering father didn't want her. She was raised by her dispassionate grandparents, who called her "the bastard girl."

A burning feeling on Christina's face and chest made her hot all over. She felt sick for Tom—sad for Maisie.

When Maisie was done with her stories, she inspected her long, red-painted fingernails and looked up into Christina's face. "Ya know—maybe you can be good for my brother. God knows he needs some happiness in this busted-up family."

They stayed at Mildred's house a few miserable days. Christina felt determined to help the man she loved, but a subtle silence grew in Tom after their furlough.

20
The Letter

It is impossible to talk or to write without apparently throwing oneself helplessly open.

— Herman Melville

*A*fter six months of wartime romance, Christina encouraged Tom to write a letter of introduction to her parents. Not only did he introduce himself, but in the same letter he also asked permission to marry her. He was thoroughly in love with the image of Christina. She distracted and enthralled him. He wanted her—he needed her.

George called his daughter long distance. "You no have permission from your Ma and me!" he shouted. "Greeks marry Greeks. Do you understand? *To ema nero then yinete* (Blood is thicker than water). Stay with your own kind! You no have our blessing."

She blinked and swallowed back tears. "But Pa, I love him!" said Christina.

"You love him! What do you know about love?" he asked. "Don't do it, I tell you! You be sorry someday, I know."

"How could you know, Pa?"

"Because I seen with my own eye. Look at your Thea Alexandra on my side. She married American boy and she's sour like vinegar. She is mean, angry woman."

"Pa, that won't be…"

"No more talk! I said NO!"

Christina knew not to pursue the conversation further.

Her parents' attitude made Tom even more determined.

⸻

Colonel Reynolds married them at a Methodist church on the Air Force base with only military friends in attendance. Beth and Mary dabbed their eyes with hankies through the short ceremony. Christina looked radiant in her simple satin wedding dress, borrowed from Captain Wood's wife. Tom stood proudly at her side.

She sent the news of her marriage by telegram to her parents a week later. Furious, her father called again.

"You married *xsenos* without permission from the parents? Who is this Tom?" her father shouted. "We say no to him and you just go ahead. Where's the respect? You no married in my eye, in your Ma's eye! You…you not our daughter."

A sharper splinter of rebellion drove into Christina's chest. Her eyes swelled with tears. *This marriage will work. I'll show them.* She bowed her head and wept.

⸻

After their first month of marriage, Christina began to notice changes in Tom. There was an increased starchiness in his voice, and he became strangely withdrawn. He'd play his violin or twist the dials of the hissing, crackling radio on the kitchen table. Some stations came in a sputter, others clearer. His vacant eyes and aloof ways felt like a betrayal to her, as if his passions had transferred to things instead of her.

One evening, he announced to Christina, "I'm gonna fix this radio, so don't bother me."

She looked at him quizzically and her pulse quickened.

"Alright," she said.

Tom turned from her and laid his small tools precisely in a row on the table like a surgeon.

He unscrewed the back plate of the radio, pulled off the knobs, and removed its wooden casing. Tom stared into its snarl of wires and circuits. He traced his fingers over and over from the power source to the glass vacuum tubes with their intricate innards: coils, diodes, and resistors. He closed his eyes, searching, drawing a map, and forming some electrical architecture in his head.

Christina stood behind him and hugged her arms to her chest. She watched with awkward fascination. He shifted, and glanced at her with furrowed brows. His eyes had a peculiar flash in them. The room seemed to fall into a slow spin. She walked away—out of his sight.

In bed, Christina could hear the fizz of static coming from the kitchen. She pushed her cheek against the pillow and clamped a hand over her other ear.

Well into the night, Tom slipped between the sheets and whispered into Christina's ear, "I fixed it." She remained silent.

Most evenings Christina went for walks or read in bed against propped-up pillows. She knew to leave him alone—otherwise he'd come unglued or sit in stony silence with knees crossed and stiff arms folded against his chest. Sometimes he'd smoke on the front stoop of their apartment and listlessly stare off into the distance. He'd get up and walk off without telling Christina where he was going. It felt like a treachery to be set aside as opposing forces of confusion cut deep into her heart, rivaling the love she had for him. She'd sit numb and pray. *Dear Theos, help me. Help my husband.*

Over dinner one evening Christina took her husband's hand and stroked the side of his head. She leaned forward and looked resolutely into his eyes. "Tom…why are you so quiet? You seem unhappy."

He bowed his head low and raked tense fingers through his hair. "It's nothing," he said harshly.

Christina flinched—his curtness stung. "I don't understand," she said. "Something's bothering you, and I don't think it has anything to do with me. What is it?"

He looked up with dull eyes and said, "Nothing! Just leave me be!"

Christina looked away with a hurt, confused look on her face. Tears welled in her eyes. Stiffness formed around Tom's mouth. He got up and walked slowly to the window.

Just then, they heard a prolonged ear-shattering noise. Dishes rattled in the cupboards. A glass skittered to the edge of the table and shattered on the floor. The windows lit up with a strange, pulsating orange glow. All sensations of reality in Christina's head vanished, and she stared dumbfounded at the window. The room spun and her eyes grew wide with terror. Tom reeled back and jerked his head around. He locked eyes with Christina, grabbed her hand, and burst out the front door. They ran towards the airfield with hundreds of others. Fire and acrid black smoke broiled up into the sky. Sirens wailed.

"Tom!" screamed Christina over the deafening roar of fire. "What happened?"

"It looks like a plane crashed!"

The intense heat stopped them abruptly at the grassy edge of the runway. Chunks of burning metal, upturned landing gear, and crumpled propellers were strewn hundreds of yards in all directions. Tom shoved Christina back and ran onto the tarmac.

"No, Tom!" Christina screamed. "Come back!" Mortified, she clutched at her chest and sank down on her knees.

He crouched low and ran to the remains of a wing. The wretched smell of burning fuel and flesh filled his nostrils and scorched his lungs. Tom lifted both hands helplessly to the carnage and cried out, knowing no one could possibly escape such an inferno. He felt a tug on his arm and wheeled around. John Driscoll, Tom's radar buddy, shouted over the firestorm, "There's nothing you can do!"

Tom backed away. "Oh, God!" he yelled. "Who was it? Does anyone know?"

John shouted over the firestorm, "I know Lieutenant Holbrook was practicing his first night landing in an A-24. I think he came down on top of a B-24 cruising down the runway!"

"What are you saying?" said Tom, disbelieving. He grabbed John by the shoulders and shouted, "How could that happen?"

"Holbrook came in on the wrong runway."

"Who was flying the B-24?"

"Colonel Reynolds and Captain Woods."

Christina heard and sank to her knees. "Oh no, Tom," she choked. "Not them. Oh, dear God…Mrs. Woods is due any day with their first baby."

Tom bent down and enveloped her in his arms. He was soaked in perspiration. "I…I didn't know." His shoulders shuddered as he drew her closer. They sat locked in a prolonged embrace on the grass. Christina pulled away slightly and saw tears streaking Tom's soot-blackened cheeks. She touched the side of his head and ran her hand gently along his face.

"Oh, Tom," she sobbed, burying her face in his chest. "How could this happen to such good men?"

"I don't know," he choked.

She looked up and studied his eyes. "Tom, I know you love me. Don't push me away."

Tom nodded, sighed deeply, and said, "I…I love you very much, Christina."

The loss of Colonel Reynolds, Captain Woods, the crew, and Jim Holbrook shattered Tom. He retreated further into his own world and refused to talk about the crash after that frightful night.

Christina couldn't eat for days. For weeks, Tom talked to her only out of necessity.

She felt utterly confused, anxious, like an intruder within their four walls. *God, please help me,* she prayed. *Help Tom. I don't know what to do.*

One evening he was tinkering with his German Luger pistol and waved it at Christina. She leaped to her feet and screamed, "What are you doing? Are you crazy? You better not have bullets in that thing!"

"You know I don't," he laughed. "I'm just playing around. Stop overreacting!"

"I'm not overreacting!" she said, clutching her throat. Her heart raced. "Are you trying to scare me?" She slumped down into a chair and bowed her head. Her chest began to heave, and tears fell onto her hands. "What's happening to us…to you?"

"I don't know what you're talking about," Tom said as he got up and walked out.

⸺

Christina felt sick and saw Tom with new eyes. Her misjudgment of him became glaring. Dread mixed with sorrow for Tom, for the life he must have had. With a sad mother like Mildred, and a mess for a father, who could blame him? *I should have known after I met his mother and sister. The warning signs were there. But I love him so much—and that will never change.*

Tom played clear and beautiful melodies on his violin. The music stirred Christina's heart but echoed loneliness in her ears. She watched Tom sitting with elbows on his knees, cradling the instrument lovingly in his hands. *He's so handsome,* she thought, *but there's a new edge to his face, like traces of the past etched into him.*

She now knew that before they married he had pretended to be something he wasn't. He romanced her, captured her heart, and now owned her like some prize. She felt superfluous, an outside observer as he nourished his wounds, his obsessions. *Maybe I can help him.*

Sometimes a morsel of attention would come Christina's way, but mostly he'd stare beyond her with a hangdog look, as if fixated on something he couldn't have. The more he made music, the more he turned inside himself.

"It seems that you love playing music and tinkering with your toys more than me," she complained, stiff-mouthed. He licked his lips and kept his head down. She could feel her world being squeezed in, growing smaller as if ropes were tightening around her.

He never tired of the warmth of her body or her delicious Greek cooking, but mostly he'd hunker down in his own world or leave the apartment without explanation.

One evening, they settled in their places: Christina standing over the stove, Tom oiling his sets of pliers and wire cutters on the gray-and-white Formica table wrapped in chrome. Christina gripped the metal edge of the countertop, turned to him, and broke the silence.

"Tom, you're gone a lot and you hardly talk to me anymore," she said. "Please tell me what's going on?"

"I've already told you! I'm busy in the radar lab, and I grab a few beers with the guys. My silence has nothing to do with you. It's just me. I…I think about things."

"I want to know what you're thinking." Christina walked over and hugged him around the shoulders. She bent down, buried her face in his chest, and whispered, "Let me in, Tom. I want to understand you." His slow embrace felt reassuring and she relaxed. "Tom, I'll always love you. I'm here for you."

"I…I love you too, but this is who I am," he said.

"Then stay with me," she said.

"You don't understand," he said, pulling his arms away. A shadow passed over his face, almost like shame. Tom stood up abruptly, pushed past her, and grabbed a beat-up leather suitcase from the hall closet.

Christina tore at the sides of her hair and ran to him. "What are you doing?" she screamed, grabbing at the suitcase.

He swung the suitcase into the wall with a loud thud and turned to face her. In a slow, dark voice he said, "Just stop pushing me! I can't be what you want!"

"Tom…please! Don't go!" pleaded Christina. He lowered his head and walked out.

Tom disappeared for hours. Christina curled up with a blanket on the couch and waited up for him, hoping his soft tread would come to the door. It did not. She listened to the radio, tried to read, and eventually fell into a fitful sleep.

In the middle of the night he sneaked back, stinking of whiskey and cigarettes.

She continued to question him, but it made him retreat even more. He spent their money and drank. Strangely enough, Christina remained willfully blind to the worst parts of Tom and struggled desperately to deaden her feelings.

Christina was accustomed to deferring to the males in her family, even the unsavory ones. Divorce never ran through her mind. She made internal excuses for Tom.

Pa's words, "You'll be sorry someday," echoed in Christina's head. *He's right*, she thought, *but I can't let them know. I will never let them know. I'll show them.*

Christina missed her family and couldn't endure the rejection, the distance any longer. It had been almost two years since she had last seen them.

An unexpected dawning flickered in her mind. What she had turned her back on were the very threads woven so deeply into the fabric of her being. She could disavow the suffocating strictness that had imprisoned her, but Christina could no longer pretend her family didn't matter. The threads that had bound her to family, to her culture, could not be undone.

She kept thinking about how her family could help Tom. If they could remarry in the Orthodox Church, they would accept him—show him what a family's about. He could learn to love them. *But how on earth can I convince Tom?*

One evening before bed, Christina came out of the bedroom wearing a slinky white satin nightgown. Tom was fiddling with the radio on the kitchen table, his feet wrapped around the chrome legs of the chair. He looked up and smiled with eyes ablaze.

"Wow, get over here, woman," Tom said, patting his lap.

Christina ran over to him and threw her arms around his neck. There were so many things she loved about him. The clean smell of his hair; how he looked deep into her eyes with his soulful gaze. Tom cradled her in his arms and buried his face in the warmth of her neck.

Christina leaned away slightly and smoothed her hair back provocatively. She took a deep breath. "Tom, I have something important to ask you. Before you give me an answer, hear me out. The war's over, and when we get out of the service in a few months, I want you to meet my family."

"Yeah, but they don't want to meet me—*remember?*" he said sarcastically.

"They will. Here's my idea. We don't have anywhere else to go, but we can move to Chicago. You've never been there and I know you would like it. But here's the thing: they'll never accept our marriage unless we remarry in the Orthodox Church."

"Are you crazy?" Tom said with astonishment. "We're already married!"

"If we go through with it, I'll bet Pa will let you help in the family business. They've even bought a couple buildings down the street from East Side Hamburgers. They're doing really well."

Christina saw a peculiar glitter in his eyes.

21
Meet the Family

You can't stay in your corner of the Forest waiting for others to come to you. You have to go to them sometimes.
— A.A. Milne, *Winnie-the-Pooh*

It felt hot as blazes the morning Tom met his in-laws. Steam rose from the blacktop when he and Christina stepped off the train. The train engine heaved and panted heavily after its long trip. Within minutes, the back of Tom's shirt became soaked as he unloaded their many suitcases onto a cart. He closed his eyes for a brief moment and silently rehearsed what he would say when he met her parents.

They won't like me anyway, he thought. *What does it matter?* He reached into his pants pocket and dragged a handkerchief across his forehead, his neck. *It's so damn hot. I can't breathe.*

"Oh, Tom, I'm so excited for you to finally meet them!" said Christina, smiling from ear to ear. She adjusted her pillbox hat, pushed a loose strand of hair behind her ear, and tugged the wrinkles out of her jacket. She knew her parents would be proud to see them in military uniform.

Christina searched his somber eyes and said, "Tom, please give them a chance."

"Hmmm." But any words he had prepared dissolved when they walked into the station to be greeted by no fewer than twenty family members, huddled together, dressed in their finest. Tom hadn't bargained for such a swarm of relatives. His head spun dizzily. The noise of them assaulted his ears as he heard a mixture of Greek and English. *They're old-country and backward, just like Christina said.* His heart gave a sudden lurch when he cast a glance at her, posing as the proud soldier with hands on her hips. Irritation and confusion grew in geometric progression upon watching her, hearing her irrepressible expressions of joy.

Sophia stood at the head of the crowd, beaming.

With a cry of joy, Christina wept openly as she ran into her mother's arms. "Oh, Ma! I've missed you so much!"

"You're home now," Sophia said in a slow, soothing voice. "My Christina." Her dress collar dampened with Christina's tears. She put her mouth within one inch of Christina's ear and said, "Pa promised to put the best foot forward with your new husband. Before, he didn't accept, but Tom's family now."

Christina embraced her again and said, "Thank you, Ma."

While Sophia and Christina embraced, George pumped Tom's hand and kissed him on both cheeks. Tom cast his eyes aside and bit the side of his mouth. He cleared his throat and said, "Uh, hello."

"*Ti kanies*, I mean, how-are-you?" bellowed a determined George as he pounded Tom on the back numerous times. George saw Tom flinch, but he forced himself to be polite in spite of his strong misgivings. "Good to meet you." George turned and swept a hand towards his family. "Look, everyone! Look: it's Christina and her husband, Tom!"

Tom set his jaw. Sweat beaded on his upper lip.

Christina forced her eyes away from Tom and looked down at Alexander's legs. She drew her breath in sharply. "Alexander!" she said. "You're not wearing your leg braces anymore!"

Alexander smiled proudly, his head cocked to one side, and said, "Yeah, I'm doing lots better with these crutches instead of those heavy braces."

"I'm so happy for you!" Christina said as she hugged him tight.

Johnny edged his way closer to Christina. He wore khaki pants and a light blue oxford shirt with a red bow tie. Thin plaid suspenders crossed in the back, paralleled in the front. The twelve-year-old looked up shyly at Christina and muttered a quiet "Hullo, Christina."

"Johnny, look at you!" said Christina brightly. "You're so grown up!" She kissed him on the cheek and ruffled his thick chestnut hair. "Ma wrote and said how well you're doing in school!" She leaned close to him and whispered with a smile, "I'm so proud of you, Johnny."

Sophia walked over to Tom with a surprisingly graceful gait, considering her broad body. She kissed him on each cheek and held him at arm's length to study his handsome face. "Welcome to the family, Tom," she said, nodding with sturdy conviction. "*Theos* brought you home to us."

Her ardent voice, her earnest eyes drove straight through him. A hesitation, a kind of weakness washed over him. "Yeah...ah, nice to meet you."

Tom stood—like a faraway figure. A strange feeling pressed in, and time slowed. His throat caught. He shook himself.

A gigantic woman with the hint of a moustache wrapped her arms around Tom and crushed him in a sweaty embrace against her bosom. Tom recoiled and took a step backwards. She leaned into him. Her eyes were bright.

"My name is Toula. *T-o-u-l-a.* I'm Sophia's cousin, and you can call me THEA Toula." She beamed proudly and clasped her hands tightly over her massive stomach.

She winked and said, "You's a good-lookin' boy!"

Tom glanced down at his watch, brought it up to his ear, and heard its soft ticking. He breathed out and stood silent. Toula eyed him with a strange expression. He looked up, caught her eye, and rubbed the back of his neck.

Christina threw herself into George's arms and whispered in his ear, "Oh, Pa, thank you for welcoming Tom. I've missed you and Ma so much."

George cleared his throat and tugged at his tie. "And I miss you," he said. "Look at you—a proud soldier." Christina stepped back and saw tears in the crackled corners of his eyes.

Demetri and Anna peeked over their Pa's shoulder. "Demetri!" Christina shouted. "You're home! I didn't know you'd be here so soon!"

Christina skirted Pa, wrapped her arms around Anna, and lifted her off the floor. "Oh, Anna, you're almost as tall as me! I can't believe it!" She set her down, cupped her younger sister's flushed face in her hands, and said, "My sweet Anna. I've missed you terribly."

"Me too, Christina." Anna's eyes shined bright.

Christina covered her sister's face in kisses.

Demetri grabbed Christina in a bear hug and gave her a smacking kiss on the cheek. "Welcome home, Sis."

"Look at you, Demetri!" said Christina. His boyish looks were gone—replaced by something somber. "You're a grown man! How did that happen?"

He cocked his head and shoved his hands into his pockets. "The Army and fighting will do that to you. I'm just glad I made it out of France alive." He shook his head. "A lot of my buddies didn't."

Christina put her hand on his shoulder and said, "I'm sorry, Demetri."

Alexander wobbled excitedly over on his crutches to shake Tom's hand but fell clumsily into his arms. Tom struggled to hold him up until Demetri pulled his brother straight.

"Forgive my brother," said Demetri. "He can't help it."

Alexander reached for Tom's hand and missed. Demetri placed his brother's hand in Tom's. Alexander's hand felt damp and weak. His neck bulged with exertion.

"I'm Alexander. I'm Christina's brother."

Spit gathered at the corners of Alexander's mouth. His white dress shirt had a dribbled brown stain on the breast pocket.

Tom's stomach turned. He swallowed hard. There was a slight starchiness in his voice when he said, "Yeah, hello."

Just when Tom thought he couldn't take another second of the heat, the family— finally, the last, the youngest cousin introduced himself.

Christina saw Tom's brow lowering and his mouth clamped shut. She moved close to him and slipped her hand into his. "Let's go, Tom," she whispered in his ear. "I know you're overwhelmed, but I'm proud of you for trying."

Tom agreed to join the Orthodox Church, after seeing the property his in-laws had acquired. Christina and her Ma organized a small wedding and reception at the Assumption Greek Orthodox Church in Hegewisch. Tom went along.

The wedding crowns, or *stephana*, which rested on top of a thin layer of rice in a silver tray, were the centerpiece of the ceremony. Connected by a white satin ribbon, they were symbolically exchanged three times over Christina and Tom's heads by Demetri, the *koumbaro*. This ritual crowned the couple king and queen of their home. Something warm crept into Tom's chest as light shined through the stained glass windows and spread soft color over the altar. Christina smiled radiantly into his eyes and seemed to open her arms to him without moving.

Father John, in his shimmering gold-and-white floor-length robe, placed their right hands together as an appeal to *Theos* to become one in spirit and flesh. They drank wine from an ornate golden goblet, which symbolized the sharing of all that life would bring: the joys, sorrows, love, and pain. The priest chanted and guided them around the altar in the "Dance of Isaiah" as they took their first steps as a couple. Anna proudly carried the train of Christina's gown. Sophia threw rose petals at the couple.

At the conclusion of the hour-long wedding ceremony, the priest took Tom and Christina's hands and proclaimed, "Be magnified and rejoice, O bridegroom and bride, for *Theos* is well pleased."

The church erupted in applause as Tom and Christina walked down the aisle. Christina glowed; Tom was flushed.

George leaned over to Sophia and whispered, "Now, they married."

After the ceremony, the guests raised their glasses of wine and danced well into the night.

Tom grew silent at the wedding table. He leaned over and whispered to Christina, "When will this be over?"

She gripped the sides of her chair.

After the wedding, Tom found her family intrusive and steeped in ridiculous tradition. He couldn't forget how they didn't fully accept him until he married Christina in their traditional way. They did their best to come around, but it didn't matter. His introverted, judgmental ways ultimately collided with their effusive, Mediterranean temperaments.

"Damn, your family is like a swarm of locusts," Tom complained. "I can't get away from them. I've never known people so preoccupied with their own heritage. They're loud and ignorant."

"If they're so ignorant, how come business is booming?" Christina spat out.

"Why are you defending them now after telling me how they squelched your freedom?" he asked. "You're the one who called them backward."

22

Sophie and Niko

The light shines in the darkness, and the darkness has not overcome it.

— John 1:5

*C*hristina and her family were overjoyed when she became pregnant. The first grandchild! Tom seemed to adopt an indifferent attitude, like a cold, pale detachment. Her increased beauty as her pregnancy progressed was the only thing that seemed to turn his head.

Christina hoped he would come around when he finally held his own baby. She tried to dismiss his ambivalence, but uncertainty menaced her.

Most of the family cemented their opinion of Tom Peters on the day of his daughter's birth. They gathered close and watched Tom as he studied Baby Sophie's perfect round face, the soft fringe of her dark eyelashes, while Christina held her close.

Tom removed his grease-stained cap and reached forward to touch the satin edging on the baby's blanket with his fingertips. So soft. His eyes moved to her tiny form. He felt momentary enchantment but took one step back and wrung the cap in his sweaty hands. Yiayia Sophia came up behind him and placed a solid hand on his shoulder. He turned to look at her. Everyone in the room disappeared as he met the sure, fervent glow in her eyes. The corners of her mouth turned up and she gave him a nod. He could feel his heart thudding and hear the ticks and hisses of a nearby radiator. Nothing was as he expected, and his soul split in two. He turned and took one deliberate step closer.

"Would you like to hold your daughter?" asked Christina, smiling up at her husband.

"Well...I..." His voice wasn't his own.

From the hospital bed she lifted the baby into his arms. The baby's eyes fluttered open. She gazed straight at him with dark, liquid eyes. Something gutted his heart, and time stopped. *Could her gaze be fixed on some star neither of them could see?* He ran a shaky finger across her cheek, and his eyes stung with tears. He drew the warmth of her small body closer and breathed in her sweet scent. "Hello," he whispered.

Christina reached to touch his hand. He looked down at her smiling face and turned to the family. A charged silence filled the room. Their curious eyes pierced him, and his breathing became ragged. He cleared his throat. With swift movement, he handed the baby back to Christina and walked out. After rounding the corner of the hallway, he put his forehead against the cool wall and stared down at his scuffed shoes. Tears dripped onto his hands.

Sophia locked eyes with her daughter and said, "It's okay. Give him a little time."

Theo Demetri became Baby Sophie's godfather. He footed the hospital bill to pay for her beginnings. Christina was humiliated by this gesture, but Tom retreated into his own world and didn't interfere. She knew he couldn't seem to jangle a meager amount of change in his pocket. Everyone wondered what he did with the money from repairing cars. Some of his profits seemed to vanish. He refused to work in the family restaurant business.

But the tenderness Christina had experienced with him before they married revealed itself in unexpected ways with the baby. Sometimes, in the middle of the night, when Christina woke with her breasts engorged, she'd find barefoot Tom cradling Baby Sophie on the porch steps, showing her the stars and humming soft tunes. He'd turn and smile at Christina with happiness that seemed to dissolve into something complete and beautiful. It surprised Christina to see him entirely at peace.

After the traditional forty days of confinement, Baby Sophie was old enough to be taken out. The family picked up Thea Toula on the way to church in Hegewisch for the baby's first public appearance. After liturgy, a throng of ladies swooped around Christina in a happy gaggle at the back of the church hall and crooned over the baby. While Yiayia Sophia was arranging Toula's mountain of *kourabiethes* cookies on a table next to a plate of feta cheese and basil deviled eggs, she looked up and saw dull-eyed busybody Cleo Kantaxis stand back and sniff her nose at Christina and the baby. Cleo shuffled her fat body over to Alexis Makris and leaned into her, swaying and smirking with her big know-it-all smile. Her nasal voice buzzed loud enough for others to hear.

"*Poe, poe*, ain't it a shame. Poor little *pethaki*, born into this world with a good-for-nothing for a father. What do you expect from *xsenos*? What was Christina thinking marrying outside her people? For God's sake, she's George's mother's namesake. Guess she had to prove something, and now look at her. The pot rolled around, but it didn't find its lid."

Sophia marched over to the women, folded her arms resolutely over her chest, and gave them a fry-your-butt look. Cleo's mouth got twitchy, and Alexis backed up.

Toula sidled up to Sophia and yanked up her saggy nylon stocking in one angry motion. "You're a fine one to talk, Cleo Kantaxis," she spat. "Marryin' that stinky, no-count Gus. Everyone knows he's fallin' off the stool at Banners' just about every night."

Cleo flinched and said, "Well! I never..."

But Toula wasn't finished. "You got so much foundation on, I bet you need a damn bulldozer to scrape it all off before your face hits the pillow at night. AND, I happen to know that farty-smelling hair spray on your head is the cheap stuff."

Cleo lifted her hand to her voluminous bouffant hairdo, got in Toula's face, and said, "Bitch!"

"Enough!" interrupted Sophia with a cool, dipped-down voice. "Time for you to leave, Cleo."

Cleo huffed loudly, grabbed her purse, and marched out the side door.

As Sophie grew into a playful little girl, her entire being was clothed from head to toe in delight. She'd tap with a blur of feet in her shiny Mary Jane shoes, and her lilting, happy laugh, bright eyes, and sensitive nature made everyone love her all the more.

At a tender age, Sophie noticed that her Pa would disappear when family and friends got together. Sometimes, when he happened to be around them, she'd see him smile a little, but never laugh. He'd stare at his hands or pictures on the walls if they were inside, at the trees and the sky when they were outside. At home, the three of them would dance in the kitchen to bebop on the radio, and he would swing her around in his arms until she got the giggles. "You're my little glass of lemonade!" he would say.

Sometimes, she'd hear grownups' voices whispering how they didn't think very well of him. It confused Sophie and burned in her ears. She heard that he didn't pay for her when she was born. Sophie didn't know whom he didn't pay or that she even cost anything. She'd always heard Yiayia say, "The best things in life are free." Somehow this story seemed to be the lightning rod in the family's estimation of her father.

Sophie would also hear the story about her name. Her parents were all set to name her Mildred, after her Pa's mother. Grandma Mildred had said over long-distance telephone, "I hate my damn name. Don't do it to that kid."

Sophie was glad that Grandma Mildred rescued her from being her namesake; she was honored to be Yiayia's namesake and proud, as the name Sophia means *wisdom* in Greek. It had dignity and the sound of a warrior, like Athena: both three syllables.

Papou wouldn't let the name thing go as the years went by.

One evening, behind the closed doors of her grandparents' bedroom, Sophie overheard Papou say the name thing again. "Oh, Ma, remember? What kinda fool name was Mildrip? We can no turn into Greek language."

"*Stamata,* Pa!" said Yiayia. "For god sake, when are you going stop this? The child is almost five years old and you're still bringing it up. It's done, and you don't want Sophie to hear this nonsense. Besides, we say *doxa ton Theo.* Sophie is no Mildred. She has the eyes of Byzantium."

Sophie ran into the bathroom, climbed up on the toilet seat, and leaned over the sink to study her eyes in the medicine-cabinet mirror. *What are Busy Town eyes? They're just brown.*

Trouble seemed to swirl around her Pa from different directions, but she loved when he played happy tunes on his violin for her, and when he showed her the evening star, the constellations, and the moon when no one was looking.

The second grandchild was born after Sophie's third birthday. Niko, short for Nicholas, was named after Tom's father. His middle name, George, came from Papou.

Tom's father had died in his late forties, from "the drink and the clap," as Tom's sister, Maisie, had informed Christina. It was providential his name was Greek.

"*Na zisi!* (May he live)," said the many theas, theos, and cousins who visited Baby Niko on the third day after his birth. Sophie was given the honor of placing the first gold in his bassinet. Christina handed her daughter a small gold cross. Sophie smiled proudly, patted Niko's soft head, and placed the cross by his tiny clutched hand.

"*Yasou,* Sophie! *Bravo!*" said the relatives in unison. They, in turn, placed gold coins around his swaddled form.

Christina pinned a small blue satin pouch with beaded edges to the back of baby Niko's T-shirt to protect him from all things unsavory. The triangular *filakto,* blessed by the priest, contained holy flowers and was embroidered on one side with a delicate cross.

When no one was looking, Tom showed Niko the evening star, the constellations, and the moon.

As he grew in strength and stature, everyone adored good-natured Niko. He turned heads with his ready, dimpled smile and expressive hazel eyes, which were framed with long, dark lashes and fine, sculpted brows.

Christina was a proud, natural mama. She loved her babies and nursed them until they walked, even when feeding with formula and sterilizing bottles was the trend. But as they grew, Christina forgot to protect the sanctity of her children's spirits when it came to her husband and their strained relationship.

She watched how Tom doggedly worked to create emotional distance between the Greek family and the children. He was unaccustomed and blind to the goodness that sifted through his fingertips and the integrity of the rich soil in which his children were planted and rooted. Tom the Intellect, beyond all their foolishness. Christina knew he didn't understand them, as if he were crosshatched with confusion, maybe as she was in her younger years.

For Sophie and Niko, it was a burden being the bearers of secrets about their father and mother—a confusion being caught in the middle of two worlds. The fighting throbbed in Sophie's head, and it stung watching what it did to her little brother.

Tom tried to muzzle Christina's protests, but it didn't work. Christina may have feared him with his cool, surly ways, but she became increasingly mouthy. Somehow, they loved and needed the arguing.

"Your crazy family doesn't know when to quit and leave us alone," Tom complained to Christina. "The kids spend way too much time with them."

"Don't you get it?" asked Christina. "The kids worship their grandparents. My family!"

"They don't know any different," Tom said resolutely. "I swear their brains are getting soft."

"Would you rather them be around your sad mother and sister?"

He got in her face and said, "Don't ever bring them up!"

"Just play on our block," Tom would say to the kids. "You don't need to run over to your grandparents all the time."

They heard the same message over and over from him, but it never worked. Sophie and Niko sneaked over to the family restaurant or their grandparents' apartment. They spent most of their time with Yiayia and Papou.

Even if the air seemed to go black between his parents, Niko worshipped his father. Rather than draw nearer to his son, Tom started to use Niko's adoration as opportunity.

PART FOUR

23

It's Ours Now!

The world is indeed full of peril, and in it there are many dark
places; but still there is much that is fair, and though in all lands
love is now mingled with grief, it grows perhaps the greater.
~ J.R.R. Tolkien, *The Fellowship of the Ring*

1956

$\mathcal{I}$t was the second week in September and the weather already had a crisp, fall feel. The mosquitoes stopped their hunt for blood, and the flowers drooped their heads. Sophie started seventh grade, and Niko was a fourth-grader at Gallistel Elementary.

"Now we're gonna do some real work, like detectives, Niko," said Tom, a Camel cigarette hanging from the corner of his mouth. Tendrils of acrid smoke rose above his head. Niko wrinkled his nose at the smell.

"See this here device? It's a hook-switch bypass that we're gonna put in some bad guys' telephones so the cops can listen to what they are sayin' and doin'. This switch bypasses the hang-up button."

A black telephone sat on the worktable. Tom unscrewed the round listening-and-talking part of the receiver and showed Niko the jumble of wires inside.

"The phone's microphone can be turned on remotely as if it were off the hook," he explained. "Someone from miles away can listen to what people are saying."

"Ooo, Pa. It's like magic!"

"Niko, Sergeant Bernaski and the police chief are very important people, and they trust me to stop bad guys from doin' bad things."

Tom held up a tiny square piece of metal between his thumb and forefinger.

"This here's an electronic bug or transmitter," said Tom. "It can be hidden in a room, and nobody knows it's there because it's so small. Same as the phone; people from far away can listen to what's being said."

"Wow, like spies, Pa," said Niko. "What do I gotta do?"

"You're gonna help me carry stuff, and we're makin' sure people are gone from their place. First we got to have patience and the eyes of a falcon, then we do fast work. We're gonna get paid real good for this, Niko."

Tom popped the cap off a bottle of Pabst Blue Ribbon beer, took a swig, and wiped his mouth with the back of his oil-greased sleeve.

"Pa, we're gettin' lots of money from the cops. Fixin' cars, buggin', and helpin' them."

"Yep," he said. "Like I said, we're helping the good guys. Now watch what I'm doing."

After tinkering on the phone for fifteen minutes as Niko looked on, Tom said, "Okay, get to work on the Lincoln's trunk. I want that spare tire unscrewed from its fittings. It's dirty and needs washin'."

The black Lincoln Capri was a beauty, with sleek running boards and a black leather interior. "It has a dual-range Hydra-Matic transmission," Tom told Niko. "It changes gears like butter, and the big V-8 engine purrs like a tiger."

"Whose car is it, Pa?" asked Niko.

"A guy named Blue, friend of Vitto's," Tom said in an offhanded way. But then his eyes went dim, and he swallowed hard. *Why did I tell him that?*

"But Pa! Yiayia says that Vitto is a bad guy and to stay away from him."

"She doesn't know everything. They pay me good. I fix their cars. Doesn't matter who they are."

Niko knotted his hands together. "But Pa!"

Tom's brewing silence filled the room, and his eyes narrowed to slits. "Get to work."

Niko crawled into the cavernous trunk. He tried to loosen the big wing nut from the center metal rim of the tire with his fingers. It wouldn't budge. He tapped on one side of the wing with a small ball-pein hammer to loosen it. When it was free of the long bolt, he tucked the nut deep into the side pocket of his denim overalls so he wouldn't lose it. He started to jimmy and rock the tire loose. The heavy weight of it tipped over onto his lap. Niko wrestled the tire to the edge of the trunk and rolled it up and out. The tire should have bounced, but it landed with a thud.

"That's a flat," Tom said over his shoulder. "Get the tire iron."

"Okay, Pa."

Tom pried and labored. "Peeling a tire off its rim is tough work," he grunted. Finally, the tire started to pull away.

"Look, Pa!" exclaimed Niko. "Look! Something's inside!"

"Damn, you're right!"

Tom finally freed the tire, and a couple of bundles of money spilled out.

"What the hell!" Tom gasped.

Tom reached inside the tire and scooped out eight strapped bundles of one-hundred-dollar bills. He sat back on his haunches and whistled under his breath. "Whew—I'll be damned! Look at all this dough!" he said, thumbing through one of the bundles. "Niko, look at the straps around the bundles. Each one is labeled 'ten thousand dollars'!"

Niko grinned to see his Pa so happy. "Wow, Pa!"

"Quick! Lock the doors and grab that burlap sack over by the wall!"

Niko did as he was told, and Tom shoved the money into the bag. He poured the bundles onto the workbench. "Eighty thousand! Think of it, Niko!" Tom exclaimed, running his hand though his hair. "Mmm…why not," he said to himself. "I think I'll take some out. They'll never notice."

Niko took a couple of steps back. "But Pa! It belongs to someone else! Won't we get in trouble?"

"Naw. We'll only take a little bit for all our trouble fixin' cars!" Tom grinned. "I'll tell ya what. We won't be greedy. These guys have so much money—we'll just take a few hundred out and put the rest back in the tire. They'll never miss it!" He pulled one bill out of three different bundles and tucked them into his back pocket.

Tom washed and oiled the tire and placed the money back inside. He muscled the tire around its rim with a crowbar and pumped it up with the noisy air compressor.

A knock on the locked side door startled both of them.

"Yeah, who is it?" Tom said with an edge in his voice.

"It's Sophie. Ma wants Niko to do his homework."

"He'll be there in ten minutes," Tom shouted.

Tom took Niko by the shoulders and bent down eye-level. "Don't say a word about this, ya hear?"

His breath, stinking of cigarettes and beer, made Niko's stomach turn. "I …I won't tell," said Niko, pulling back. "I promise."

"Yeah, well, I happen to know that you showed your Slim Jim to that Jake kid. Pull anything like that again and you'll be answerin' to me, not just Taki."

Niko looked at his father with confusion and shuddered as coldness cut through him like a knife. "I won't, Pa."

"This is our chance to tuck some money away. I'm thinking we'll move out west someday for some peace and quiet. This will be our little nest egg, so don't ya ruin it!" A bead of sweat trickled down Tom's cheek, the veins stood out on his neck. Niko turned away from his father's face and then his eyes got wide. He wheeled back around on his heels.

"Pa! We can't move! Our family's here, and that's too far away!"

Tom flung his hand an inch from Niko's nose and pinned him to the wall with his stern gaze. "Go! Your Ma wants ya. I'm gonna seal this money up and hide it good for now." He turned to the workbench, reached for his soldering iron, and pulled out some metal scraps from a small wooden box on the floor.

Niko moved slowly, placed his hammer on a shelf, and shuffled backwards, looking at the floor. He unlocked the door and squeezed through quickly. He heard the bolt lock behind him.

Niko sat on the back porch steps and put his forehead into his cupped palms. Fearful thoughts exploded in his head. Christina opened the screen door.

"Niko, what's wrong?" she asked.

He raised his head. "Nothing, Ma, I…just, I'm kinda tired."

She took his hand and walked him into the house. Under the kitchen light, she said, "Niko, you look like you've seen a ghost! You're so pale. Are you feeling okay?" She felt his forehead and examined the dark circles under his eyes. "Hmm, no temperature."

"Yeah, Ma, I…I just, I'm thirsty and tired."

She lowered her voice and looked him in the eye. "What are you doing in the garage with Pa?"

"Just, just learning about cars and stuff."

"Is that all, Niko?"

He took in a slow breath and said, "Yeah, Ma. That's all."

Christina hugged him close and stroked his head. He buried his face and listened to the gentle sound of her breathing, the faint rub of his ear against the fabric of her dress. He stood—isolated in thoughts—not able to tell her the stinging secrets that followed him everywhere. She turned to the sink and poured him a glass of water.

She placed it in his hand and put her cool hand on the back of his neck. "Now, you drink all of this down. See how you feel in a little bit."

"Okay, Ma."

Niko walked upstairs to his bedroom and threw himself facedown on his Lone Ranger bedspread.

24

I Done Good

Nani (Sleep)

Nani, my child, nani, nani
And wherever it hurts will heal
Nani, my baby, whom I enjoy
As the olive of its leaf.
As the little birds of the water
And the mountain of the sun.
Nani, my child, nani, nani

— Greek lullaby from the Island of Kalymnos

"What's wrong with you, Niko?" asked Sophie as they walked to school bundled from head to toe against the frigid weather.

Niko shivered. "I don't know whatcha mean," Niko said quickly. He curled his fingers into fists inside his woolen mittens.

"You're quiet and tired-acting all the time," she said. "You don't eat very much."

Sophie grasped Niko's arm and turned him to face her. "Look at me," she said sternly. Reluctant, he brought his gaze up to hers. "I've asked you over and over, and you always say *nothin's wrong*. Well, I don't buy it. I know Pa's making you do his dirty cleanup work in the garage. He's treating you bad."

"He is NOT, and I like to help him," he said.

Sophie bristled. "Is that Jake makin' ya do stuff you shouldn't?"

"Naw."

"I know. It's that slimy Taki, isn't it?" she asked.

"Naw. If he comes to see Pa, I leave. I hate 'im."

"He and Pa are doing bad business with that hoodlum Vitto, and Taki did a very bad thing scaring and hurting you just because you busted his stupid watch."

Tears stung Niko's eyes. "I told ya, Sophie! I stay away from him!"

"Something's going on, Niko," said Sophie. "Nobody knows ya better than me. Just so ya know, I asked Ma and Pa about you."

"What! Why? What did Pa say?"

"Nothing," she said. "Pa makes ya work hard. Is that it?"

"Yeah, sometimes. I get tired and all."

Sophie rested her hand on Niko's shoulder. "Niko, you gotta know by now, Pa cares mostly about himself. Be careful what he asks of you. Okay?"

Niko took in a sharp breath. A flash of momentary animation kindled in his eyes, but he thought better of it and quickly looked down. "Yeah, I know. I will."

Niko's heart was bursting to tell Sophie everything, but he felt trapped. He couldn't forget Pa's threat. If Niko told, maybe Pa would make Sophie do something she shouldn't, or hurt her. He found Noops walking by the Piggly Wiggly on his way home after school. He gestured wildly to his friend and told him everything.

⸻

The next Sunday, Tom drove to Calumet City after dinner to buy a car part from a fellow garage mechanic. Sophie put on a heavy wool cardigan sweater and sneaked into the garage, while Niko and Ma sat in the living room watching *The Ed Sullivan Show* on television. The two of them were laughing at comedian Carol Burnett. She knew they wouldn't budge until the show ended.

Sophie turned on the overhead lights and started rummaging through drawers and searching under workbenches for clues—any hint that Niko might be doing something he shouldn't. She scooted a wooden stepladder to reach into the cupboards above the workbench. One of the cupboard doors had a small round lock under a sturdy-looking latch. She flipped the lever of the latch, but the door was firmly locked. Sophie climbed down the ladder and went through every drawer again looking for a key. Nothing. Discouraged, she sat on the lowest rung of the stepladder to think.

She got up, opened each drawer, and felt along the inner rough-hewn wooden sides. Her hand brushed up against a small key hanging on a nail in the back of a middle drawer. She grasped the key and climbed up the stepladder. The lock clicked open with a dull, tinny sound. Sophie opened the cupboard slowly but stopped when she heard a car drive by. She jumped down and looked through a tiny knothole onto the street. Nothing. Sophie went back to work and found rumpled child-sized pants, a torn shirt, a jacket, and gloves—all black with grease stains and smelling of motor oil. A stack of three little books sat in a back corner. She touched the top book with her fingertips, but it felt soft. Sophie pulled it out and saw that it was a fine black leather wallet. "What's this?" she whispered. She opened it and found an Illinois driver's license with the name John Pulasky.

She took out the other two wallets and realized they also belonged to other people. The last one was empty. A wave of weakness ran through Sophie's body. She held onto the edge of the cupboard door and leaned her forehead against it.

Just then, she heard a key click in the garage door lock. She froze. The door creaked open. Sophie saw the shadow of her Pa at the edge of her vision. Her mouth dropped. She turned and met his eyes. The sight of his catlike stare under the bill of his cap paralyzed her.

He dropped a bag on the floor and rushed over to Sophie. "What do you think you're doing?" he boomed.

She leaped off the ladder and backed away.

"Sophie, you have no business in here!" He turned around, scooped the wallets and clothes back into the cupboard, locked it, and pocketed the key.

An angry spark wired into her brain. Suddenly, she felt wild inside. "What *is* that stuff?" She lifted her chin and girded herself. "Those wallets belong to other people. You're stealing! I bet you're making Niko steal too!" Sophie saw a faint twitch of his mouth.

"That's ridiculous. Those wallets are from my Army buddies," he said, pushing his cap to the back of his head. "I'm keeping them safe." He stepped forward and swept a stiff hand out from his side. "You know nothing!"

"Well, I know those clothes could fit Niko." Her voice edged with sass. "How come they're all black?"

He waved her words away with his hand as if fanning an annoying gnat and then glared at her with steely eyes. "Okay, nosey. Since you need to know, I'm teaching Niko how to repair cars from under the hood and chassis. Your Ma would be damned upset if she knew I put him under jacked-up cars."

"I don't believe you!" She began to feel sweat gathering at the edges of her hair.

"Grease doesn't show up on black. Sophie, your brother is a smart kid. He picks up anything I show him, faster than anyone twice his age."

"But Niko seems nervous a lot of the time. Something's bothering him," she said. "What is it?"

"Could be your crazy Greek family provokes him into being a worried kinda kid," he said. "Everything's high emotion in that family."

"Well, we like the emotion in *that* family," she said with an impudent nod. "Why can't you see how good they are and how much fun we have with them?"

"I don't see them with the same eyes you do, Sophie."

She folded her arms across her chest and sensed the futility of trying to change his mind. "You don't care about any of us."

He was silent for a moment. "I do care about you, Sophie." She looked up and saw his eyes give in to a little bit of grace. "I always have."

"You just act like I'm annoying you all the time!"

Pa reached his hand out and took a couple of steps towards her. "Sophie, I don't mean to." He shook his head. "I just…"

She backed up and said in a low voice, "I don't trust you, Pa."

He cleared his throat and said, "Young lady, this conversation is over. Remember, the garage is off limits unless I invite you in. There are valuable tools in here."

Sophie saw the familiar arrogance in his face and posture. She turned her back on him and stomped out of the garage.

After Niko got into bed that night, she peeked into his darkened room and found him sitting up in bed. She whispered, "Niko, can I talk to you a minute?"

"Yeah, okay," he said.

Niko scooted over and Sophie sat down on the edge of the bed. He pulled a blanket over and piled it on his lap. She rested her hand on the other side of him, leaned forward, and said, "Niko, when Pa drove off to get that car part and you were watching Ed Sullivan, I went into the garage and found some black clothes belonging to you. Even some black gloves. What's going on?"

Niko's eyes flickered at her, and he fiddled with a button on his pajamas. "Nothin'. Whatta ya mean?"

"Why and when do you wear black clothes?"

"I...um, I don' know. Well, I mean, sometimes I wear them when I work on cars, so's, you know...my other clothes won't get messed up."

Sophie's brows knitted together. "Is that true, Niko?"

"Yeah, Sophie." He perched himself up on his knees and looked into her face. "See, cross my heart." He traced two fingers across his chest in an *X*.

Sophie looked at her curly-haired brother with tenderness. She scooped him up in her arms and hugged him. His scent—familiar and sweet. A soft quiet in the darkness blurred the lines between them, and she drew him in closer.

"Promise you'll tell your big sister if anything bothers you."

Niko shifted. "Okay," he whispered. "I love you, Sophie."

She kissed his forehead tenderly and said, "I love you too, Niko."

"We're gonna be just fine, kid," Tom said to Niko while they worked together in the garage on a Saturday evening. Tom looked at his son, who was bending over a set of spark plugs. *Maybe I've pushed him too far.* He wadded a greasy rag like a baseball in his hand. *Damn, he's a smart kid…a nice kid.* Niko felt Tom's eyes on him and looked up. He ran a finger over the length of a spark plug and gave Tom a cockeyed grin, seeing the calm look on his face. Tom looked away.

Sophie's accusations stung, but Tom knew he was finally getting ahead of the game. *After these next jobs, I'll cut him some slack.*

"We'll just finish buggin' two more places, kick back, and start living like kings. No more of this running around at night."

"Whatta ya mean, Pa?" asked Niko.

"We'll be done with the jobs I agreed about, then we can stop," he said. "I got a feeling to quit this business while the quittin's good. Besides, it's getting damn cold at night. I've had it with the wind and snow. It's better out west. I'm thinking we can get away and move clear across the country to Oregon some day." Tom casually flicked his hand at one of those slow-moving, ready-to-die fat winter flies buzzing around his head.

"Pa! Why?" exclaimed Niko. "We can't move! We got everyone here!"

"Yeah, that's what your Ma says."

Tom pulled out his whiskey drawer and showed Niko a calendar picture of a pristine mountain in Oregon.

"Look at this," said Tom. "Open, clean air, no one buggin' us all the time. I'm sick and tired of Greeks!"

"But Pa, they're our family! They love us! I…I love them."

"Is that what ya call it? Love? I'll tell ya what, they're ignorant, loud busybodies."

"But Pa," said Niko, stinging tears wetting his lashes.

Tom lifted his hand, hesitated, and then stroked Niko's soft cheek with his forefinger. "You're so young. You don't understand nothin'."

Just then, one side of the double garage doors crashed open. The huge frame of Vitto pushed a desperate-looking Taki ahead of him. He kicked him to the floor with his steel-toed boot and slammed the door shut. Taki gave a bone-shaking cough and grabbed at his thigh. Tom heard Niko whimper, and his mouth went dry.

"Lock them doors!" Vitto roared. His luminous, evil eyes cast about. "Now!"

Tom rushed over to latch the big doors shut and flip the bolt on the side door.

"You got somethin' that don't belong to you!"

Tom felt ringing in his head, and he choked, "I...I don't know what you're talkin' about."

"Don't play like you don't know. Hand over da money you stole!"

"What money?" asked Tom, standing to his full height. "I don't know what ya mean."

Vitto reached into his overcoat pocket and slowly pulled out knobbed brass knuckles. He wriggled his stubby fingers into them, never dropping his fiery gaze from Tom. Niko shrank into the shadows and hid behind the workbench.

Vitto grabbed Taki up by his shirtfront, reeled back, and slammed his face with the glinting knuckles.

Taki crashed to the floor clutching his bloody, torn cheek. He let out an ungodly scream and cried, "*Theos*!"

Tom clenched his fists and sidestepped in front of the workbench.

Vitto growled, "Do you's or that boy want the same?"

"Be reasonable," implored Tom. "What money are ya talkin' about?"

"Ya know damn well!" Vitto sneered. "Beside takin' money that don't belong to you, the boys and I know you been helpin' the cops."

Tom gave Vitto a puzzled look and raked stiff, shaky fingers through his hair. "I don't know what you're talkin' about."

Vitto laughed. "You know damn well what I'm talkin' about. Pullin' in the dough from both sides. Ya think you's so smart."

A flash of plain fear came into Tom's heart.

Just then, the side door handle jiggled. "Tom! Tom, open up!" shouted Christina. "Is Niko in there? What's happening?" She pummeled the door with her fists. "Open up! I've called the police!"

Vitto reached inside his suit coat and pulled out a silver snub-nosed revolver. Without a moment's hesitation, he turned and shot the prostrate Taki in the head.

Christina screamed and slammed into the door full force with her body. The door didn't budge. She heard Niko cry out.

"Ma!" Sophie screamed from the back door of the house. "What's happening?"

"Go back inside NOW!" yelled Christina. "Hide!"

Niko gasped and clamped his hands over his eyes as a great, dark pool of blood spread on the gray cement floor under Taki.

"Your kid's next!" Vitto snarled as he pointed the gun at Niko. His crimson, sweaty face became distorted with evil rage.

At that moment, the double garage doors burst open; Tom swung around and leaped in front of Niko as the gun fired. Heart, bones, brain all imploded, like being hit with a sledgehammer, when the bullet entered under Tom's right shoulder blade.

Four cops stormed in. They tackled the gun away from Vitto, slammed his face against the cement floor, and locked his wrists tight into handcuffs behind his back.

Tom writhed in searing pain as a dark stain spread across his shirt. His left arm jerked protectively around Niko. He slumped and felt Niko's body go limp beneath him. Choking dread entered his heart. He lifted himself with his good arm and pulled away enough to see pain distort Niko's face. Blood was spreading on his chest. *Maybe it's mine.* With a frantic movement, he yanked up Niko's T-shirt. Blood oozed from a hole in his small chest. "NO!" He pressed his hand on his son's chest, but the blood kept coming.

Niko's frantic eyes grew wide and shadowed with stark fear. "Pa!" he gasped. "Help me."

It felt like the ground had buckled beneath Tom and he was falling into a ragged pit. "Oh, Niko! Look what I did to you," groaned Tom.

Just then, Christina shoved her way through the carnage and knelt on the floor beside her husband and son.

"Oh, *The-eh-mou!* No, not my Niko!" screamed Christina, cradling his legs onto her lap. She placed her outstretched hand on his bloodied chest.

"Here I am, Niko! It's Ma! You'll be alright now." Christina pressed her hand on the wound, but blood kept oozing between her fingers. She wailed, "Oh no! *Theos*, make it not be!" She turned to the cops and screamed, "Someone help him!"

Niko's breathing became uneven, raspy. He whispered, "I did good, Pa. Didn't I?"

"Oh, Niko, you always did good," Tom choked. "I'm so sorry. I love you, son."

With that, Niko turned his eyes to Christina and gave her just a flicker of a smile. "Mama."

"*Agape mou*, Niko," cried Christina.

His eyes fixed on something she couldn't see, and then his face softened. An otherworldly peace rested on his face.

"No, Niko!" she screamed. "Wake up!" She lifted him onto her lap and cradled his head to her breast, caressing the name as she spoke it again: "My Niko."

Tom could hardly tell if wailing was coming from inside or outside of himself. It was Christina.

Sophie came in and froze in her tracks, not comprehending the sight before her. A look of horror etched her face. She shut her eyes tight, sank to her knees, and screamed like a wounded animal. Sophie clutched her stomach, ran outside into the bitter cold of night. She became sick, and everything turned black.

25
Αποχαιρετισμοζ - Farewell

Farewell, thou child of my right hand, and joy;
My sin was too much hope of thee, lov'd boy...

— Ben Jonson, "On My First Son"

The shrill wail of sirens caught Yiayia Sophia's attention as the last customer left the hamburger store. She locked up, finished mopping the floor and scrubbing the grill. Sophia buttoned up her long wool coat and began walking to Christina's house. George was in Calumet City helping relatives set up a new business, and Christina was expecting her for dinner.

From less than two blocks away, she saw the eerie red flashing lights of police cars and neighbors congregating. She pulled the collar of her coat snug around her face.

A burly young man brushed by her and yelled, "I heard someone's been shot!" Her heart thumped and she quickened her pace. She adjusted her glasses, squinted, and saw a crowd—a bombardment of confusion on Christina's block. There were shouts, more police cars; blinding red lights whirled and flashed. "*Theos*...I beg you...make it not be their house," she prayed frantically, and squeezed her arms to her chest.

With each step, a sickening dread crept into her senses. She saw a couple of emergency vehicles pull away from Christina's house. Panic dashed into her chest. "*Oxi, oxi!*" she screamed.

She shoved her way to the garage. The sight of spilled blood was terrifying, overwhelming. "What is this?" she shouted. "What's happened?" Suddenly, the faces, the garage spun dizzily before her. She dropped her purse, staggered inside the garage, and leaned against the door frame to catch herself from falling. She saw her daughter on the floor, covered in blood, cradling and rocking Niko's crumpled body. Her tortured face was buried in his thick, tousled curls. Sophia closed her eyes and clutched her chest, sinking to her knees. A policeman caught her by the elbow.

"Ma'am, let me help you," he said. Soon a circle of other policemen drew closer.

"Leave me," she cried, gasping for air. "Leave me!" She gripped her throat, slowly crossed herself, and prayed, "*Theos*…give me strength."

She crawled, heavy and slow, over to Christina and Niko. Her glasses clattered to the floor. She reached a tentative, trembling hand to touch Niko's slender leg. His skin felt cold. She took in a sharp gasp of air, bowed her forehead to the wretched, cold floor, slick with blood, and whispered inaudibly, "Oh no…my Niko."

"Ma! Ma, help me!" Christina pleaded hysterically in a spasm of terror. "I…I can't wake him."

Sophia slowly lifted herself and enveloped her daughter in her arms.

"He's gone, *pethie mou*." Her voice was not her own.

A shudder coursed through Christina's body. She uttered a low groan, a strange shallowness in the sound. "No, oh please, not Niko!"

Sophia pulled back and locked eyes with her daughter. "Christina…he's gone."

Christina lowered her eyes and said, "Oh, Ma. I can't. I can't live without him."

Sophia shook her head and said, "Christina, where's Sophie? Where's Tom?"

"Sophie saw Niko and ran out."

"And Tom?" Sophia saw her daughter's eyes darken and her chest heave.

"Don't say his name to me ever again."

Their tears mingled and fell onto the cold, lifeless body of their beloved Niko. With silent respect, the police averted their eyes and closed the doors to onlookers.

Thus they sat, suspended in an otherworldly state between utter disbelief and incomprehensible sorrow. Their agony somehow intertwined with that of all grief-stricken mothers echoing back to their ancestors—to antiquity.

"*Ella,* Christina," choked Sophia. A profound weariness consumed her body. She forced herself to move.

Christina clutched Niko's body to her chest. "Don't let them take him, Ma! They tried to already!" she exclaimed with frantic, wild eyes. "Don't let them!"

"I won't," she said softly. Sophia motioned to Sergeant Bernaski, who was a regular customer at the store. "John, please. Please leave us be," she said tearfully. "We need to take care of Niko our way."

"Yes, ma'am," he said, tipping his cap. He wiped his eyes with the back of his gloved hand. "I'm sorry for your…We'll wait outside. Take as long as you need."

Rookie Officer Jack Hale stepped up to Sergeant Bernaski and whispered harshly, "Shouldn't we get the body to the morgue? This is a murder."

John Bernaski said, "I'll take responsibility."

Sophia said, "*Ella, pethie mou*, let's take Niko out of here. We'll carry him into the house."

Careful to hold his head still, they lifted him slowly. John reached to help them. "No, John. We carry him." The two women tenderly carried Niko through the side door of the garage to the back of the house.

Sophie had collapsed on the grass in the backyard and sat propped up against the clothesline pole like a rag doll. She too felt at the precipice of death, wanting to join her brother. His blood, his body—shattered. Niko, who ran and laughed with her, his soft cheeks dimpled clear through with happiness; she'd squeeze his hand in loving protection. *My Niko.*

She willed her eyes open and looked up. Tears blurred the starry nighttime sky. She knew right then that the universe had shifted.

Voices roused her. She turned to see her Ma and Yiayia carrying her brother. Niko's arm dangled. Sophie forced herself to stand and staggered over to them. She reached to touch his hand and stopped breathing. It felt icy. She slowly draped his arm across his bloodied chest, fell on her hands and knees, and became sick. Yiayia Sophia reached down with one hand, touched and then stroked the top of her head, and said, "Stand up, honey. Stand up now. I need you to help us." Sophie obeyed, got up awkwardly, and opened the back door.

She turned around, met her Ma's eyes, and cried out, "Oh, Ma, why— how did this happen?" Christina couldn't speak.

Yiayia Sophia helped her daughter sit on a kitchen chair, with her son clutched to her breast. Niko's lanky legs hung out of his too-short trousers. His shoelaces were untied as usual.

Sophie watched as her Yiayia cleared the kitchen table, then fetched clean sheets, towels, blankets, and a pillow. With deliberation, she formed a soft bed for Niko, lit two candles, and turned the kitchen lights off. Ever so slowly, Sophia took him from Christina's reluctant arms and cradled him to her breast. With tender care, she laid him on his back and removed his bloody clothes. Slowly she began to wash his young form with graceful, fluid movements.

The cruel wound in his chest seemed smaller as she washed. She folded a clean sheet over his lower body. With drops of olive oil rubbed between her hands, she caressed his face, arms, and hands. From her great position within the family and a heart familiar with the art of love and healing, Sophie's Yiayia looked dignified. Within the brokenness of the moment, it was a calm and clean beauty. She had restored the image of the child.

Yiayia Sophia poured drops of olive oil onto Sophie and Christina's fingertips. She formed the sign of the cross on Niko's forehead, eyelids, and open palms and guided their hands to do the same.

When finished, she drew the sheet up to his chin and placed his arms outside to his sides. His palms fell outward, open, with the oil glistening in the creases of his young hands.

"*Nani,* Niko, sleep," she whispered.

The dark of night became indistinguishable from the light of day. The family changed overnight, and there was no stopping it from growing into some new kind of life—one that nobody wanted, without Niko.

It was Yiayia Sophia who took hold of the tragedy and willed the broken family forward. Her courage and resolve became legend from the moment she gazed upon her grandson's lifeless body.

The tragic story of Niko's death swept the Southeast Side like moving water. The Greek community and a large cross-section of the city spoke in pained whispers of the young child so cruelly cut down by evil. Their heads bowed, searching to comprehend, imagining losing one of their own.

The many ethnic groups joined hands like one tribe and poured out their collective grief for young Niko and his family. With quiet respect, hundreds braved the frigid weather and wound their way around the block of the funeral home to gaze upon Niko's face lit with soft candlelight. For Hasidic Jews wearing round caps and tassels, Catholic and Orthodox priests, Russian women with babushkas—he was everyone's child.

Noops Potter approached the casket and hovered over Niko's body with an expression of mixed sorrow and confusion. He panted audibly and studied Niko from head to foot. A slight spasm rippled through his body. He reached forward with timid curiosity but quickly withdrew his hand.

Sophie walked up to him and rested her hand on his shoulder. She whispered, "I know Niko told you everything."

Noops twisted his hands together and nodded. "Ah…"

"You were his best friend, and he loved you."

He met her face with a knowing, fretful look and said, "Niko." His eyes darkened and he looked back at the prostrate body of his friend.

"It's okay, Noops," she choked. "You can touch him."

Noops placed his fingertips on his friend's stone-cold cheek and whispered, "Ah…ah be Noops." He jerked his hand back, buried his head in the crook of his elbow, and whimpered. Mr. and Mrs. Potter led him out.

26

Cigar Box

As he stepped off, the ground came up slightly to meet his foot.
— E.B. White, *An Upheaval*

*T*om recovered from his gunshot wound and fully cooperated with the police and FBI. He told them where to find the three one-hundred-dollar bills: encased and buried under one of the metal clothesline posts anchored in cement in the backyard. The Feds were amazed by the precision of Tom's handiwork, from the electronic bugging devices to the waterproof metal box he created to seal up the money. It baffled them that he had managed to juggle both sides for as long as he did.

After a brief trial he was sentenced to five years in the notorious Joliet State Prison for robbery, endangering and contributing to the delinquency of a minor, hiding evidence, and repairing cars for criminals. As an informant to the cops, he remained in an area sectioned away from imprisoned members of the Mob.

The day after the funeral, Sophie rummaged through Niko's dresser, took out his favorite flannel shirt, and hid it under her bedcovers. At night, she hugged the shirt and buried her face in its sweet boy scent. Bitter tears wet her pillow. She blamed herself for not telling her Ma the truth about Taki—for not pressing Niko harder for information. She hadn't even tried with Noops.

The next morning Sophie went back into Niko's bedroom, got on her knees, and lay down on the hand-braided rag rug next to his bed. Her eyes were puffed, wasted from tears. She wrapped her arms closely to her chest, rocked from side to side, and moaned. She forced her eyes open, lifted the Lone Ranger bedspread, and looked under his bed. Sophie saw Niko's cigar box. Slowly, she pulled it close and sat up. Her fingertips glided carefully over the raised letters: "El Producto."

Sophie hesitated, and then opened the lid. It was brimming with a little boy's treasures: the spring Niko had shown her; a perfectly shaped, solid cube of smashed aluminum foil; a rock speckled with glints of mica and a piece of shiny black obsidian shaped like an arrowhead; BBs in a plastic tube-like cylinder with a corked top; a photo of Yiayia and Papou; a coiled Slinky with a few kinks; a bottle cap; an Ernie Banks baseball card; a rubber cigar; three cat's-eye marbles; Bazooka gum comics; eraser shavings in a tiny plastic box; a dirty spark plug; two white feathers; a shiny plastic Lone Ranger bullet; and a blue pom-pom Easter chick with one orange leg sticking out sideways.

Sophie cradled the frail chick in her hand, brought it up to her mouth, and rubbed its feathered wings softly across her lips.

As Christina struggled in her own agony, she tried to keep going for Sophie, but words rang empty even in her own ears. Her son was gone and her husband in prison. The world was black. She wanted to die. Yiayia and the family made sure she didn't.

Yiayia came over every day and stayed with Christina and Sophie. She got them out of bed, fed them, and made sure they kept breathing.

Within a week, dark shadows formed under Sophie's eyes. She could barely eat, and her lanky, coltish body thinned even more. She avoided Christina and stayed up in her room.

Yiayia decided to move in. The first night, she slept with Christina.

The next morning Sophie said to Yiayia, "Ma has you at night. I don't have anybody."

Her arms went around Sophie. "Would you like Thea Toula to come and stay?"

"Yes," said Sophie.

A bed was set up in Sophie's room for Thea Toula. The first night, Toula watched Sophie sit dumbly in bed, staring out the window into the dark. The unconcerned moonlight moved across the floor. Toula cracked the window open. Someone down the alley must have been burning leaves. The air smelled like smoky earth.

Sophie whispered, "Thea. The day before Niko died, we crunched through leaves on the sidewalk."

Saying nothing, Toula moved over to Sophie's bed. With aching tears coming down her face, she hugged Sophie into her large girth and rocked her back and forth. Sophie began to sob and claw frantically at Toula's flannel nightgown. Toula let her.

Sophie went back to school a few weeks later, glad to get away from her mother, but it surprised her to see the world didn't stop just because her brother did. She wore a downcast look in the hallways, the classrooms. Friends ate lunch with her, teachers were kind, but it felt like the world of bystanders to her tragedy were in ready position, waiting for her every reaction.

When Sophie couldn't cry anymore, she turned within a gloomy world, withdrawing from everyone except for Yiayia and Thea Toula. She stayed away from the store, stopped speaking Greek, and gave up searching for something to relieve the anguish. It felt like an irreparable hole tore permanently into her soul, and a cold wind flowed through her wounded heart. *Where were you, Theos? How could you let this happen?*

Sophie stiffened when Christina reached to hug her one morning before school. She wheeled backwards and screamed, "Why didn't you know what Niko was doing with Pa? I hate you! I hate him!"

Doors slammed behind her. Her light became extinguished and the world seemed a hollow, cruel place. The confusion and awkwardness of her age, compounded even further by the unbearable loss of her brother.

Three months after Niko's death, Christina mustered an anger-driven courage to face Tom in prison. She sat in front of one of five rectangular openings carved into the thick cement wall. Heavy iron bars separated the visitors from prisoners.

Tom staggered to the window—head bowed, ankles shackled in chains. She saw a flash of plain fear come over his dirt-smudged face when he looked up at her. A strange, dazed feeling came over her, momentarily not knowing where she was. *What happened to him? The man I knew before we married? The smart, proud soldier.*

He stared down at his clenched hands. In a pained voice he said, "Christina. I'm…I'm so sorry. I caused our son's death."

Christina saw a broken man, swallowed up by his own grief. Her head throbbed hot, but her heart remained stone cold—brimming with unbridled, raw anger, and closed off to any notion of grace. "How blind I was to not see what you were doing. I can't forgive you! I can't forgive myself!" she choked. Angry tears streamed down her face. She stood up so fast, her metal chair fell backwards with a deafening clatter. She grabbed the shelf in front of her, leaned into the bars, and seethed, "Damn you to hell! YOU killed my Niko!"

He saw her face contort with hatred. "Christina, I don't blame you," he said. "I…"

She turned her back on him and ran out. The heavy steel door clanged shut after her.

His heart pounded. Spokes of light from the caged bulbs spun throughout the room. His eyes saw tunnels, then darkness.

A guard jerked him up from the chair. Chains clattered. Tom fell to his knees.

Inside his cell, Tom sat erect on his grimy ticking mattress. His eyes traced the architecture of the bars and pattern of cracks in the cement wall. Christina's words burned like a fiery hand in his heart. *You killed him.* A gray fringe clouded his vision. *I killed him. I made that innocent boy do bad things.*

Help me, God. Forgive me, God. Over and over, the repetition of those two phrases softened the strangeness of his supplication.

His feverish hands brushed frenetically down one arm, then the other. He cried out.

﹏

After Niko's funeral, Papou started having chest pains and needed to be put on nitroglycerin pills. His humor returned after a few months, and he told his grandkids, "Watch out! I might blow up!"

Over a quiet dinner with Yiayia one evening, Papou glanced out the window. He saw a soulful, silver moon show itself full and high above the surrounding brick buildings. The rise and fall of his wife's breathing, the proximity of her hand resting on the table made his throat constrict. He pushed his plate aside, took her warm hand in his, and said, "*Poe, poe,* Ma, this is no good. Christina and Sophie doin' bad no matter what we all do. I'm thinkin' we should go to prison and see that Tom."

She sank lower in her chair. "Do ya think so, Pa?" she asked. Her eyes shrouded over. "I don't know if I can ever look at 'im again."

George reached to touch her cheek and said, "Somethin' tells me we should."

Without telling their daughter, they packed some plates of Greek food and headed to Joliet. The towering limestone structure encased in tall fencing and razor-sharp barbed wire loomed forebodingly.

They sat behind the visitation bars as Tom was brought in, dressed in his prison stripes, to face them.

"What? Why are you here?" asked Tom, scarcely believing who sat in front of him. "Ya both hate me. I know it." He lowered his eyes, shame coursing through him. He wiped sweaty palms on his pants; his breath came quick.

"Tom," said George, shaking his head side to side. "We can no hate ya. You Christina's husband and the children's Pa."

A heavy silence fell between them. With a tortured look, Tom choked, "I, I didn't mean for Niko to be hurt, and now he's gone." He bent down and sobbed into his hands. "I can't bear it. It's all my fault. He was just a little boy and I even hit him. I threatened him. I…I was only thinkin' of myself."

"Did ya love 'im, Tom?" George asked.

Tom took a deep breath. "I loved him more than I even knew. He was everything I'm not. I should be dead, not him. I want to die."

Sophia took off her glasses and wept quietly. She pulled George's over-sized handkerchief out of the breast pocket of his brown suit coat and buried her face in it. George reached over and rested his hand on hers. Tom cupped one hand over his eyes.

"Tom, I'm thinkin' you don't know important things," said George in a somber voice that rang with conviction. "What Ma and I are thinkin' is that we started on a bad foot. Our Christina went off and joined the Army and married you, *exeno,* without the permission. In our ways, is no respect."

He paused and took off his glasses. "But it's a new country, a new way. She musta seen somethin' in you, and we didn't give that a chance."

"But, you gotta hate me."

"We can never forget you put our Niko in bad ways. But Tom, there's somethin' you don't seem to know. When you married Christina, you family."

Tom bent over and wept silently into his hands.

"I have two more things to say, Tom," said George. "I tell you first in Greek. *Eki pou ise imouna, ke etho pou ime tha elthiis.* Where you are, I been; and where I am, you be. *Yiatrepse ta pathi sou keh ystera ta thika mou.* Mend you faults, then look at mine. *Theos* knows you name. He can know the hiding places, the dark places in you heart and shine a light. He who threw the stars up into space and shaped the mountains and oceans with His own hands—He knows you."

Tom brought his chin up and gazed into George's wise brown eyes.

Sophia looked over at her husband with surprise mixed with pride and dabbed her eyes. She stood up and gave the bag of food to the stern-faced guard. George put his hand on the back of the chair and got up slowly. He reached into his deep coat pocket and pulled out a leather Greek-English Bible. He paused and rubbed his hand over the gold letters on the front cover.

George turned back to Tom and said, "Read this book. It will show you the way." He handed it to the guard and reached for his wife. They walked through the heavy metal door clutching each other's hands.

Tom sucked in a deep breath and shook his head, as these were people he had judged to be simple-minded fools. This thought gripped him. Every notion Tom had ever conceived became subject to a new truth.

27
Make Haste, the Light

We never know how high we are
Till we are asked to rise...

— Emily Dickinson

Sophie charged into the kitchen to find Papou sitting at the chrome-leg table with his nose in the *Calumet News*. Papou was someone you didn't talk to when he read the paper with tranquil evaluation, but she was brimming with unbridled anger. She grabbed a Coca-Cola bottle from the refrigerator, flipped the cap off with the opener under the countertop, and plopped down across from him.

"Papou, how come?" asked Sophie. "Why'd you and Yiayia go see him?" The blood ran dizzy-hot in her head.

George calmly laid the paper down, took a cigar out of his coat pocket, and examined it thoughtfully. "He's your Pa, Sophie."

"But you should hate him!" she blurted. "I do!"

"I know," he said solemnly as he reached to take her hand. He raised his bushy eyebrows and said, "Someday, I think—I hope, you can know about your Pa. It's like he swallowed somethin' bitter in him a long time ago, but I'm thinkin' he knows it. Sophie, I don't want you swallow that bitter taste like he did. Niko was our boy, your brother. He would want you heart happy."

She closed her eyes and formed the image of Niko in her mind. She gripped the neck of the sweaty Coke bottle and sank down in her chair. "Oh, Papou, how can I ever be happy?"

"By remembering Niko and the good," he said in a soothing tone. He squinted his friendly eyes into Sophie's. "Do you like plums, Sophie?"

"Yes."

"Think of a nice plum that ripes on the tree with the sun shining down on it." Papou reached up and pretended to pluck it from a branch. "Hold the warm plum in you hand. You can eat and drink da sweet juice and it fill you, or remember it by only da sour skin. What life or people done bad to you, turn round and give somethin' better. When there is dark, shine a light."

Sophie couldn't speak as tears swelled painfully in her throat. Something in her limbs collapsed, as if she had been running for miles. Papou stood up, drew her into his arms, and rocked her gently. She cried and cried.

If it hadn't been for his father-in-law, Tom wouldn't have survived his grief. George came to visit him every week with a sack of hamburgers, shakes, and fries from the store. Tom counted the days between visits.

For the first time in their long marriage, George saw his wife's strength waver. Sophia couldn't go back to Joliet.

"It's too much, Pa," she said bleakly. "I can't do it."

"It's okay, *pulakee mou* (my bird). I go."

The same friendly guard escorted George each time to the visiting area. They'd weave their way through the bleak corridors. George would hand the sack of food to the attending guard and sit in his usual chair. He noticed everything clang with sharp sounds: metal on metal, bundles of keys opening locks, shackles, doors slamming.

When Tom was ushered in he would raise his eyes to his father-in-law, and every time, with fresh force, he would feel conscious of himself, the criminal who caused the death of this man's grandson. George would give him a calm, friendly look. Tom would shake his head in disbelief and then lean close to the bars, an elbow propped on the shelf between them, his fist always resting against his cheek. Roused from the shameful condition in which he found himself every day, his heart would give some flicker of hope upon looking into George's dark eyes. Tom admired the absolute certainty of his countenance and faith in God.

He spent each week rehearsing questions in minute detail about Christina, Sophie, and the family. George would answer his questions and then reach inside his coat pocket for the latest newspaper. He'd adjust his glasses and read the news to Tom.

One Sunday, George asked Tom to describe the prison behind the visiting area.

"Are you sure?"

"Yes," said George. "I'm sure."

Tom rubbed his temples and stretched his hand across his eyes. "The cells are stacked in rows, with walkways and rails in front of them. There's no privacy, but I'm lucky to be at the end of a cellblock. A metal toilet and little washbasin stick out of the wall. Everything is cement and metal, except for my mattress. It's infested with bugs, but I'm killin' 'em. Everything stinks. I stink. Lights click off at nine except for a few bulbs. Some guards are cruel, but I keep my head down. Cons get beaten with rubber hoses if they're defiant. I hear screams."

Tom put his hand up and said, "No more. You don't need to hear this."

George reached through the bars and touched Tom's hand. He smoothed his tie with his other hand and said, "Let's practice speaking the Greek."

Tom memorized the Greek alphabet and sounds.

⁓

At the end of October, a year after Niko's death, freezing weather gripped the city of Chicago. The numbing cold and steely skies transformed Sophie's raw, anger-driven sorrow into a dull ache.

Sophie knew Papou left every Sunday after church to visit her father. With trepidation, she decided to face her Pa.

Before walking out the front door of her house, Sophie caught her image in a mirror. She stared into her eyes. *What will I say? I hate him.*

She stepped into the icy air and pulled her coat collar up around her neck. The fierce, biting wind blew in every direction. The remaining leaves on the trees quaked, and the dead-brown grass poking up from the frosty ground crunched under her boots. Awnings, tree branches, telephone wires, and power lines collapsed as if they had made a collective decision to give up. Sophie shivered and leaned into the wind.

Just as she rounded the corner of 106th Street, she saw Papou taking careful steps on the sidewalk with two sacks clutched in his hand. His breath puffed like steam. He made his way to the yellow Olds parked parallel to the curb and then reached into the deep pocket of his wool overcoat and fumbled for the keys. Sophie waited for him to settle behind the steering wheel and then knocked on the passenger window. He turned in surprise, reached across the seat, and pulled the lock up.

"Why, Sophie, what you's doing here?"

"Papou, I'm going with you to see Pa." She folded her arms tight against her chest and said, "I'm scared of the prison." She closed her eyes and reeled, thinking of that hideous day when she lost Niko. "I'm scared of him."

He reached across the seat and pulled her close. "Come, *koukla*. I be with you."

George distracted Sophie with family talk during the hour-long drive on Route 66 to the city of Joliet. As the heater cranked up, Papou's car seemed like a snug boat in the winter sea. She looked at him sideways and studied his hands on the steering wheel as he navigated the streets. They were splotched with brown spots and wrinkled in crisscross lines, like a road map. *What is it like to be old? I wonder if he studies his worn-looking hands.* She broke away from her reverie as he cruised slowly onto Collins Street and parked the car along a curb. The tires crunched on the ice.

Sophie looked up through the windshield at the looming castle-like entrance of the prison. Her heart began to thump. She stared down at the floor and sank back into the seat. George came around to her side of the car and took her hand. "Come, Sophie. You be okay."

She gave him a weak smile and swallowed, her throat dry as paper.

The medieval-looking stone building looked gloomy with its towers, turrets, and arched, Gothic windows. It rose up menacingly and stood starkly out of place in the neighborhood of squatty, conventional buildings. A solid limestone wall, topped with hideous barbed wire, stretched blocks in either direction. Sophie spotted a little brown bird perched on the razor-sharp wire. She stared at its miserable position, but it fluffed its wings, arranged them in order, and took flight.

Sophie bit her lip and leaned into her Papou's side as they walked through the front entrance. Her eyes fixated trancelike on a large moth, strangely posed upside down, spread-winged, halfway up a cement wall just inside the entry hallway. The wings had dark circular eyespots that seemed to stare at her. *How odd to see a moth during the day.*

"Hey, George, how ya be?" asked a Negro guard at the sign-in desk.

Sophie shivered out of her contemplation of the bird and moth.

"Good, Jim," said George, touching the brim of his fedora. "This is Sophie, my granddaughter. Tom's girl."

"Well now," drawled Jim as he tipped back his cap and grinned. She stood up a little straighter and shook his extended hand. Jim bowed slightly. "You be one brave girl to come here, but doncha worry now," he said warmly. "No one's gone hurt ya."

Sophie liked him right away. He stood proud in his crisp blue uniform. His pants, with a wide darker blue stripe on each leg, were tucked into polished black boots with silvery metal eyehooks. His bullet-studded belt held a pistol in its holster.

Jim grabbed a ring of keys from a pegboard and led them down a long limestone-walled corridor. Sophie grimaced as a wretched waft of dank air hit her nostrils. The heels of their shoes echoed on the cement floor as they fell into step behind Jim. She leaped sideways when she saw a big brown cockroach skitter into a corner. Its wings crackled. Prickles ran along Sophie's skin.

A waft of cold, vile air filled the corridor. Caged light bulbs casting strange shadows and clusters of pipes ran along the low-slung ceiling. She felt the walls closing in on her. Sophie shuddered upon hearing a distant scream and what she thought was the eerie drone of hundreds of voices. George wrapped his arm around her shoulders and pressed her close.

They walked through a heavy steel door into a room dotted with small, waist-high windows reinforced with bars. They were the only visitors. Sophie trembled.

"This is where I leave ya, but Emerson here, he take care of ya," said Jim. He bent down close to Sophie's ear and whispered, "Don't be scared a Emerson. He one of them types—tough guy on the outside, but soft inside." He tipped his hat and winked at Sophie. Emerson had a craggy, stern face and a savage-looking scar along his cheek. Despite Jim's reassurance, Sophie figured Emerson was not someone she would want to cross.

Emerson motioned for them to sit on metal chairs by the last window. Sophie turned and eyed the door anxiously, wanting to follow Jim. George looked at her pale white face and took her hands into his. Their eyes connected, and the momentary quiet seemed to smudge the lines between them.

With a sure, steady voice, he said, "Sophie, *Theos* is here with you, with us."

Sophie stiffened in her chair when she heard a loud buzzer, a clanging door, and the jangling of chains. She looked up to see her Pa, head down, shuffling towards her in jerky steps. His ankles were shackled, with a thick chain between them. He lifted his head, took in a sharp breath, and gripped the back of the chair.

Sophie's heart gave a terrible jolt and her stomach turned. She squeezed her hands together until they hurt. George preoccupied himself by polishing his glasses with his white handkerchief.

Her Pa sat down slowly and scraped the chair legs close to the worn wooden shelf in front of the window of iron bars. He ran a shaky hand over his stubbly beard. His dark hair was short and graying at the temples. A strange pastiness marked his face, and he had purplish circles under his eyes. The uniform of black-and-white stripes surprised Sophie. *He looks like a cartoon jailbird.* The fabric was smudged with grime and frayed at the collar and cuffs.

His gaunt face warmed when their eyes finally met, but darkness entered her heart and she looked away. His tentative fingers reached between the rigid bars. She scooted back in her chair and regarded him with pure resentment. The thought of his touch revolted her.

"Sophie, look how you've grown!" he whispered.

Nerves tingling, Sophie shifted in her chair. Her throat felt strangled. She looked down and rubbed her damp hands over her skirt. Unwanted tears ran down her hot cheeks. She wiped them away in a furious motion with the backs of her hands.

"Sophie," he said in a ragged voice. "I'm…I'm so sorry for your pain and how I've treated you." He looked away, tears of humiliation running down his cheeks. "I've been a bad father. Niko's gone, and I blame myself."

She clamped angry arms across her chest, leaned forward, and heaved her words at him. "You *should* blame yourself for taking my brother away! I'll never forgive you!"

He closed his eyes and said, "I understand." He got a distant look and breathed Niko's name. "All he wanted was my attention. He was a smart boy …a good boy." He looked back at Sophie. "I have no excuse for my terrible behavior." His voice sounded strained. "I didn't listen to your Ma…to you."

Sophie sat silent for a moment forming a picture of her brother in her mind—looking smart in his red jacket and plaid bow tie at church. Her voice caught. "It's too late. Niko's gone." Her own ears rang with the finality of the word.

Sophie saw his face contort, and she looked at him head-on. She didn't feel afraid of her Pa right then, but she wouldn't extend an ounce of forgiveness. As she turned away from him, everything seemed to go gray. Papou put his hand on top of hers. She met his eyes, and he searched hers.

"I want to go, Papou."

He nodded and said, "Okay."

Tom watched them walk out. He shielded his eyes with his hands and wept, blaming himself for being the author of everyone's misfortune.

⌒

When Christina found out about Sophie's visit, she mustered her courage and drove to Joliet. Raging in her head, she clutched the steering wheel so hard the entire way that her hands were numb when she got out of the car. The glaring harshness of the stony building gave her a peculiar, sick sensation in the pit of her stomach. She wanted to bolt but felt pulled, somehow dedicated to an invisible course, one that her daughter had laid.

The second time seeing Tom confused Christina. As her eyes bore into him, she saw a different man—thin, worn-out, but somehow softer around his eyes and mouth. Nevertheless, coldness gripped her heart. Coldness mixed with sorrow so deep, she didn't allow herself to cry in front of him. "My Niko is gone because of *you.*"

Tom rubbed his temples hard and met Christina's eyes. Subtle lines had formed around her haunted yet beautiful eyes. He looked down at her hands and noticed her wedding band was gone. His voice came from far away. "Most cons blame everyone else for their troubles, but they only have themselves to blame." His hand sought the back of his head. "That's me, Christina. It's my fault."

Her eyes flashed and she gave a short, harsh laugh. "You're right. You tortured us with your rotten attitude towards my family, your drinking and illegal dealings. You used Niko, knowing all the while how he worshipped you. I should have left you a long time ago and spared the children, spared Niko's life." She tapped the shelf with a soft fist and whispered, "We didn't care what they heard between us. Poor kids. You never listened, and I pretended to my family. I stayed with you because of my stupid pride." She looked sideways at the cement wall and shook her head. "What a fool I've been."

"No, I've been the fool. You were a trusting, loving woman when we first met. I adored you, but I threw us aside because of my own confusion. I've been sick in my heart, sick in my mind. I pulled you down, and didn't deserve any of you with my selfish behavior. Look at your father—reaching out to me after what I've done. If I could only be the man he is…"

Christina looked him curiously. *Has he changed? Can I trust this newness? I saw something in him when we met. Pa says his thinking is right but he needs to practice love—getting and giving.*

28
George

Love is composed of a single soul inhabiting two bodies.
— Aristotle

1959

*T*hree years after Niko's death, on a sweltering June day when the humidity felt high and thick in the morning, George and Sophia decided to drive by themselves to visit relatives in Kankakee. George seemed fidgety, uncomfortable, and jerked his arms like a horse shedding flies. He wiped the back of his hand across his forehead.

"Are you okay, George?" asked Sophia.

"My stomach don't feel so good, Ma. It has the…the indigestible."

"It must have been Pasquale's pizza we ate last night," she said.

About ten miles later, George unbuttoned his shirt collar and complained, "Oh, Ma, it's *so* hot!"

She took a thermos of cool water, drenched his handkerchief, and mopped his face and the back of his neck. He clutched his chest with one hand and started gasping for air.

"Pull over, Pa!"

His foot slid off the accelerator. His head lolled to the side. "George!" Sophia screamed. She grabbed at the steering wheel. The car cruised to the gravelly side of the road and finally came to a jerky stop after scraping along a rusty guardrail.

"George!" Sophia shouted. She fumbled in her purse for his nitroglycerin tablets and shoved one under his tongue. She cradled his head against her chest and cried, "Pa! Pa, breathe easy! You'll be okay." George moaned and slumped over into her arms.

Yiayia Sophia Poulos laid her husband to rest next to their parents' graves in Evergreen Cemetery. The air felt crisp and the sky was clear that woeful afternoon. There had been a downpour in the middle of the night, leaving the earth fresh and new. The leaves, grass, and bushes glistened—polished with faded raindrops. All seemed quiet except for a lone sparrow that sat on a tree branch above Papou's grave. It cocked its head sideways and chirped a sweet song. It landed on a low branch by Sophie. She held out an open palm. The sparrow tilted its head, considering, and then flapped away.

Yiayia Sophia straightened her glasses, leaned into the casket, and kissed her husband one last time. She laid her folded handkerchief, edged with lace, on his chest and placed one of his crisply ironed handkerchiefs next to hers. Toula watched her cousin teeter as if she were going to crumple to the ground. She rushed to her side and propped her up. They bunched their faces in grief and cried. Sophie walked to their sides and cried with them.

Yiayia Sophia's children took turns driving her to the cemetery once a week through the summer months. She ambled slowly from the car to the Greek section of the cemetery with her picnic basket. Like all ethnic groups, the Greek community knew one another. The names on the headstones were familiar—"Papou's neighbors," as she told her grandkids. It was a rare visit that Yiayia Sophia didn't see someone she knew, but mostly she visited her George alone.

She bent her sorrow over the little clear glass vase propped against the rose-colored granite headstone inscribed with large block letters: "POU-LOS". The week-old flowers were replaced with a fresh bouquet of fragrant white stephanotis, George's favorite. Sophia lit pungent incense in a little brass censer with a cross on top. The incense crackled upon being lit and then settled down to a soft, fragrant ribbon of smoke. She crossed herself and bowed slightly three times. Yiayia Sophia spread her small red-and-white-checked tablecloth on the grass, ate lunch, and talked to George.

The diminutive sparrow visited Yiayia Sophia. It hopped along George's headstone, looked at her with its bright, round eye like a black raindrop, and trilled its song for her. Each time Sophia visited, George sent the sparrow to her. She smiled, remembering what George had said about his family surname: "Poulos—it mean nesting for the birds."

Late in August, Yiayia Sophia had a mild stroke. It left her with slightly halted speech—imperceptible to those who didn't know her. The family trembled at its core whenever Yiayia swayed with weakness.

"Christina," she said from her hospital bed. "Last week I prayed to the East and fell asleep. I saw your Pa in a dream. He smiled his sweet, slow smile, folded one arm over his chest like a proud warrior, then reached his hand out to me. I wanted to join him right then, but I told him, 'Not yet, Pa.' " Her glasses slipped down a little. "Christina," she said, looking over her glasses with a small grin, "I know he's flying with the sparrows."

"Oh, Ma, all of us love you so much. We need you."

"I know, *koukla*. I'm so lonesome for your Pa, but I got reasons to stay."

When Christina broke the news of George's death to Tom, he put his head down onto his arm and wept openly. Tom knew he had experienced a glimpse of virtue and forgiveness in the most pure form through George Poulos. He lifted his head and touched Christina's fingers through the bars.

"First Niko, now George," he groaned. "Christina, I'm so sorry. I...I loved your Pa. He was good to me when there was no reason. Your parents are fine people, and it took me this long to figure that out." With clarity in his voice, he said, "Christina, I love you more than I can say. I broke your trust from the beginning. Please believe me. We can help each other now."

To change from her determined, unforgiving position was like lifting a huge piece of furniture, but something unnatural stirred in her head and she surprised herself by giving a subtle nod.

PART FIVE

29

Fresh Water to Drink

Atticus was right. One time he said you never really know a man
until you stand in his shoes and walk around in them.
Just standing on the Radley porch was enough.

— Harper Lee, *To Kill a Mockingbird*

1961

In the middle of the night, Tom sat up straight and still on his filthy ticking mattress. It was late summer, but he had dreamed about rows of wintertime trees stripped of all their leaves. The desolation of the gray sky and bare branches not touching one another made him shiver. He pressed his thumb into his hand and took a deep breath. *How can I expect Christina to trust me after what I've done? Can I trust myself? I should be dead, not Niko.*

He replayed the years when he had first met Christina. How he wished he could turn back time and start over. Christina had suffered the loss of her son; now her father.

George—always funny, yet dignified. The smell of spent cigars, his crisp white shirt and Sunday coat, his thick accent and warm brown eyes. George had told him, "If ya know you wasn't a good husband and pa, you could learn and try. Ya gotta be ready to think of them first, take care of them, and ask *Theos* to help ya all the time. You was blind and now you starting to see. Remember, Tom, a candle don't lose nothin' by lighting another candle."

Tom lay back on his mattress and stared up at the low ceiling. A waft of stale urine filled his nostrils, and the caged bulb a couple of cells down flickered. It was a new notion to even imagine having a chance of being a husband to Christina and a father to Sophie. *Why would they want anything to do with me?*

Christina picked up where George left off. She knew her father would want her to keep seeing Tom. Habit turned into a dull desire that surprised her. Every week she went to the prison and brought sacks of hamburgers to Tom, Jim, and Emerson. Sophie came with her once a month because she was asked.

At unexpected times Sophie would well up with impossible sadness, missing Niko and Papou. She'd clamp her hand over her mouth so she wouldn't cry. If she started, she wouldn't be able to stop. Yiayia told her to keep praying, so she whispered long pleading sentences to God, asking for the pain to be easier. When she played with friends, she'd forget and then, later, feel guilty about forgetting.

The visits were made tolerable by seeing the kindly guards Jim and Emerson. Sophie saw her father for precisely ten minutes. The rattle of his chains, coupled with his soft voice, clanged in her head. She'd answer his boring questions while watching the minutes tick by on the school-sized wall clock and then look to Emerson with a nod. He would escort her back to the front desk to play card games with Jim.

Sophie noticed how Emerson's hardened façade softened whenever he looked at her or spoke. The hollowness in his cheeks and downturn of his eyes went away with his smile—a delicate, vulnerable look. He told her how he missed Papou's visits.

The cockroaches and Sophie were on better terms, and she wasn't terrified of the musty-smelling, shadowy passageways like she had been. Sometimes she felt like a steady-eyed cat studying the hallways in that prison wing. The few windows slanted light onto the limestone walls and made them glow yellow-orange. The network of interwoven pipes hanging from the ceilings reminded her of a busy train yard.

After a few months of visits, Sophie finally dared to ask Jim what he thought of her Pa.

"Well now, Sophie, I've been savin' up my thoughts about your pa fer a while. I go see him just about ever day, and my thinkin' is that Tom's a right good man," he said. "He got privileges other cons don't. He reads a lot and he different than the others. Most go blamin' and fightin' each other, but your Pa stays outta trouble and be kindly—even to the ol' broken-down cons."

Sophie looked at the floor and said, "You know why he's here, don't you?"

"I does, Sophie. It bad, and I feel sorry," he said. "But there's somethin' about 'im. Different, I suppose. Sometimes I wonder if he'll get outta here early with his good behavior. We put him under watch in the prison shop and I tell you, that man can fix anything. He smart. It all started when Emerson complained about his watch not workin'. Somehow, Tom talked 'im into lettin' 'im fix it. After thinkin' about it, Emerson decided to pass his watch through the bars to Tom. A few days later, Tom handed the watch back to Emerson tickin' like it brand new. Emerson found out that Tom had jimmied out two wires from the woven metalwork under his mattress and scratched 'em on the cement wall until one turned into a sharp point and t'other into a miniature screwdriver. With those tiny tools, he fixed up the watch. Tom tol' Emerson he could patch up just about anything with electricity and parts that move. Word spread and guards started bringin' 'im all kind of things to fix."

Sophie sat in wide-eyed silence, imagining Emerson with his hulking shoulders, thick neck, and stern face handing Tom his watch. Trusting him with it.

"Any busted-up kitchen mixer, watch, or radio—why, he can put 'em together good as new. With his good behavior, he works under a guard in the prison shop most days. He's even been overhaulin' car and truck engines. That Tom reads the Bible your good grandpa gave 'im all the time. I think that man learned the Greek in it too."

"Why didn't you tell me this before?" Sophie asked.

Jim tipped his chair back and rubbed a brow thoughtfully with his fingers. "I don't blame ya for all the pain and anger ya feel. I guess I just wanted the askin' and tellin' be your idea."

Sophie asked Christina, "Ma, do ya trust Pa? He seems different and all, but I don't know. I miss Niko so much. I don't see how he can be different."

Christina placed her hand on Sophie's shoulder and met her eyes. "I know, honey. Life will never be the same for us. Let's just say…I'm just giving it time. That's why I keep visiting him. Papou wanted me to try, and it seems like I should."

30

East Side Hamburgers

For the strength of the Pack is the Wolf, and the strength
of the Wolf is the Pack.

— Rudyard Kipling

The years went by and Sophie blossomed into a willowy seven-teen-year-old junior at St. Francis De Sales High School. Each morning before the first bell rang, the whole student body gathered in the chapel to sing. It was Sophie's favorite time of day, when she sat shoulder to shoulder with her good friend Charlotte. In contrast to her thin body, Charlotte's hands were plump and delicate. Her full face and earnest eyes seemed to have a perpetual look of wonder. Sophie could be herself around Charlotte.

All the girls, with their matching plaid skirts, navy sweaters, and white blouses monogrammed with the initial of their first name on the rounded collars, made Sophie feel like they were a big family. Their voices lifted to the vaulted ceiling and echoed gloriously throughout the chapel.

She played on the girls' field hockey team and could have gotten better grades if she had tried harder. Sometimes she felt so changed inside, like her world was lopsided.

The nuns, in their floor-length habits, were kind to Sophie under their stern façades. She continued to be a voracious reader and did well in English but wasn't motivated in her other classes.

Sophie's elegant cursive handwriting and insightful stories caught the attention of the youngest nun, Sister Margarita, who taught literature. She would often ask Sophie to come before the morning bell to write poems on the blackboard. Sophie loved the rhythm of poetry, and how the white chalk flowed velvety across the smooth slate.

Sister Margarita's sky-blue eyes framed with dark lashes had a crinkle of humor and intelligence in them. When she recited poems or passages from books, her voice was vivid with expression, and her long black habit brushed desks as she waltzed through the rows of students. Sometimes a curl of dark brown hair would come loose and peek through her wimple. Sophie found herself smiling through literature class.

One morning, after Sophie finished writing the Emily Dickinson poem "Hope is a thing with feathers that perches in the soul" on the board, Sister Margarita startled her by saying, "Sophie, have you lost some of your hope?"

Sophie pulled a loose thread off her skirt. "What do you mean?"

"You do so well in literature class, but your grades don't match up in your other classes."

"I guess I'm just not as interested," she said.

"Well, Sophie, I know you have it in you to do better," she said kindly. "Maybe some other things are in the way."

Sophie felt tired just then and tried to smile.

Sophie and Cousin George worked at East Side Hamburgers after school. They wore long white aprons and yellow paper lieutenant-type hats emblazoned with the words "East Side Hamburgers" in red letters on each side. Two little black musical quarter notes danced on either side of the words— "to show family harmony," said Yiayia Sophia.

The inside of the store would be awash with a soft light coming from the big window by the door, and Sophie would notice.

Cousin George kept the records spinning on the lighted Wurlitzer jukebox, and Sophie would bebop in her black-and-white saddle shoes behind the counter. Sophie loved her unpredictable cousin and saw that his clear green-blue eyes had a look of perpetual mischief. George would slide behind the counter on his slick-soled shoes and toss cherries high into the air, catching them in his mouth every time like a baseball player catching a pop fly.

The neighborhood kids came in just to see the two of them. Sophie personalized their ice cream sundaes and slipped pennies in their hands for the gumball machine from her stash under the cash register. She scooped ice cream with a flourish into the thick sundae glasses and skipped between containers of toppings, dropping small handfuls of sprinkles and nuts onto the whipped cream like a waterfall from above. A bright-red cherry would be the finishing touch.

One quiet Saturday afternoon, the little store bell tinkled as the door opened. Sophie looked up, blinked hard, and saw Niko, with his hiked-up pants, slight swagger, flashing dark eyes, and dimpled smile. The floor tilted. She squeezed her eyes shut and pressed her fist against her cheek. Heart pounding, she leaned against the freezer and opened her eyes to Avram hopping up on one of the chrome barstools topped with a red leather seat. He propped his elbows on the marble countertop and said, "Hey, Sophie, I want a one scoop vanilla, one scoop strawberry ice cream sundae with hot fudge and caramel on top. You know: the works!"

Feeling numb, she stuttered, "Oh, uh…hi, Avram."

Avram cocked his head sideways. "You look kinda strange, Sophie. Are you okay?"

"Uh, yeah, I'm okay. I was just thinking of something." Her arm disappeared into the freezer case as she scooped the ice cream. She dipped her head down and inhaled the frigid air. The vapor of her warm breath billowed around her face. Her throat constricted. Avram was nine years old. Almost the same age as Niko when she lost him forever. In spite of her surviving the calamity of Niko's death, it didn't take much to bring her back to the crushing loss.

Noops was a steady customer at the store, and his very presence, although happy, made her feel fragile.

A young man of routine, he'd bat the little bell hanging above the door in his awkward way to announce his arrival.

"Hey, Noops!" everyone would shout.

"Ah, ah, ah," he'd pant heavily with his smiling mouth hung open. Noops threw his head back as gladness shivered over him.

He'd always sit at the same low stool by the door and make friendly gestures and sounds to incoming and outgoing customers—like the store's ambassador. He'd wrap his untied oxford shoes around the stool's thick post and rest his forearms on the countertop for balance. After he got his cheeseburger, fries, and a shake, he'd shake like a rabbit with excitement and tap the pattern of sesame seeds on the top bun with a bent forefinger before starting to eat.

When finished, he'd amble up to Sophie and jerk his face up so she could wipe him with wet napkins. He'd croon upon her soft touch.

One crisp fall afternoon, Noops seemed different after Sophie cleaned him up. He stared into her eyes with an unexpected gleam and said, "Niko," so clearly it startled her.

She rested her hand on his shoulder and said, "Yes, Noops. Niko was your friend."

Noops lowered his head and squeezed his eyes tight. One large tear rolled down his cheek. He breathed a half-sigh and wiped the tear and his nose with the back of his sleeve. Sophie took him into her arms and whispered, "Thank you for being Niko's good friend. He loved you, Noops."

"Niko," Noops said. Thus they stood, forming the image of Niko in their minds.

Within seconds, new life breathed into him. He crossed his arms, all business, and said, "Boom."

"Sure thing, Noops, but first I need to tie those shoes."

Sophie bent down on one knee and double-knotted his shoelaces. Noops patted her hair with his fingertips.

She gave him a wide, bristly broom, and he swept in a clumsy waltz across the floor. Sophie watched him, enchanted by his broad and jerky movements. He mumbled and smiled to himself, as if in his own twilight world. She wondered what floated around within his dreamy thoughts. Sophie imagined mostly lovely things.

After sweeping a bit, he looked up and announced, "Ah be goo!" It was as if all the agreeable sensations possible to a human being were embodied within Noops's flesh and blood.

⌒

Yiayia Sophia wasn't as robust as she had been. She still grilled onions, flipped burgers, and made shakes for her customers, but she moved slower. Christina took over the bookkeeping, ordering of supplies, and management of the workers.

George never left Yiayia Sophia's thoughts. She wore his gold wedding band on a necklace with her ornate gold cross, carried a big black purse, and wore black dresses, hose, and shoes every day.

"Ma, why don't you wear a little color?" Christina asked. "Pa would like it."

"No, honey, I honor your Pa. It's my way."

Christina decided to buy Yiayia Sophia a dark blue sweater. It was a big leap for her Ma to wear it, but after that, she wore modest accents of color, like black dresses with white lace or colorful piping around the collar. Her red-white-and-blue rhinestone American flag was unfailingly pinned to the bodice of every dress.

The family, grandkids, neighbors—the entire community of the East Side kept Yiayia Sophia going. Since the stroke, she talked more to herself, to George at odd times. She quietly confided in George while cooking at the grill, watering her houseplants, sweeping, smoothing her hair, and walking down the sidewalk. Everyone understood as she was greatly respected—greatly loved. Her family and the neighborhood kept vigilance over her. One of her adult children or grandchildren walked everywhere with her.

"Give me a wing, honey," she'd say, grabbing Sophie's bent arm for good measure and balance. Sophie remembered how Yiayia and Papou always walked down the street holding hands.

Sophie noticed how gentlemen swept their hats off and waved gallantly from across the street in deference to her. She looked into her Yiayia's soulful eyes, which regarded the world fearlessly, and thought she was the most extraordinary woman she had ever known. Sophie felt great ambition to be like her.

During Christina's regular visits with Tom, a quiet friendship reminiscent of their courtship surfaced. Every visit began with Tom asking Christina questions about herself, Sophie, and the family. He leaned closer to the bars and genuinely listened—thoughtful of her every notion. Tom made no excuses and gave her the feeling he needed to right all the wrong he had done. They began to get acquainted with their new reality, but Christina needed the proof of time. Nothing could bring Niko back. Can he be trusted?

Before Christmas, Tom found out he would be released from Joliet in February—nine months early for good behavior. Christina had been forewarned, but it still spun her world sideways. There would be no bars between them. What would it do to Sophie? Christina recoiled, knowing this unexpected news would be a shock to her. She mustered the courage, a few days later, to tell Sophie after school.

Christina girded herself as she heard the back door slam shut. She walked into the kitchen just as Sophie plopped her schoolbooks down on the table. Sophie shook the snow out of her hair and shrugged her coat off.

"Hi, Sophie," said Christina. Her heart drummed, and she raked an unsteady hand through her own hair. "How was your day?"

"Okay. I have a lot of homework."

"Honey, I need to tell you something important." Her own voice sounded strange and thin. She brushed some crumbs off the kitchen table and motioned for Sophie to sit down.

Sophie's chin came up and she glanced sideways. She had cultivated an expression devoid of interest around her mother.

"It's about Pa."

Sophie sat down, drew her knee up to her chest, and felt her jaw tighten. "I *don't* want to talk about him."

Christina reached for her hand. Sophie pulled away. "Your Pa's getting out of prison early, and he needs to move away immediately."

"What?" Sophie shook her head as her fists went to her hips. "Well, good. He can just move away," she said in a rush.

Christina ignored her comment. "The Mafia has left you and me alone because we're nothing to them, but they'll be after your Pa. He knows too much about their operations. He needs to disappear far away."

"Where's he going?" asked Sophie.

"I can't tell you right now, but far."

"That's okay by me."

"He also needs change his last name—our last name."

"What's that got to do with me?" Sophie challenged. "I'm not changing *my* name!"

"I understand what you're thinking, but eventually we won't have a choice."

Sophie stood up defiantly. "Maybe you don't, but I do!"

"I have more to tell you." Christina lightly touched her daughter's cheek. Sophie took a quick step back. Christina sucked in a deep breath, and it felt like bees were buzzing in her head. "I'm planning for the two of us to join him away from here."

Sophie's mouth fell open and her face paled. Her body looked unhinged to Christina.

"Are you crazy? No, Ma! I don't want to be with him—ever! I'll never trust him! Why would *you* want to be with him? All you ever did was fight, and then look what happened to Niko! I don't understand. Please, Ma!" she begged. She stopped abruptly and stared, eyes flaming. Her voice dipped down, low and calculated. "You go right ahead. Be with him. I'm staying here with Yiayia and our family."

Christina forged ahead. "He'll go by himself and find a job first," she said. "I'll join him after you finish the school year."

With sass in her voice Sophie said, "Then what?"

"You'll stay with Yiayia, and I'll join Pa and make sure everything's okay. We'll send for you before school starts in the fall," she said. "The family will take care of Yiayia and the business." She rushed on, "I believe your father has changed and I need to see if we can work things out. After you finish high school, if you still want to be with the family in Chicago, you can leave."

"So it's okay to ruin my senior year of high school? Make me leave my friends? You didn't even ask me before you decided all this!" shouted Sophie. "Isn't it enough I lost my brother?" She backed away, shaking her head. "No! I can't! I won't! You'll be sorry. We've never lived anywhere else. It will break Yiayia's heart."

"She's encouraging me, honey, and feels it's the right thing to do. I know Papou would want me to try, and Yiayia understands that I need to give this a chance."

"I don't believe you! Yiayia would never want me to move away!"

It seemed her world was spinning out of control—the same feeling she'd had after Niko's death. *How can I leave and not even graduate from high school with my friends!*

Sophie heard a roar in her head and squeezed her eyes shut. Her stomach contracted into a tight ball. She wiped hot tears away with the palms of her hands. Christina reached to touch her shoulder, but Sophie jerked away and burst out the back door. With clenched fists she trudged through the slippery snow as fast as she could to Yiayia's apartment. The dirty slush in the streets was furrowed in haphazard ways from passing cars.

Tears froze on her stinging cheeks. *Ma will hate it and come back. I won't even have to go.* Her heart beat in dark confusion.

She pushed the front door of the apartment building open and took two steps at a time up the floral carpeted stairway. Sophie found her Yiayia sitting in Papou's upholstered easy chair, with a blanket over her knees and watching her favorite soap opera, *The Edge of Night.* She was wearing a familiar black dress and her black Dr. Scholl's shoes. Her thick white hair hadn't been brushed. It sprang wild and made her face look soft—vulnerable.

Sophie ran across the room and collapsed on her knees at Yiayia's feet. She wrapped her arms around Yiayia's legs and buried her face in her dress's skirt. She inhaled her familiar scent. "Shh, shh," Yiayia comforted. "I know why you're here. It will be okay. You know, your Ma is a brave lady."

"Brave?" Sophie raised her head. "After letting Pa do bad things with Niko! How was that brave?"

"I hope you see something about her—I want you to see that she has courage to imagine a different life. To imagine forgiveness after all that's happened. It doesn't seem like it to you, but your Ma is trying see things differently for you, for herself."

Sophie fingered the hem of Yiayia's dress and shook her head. "But Yiayia! Ma says *I* have to move!" she moaned, renewed tears springing up in her eyes. "I can't! I won't leave you!"

"I know, honey. We've never been away from each other." She coaxed her tall granddaughter onto the arm of the chair and her lap. She covered Sophie's cold arms with the blanket and stroked her wet cheek. "This is all hard for you to hear, to understand. I promise to visit, and you'll come back to see us, even spend summers here."

"Yiayia, no," Sophie sighed. "I can't go away from you."

"You've been through more than a girl should, but you are turning out like that nice loaf of bread.

"I'm proud of you. Where you go, I'll be right there, inside you." She patted Sophie's chest. "Your goodness will bring a happy heart to you, to everyone," she reassured. "Trust and watch how the light will scatter the darkness. *Feggaraki mou lambro* (My moon shines brightly). *Theos, foto mou na perpato* (God, light my way to walk). Try not to fight so hard. *S'agapo, angelaki mou* (I love you, my angel)," she sighed. "Everything will be all right. I know. You see."

Folks said Tom Peters came out of prison a changed man.

Christina's breath rose like steam as she waited in the cold for Tom to come out the back door of the prison. She gripped the chainlink fence with her gloved fingers until they hurt. Looking down at the shallow puddles on the sidewalk, she saw reflections of the streetlights in the darkening gray sky. She squinted her eyes and the light became tiny points in the puddles. *What will it be like with no bars between us?* The sound of jangling metal startled her. Her breath came fast and she sidestepped into the shadows.

The heavy door scraped open and light poured out. She saw Tom's profile and Emerson standing next to Jim. Her heart pounded.

She heard Jim say, "Here ya go, Tom. Freedom."

Tom shook hands with both men and said, "Thanks for everything you did for my family and me. I'll never forget."

Emerson sneezed, swabbed his nose, and said nothing. Christina saw him smile. It made the rough etchings on Emerson's face disappear.

Jim put his hand on Tom's shoulder and said, "Good luck to ya."

Tom took a few steps out and looked up as if he were exploring the expanse of sky. He turned and waved to the men. Christina waited a moment and then stepped around the fence into the light. He spotted her.

"Christina! You came." He ran over to her and took her in his arms. He brushed his lips against her cheek. Her back stiffened.

His face smelled clean like soap to Christina, but his wool overcoat had the dank odor of mildew. She placed her shaky hands on his arms and took a step back. She pulled him under the streetlight and studied his face. It startled her to see the measures he had taken to disguise himself. He had a neatly cropped beard and moustache. His hair was a little longer and combed back on the sides. The light seemed to seep far into his blue eyes, and it picked out flecks of deeper blue. Christina dropped her gaze, unable to meet the new, naked honesty in his eyes. "You're so different."

"I feel different—grateful," he said.

They walked to the car. "Tom," she said, "I'm not sure this will work."

He looked at her and said, "Niko's gone. I understand."

To protect Tom and his family, his release was kept secret and the FBI facilitated a formal name change to erase any links or connections to the Mafia. He became Tom Elias. He wanted a Greek name to honor Christina and Sophie. The FBI wasn't in favor of the Greek name, as they felt it might create a tie to Chicago, but Tom was adamant. Eventually, they agreed.

Christina and Tom were cautious—timid together. Tom hungered for her body, her warmth, but he waited. He'd look in her eyes and wonder if he should disappear for all the heartache he caused. *God help me not to mess up.*

They stayed with relatives in Cicero for a few days and ventured out for a long walk one evening on the snowy sidewalks and through parks. Tom offered his arm to Christina, and she took it. He smiled. A metallic wintry atmosphere settled from the sky to the ground. Ice crunched under their boots. The red sun sank down, leaving a pink blush on the snowy rooftops. The sagging wires strung on the poles edged the roads. Tom heard the doves coo softly in the bare branches of the trees, and their wings made a whistling sound upon takeoff. The sights and noises that shivered over the earth rang joyful to Tom. Perhaps he finally felt a part of something, and when it came to him, it came like the sun and air with the knowledge of what is true.

31

The Great Northern Empire Builder

I am not concerned that you have fallen,
I am concerned that you arise.
— Abraham Lincoln

*C*hristina drove Tom to Union Station to catch the Great Northern Empire Builder train heading west to Oregon. Before boarding, he looked down and studied the wheels of the train poised on the tracks—their machined surfaces—grooves polished shiny from steel running over steel. The blackened earth between the creosote-soaked railroad ties was pounded rock-hard by the heavy trains. "Look at the wheels, Christina. Aren't they interesting?"

She propped her hand under her chin and said, "If I see them with your eyes—yes."

He rested his hands on her waist and looked into her eyes. "I'll try to be worthy of you and Sophie. I'll always love you." He kissed her tenderly and then boarded the train with his two scuffed leather suitcases. He found a seat next to the window and spread his hand against the cool glass to Christina. She put her hand out to him. The diesel locomotives heaved as the train moved away from the station. Her image became small between his fingers and then disappeared. Tom wiped the sweat off his brow and became aware of an elderly man sitting down in the seat next to him. The man's broad, knotty hands were wrinkled like dry leaves.

He reached his hand out to Tom. "My name is Noah. Noah Shapiro. How far are you going?"

Tom looked up at him, drawn by his sure, soft voice. His face was ruggedly formed, and everything about him was dignified. He was neatly dressed and wore a dark brown vest under his coat. A little gold baseball hung on a slender chain across the vest. His trimmed moustache matched his thick snowy-white hair, which was striking against his dark skin.

"My name is Tom Elias. I'm going all the way to Oregon."

"Well sir, that's a long way. I'll be stopping in Whitefish, Montana, to visit my daughter, her husband, and three grandkids." He looked wistfully past Tom out the window. "Lost my wife last year."

Tom looked into his face for a moment, then down at the floor. "I'm sorry."

"Makes a fella lonely, but I've got my kids and friends."

They lapsed into silence. Tom opened his lunch sack and took out a turkey sandwich wrapped neatly in wax paper. He settled back in his seat, stared at it, and left it on his lap.

The train skirted the Great Lakes and then wound its way across the northern states. Noah had been a structural engineer working on the design of bridges in Chicago. Tom and Noah's mutual interests kept them engaged in conversation almost the entire way to Montana. The motion of the train lulled them to sleep in their seats at night.

Tom was sorry to lose the physical presence of Noah when he got off the train at Whitefish two days later. He stepped off the train and helped Noah with his luggage. They shook hands warmly and Noah departed.

Melting water came out like little streams towards the tracks from the snow banks around the platform. The air seemed crisp and thin to Tom. The shrill train whistle blew and Tom got back to his seat. He spent the day gazing out the windows into the stunning beauty of the Rocky Mountains. When nighttime came and the inside lights of the train car switched off, Tom looked into the black of night and saw the evening star shine like a beacon. He thought of Niko, he whispered to Niko, keeping him alive, as if he had never died.

Tom knew that Oregon was a state of every kind of geography. Fertile green valleys dipped between the coastal and Cascade mountain ranges. He had seen photos of the scrubby high desert in Central Oregon. Those colors were of a softer palette—splashes of sage, yellow, and brown. He remembered showing Niko the photograph of an Oregon mountain, and he lowered his head into his hands and wept.

When Tom disembarked from the train at Portland's Union Station, he breathed in pure, clean air. He filled his mouth with water at the station's drinking fountain. It tasted cool and fresh.

Tom moved into a studio apartment and found a good job developing, troubleshooting, and repairing electrical components for aircraft at a Boeing subsidiary in Portland. He had placed a handmade radio on the interviewer's desk and described his work with radar and airplanes during the war. He was hired on the spot.

Tom played the violin with his eyes closed, the way he always did when sorrow about Niko entered his heart. He thought about Papou and talked to God. Was it the wounded places in his heart that made him want to love more, to do things better?

He figured out how to live frugally and was proud to save every spare dime. His letters to Christina were prolific and upbeat. He sent pictures and wrote letters to Sophie describing the rugged Pacific coast, pristine volcanic mountains, profusion of trees, ferns, and lush flowers which burst forth in the spring. The dinner-plate-sized rhododendrons were glorious. The bustling city of Portland, known as the "City of Roses," was tiny compared to Chicago but surrounded by beautiful tree-studded hills, rivers, and sweeping landscapes.

Tom loved music and poetry, but Christina hadn't known him as a writer. The depth and imagery in his descriptions of Oregon and his job surprised her. She reread a paragraph of one letter:

I walked through the forest today and knelt down on the moss to study a snail with my jeweler's loupe. It floated along on a slime trail, and its complicated eyes on top of long tentacles swiveled around in my direction. They shrank down for a moment and then rose back up. I touched its striped shell with one soft tap. A couple pill bugs, like little armadillos, seemed to follow the snail on their many feet.

He also wrote Yiayia Sophia to help her form a picture of where her daughter and granddaughter would live.

Before Christina left for Oregon, she sat at the foot of Niko's grave, under the shadow of the large Poulos headstone where Papou was buried. She choked on her tears and rubbed her hand across his etched name, Nicholas George Peters.

Saying farewell to her Ma was unbearable; she wondered if she would see her again.

Yiayia Sophia said, "Remember what I said to you when your train left for Virginia? We look at the same stars in the sky."

"Will you be okay, Ma?" Christina asked.

"I got lots of years left, honey. Now, go fly with new wings."

Sophie wanted to protest watching her Ma pack, but she had already exhausted all of her words. For the first time in years, Sophie let her Ma hold her. Christina kissed her forehead and cheeks. "Try not to be afraid, Sophie. I'll do my best for you when you come out west. Trust me."

Sophie knotted her hands together and said, "I may not come."

"I promise things will be different than they were before Niko died." She unhooked her Athena necklace, took Sophie's hand, and placed it into her palm. She curled her daughter's fingers around it and cupped her hand. "This is yours now."

"Why are you giving it to me?"

"Yiayia gave it to me when my life was about to change. Her Ma gave it to her. It's a reminder of our family's courage and strength. It's yours now."

Sophie's eyes welled with tears.

It was also by train that Christina discovered America west of the Mississippi. She knew the plains and small hills of the Midwest, but nothing could prepare her for the grandeur of mountains and wild, rushing rivers. Her eyes filled with wonder upon each passing mile. She turned her wedding band around and around on her finger.

Christina scrutinized Tom with new eyes and was slowly convinced that he was learning to value life. It was a new experience to observe his zeal for saving money.

Christina had sold their house in Chicago, and they bought a three-bedroom house in an established, tree-lined neighborhood on the outskirts of Portland. They planted a small vegetable garden in the backyard and beds of flowers in the front. She lined the curved brick walkway with pansies.

Christina missed everyone desperately, but it helped when she and Tom began to attend the Holy Trinity Greek Orthodox Church. She connected with the women's group called The Daughters of Penelope. Christina found a job in a bakery, which was in walking distance from their new home. In August, they sent for Sophie, who had been living with Yiayia.

The summer months had gone by too quickly for Sophie, and thoughts about leaving throbbed in her head. Each day she took a long look at all she held dear: her Yiayia, theas, theos, cousins, her friends at school, Charlotte, neighbors. Even the unique aroma of the neighborhood filled her head—hundreds of ethnic kitchens, Pasquale's Pizza, East Side Hamburgers, the factories.

Theo Demetri and his wife, Georgia, threw a lamb feast in their backyard for Sophie before she left. Friends and family came to wish her well, to touch her before she went away. Johnny and Noops were there. Sophie's thoughts bordered on bewilderment. *How can I leave everyone I love? When I graduate from high school, I'll come right back. This is my home.*

Sophie spent most of her three-day train trip staring at the scenery through the large curved-glass Vista Dome windows on top of some of the train cars. She sat mesmerized. Her breath became vapor on the glass as she rested her forehead against the window. *How can I live with them after all that's happened? This all seems impossible and wrong. I'll never forgive Pa for what he put Niko through.*

Fraught with exhausting thoughts, Sophie eventually relaxed with the gentle swaying, click-clack of the metal wheels on the tracks, and comforting rumble of the train engines. The dark green, orange, and yellow Empire Builder snaked its way through land she had only heard of or read about. The train lumbered over the mighty Mississippi, through St. Paul and Minneapolis, and across the vast Dakota prairies. From her history books, Sophie remembered this had been land of the Cheyenne and Sioux nations.

Her eyes widened as she gazed upon the water-cut ravines, so jagged and deep, in Montana and northern Idaho. The rushing rivers looked like silvery ribbons woven between towering mountains. At twilight, the deep blue, wide-open sky became streaked with purples, reds, and oranges. The thick stands of trees threw long shadows.

Sophie had noticed the same middle-aged porter walking up and down the aisles checking on passengers. He was dressed in a smart, navy blue uniform, starched white shirt with a striped tie, and short-billed cap. His black shoes were shined to a mirror finish. He greeted the passengers with respectful cheer. This time, he was carrying a round tray of Coke in small bubble glasses, just like the kind at East Side Hamburgers. When he got to Sophie, he gave her a wide-mouthed, crinkled-eyed grin, tipped his cap, and said, "Hello, Miss."

Sophie smiled and said, "Hello."

"My name is Joseph and ah been seein' ya lookin' out the windows. What do ya think 'bout the view up here?" His white teeth gleamed.

Sophie smiled back. "Oh, I didn't know anything could be this beautiful."

"Law, ah never gets tired of the view myself. Why, you could say, it changes every single trip. I'm thinkin' ah have the luckiest job. Would ya like a pillow and a nice warm blanket?"

"I would, thank you."

That night, Sophie leaned the red velvet coach seat all the way back, rested her head on the pillow, and drew the gray woolen blanket up to her chin. She rubbed the silken edge of the blanket between her fingers. Two bright stars appeared in the darkening sky. Within a short time she found herself gaping at the profusion of brilliant stars, which pierced the velvety black of night. Her eyes drank in the sight. The Chicago cityscape, with its buildings and streetlights, dimmed the glittering beauty of the night sky.

In the dark, she gazed at her reflection in the train window and slowly traced the outline of her face with a finger. She wiped tears from her eyes but sensed she was connected to a larger world, one that Yiayia would want her to see.

After leaving Spokane, Washington, the train pulled its weight closer to Portland. Summer's sun had transformed fields into a golden rust color, and the intensely dark evergreen trees painted swathes of striking contrast.

The train snaked along a deep gorge, skirting the shores of the Columbia River. It crossed the river into Oregon on the Hayden Island Railroad Bridge.

Sophie's chest squeezed tight with apprehension as the train crawled into Portland's Union Station. She pulled a small hand mirror out from her purse and studied her reflection. Worried eyes and knitted brows stared back at her. She gripped her Athena necklace, looked up, and whispered, *Theos, please help me.*

Through the thick window, she saw her mother and father standing shoulder to shoulder on the platform, holding hands. They wore wide smiles and their finest clothes. Every limb in her body weakened, and a flood of dread consumed her. Her breath fogged the thick window and dimmed their images.

The clamor of passengers reaching for their luggage from overhead racks jarred her. She turned to the window and clamped her eyes shut to block out the frenzied rush. When most of the passengers had filed out, Sophie slowly rose out of her seat to gather her belongings. Her heart raced and her legs felt shaky as she walked down the aisle to the open train door. She resisted the urge for panic despite her growing fear. At the door, the warm outside air felt light and dry.

Joseph extended his white-gloved hand to Sophie. He helped her down the steep metal steps of the train and onto the step stool. Her hand trembled in his.

On the platform, he tipped his cap and gazed into her eyes. "Now, Miss, ah hopes ya have a real nice time in Oregon. I'm a-thinkin' you'll like it."

She smiled and said in a quavering voice, "Thank you, Joseph. I…I hope so."

Sophie stood awkwardly, clenching the handle of her suitcase. She dropped it and ran to her mother.

"Oh, Ma! I've missed you!" She buried her face in her mother's shoulder. Ma hugged Sophie tight, kissed her sun-browned cheeks and forehead, and then held her away with straight arms to study her face. A slight wind arose and Sophie felt her mother's fingers under her chin.

"My beautiful girl," said Ma. "You have courage to come here."

Sophie opened her mouth to say something derisive but thought better of it.

Pa clutched the brim of his fedora with one hand and reached to hug Sophie with his other arm. She stiffened to his awkward touch. He took a step back and tugged at his starched shirt collar. "Sophie, it's so good to see you," he said.

Unwilling to hold the sight of him, Sophie fixed her eyes on the charcoal-colored undercarriage of the train car.

32
Out of Sync

Courage is fear that said its prayers.
— Maya Angelou

Sophie grudgingly admired the small Cape Cod–style house on the quiet leafy street. She walked across the wood-slat porch and reluctantly stepped over the threshold. Her breath caught as the living room looked familiar. It seemed a betrayal that it was clean and cheery.

A strange, shy look came over her Ma. "We shipped most of our things from Chicago," she said. "Your bedroom is upstairs. Look around. We'll leave you alone."

Ma stayed in the kitchen, Pa—outside.

Sophie took slow steps through the house and peeked into rooms. Her parents' bedroom was downstairs. She put her hand on the doorknob and glanced inside. A peculiar feeling surged, as if spectators were in a gallery watching her. She turned and walked quietly down the hallway—past closets, a small den, and a bathroom. Eventually, she found the door to the garage and opened it a crack. The smell of greasy car engine—steel, flint, and tires assaulted her nose. Her stomach lurched. The meticulous details of the garage at home tore her heart wide open. Niko's tall stool, the lined-up tools on the walls, crowbars, hubcaps, spark plugs, small drawers, and car parts. She backed away and wiped her eyes with the hem of her shirt.

While climbing the stairs to the second story, Sophie looked down at her feet. The groaning, creaking treads sounded like the staircase up to Yiayia's apartment. She rubbed her hand back and forth on the smooth railing, and weariness came over her. Sophie took the last steps and crossed the hallway into her bedroom. Hardwood floors, patterns—the same braided rug, the same bedding from her old bedroom—furniture in the exact arrangement. A new hi-fi and a stack of forty-five records sat on a corner table. Crisp white curtains hung in a bright paned window. Sophie sat immobile on her bed for a long time, searching the palms of her hands.

She got up slowly, walked into her bathroom, and rested an elbow in the curve of her waist, staring at the claw-foot tub. It looked like the one at home. There was another bedroom down the hall with fresh curtains and a quilt that Yiayia had made on the bed. The room was simply furnished with a small wooden desk, lamp, and chair. Sophie lay facedown on Yiayia's patchwork quilt and breathed in. She turned her cheek and fell asleep.

Ma startled her awake when she called her down to dinner. Sophie got up slowly and crept down the stairs, steadying herself on the handrail. When she walked into the kitchen, Ma said, "I hope you like your bedroom."

Sophie stared dumbly. Anger welled up, and her first impulse was to shout in Ma's face. Instead, she said dully, "It's fine."

"The extra bedroom is for Yiayia when she comes to visit us," said Ma.

Late the next morning, Sophie willed herself to get out of bed. She dressed methodically and took slow, deliberate steps down the stairs. She found Ma in the kitchen. Pa had left for work. Ma turned and placed her hand on Sophie's arm. She searched Sophie's eyes.

"Oh, honey," she said. "I'm so happy you're finally here with us." Sophie shrugged and looked away. Her mother's breezy voice and movements were irritating. Sophie ached as if someone had kicked her in the stomach, but she was too tired to resist. Silence settled over her.

That first day, she watched her Ma do everyday things around the house and wondered how she could act so nonchalant. Sophie moved through the day feeling disconnected and anxious. The inside of the house transformed into a crazy palette of colors with no form. Her mind kept shifting back home.

As the days went by, Ma cooked Greek food with fervor, filling the house with delicious, familiar smells, but the rhythm of life, the landscape, even the air in Oregon felt completely odd and out of sync to Sophie. It seemed quiet; the busyness of Portland felt subdued compared to the bustle of Chicago.

When Pa rolled in the driveway from work in the late afternoons, Sophie would run upstairs or bury herself inside the oversized tire swing in the backyard. She'd hear him drop his briefcase down on the floor with a thump. The sound had a blunt permanence about it.

The tire swing hung by stout ropes wrapped around the thick limb of a big leaf maple tree. She had placed an oversized pillow in its hollow. Curled deep inside, she would read or write letters to her family in Chicago. Waves of homesickness, so strong, paralyzed her. She had lost everything—Niko, Papou, Yiayia, her family, and all sense of the familiar in Chicago. The gentle swinging motions helped as she choked on her tears.

The cheerful letters she wrote to Yiayia Sophia contradicted her sadness, but Yiayia read between the lines. She prayed for Sophie every night within the soft red glow of her prayer lamp. She crossed her arms over her chest, faced east, and gazed at the ornate silver cross on her bedroom wall. *Theos, I ask you, please help my girl.*

33
Like Another Planet

In the middle of difficulty lies opportunity.

— Albert Einstein

*C*hristina drove Sophie to the red brick building of Jefferson High School to sign her up for her senior year. To Sophie, it looked reminiscent of St. Francis de Sales on the East Side, as they both had sweeping front steps that fanned out to the sides.

A bank of windows surrounding the double front doors lit up the hallway when they walked in. They reached the office just beyond the entrance and filled out registration forms for Sophia Christina Elias. Sophie rolled the mouthful of her new last name over and over in her mind, feeling as if she were being forced to be a brand-new person, all because of Pa. Renewed anger welled up and clouded her vision. Thoughts of Niko tore through her like the hot blade of a knife, and whatever minimal grace she had extended to her Ma disappeared.

While they walked to their car, a bead of sweat trickled down Sophie's temple. She got into the passenger side and slammed her door so hard the car rocked on its springs. She shot a furious glance at her Ma and yelled, "How can you do this to me? You act like everything's okay. It's not! Now you make me have a new name! Niko's dead! You made me leave Yiayia and our family, and now we're pretending to have this wonderful life? It's your fault! I can't even stand being around Pa!"

Sophie saw her Ma's jaw tighten and her hands tremble on the steering wheel. Her Ma looked straight ahead and said, "I'm sorry, Sophie."

Sophie dug her heels into the floor mat. "Nothing you say will help!"

"Look at me, Sophie."

She turned away and glared out the side window.

"I felt the same way as you for so long. Anger ate me up. I don't blame you for feeling the way you do, but Pa *has* changed. Papou saw it and so do I. Can you try and give him a chance, give us a chance to be better parents?"

Sophie bristled. "Why should I?"

She had worn uniforms at St. Francis's. Her limited palette of school clothes consisted of plaid and plain pleated skirts, navy blue and dark gray jumpers, vests, and white blouses with rounded Peter Pan collars. Clothes were easy. There was no rich or poor.

Jefferson was a public school and there would be no uniforms. Sophie and Christina shopped for the kind of clothes they saw other Oregon teens wear.

The morning of her first day of school, Sophie spent an hour in the bathroom rearranging her thick, shiny hair and staring at her somber reflection in the mirror. The only makeup she put on was a natural pink lipstick. Sophie's rosy cheeks and her dark brows and lashes were enough.

Her sleeveless soft pink dropped-waist dress, with its white collar, little black buttons, and gray plaid skirt, was stylish. She gripped her Athena necklace, turned it over in her hand, and let it drop from her neck under the bodice of the dress. The gold felt cool. She stared into the mirror and recognized Niko's eyes within the shape of her own. She lowered her head, crossed herself, and thought of being strong for Yiayia, for herself, for Niko.

"Oh, honey, look at you!" said Ma. "You're so lovely. I know you, Sophie. Just watch how well you'll do."

"I'm scared, Ma," she said, gripping a three-ring binder to her chest.

"I know."

Sophie had never ridden a school bus before. She walked to the bus stop at the end of her tree-lined block and saw a tight cluster of preppy-looking kids from a distance. Her stomach turned queasy, and her first instinct was to bolt. She glanced down and studied the small tufts of grass and weeds sprouting from the sidewalk cracks. As she approached, a boy wearing a letterman's jacket, jeans with cuffs rolled up, white socks, and brown loafers eyed her up and down. He elbowed a guy standing next to him.

"Hey, look what we have here," he drawled. "What's your name, good-lookin'?"

Sophie's already thumping heart skipped a beat. He was tall and hand-some, with thick brown hair, intense blue eyes, and a beautiful smile. Sophie shyly looked down and fixed her gaze on a tarred crack in the street.

"What's your name, brown-eyes?" he repeated smoothly.

She slowly raised her head and said, "Sophie."

"Hey, Sophie," he said, flashing a sideways grin. "Sam Tucker's the name. If you need anything, just ask Sam."

"Uh, okay."

One of the white-lipsticked girls with a perfect blonde flip hairdo, stiff and sprayed, grabbed Sam's arm and said rudely, "Oh, honey, he's mine. Got it?"

"Who says?" said Sam sarcastically, looking down at the girl. "You don't own me, Shelli."

Sophie smiled uncomfortably and glanced away.

"Hey, girl, pay them no mind," whispered a colored girl who joined the cluster of kids and sized up the scene. The yellow bus slowed with its lights flashing and stopped next to the curb. "Come on, sit by me."

The doors of the bus flung open. The girls climbed up the steep, rub-ber-treaded steps and sat in the second seat.

"My name is Margaret Edwards. I've never seen ya before," said the girl, tugging at one of her bobby socks. "Are ya new? What's your name?"

Sophie grinned, "I'm Sophie E-Elias. I live just down the block."

"You sure do talk different, girl," said Margaret. "Where ya from?"

"Chicago."

"Sweet Jesus, girl, that's far from here, just like me," she whistled. "I moved from Alabama two years ago, so I know about bein' new. I think you're gonna like Jefferson, but I'll tell ya what. It's like being on another planet."

"Yeah, that's how I feel," said Sophie. "Oregon is pretty, though."

"It grows on ya," said Margaret. "I'll tell ya what, stay away from those preps. The girls are like a pack of cats. They eat their own, then they scratch your eyes out if you don't watch out. Just stick with me and I'll show ya around. I'll introduce ya to *my* friends."

She reminded Sophie of Charlotte, her good friend back home. Margaret was a stout girl with a brilliant smile and a sure, no-nonsense voice. Her velvet-looking skin was a rich cocoa color, except for her dark brown elbows and knees.

When the bus rolled up to the school curbside and let loose the whoosh of air brakes, Sophie asked Margaret, "Will you sit by me at chapel?"

Margaret raised her brows and whispered, "Public schools don't have chapels."

Sophie verged on tears as she bumped through the throng of students—not one familiar thing—faces that meant nothing to her, let alone shared her blood.

After a couple of months, Sophie's awkwardness slowly melted away as she met kids in her classes. She steered away from the preppy group and joined Margaret and her friends in the cafeteria. When she shared lunch and laughed with her new acquaintances at school, she pushed away her confused feelings to a place where she didn't argue with them in her head.

Shelli and her groupies snubbed Sophie. Her warm, dark looks and easy, friendly smile turned heads and caused a stir. Sophie walked the halls of the school unaware of her wholesome, yet striking appearance. That made her even more beguiling.

In November, Sophie's social studies teacher took a group of seniors on a field trip to some nearby colleges. Sophie had never been to a college campus before. The stately brick buildings and the grounds were beautiful; the students seemed energized and happy.

For weeks afterwards, all Sophie could think about was college.

Every Sunday afternoon, Christina and Sophie talked to Yiayia on the phone. One Sunday, when her parents were out of the room, she whispered low into the heavy black receiver, "What do you think about me going to college, Yiayia?"

"Oh, Sophie," Yiayia said with excitement. "This is good. Yes. You're a smart girl. You can do anything, I know."

"I'm going to talk with Ma and Pa and see if I can get in," she said. "I'll call you soon."

"Okay, honey. You can do it," Yiayia said.

Sophie held the receiver to her chest before hanging up. She talked to Tom and Christina over dinner that night.

Tom looked reflective and smiled. "That's a great idea, Sophie, but we need to look into it. Why don't you talk to an advisor at school?"

Sophie stared at her Pa.

⸺

"Sophie Elias, hmm, what kind of name is that?" asked the pinched-faced dean of girls. Mrs. Duncan's lofty chair made her look as if she were perched on some kind of throne behind her cluttered desk. Sophie felt small sitting on the wooden student chair.

"It's Greek," said Sophie.

"Hmmm, interesting."

Sophie thought the downward turn of her mouth, frizzled hair, and rouged cheeks made Mrs. Duncan look like the caricature of an unhappy clown. She tapped the sharp point of a yellow pencil impatiently on her desk.

"Your records show that you moved from Chicago this year. Inner city, I imagine," she said, peering over her black wing-tipped glasses with a rhinestone embedded on each corner. Sophie shifted in her chair. Her foot jiggled.

Mrs. Duncan cleared her throat, leaned forward on her pointy elbows, and said smoothly, "I've noticed you've been keeping company with some of the colored girls. Oh, yes, I know what goes on in my school. I would suggest that you think about your reputation, young lady." A chill shot through Sophie.

"What do you mean?" asked Sophie, disbelieving what she had just heard. She leaned forward and said, "They're *my* friends! I don't care what color they are!"

"Well, dear, if you can't figure out why, then never mind. My point is: even if you get accepted into a college, you won't make it with your average grades and financial situation."

Something popped inside Sophie's head. "How do you know about my financial situation?"

"That's easy," said Mrs. Duncan, hissing like a snake. "Your address."

Sophie scooted to the edge of her chair. "What kind of advisor are you to say something like that?"

Mrs. Duncan eyes became cold, demeaning. A maddening superiority oozed from her ugly face. "Honey, get this through your head. You're not college material. Just get a job, and remember what I said about who you choose as friends."

"But I want to try!" Sophie exclaimed defiantly. She stood up abruptly, fists balled at her sides. "I think I could be a teacher!"

Mrs. Duncan smirked and waved her hand dismissively.

Sophie snatched up her books, wheeled around, and stormed out of the office into the hallway. She wiped hot tears off her cheeks with the back of her hand.

"Nobody's going to tell me what I can't do and whom I should keep company with!" she said under her breath. "Who does she think she is? I'll *make* it work!"

That evening she found Tom in the garage, leaning under the hood of the car. She told him what happened with Mrs. Duncan. Her voice dripped with hurt sarcasm.

He folded his arms and looked at her mildly, amusement in his eyes. With a quick nod, he said, "Well now, Sophie, I believe this woman did you a favor."

"Why would you say that?" Sophie challenged.

"Because she made you mad." Sophie gave him a glimmer of a smile and walked off.

Mrs. Duncan's presumptions made Sophie more determined by the day. She studied hard, highlighted her books, and outlined notes from class. She met with teachers and compared notes with Margaret. They quizzed one another and proofread each other's papers. Margaret could add and subtract faster than lightning. She taught Sophie the magic of her strategies. Her reading lamp burned well into the night. Within a short amount of time, her test scores and grades improved. She researched entrance into different colleges and found out that she could get into a state university. She applied to Oregon State University and was accepted before school got out in June.

Yiayia Sophia, Theo Demetri, Cousin George, and Thea Stefania flew out for her high school graduation. Sophie's heart soared with happiness upon seeing her Yiayia. She looked the same but ambled along a little slower with a cane. "Just a stick to hold this old lady up!" she laughed. "My first grandchild—a high school graduate!" she boasted. "Sophie, I never made it past eighth grade. Look at my girl!"

Yiayia Sophia, Demetri, and Stefania were thoroughly enchanted with Christina's home and Oregon. Tom and Christina drove them to the coast and mountains. It surprised Sophie to feel her heart swell with pride while showing them the sights. Yiayia clutched Sophie's arm in the back seat of the car when they drove on curvy roads.

"*Poe, poe*, the mountains are so tall, *koukla*, and the roads wind all over the place! It's a little dizzy in the car."

"It's okay, Yiayia, I'll hold you," Sophie said with a smile. It seemed peculiar to comfort the person who had soothed her so many times.

Yiayia Sophia sensed a difference in her son-in-law. His face looked softer and his sullenness was gone. He didn't retreat from their company. Tom's hand was perpetually around a cold, sweaty bottle of Coke. Christina told her that he had given up drinking alcohol. He still liked his unfiltered Camel cigarettes. He smoked outside.

They all stayed up late every night talking, playing games, and laughing uncontrollably, mostly about funny family stories.

"Remember Thea Toula and Riverview?" asked Yiayia Sophia.

Sophie's family loved Riverview, one of Chicago's great amusement parks on the Northwest Side. The "Bobs" wild wooden rollercoaster, "Pair-O-Chutes" tower, "Shoot-the-Chute" water ride, "Tunnel of Love," "Wild Mouse," bearded lady, snake charmer, and Chinese finger traps all held a fear factor and appeal for her.

"Tell us, Sophie," said Theo Demetri. "You and Cousin Peter were with Thea Toula when she hung upside down on the Moon Saucers!" Sophie remembered the fearsome ride, especially at night. It was a dizzying display of multi-lighted, twirling egg-shaped cages that spun around within a revolving vertical Ferris wheel.

She had been just a gangly eleven-year-old in pedal pushers when her family, including her Ma, Niko, grandparents, cousins, theos, and theas, went to Riverview that sultry July day.

"Thea Toula, me, and Cousin Peter dared one another to get into the Moon Saucers. We could barely squeeze into the seat together. Thea sandwiched her big body between us. We each had our own leather belt and buckled ourselves in tight," Sophie explained. "We gripped the metal bar in front of us and hung on with slippery, sweaty hands. Thea's eyes looked like they'd pop right out of her head. The carney man leaned into the lever, and off we went spinning wildly in two speeds. Our sides ached from laughing and screaming so hard. The ride came to a stop when we were at the very top of the wheel, I suppose to let people on and off, but something happened to our cage. It got stuck upside down."

"This is the funny part," said Yiayia, clapping her hands together. "What happened next?"

Sophie pretended to be Thea Toula. "Mmph, mmph, help, I can't breathe!" she muffled with her hand over her mouth. "You know how Thea's bosoms are so gigantic? Well, they flipped over onto her face. She let go of the bar and dangled from the leather strap, kicking her legs while trying to push them away. She was smothering! I started laughing and then thought, 'Oh, my god, why am I laughing?'"

Tom's eyes glistened as his daughter thoroughly captivated him.

"Cousin Peter frantically tried to raise her breasts away from her face. He was mortified with embarrassment," Sophie said, covering her own blushing face with her hands. "Do you blame him? He was sixteen years old and Thea's godson! Well, I tried to help, but they were too big and we were upside down. It seemed forever before the wheel moved and the cage fixed itself, right side up. Thea Toula was white as a sheet and gasping for air. Cousin Peter was as red as a beet. Thea's pale yellow dress was smeared with her lipstick. When she caught her breath, we all started laughing hysterically and couldn't stop."

Tom joined in the laughter.

Yiayia Sophia, Demetri, George, and Stefania stayed for two weeks and took Sophie back with them for the summer so she could work at the store to save money for college. She had never flown on an airplane before. Sophie sat spellbound, staring out the window at the cerulean sky and patches of land below.

When they got off the plane in Chicago, Sophie searched the throng of people and saw Cousin Angie and Thea Anna waving crazily and jumping up and down. She laughed out loud and ran to them.

"Look at you guys!" she said. "You're all here! Oh, I've missed all of you so much."

"We've missed you, Sophie!" said Cousin Angie.

Sophie stretched her arms wide and they all hugged in a tight embrace. Yiayia Sophia, Demetri, and Stefania caught up.

Sophie looked at all of them and said, "I'm dying for an East Side cheeseburger. Can we go to the store right now?"

"That's just where we were planning to take you," said Cousin Angie with a sideways grin.

Family and kids from the neighborhood streamed through the door of the store to celebrate Sophie's return. The party lasted well into the night.

The kids in the neighborhood and her little cousins peppered Sophie with outlandish questions about Oregon.

"Do you see cowboys and Indians?"

"Do people drive cars?"

"How do ya get food?"

"Well, I saw cowboys riding bucking broncos in a rodeo, and I know Indians have powwows, but there are lots of cars just like here," she said with an amused smile. "They even have grocery stores and restaurants!" Sophie happily painted pictures of her new home with words.

When the crowd thinned out, Cousin George looked thoughtfully at Sophie. He tugged on his ear and said, "Ya know, Sophie, I think you're a little different."

"Like how?"

He walked his easy stride over to the cash register, turned, and smiled a toothy grin. "Well, cousin, I notice—maybe more glad of yourself or somethin'."

Sophie smiled.

34
Sparrow's Song

It's not what you look at that matters, it's what you see.

— Henry David Thoreau

The day Sophie came back to Oregon at the end of August, the sunflowers Christina had planted in the front of the house greeted her. They were like straight little trees with dozens of yellow-orange blossoms nestled in rough heart-shaped leaves. After setting down her luggage, she opened the screen door to the backyard and went outside. The air smelled fresh and the sun felt hot on her head. She walked over to a wild thatch of ever-bearing strawberries clustered by the lush vegetable garden. Sophie picked a large, shiny strawberry and studied the delicate tracery of tiny seeds. She brought the strawberry to her lips, smelled its sweetness, and plopped its juicy warmth into her mouth.

Sophie walked under the cool shade of her big leaf maple tree and climbed halfway up. She stopped, looping her long arms around a big branch. The outermost leaves of the tree took on a warm golden hue, giving a hint of fall to come. She crouched down, pushed her hair back from her face, and settled herself. A slight wind stirred the branches and she closed her eyes. There was singleness between the tree and Sophie. Resting and still, she heard a sparrow's song.

Ma and Pa liked their jobs and acted peaceful in one another's company. Pa still tinkered and had his world of inventions in the garage, but he was connected. Sophie's heart remained skeptical—guarded. She maintained a casual distance from him.

Pa fixed up their light-green Oldsmobile, reminiscent of Papou's. He polished it fender to fender until it gleamed. In mid-September, they packed the car and drove Sophie down a less-traveled road to the university. After moving in, she waved a tentative goodbye to her parents in front of her six-story dormitory. Sophie's roommate was from a tiny town by the Umpqua River in Oregon called Toketee Falls. Peggy had a slight backwoods drawl. They sized one another up—city and country girl—and eventually became tight friends.

Mrs. Duncan had been partially right. Sophie's grades were shaky after her first term. The muddiness of anxiety entered her heart as she realized her ways of studying were not refined enough for college classes. The idea of rising above plagued and enthused her at the same time. She dreaded changing her study habits. She invited it. Sophie dedicated herself to scribbling copious notes and color-coding them. She joined study groups and pored over passages in her books until she knew the material. Sophie confined her activities with one purpose in mind—to get better grades. Within a couple of months, she gained a cautious sense of confidence.

On a blustery winter day, while poring over her history notes on index cards, Sophie tripped over a raised crack on the sidewalk in front of the Women's Building on campus. She fell hard onto the sidewalk, and daggers of pain shot through both knees. "Oh no!" she groaned as her cards went flying out of her hands into the wind. She struggled to her feet and saw blood trickling down her shins.

"Here, let me help you," said a young man. She watched him run after the cards and then joined the chase. Like running to catch swirling leaves, the two of them rescued all of the cards. He placed them in Sophie's hands, gave her a shy, cockeyed grin, and held her gaze for a moment. "That was a nasty fall. Are you okay?"

Sophie studied him. His dark, wavy hair was parted on the side and fell over one eye. His boyish, dimpled cheeks were flushed. Under his jacket, Sophie noticed, he was wearing a crisp blue oxford shirt. She looked down and saw that he wore low-top black Converse tennis shoes.

"Well, I'm more embarrassed than hurt," she said, dabbing her leg with the hem of her skirt. "Thanks for helping me."

"No problem," he said. He looked down at her knees and rummaged deep into his jeans pocket. "Here you go—a clean handkerchief for your knees."

"Oh no, I couldn't."

"It's okay. Keep it." One side of his mouth turned up, and he shuffled his feet like he was ready to say something. "Ah...well, bye. Gotta run! I'm almost late to class." He started jogging down the sidewalk and turned back. "What's your name?"

"Sophie!"

"See ya around, Sophie! I'm George!" Sophie smiled at his name. A wind stirred and rustled the leafless branches of the trees. She smiled and whispered his name, *George*.

—

As Sophie's grades improved, she walked to classes with clipped sureness in her step. She was getting mostly As and some Bs. Campus in the spring was glorious. Daffodils and tulips dotted the planting beds with splashes of color. Swollen buds on the flowering cherry and magnolia trees finally burst open with a profusion of dazzling blossoms. Some rhododendrons were as tall as buildings. She stood under their broad canopies and gazed up through the branches to geometric spots of blue sky.

—

Sophie embraced learning and loved college. By her sophomore year, she enrolled in the School of Elementary Education. She continued to live in the dormitory with her friend and roommate Peggy.

Every summer Sophie took the train back to Chicago to stay with Yiayia and work at the store, but the summer before her senior year, she decided to stay in Oregon. She needed to gather information from school districts in hopes of finding a teaching job after graduation.

Sophie found a summer job at Rube's Deli, a block down the street from the bakery where Christina worked. They walked to work together in the mornings. Sophie chattered about college. Christina smiled in unaccustomed comfort, as her daughter's voice seemed soft and light to her ears.

35
Cool Your Jets

Good people know about both good and evil; bad people
do not know about either.

— C.S. Lewis

*O*ne warm day in July at the Deli, while Sophie was neatly smoothing mayonnaise on rye bread with a wide spreading knife, she heard, "Hey there, brown-eyes. How ya doing?"

The familiar voice caused Sophie to drop her knife.

"Whoa, I didn't mean to scare you!" said Sam.

She looked up and said, "Oh! You just startled me." Sophie's words came in a rush. "I was, uh, daydreaming."

Sam flashed his brilliant smile and leaned closer with his hand on the deli case. "I hear you go to Oregon State. How do ya like it down there?" he asked with a gleam in his eyes.

Sophie blushed and offered, "I like it a lot."

"How come I don't see you around in the summers?"

"I've been staying with relatives in Chicago and working. This is the first summer I've been home since high school." Sophie began to relax. "What have you been doing since high school?"

"I'm a car mechanic at my dad's garage down the street," offered Sam with a proud grin. "Ya know, Johnny's?"

"Yes, I know where it is," said Sophie.

"It's a great job."

"That's cool, Sam. Uh…I better get back to work," she said, picking up the knife. The air felt hotter and she noticed the smell of burnt coffee.

"Hey, would you like to check out a movie at the Paramount this Friday night?" he asked with a boyish grin. "I'll pick you up when you're off and we can grab a bite to eat first. How's that sound?"

Sophie looked up surprised and felt light-headed for an instant. She ran her hand down one arm thoughtfully, smiled, and said, "Okay. I get off at five."

"See you then, brown-eyes."

Sophie felt giddy. Sam was so handsome, and she hadn't left any room for dating in college. She was too busy studying.

Christina walked home with Sophie after work that day. Sophie hummed a little tune. "You seem happy today, honey."

"Uh, well, I guess. Ma, remember that Sam from high school?"

"The tall boy with brown hair?"

"Yeah, that's him. He lives in our neighborhood. Well, um, we're going out this Friday."

"Oh, that should be fun. Is he a nice boy?"

Sophie rolled her eyes and smiled, "Yeah, Ma."

Sophie brought a change of clothes to work on Friday. Sam strolled into the Deli to find his date dressed in a button-down flowered blouse tucked into a slim blue belted skirt. Her thick brown hair was swept to the side with a barrette.

Sam feasted his eyes on her graceful body. He leaned his hip into the counter, crossed his arms, and said in a smooth voice, "Hey, Sophie. You're lookin' good."

Sophie moistened her lips, gazed down shyly, and said, "Thank you."

Sam placed his arm around Sophie's waist, opened the door, and led her out to his black Pontiac GTO with chrome wheels. Large, fuzzy white dice hung from the rearview mirror, and red fringe encircled the back window. Sophie smiled, as his car reminded her of a carnival booth.

"So, how do ya like my car?" winked Sam.

"It's really cool."

Sam slid into the driver's seat and started the engine with a roar. He cranked the volume up on the radio's rock-and-roll station and peeled away from the curb. Sophie gripped the armrest with her right hand. Sam careened between cars on Sunset Highway and drove well over the speed limit towards downtown Portland.

Sophie ran tense fingers through her hair. "Hey, Sam, slow down. You're driving too fast."

"That's my game, girl. I like to live fast," Sam boasted. Sophie looked at him sideways with surprise. Her stomach churned.

He pulled into a slot at the drive-in of Jake's Hamburgers in downtown Portland. A roller-skating carhop, wearing a plunging black blouse and little apron over a short pink pleated skirt, leaned into the car window and asked, "Can I take your order?"

Sam stuck his elbow out the window and leered at her cleavage. "My date and I will have a couple cheeseburgers, fries, and Cherry Cokes." Sam cranked his window up for the food tray and turned to face Sophie. "So, what do you do for fun at college?"

"Well, lots of things."

"I bet the guys are hot on a pretty girl like you. Do ya date much?"

Sophie sat silent. Sam shifted in his seat. She finally said, "Um, not really." Sam whooped and slapped his leg. "You gotta be kidding!"

"I study a lot and my friends and I go to football, basketball games, you know, stuff like that."

"Do ya hang out with the niggers too?"

Sophie turned slowly to face him and said tersely, "That's an ugly word, Sam."

He lifted his chin with an airy, smug smile and said, "Well, girl, you need to know your place. I've seen you with 'em. We don't hang out with those kind."

"What do you mean by that?"

"Simple. They're black—we're white. That don't mix."

Sophie jerked her head around and locked eyes with him. His handsome face turned ugly. A thick sliver of dread rose in her chest. "No, *you* don't get it," she said. "I don't look at color. Frankly, judgmental people like you miss out and spread hatred and fear."

"Listen to you—another Martin Luther King."

"I don't care to talk about this with you."

Sam clenched his teeth and then looked at her with a fake smile. He slid his hand onto the back of her neck and stroked. "What's this?" She backed away. He pulled the necklace out from her blouse and yanked on it to draw her closer.

"Hey, what are you doing? Let go!"

He turned her medallion over in his hand and said, "What the hell! Who's this?"

She grabbed it out of his hand. "It's just something from my family."

"Yeah, but who is it?"

"If you have to know, it's the Greek goddess Athena, and an owl on the other side." Sophie took it out of his hand and turned to face him. "It's been handed down to me by the women in my family." She turned her head to the side abruptly, angry with herself for bothering to tell him.

"Hmm, Elias," he said. "Yeah, I get it. You're Greek." He gave a sudden laugh and said, "Hmm…interesting. Isn't Greece close to Africa?"

Sophie turned away in disgust. "I don't want to be here with you. Take me home."

Sam ignored her.

"So, Greek girl," he crooned, "are all the women in your family as sexy as you?"

She didn't answer. His voice sounded obnoxious, like broken glass grating over a large, rough rock. Their order came and Sam promptly wolfed down his burger; Sophie lost her appetite. She felt claustrophobic, suffocating even with the window open.

"Sam, I don't feel well," she said, touching her throat. "Take me home! Now!"

"Let's go to the movie. I'll bet you'll feel better once it starts."

"No!" she said forcefully. "It would be better if I went home."

The carhop took their tray away and Sam turned the key to the ignition. He gave Sophie a crooked smile and backed out of the parking spot. "Let me know how you feel after the movie," he said. "I'll take you home if you're still feeling bad."

Sophie tugged at her skirt. "I said—take me home."

"Look, I will after the movie. Let's go have some fun."

Sophie pressed her back against the seat. *Was I ever wrong about this guy. He's a total jerk.*

Sam drove downtown and pulled into a parking spot on Sixth Street. He got out, walked around the front of the car, and opened the passenger door for Sophie. He leaned in and took her hand. His rough hand felt hot and sticky to Sophie. They walked up Broadway to the Paramount Theater, with its lavish lighted marquee. Sam slid his money under the window at the ticket booth. He opened the heavy brass door of the theater. Sophie walked over the threshold and immediately looked up to the high domed ceiling and enormous, sparkling chandelier. They walked across the lobby and through heavy curtains into the darkened theater. Sophie slid into a plush red velvet seat near the back.

Without looking at Sam, Sophie said, "I need to use the restroom." She was out of her seat before Sam could respond.

Sophie walked out through the curtains, past the usher, and down the floral carpeted hallway into the bathroom. She placed her hands on the edge of one of the sinks, leaned forward, and looked into the mirror. She saw that her face had a glimmer of sweat. Just as she reached for a paper towel, a middle-aged woman came out of one of the stalls and cranked on the faucet at the sink next to Sophie's. She looked up at Sophie in the mirror and furrowed her brow. "Honey, you looked a little peaked. Are you okay?"

"Oh, I…I'm fine."

"You sure, now?"

"Yes, thank you."

"Okay. I hope you enjoy the movie. I love Clint Eastwood."

"Yeah, *The Good, the Bad, and the Ugly,*" she said mockingly. "I'll try."

Sophie went back into the darkened theater and stood at the top of the aisle until her eyes adjusted. The previews had just started. *I'm silly to be afraid of him.* She lifted her chin and found her seat next to Sam.

"You sure took a long time," Sam said.

"Well, I'm here now."

Half an hour into the movie, Sam leaned over the armrest and draped his arm heavily around Sophie. She squirmed away from him, but he drew her closer. Sophie felt his hot breath on her neck and froze as he rested his other hand on her bare knee. He stroked her leg. Sophie picked up his hand and flung it back into his lap.

"Come on, girl," crooned Sam. "Don't be such a prude."

Sophie glared at him in the dark. With a swift motion, his hand moved up between her warm thighs.

Sophie slapped his hand away and seethed, "Take your hand off me!"

Sam leaned over and nuzzled her neck with his wet lips. "Let's get out of here," he said hoarsely.

Sophie shoved him away with both hands and stood up abruptly. She marched up the aisle and heard Sam's footsteps right behind her. In the lobby, she turned to face him. "I'll find my own way home." She saw him shrink from her fiery gaze.

"Sophie, I…" She turned and walked through the lobby. He followed her around the corner and saw her rummaging in her purse. She took hurried steps towards the pay phone in an alcove.

Just as she was about to drop a coin in the slot, she felt a hand on the small of her back. Her heart gave a lurch.

"Who are you calling?" Sam asked in a menacing voice.

Sophie whipped around to face him. "None of your business!"

His voice softened. "Look, Sophie. I read you wrong. I'll just take you home."

She lifted her chin and stared directly into his eyes. "You know, Sam, I don't put up with this stuff. I'm not someone you can play with, like other girls."

He sucked in a slow breath, ran his hand through his hair, and said, "Okay, I get it. You're not at all the girl I thought you were."

"If you have other plans, I'll find a different way to get home. Got it?"

"What do you think I am?" Sam said, looking slightly wounded. "Let's go. I'll take you right home."

"You better swear, or I'm not going anywhere with you," she said.

He trailed a single index finger diagonally across his chest in an *X*. "I promise. Don't worry. I made a mistake about you."

She studied him carefully and saw a sincere, almost defeated look to his face, as if he were acquiescing with a little grace. There was a palpable silence between them.

"Well...okay."

They walked without speaking down the sidewalk to his car. Sam opened the car door for her. He got behind the wheel and started driving out of the city. After a couple of miles, he suddenly stepped on the gas and diverged onto a side street. Sophie looked at him incredulously. "What do you think you're doing?"

Sam didn't say a word. He took another turn and started driving up winding roads.

"What *are* you doing?" Sophie asked with anger in her voice. She glanced sideways at him and saw a grin on his face.

"Just going for a little drive," Sam said, reaching across the seat back to draw her closer. She scooted towards the car door and hung on to the armrest.

He took the curves fast, with one hand on the wheel. Sophie shouted, "You're a despicable liar!"

"Cool your jets, girl. I just want to show you the city lights and the stars from Council Crest. It's really amazing. I promise to take you home after."

"I'm not interested in the sights."

"God, Sophie. You gotta trust me. I swear I'll take you home."

Sophie sat fuming but decided to stay quiet.

As they wove on switchback roads to the top, Sam turned off the car lights and cruised slowly to the side of the road behind other parked cars.

"What do ya think of this, brown-eyes?" The stars spanned the sky and the city lights glittered.

"It is beautiful, but I've seen enough. Let's go."

"I will, when I'm ready," he said with smooth sarcasm.

Sophie sucked in her breath and bit her bottom lip. Her heart hammered.

Sam slowly slid towards Sophie and put his muscular arms around her shoulders, pressing his body close to hers. A ferocious anger erupted out of her. Sophie shouted in his face, "That's enough!"

"You're gonna learn your lesson who you hang around with."

Sam yanked her blouse up out of her skirt and reached around to unhook her bra. Sophie shoved him and slapped his face hard. "Get your dirty hands off me!" she screamed.

"Ooo, a feisty one! Usually the girls are beggin' me by now."

Sam pinned her arms down and grappled her breasts with his other hand. Sophie shrieked and kicked his shin hard.

A startling metallic crack against the driver's window immobilized Sam. Bright light flashed into the window. Several seconds passed. Sam jerked upright and froze.

"Open the door!" commanded a male voice.

Sam grasped the door handle of the car with his sweaty hand and slowly pulled upward. He cracked the door open to find a bulky policeman shining a large flashlight in his face. He squeezed his eyes tight against the blinding light. The officer flung the door open.

"Get out of the car!"

Sam reluctantly got out and stood by the side of his car.

"Oh, Officer," he panted with a nervous laugh. "We're just having a little fun."

The policeman flashed the light into the car. "Young lady, are you here of your own free will?"

"No!" Sophie cried. "He won't leave me alone! I want to go home now!"

"Well, hotshot, the lady wants you to drive her home," he said. "Where do you live?" he asked Sophie.

"Not far, Officer. Just off Sunset Highway."

"Good, I have nothing else going on. I'll follow you."

Sam reluctantly got back into the car and drove to Sophie's home with the white squad car following.

"You nigger-lovin' bitch," snarled Sam with a clenched fist. "Nobody says no to Sam Tucker. I don't get your game. You've been beggin' for it for years."

"Well, you're wrong. I never want to see you again! You disgust me!"

Sam pulled up to the front of Sophie's house. He turned to her and seethed, "I'm not finished with you." A new fear wrapped around Sophie's heart. Sam smirked at the frightened expression on her face.

She opened the passenger door and slammed it hard. The officer got out of his squad car and met Sophie on the sidewalk. As they watched Sam drive off, Sophie let out an exhausted sigh.

"Are you okay, young lady?"

Two tight lines appeared at the corners of her mouth. "I am now, but I'm afraid he won't leave me alone."

His eyebrows drew down into a scowl and his shook his head. He handed Sophie his card. "I've run a check on him. If Sam Tucker harasses you in any way, call this number. Ask for me, Officer Tim Dawson. And your name?"

"Sophie Elias."

He jotted her name down in his small notebook and stabbed the paper lightly with his pen. "Okay, Sophie."

The events of the night hung over her like choking smoke, but she lifted her chin and met his eyes. "Thank you for your help."

He politely touched the bill of his police hat and said, "Of course." He got into his car and rolled the window down. "Now, you take care, young lady."

"I will."

She walked halfway up the brick path to her house and turned to watch him drive off. Just then, she heard a crackling sound in the bushes. She spun in the direction of the sound. An animal-like growl came at her. It was Sam! Sophie leaped backwards and turned to run. He grabbed her arm in a viselike grip, spun her around, and jerked her towards the street.

"What are you doing?" she yelled. "You're hurting me!"

He slammed her backwards against the side of a parked car and viciously ripped at her blouse.

"Leave me alone!" screamed Sophie, grabbing her blouse. She clenched her other hand in a tight ball, reared back, and punched him across the cheek with all her strength. He laughed, grabbed the back of her neck, and clamped her mouth shut with his other hand. She bit down violently and stomped on his foot. The sickening taste of blood oozed into her mouth. He groaned and let go of her. She turned and ran.

"You dirty bitch!" he growled, tucking his wounded hand under his other arm. Sam leaped, caught her by the arm, swung her around, and threw her down onto the grass. She quickly got to her hands and knees, but he shoved her onto her back, straddled her, and slapped her face with his open palm. Sophie pummeled him with her fists and screamed. Her fighting fueled his rage. With a vicious sneer, Sam fumbled at Sophie's neck and ripped her necklace off. He laughed maniacally and tossed it into the street.

"No!" she screamed. "Stop!" He turned back and pinned her arms to the ground.

"Oh, God!" Sophie screamed. "Help me!"

36
A Soothing Voice

I can see the stars come through my room.
— Duke Ellington

Like vapor, Sam's weight left her. Sophie saw a fleeting vision of her father's face—craziness burning in his eyes. She heard a growling voice, a scuffle, what sounded like slaps, high-pitched shrieking, and moans. Sophie's vision blurred, her mind faded, and everything went mercifully dim.

After calling the police, Christina ran outside to see Sophie on the ground and Tom ravaging Sam with both fists. She barged into the fray and kicked Sam hard on the side of his leg just as Tom threw the final blow square into his face. Sam sputtered and groaned as he fell backwards. He hit the ground with a thud and lay unconscious.

Tom stepped back and looked over at Sophie on the ground, curled up on her side. He wiped his hands on the grass, peeled off his blood-spattered T-shirt, and threw it aside. Tom knelt down close to her. His breathing was labored. Christina staggered over and fell onto her hands and knees. She struggled to catch her breath and turned Sophie onto her back. "Sophie! My Sophie! Are you okay?"

Sophie felt a gentle hand on her forehead and a strong arm under her shoulders. "I'm here," said Tom. "Thank God. You're okay now."

Sophie's eyes fluttered open. She was aware of red lights flashing, a soothing voice. It was her father.

"Oh, Pa, I, thought…he…"

"No," he said. "He roughed you up, but everything's okay now. You fought him strong and hard, Sophie. I went crazy when I saw him hurting you. Don't you worry now. Ma and I are here. I stopped him."

In the half-light, Sophie gazed up at him. His face took on an expression of anguish. He lifted his eyes to the sky and Sophie heard him whisper, "I stopped him." His breath was fragmented and his chest heaved.

She looked over at her Ma and then saw Sam being handcuffed by two policemen. His face was barely discernible, covered in blood. She quickly averted her eyes, feeling sick and hot. Sophie started crying, muffled at first, and then sobs took hold of her. Christina shuddered and cried softly with her. Tom put his hands on each of them and then stroked Sophie's brow.

When Sophie could no longer cry, she exhaled a long breath and suddenly remembered something. She sat up. "Ma! My necklace! He threw it in the street!" Christina looked sideways, stood up, and ran to the curb. The streetlight cast sharp shadows on the street. It was hard to see, but there it rested, tucked against the curb, just a bit of Athena's helmet glinting in the light. She scooped it up, pressed it hard to her chest, and plodded back heavily. She sank to her knees. With a quavering voice, she said, "Here it is." She gazed down at the necklace. "The chain is broken," she said. "But it can be fixed."

"Oh, Pa," Sophie murmured, "Pa, thank you." Tom smiled and drew Sophie closer. She did not resist his gentle embrace and became dissolved into something beyond herself, something peaceful. He tenderly picked her up in his arms and carried her into the house.

Sam Tucker was hospitalized with a badly broken nose. It couldn't be aligned properly, and part of his lower right eye orbit needed to be permanently screwed into place. After a period of recovery, Sam's handsome face looked slightly askew.

Sam's father, Johnny Tucker, filed suit against Tom for assault and battery. He had his own connections with the underworld. He and his cohorts did some digging. Something didn't add up about this Tom. He seemed to have no history.

Johnny's accusation quickly lost momentum in court as the judge reasoned that Tom defended the life and sanctity of his daughter. Testimony from Officer Tim Dawson, who had followed Sam and Sophie home, vindicated Tom. The assault claim was thrown out. Sam received strict instructions from the court: if he ever harassed Sophie or any other girl again, he would go to prison. Sam was ordered to pay restitution for Sophie's emotional trauma and physical injuries. He was sentenced to six months in the City of Portland's jail. Tom thought he got off easy.

Johnny Tucker was enraged. He vowed to his son that he would get revenge.

The terrifying episode left Sophie traumatized, but as her bruises disappeared, she felt a strange lightness, like an unexpected awakening. She started to talk openly with Tom for the first time.

37
Busted

Fear is the mother of foresight.
~ Thomas Hardy

After work one late August afternoon, Tom walked onto the hot pavement of the parking lot and spotted a small white envelope on the dashboard of his car. He unlocked the car and slit the envelope open with his pocketknife. A paper was inscribed with blocky penciled words: *We know who you are.* He gripped the paper with both hands and closed his eyes. *Oh no!* On the outside of the driver's door he saw a slight indentation and scarring on the upper rubber gasket of the car window. A Slim Jim had been inserted to unlock the car. He walked around and didn't see any other evidence of tampering. He shoved the note into his pocket and drove to a phone booth to call the FBI.

Several mornings later, Tom backed the Olds down their driveway and headed off for work. The sky had lit up with a crackling thunderstorm the night before, and the hot morning sun brushed most of the clouds aside. The pavement steamed.

While exiting down a hill onto the freeway at forty-five miles per hour, he pushed the brake pedal down to ease into traffic. The pedal felt mushy. He depressed it again and it shot straight to the floor. Tom leaned forward with disbelief. The heavy car started gaining momentum. He pulled the emergency brake handle with his left hand. Nothing! He knew instantly the cable had been cut and the brake fluid drained.

Sweat gathered on Tom's furrowed brow. He slammed the horn steadily with his palm and, with frantic, jerky movements, wove in and out through traffic that seemed to be crawling. While manhandling the big steering wheel, he saw his chance. The freeway flattened out and there was a large, grassy expanse beyond loose gravel on the right side. He bit his lower lip. *I must concentrate! This is where I could lose control!*

Tom carefully turned the wheel into the gravel and the car instantly began to fishtail. *Don't panic.* He eased the car through the small flying rocks and felt the right-side tires cross into the mushy grass. The steering wheel jerked wildly in Tom's hands. He put every ounce of strength into fighting the two surfaces. If he lost control now, the car could flip. He held steady and the car began to slow. He could see a telephone pole directly in his path about fifty yards ahead. The car decelerated to about twenty-five miles per hour, but the pole was coming fast. He jerked the wheel to the right and the car careened down a steep embankment. It plowed down small saplings and bounced through thick underbrush. The car came to an abrupt stop after hitting a stout birch tree, and Tom's forehead smacked into the windshield. He fell back into his seat and breathed out a low groan.

Dazed, Tom realized he was holding the steering wheel in a viselike grip. He pulled his hands away and slowly stretched out his cramped fingers in front of his face. He reached up and felt sticky blood and a painful goose egg above his brow.

I know my brake lines have been cut. Who could have tried to kill me? Tom could think of two possibilities. Either the Mafia had caught up with him or Sam's car-savvy father, Johnny, had.

Tom couldn't push the door open, and the bench seat had become unbolted from the passenger side. He was trapped inside. Within minutes, he heard a soft tapping on the driver's window and a man's voice yelling, "Police! Are you okay?"

Tom couldn't see through the mud-smeared windows. He yelled, "I can't open the door!"

"Sit tight. I'll get a crowbar."

Within ten minutes Tom heard the man again. "Lift up on the handle and push if you can. I'll try to pry the door open." Tom caught a string of swear words, grunting, and sharp sounds of steel cracking under pressure. When the door was finally wrenched open, Tom gaped into the muddied face of a burly policeman. "Hey, buddy, you're damn lucky. That's a nasty bump on your head. Are you okay?"

"Yeah, I…I'm okay."

"What's your name?"

"Tom. Tom Elias."

"Okay, Tom. I'm Officer Jonah Ridley. Here, give me your hand." They linked hands and worked together to pull Tom out. "I saw you driving way over the speed limit and weaving between traffic." He leaned into Tom's face. "Been drinking?"

"No! Officer, someone cut my brake lines!"

Ridley put his hands on his hips and eyed Tom suspiciously. "What makes ya so sure?"

"I know cars like my right hand," Tom said in a sure voice. "I used to repair and rebuild them."

"Let's climb up to my squad car. I'll radio for a tow truck and we'll see about your theory."

The heavy Oldsmobile was pulled backwards out of the woods by the tow truck's metal cable and hook. When the car came to a rest on the side of the highway, the truck operator hoisted the front end high off the ground. All four tires were flat and sagged from the rims. Tom and Officer Ridley shined two bright flashlights under the chassis of the car. They saw a cleanly cut cable and gold-colored brake fluid dripping out of severed hoses.

38
Awakening

You are the breathless hush of evening.
— Ella Fitzgerald

1965

Lugging a box of pots and pans under one arm and pushing a blue Schwinn bike by its spring-cushioned seat with the other hand, Sophie awkwardly maneuvered her way towards the front of her new apartment building. Her cheeks flushed with excitement upon starting her senior year in college. Just as Sophie was about to reach the bike rack, the front wheel suddenly jerked sideways as it dropped off the edge of the sidewalk into soft dirt. At the same time, Sophie lost her balance and started falling forward. The box of pans fell sideways and clattered loudly to the cement. Suddenly she felt a strong hand grab her from behind. She started to stumble backwards but her momentum was stopped.

"Whoa, that was close!" said a male voice.

Sophie whipped around and faced a vaguely familiar, handsome face. "Oh, oh thank you," she sputtered. "You caught me from falling!" Sophie eyed him closely and touched her cheek thoughtfully. "Do I know you from somewhere?"

George gave her a bashful grin, looked down, and hooked his thumbs in the front pockets of his jeans. "You fell in front of the Women's Building a long time ago and we chased your notes. They were blowing around in the wind."

"Oh, now I remember! That was my freshman year!" said Sophie as she recognized the tall, slender young man. "You're George! Here I am, falling down in front of you again!"

"And your name is—Sophie." George uttered her name with a distinct air of reverence. He looked down quickly, mortified. Sophie smiled.

"George was my grandpa's name," she said. "That's how I remember."

"I'm named after my great-grandfather on my mom's side."

"Everyone in my family inherits a name from someone," said Sophie.

"Who are you named after?"

"My grandma, Yiayia Sophia. That side of my family is Greek."

"I sure love Greek food!" said George with a knowing smile. "I'm George Littlefox. My dad was Navajo Indian and my mom is Irish."

His bright blue eyes had a fresh sparkle and were framed by dark lashes and shiny black hair, sweeping sideways just above his brows. He was well muscled, with finely chiseled features and a healthy, tanned complexion. Sophie caught herself staring open-mouthed at George. Her face felt hot and she lowered her eyes.

"How embarrassing! You must think I'm the clumsiest person!"

"Oh no, we all have accidents," said George in a sympathetic voice. "I'm just glad I could help."

"I haven't seen you since my freshman year."

"I've been at the University of New Mexico to be closer to family in Santa Fe. My dad just passed away a few months ago."

"Oh, I'm sorry," said Sophie.

George looked to the side for a moment. "I'm glad I could be with him. He was a good man." He met Sophie's eyes and smiled. "I wanted to finish up my engineering degree here. It's a great school."

"We're both from somewhere else," said Sophie. "I'm from Chicago."

George's dimpled smile reminded her of Niko's. He picked up the bike and placed it in the rack with a dozen others. Sophie bent down at the waist and wriggled her fingers under the box to pick it up. George said, "Here, let me." His hands brushed hers upon the exchange. She smiled wistfully at the moment and glanced at George. Patches of yellow sunlight filtered through the trees onto his face.

Sophie opened the front door of the building for him and led him up the stairs to her apartment on the second floor. She turned to face George, and he carefully placed the box into her hands. She felt at once a deliberateness and subtle poise within his movements.

"Do you suppose…uh, may I see you again someday?" George asked shyly. "There's a great ice cream shop down the street, uh, that is, if you like ice cream."

"I do. I'm free this Saturday. Maybe after dinner."

"How about I pick you up at seven."

"That sounds good, and George…thanks for helping me again."

George gave a slight bow and said, "My pleasure." He turned and grinned from ear to ear. Sophie paused with her hand on the doorknob just to hear his footsteps retreat down the stairway.

She whirled into the apartment and exclaimed to her roommates, Peggy and Jenny, "I just ran into the same nice guy I met freshman year!"

Sophie savored the sweet details of those first months with George while she worked as a student teacher at Madison Elementary. She shared her observations about the kindergarten children in her class. George joined in her laughter when she told him about freckle-faced Connor, who explained how he smashed a squishy tomato with the toilet seat lid behind a locked bathroom door at his grandma's house, just to see what would happen. He said, "The tomato exploded, so I ate the seeds off my pants and tried to wipe the mess up with toilet paper, but I couldn't fool grandma. She didn't get mad but said I had a flip-flop time in the bathroom."

Then there was Annabelle, who shied away from people wearing buttons, and Hallie, who said, "Look, Miss Elias, my tongue is like a pink fairy princess sticking through my missing front tooth." Sophie knew within the first weeks that she had found her calling.

It was during those happy months that Sophie and her roommates started to receive phone calls at random times during the day and night. The first time it happened, Sophie was in her bedroom writing lesson plans in a spiral binder at her desk. The loud ring jarred her. She walked into the living room, picked up the heavy black receiver, and propped it between her chin and shoulder. "Hello." Silence. "Hello," she said again. She took the receiver into her hand and pressed it closer to her ear. Her skin prickled when she heard heavy breathing and her name whispered slowly—ominously. She slammed the phone down and closed her eyes. The vision of Sam's steely eyes came into her mind, and her breathing felt squashed.

After a couple more days of the same calls, she and her roommates decided to call campus police, unplug the phone from the wall jack, and keep the curtains shut. George spent more time studying at their apartment in the evenings. He put a deadbolt on the door, and the girls changed their phone number. The phone calls had left them wary—especially Sophie.

She had put the terrifying episode with Sam away in the recesses of her mind, but it all resurfaced. She told George every detail. The thought of her being hurt infuriated him. "Don't go outside alone, Sophie," George cautioned.

George and Sophie began to covet every moment together between the busyness of college and studying. They walked side by side, holding hands in the glorious fall days as the earth's colors softened to the spectrum of yellows, reds, and browns. In the cool of twilight, the fragrance of dried leaves mingled with the pine scent of fir trees. When the dry days gave way to the valley's steady rain in November, they'd walk through campus huddled under a big umbrella.

Sophie spilled her heart out to George. He listened with rapt attention when she told him about her Greek family, her father, the losses of Niko and Papou. She held nothing back. George cried with her. He held her, and never tired of listening to her lilting voice. Sophie's fervor for life moved him.

George caressed her name just by uttering it, and everything was made bright by her smile. He thought she was far above anything earthly. The delicate beauty of her movements, the soft, serene, truthful expression in her dark brown eyes—all touched his quiet heart.

One evening, in the shadows of a streetlight by a gnarly old tree on campus, George took Sophie's hands in his. There was a lump in his throat and a catch in his breath. His eyes shined with happy tears. "Sophie, you are the most wonderful person in the world. I know we are meant to be together." He leaned forward and kissed her softly. She returned his kiss and tender embrace. George whooped and did a clumsy cartwheel on the grass. His slide rule fell out of his back pocket. Sophie laughed and flopped down on the ground to hug him.

Sophie brought George home one weekend in late March. As an electrical engineering student, George instantly clicked with Tom. It was apparent to him that Tom had an innate understanding of anything mechanical or electrical. George sensed Tom's reticence to discuss his knowledge, but he asked questions anyway.

Sophie found her Pa in the garage before they said their goodbyes early Sunday morning. He looked up from his wooden workbench and gave her a warm smile.

"Pa, thank you for welcoming George. He really likes you and Ma."

"He seems to be a very nice, bright young man. Your Ma and I can see that he's crazy about you." He took a step close to her. "Sophie, I have something to give you." He reached inside his inner jacket pocket and took out what looked like a shiny silver coin. He took her hand and placed it in the middle of her palm.

"What's this, Pa?"

"Look at it closely, Sophie."

She saw a warrior on a reared-up horse holding a spear poised to slay a dragon. "It's Saint George," he said. "Papou gave it to me for protection when I was in Joliet. I want you to have it."

"From Papou?" Her eyes brimmed with tears. "Oh, Pa."

He curled her fingers around the medallion and held her hands in his. "Thank you for giving me a chance, Sophie. For letting me love you."

Her face softened with a smile. "Pa, are you afraid someone's after you?"

Dimness entered his eyes and the air half froze in his mouth. "I'm more concerned for you and your Ma."

Before they headed back to school early Sunday morning, Sophie and George decided to take a side trip to Multnomah Falls, in the Columbia Gorge.

There was a fresh consciousness that winter was over, and Sophie saw signs of spring across the emerald landscape as they drove on Interstate 80 North—the Columbia River on the left and the mountainous forest on the right. She rolled down the window of George's powder-blue VW Bug and let the fresh breeze blow in her face. The temperature hovered in the low seventies. She took off her cardigan sweater and straightened her black-and-white-checked blouse.

They talked about their visit. "Your Ma's very kind and she's a great cook, Sophie," said George.

She laughed. "I come from a long line of great cooks, George. I can't wait for you to meet Yiayia and the other Chicago family. Yiayia came to my high school graduation, and she's planning to come for college too. She's so proud."

"Your dad's radar research during World War Two was cutting-edge stuff back then. I kept questioning him, and finally he showed me schematics of the rotating radar units used in the fighter planes and explained how they worked. He knows more than he lets on."

"I never thought I would have any room in my heart for Pa, considering the mess he made of our lives, but…he's different." Sophie put her hands together and looked out the side window. She squinted in the sunshine and said, "I miss Niko every day."

George reached over and rested his hand on hers. "I'm sorry, Sophie. I do like your parents." He looked over to her. "They made you." They rode along in comfortable silence.

After they rounded a bend on the freeway, the waterfall loomed glorious before them—a silvery ribbon cascading from a great height. George pulled into a parking spot, and they walked through a tunnel under the freeway to the base of the falls. They hiked up to an old stone footbridge and leaned out against the stout fencing. The water from the falls misted cool against their faces. A lush profusion of ferns and mosses encircled the turbulent pool below.

"Sophie, look up," George said, after reading a sign about the falls. He whistled and said, "Wow—the sign says it's over six hundred feet high! It's beautiful!"

Sophie brushed George's hair from his eyes and smiled, "I knew you would love it. This is a perfect time to be here. It's usually packed in the summer." She grabbed his hand and started running across the bridge. "Let's hike up to the top!"

As they began to climb, Sophie looked into the woods. The deeper colors of conifers, intermingled with the rich limes and pale yellow-greens of the budding deciduous trees, painted a mosaic of lushness in the forest around them.

She breathed in the tangy air. "You don't see this on the East Side of Chicago."

George smiled and put his arm around her waist. "My town of Santa Fe, New Mexico, looks like another planet compared to this."

After twenty minutes of hiking up the steep switchback trail, they were winded. They slowed their pace and Sophie heard the sound of twigs crackling softly behind them. She looked over her shoulder to see if someone was off the trail. She shrugged and tucked a tendril of hair behind her ear. *Probably a deer.* "There's a bench ahead, George. Let's stop and catch our breath."

"Okay by me." He blinked his eyes in the dappled sunlight. They sat on the wooden bench and took in the sweeping view of the Gorge. Within seconds a strange sensation crawled up Sophie's spine. A wind blew and the tree branches started to seethe and clatter. She clasped George's hands stiffly as she felt something staring at her.

Sophie sprang to her feet and scanned the trail below them.

"Is there something wrong?" George asked. Sophie stepped down the path and shaded her eyes to have a closer look. She didn't answer.

Barely a shadow of a figure disappeared behind a boulder. Sophie couldn't make out if it was a man or woman. She waited until an older couple walked by the bench, grabbed George's hand, and said, "Something's giving me the creeps. Let's keep going."

"What's bothering you?"

She exhaled slowly. "Maybe I'm being paranoid, but it feels like we're being followed. I saw someone duck behind a boulder when I looked back."

George scanned the trail and brush behind them. "Mm, I don't see anything. Let's catch up to those folks."

"Okay."

With each passing minute, Sophie felt a deepening awareness that they were being followed. She held George's hand tighter. For a while they stayed right behind the other couple, who then stopped abruptly. The man turned to Sophie and George and rested his hands on the small of his back. "Whew! This trail is steep!"

"I'll say!" said Sophie. She looked back down the trail again. "How about we all catch our breath and walk up the final bit together?"

"Well…that's a nice idea, young lady," said the woman. "I'm Annie, and this is my husband, Jacob. We don't have hills like this in New York City!" They all laughed.

Sophie and George introduced themselves and everyone shook hands. After fifteen minutes of resting and visiting, Sophie said, "Is everyone ready to go? We're almost there! It's just a little ways ahead!" She looked around and pulled on George's hand. Within a few minutes they stood at the crest of the falls. The roar of cascading water filled their ears. Sophie gazed back over her shoulder, turned around, and leaned over the stout wooden fence to look down. The height and view took her breath away.

Sophie tugged on George's arm and said, "Okay. Let's go."

"But Sophie, we just got…" They heard branches snap and suddenly something crashed through the bushes behind them. Before they could turn around, someone grabbed Sophie around the shoulders and roughly jerked her backwards. She screamed, turned her head, and saw Sam Tucker wielding a knife.

"Sam!"

Sophie shouted and flailed her fists at whatever she could hit. George kicked him hard in the back and yanked him away. She fell to her hands and knees, staggered to her feet, turned, and looked into Sam's crazed face. She gasped and clutched her chest.

He breathed through his teeth like a prowling animal. His eyes were blazing. "You bitch! I told you I wasn't finished with you." George lunged forward but Sam jumped to the side and swiped her with his knife. She felt the hot blade graze her upper arm. She looked at him in horror, clutched her arm, and backed away towards the fence. Sam sneered.

George grabbed Sam's wrist and wrenched his arm backwards. Sam groaned in pain and fell to his knees. The knife hit the ground. He twisted free just as Sophie grabbed the knife and pitched it over the falls. George ran to Sophie and stood in front of her. He felt an inferno of rage inside. He wasn't about to let Sam get at her again.

Jacob yelled, "Hey!" as he lunged at Sam and yanked on his T-shirt. "What the hell are you doing?"

Without looking back, Sam elbowed Jacob in the stomach. Jacob reeled backwards, clutching his stomach, and Annie screamed. Sam crouched low, like a lion ready to kill. He charged George and Sophie with clenched fists. George threw his body forward with superhuman force. He punched Sam in the chest and tackled him to the ground. He flipped Sam onto his stomach and held him down with his knee. He grabbed Sam's wrists and pinned them behind him. George leaned his full weight into Sam's back. Sam breathed out a gush of air and struggled.

"You better lie still or I'll really hurt you."

Sam moaned. Jacob and Sophie rushed in and helped hold him down. He gave up fighting but let loose a string of obscenities. Jacob pushed Sam's face into the dirt and said, "Shut up."

Sophie dug her fists harder into his back and shouted in his ear, "You're finished, Sam." He growled like a wounded animal.

Annie knelt down by Sophie and pulled up her short sleeve to have a look at her arm. "You're okay. It's just a graze, and the bleeding has stopped." She looked at all of them and said, "Hold him. I have an idea." She shrugged off her small cotton knapsack and pulled out the shoulder cords. "Let's tie his wrists with these."

"Good idea," said George. He wound the stout cord around and around Sam's wrists, like a calf roper at a rodeo, and tied the ends tightly. Sam swore again.

Annie bent down to Sam's face and said, in a tough New York accent, "Okay, buddy. We're gonna shut that big mouth of yours, too." She dumped a couple of wrapped-up sandwiches out of the green knapsack, pulled on a seam, and tore the fabric into long strips.

George looked at the two of them in amazement. "Are you okay, Jacob?"

"Yeah, I'm good. Just got the wind knocked outta me for a minute."

They gagged Sam and all four of them jerked him to his feet. A strange spasm shook him. Sweat glistened on his forehead. Except for the dirt smears, his face looked colorless, defeated. The green cloth wedged in his mouth was wet with spit.

Sophie glared into his dull eyes and said, "I feel sorry for you, Sam."

He looked away.

George and Jacob gripped Sam's arms and led him down the long path to the lodge. Sam didn't fight. George looked over at Sophie. Her face was streaked with tears.

"He'll never touch you again."

The clouds had rolled in by the time they reached the lodge. The air felt thick and heavy to Sophie. The security guards rushed over to the scene of four people walking a bound man. They told the guards what happened at the top of the falls, and Sophie filled them in about Sam's prior attack and his time in jail. The guards led Sam into the lodge and called the police.

When they walked off, Sophie watched Sam's slumped image grow dim. She stood taller and took George's arm. "Are you going in too?"

"Yes."

 "I can't stand to be near him. I'll stay out here."

George reached to stroke her hair, her face. "Thank God you're okay." He searched her eyes and then held her in a tight embrace.

They walked over to Jacob and Annie, who were standing just a few yards away. George looked down at Jacob's socks, which were bunched around his ankles and hanging over his sneakers. Annie looked like a tired rag doll.

"I want to thank both of you for helping Sophie and me up there. You could've run off, but you didn't. We'll never forget what you did."

Annie's eyes glistened. "You would have done the same." She took Sophie's hand and said, "I'll stay with you."

"Can you help Sophie clean up that wound on her arm?" asked George.

"Of course."

"I forgot all about it," said Sophie.

George kissed Sophie's forehead and walked into the lodge with Jacob.

After cleaning Sophie's arm and drinking cool water from the outdoor fountain, the two women walked halfway up to the footbridge and sat down on a bench. Sophie's hands dangled limply between her legs. The falls thundered in her ears.

 Annie put her arm around Sophie's shoulders. "You're a strong girl and you have a fine young man." She chuckled, "And I have a fine old man."

Sophie looked into Annie's eyes and smiled.

39

The River

The skies are painted with unnumbered sparks.
They are all fire, and every one doth shine.

— Shakespeare, *Julius Caesar*

Sophie and Annie heard sirens over the roaring falls. They waited for twenty minutes and then walked down to the lodge. Sam's back was to them. His hands and ankles were shackled with chains. Two policemen escorted him away. A burly officer stood by George and Jacob with a notepad in his hands.

George reached for Sophie's hand. "Sophie, this is Officer Elliot. He wants to see your arm."

She pulled up her sleeve, stained with blood. "Well, that's lucky," Elliot said. "It's a superficial wound. I'm sorry for all your troubles with Sam Tucker, young lady. He's got quite the record."

By the look on the officer's face, Sophie got the distinct impression that Sam would be going away for a long time.

He handed Sophie a card. "I need all four of you to meet us at the Portland police station, this address. Shouldn't take long."

George said, "We'll be there."

"Anything we can do to put that sucker away," said Annie.

The interrogation continued at the police station. Annie and Jacob told the same story separately.

When the questioning was over, Sophie called home to tell her parents. Christina answered. Sophie hesitated and said, "Ma...first I need to tell you that George and I are okay, but..." Her voice tapered off.

"What, Sophie! Tell me!"

"Ma, something bad happened." Sophie heard her Ma gasp. "That horrible Sam came after us at the Falls, but George beat him up. The police have him now."

"Sophie, how terrible. Come home now!"

"Where's Pa?"

"He left for the store after you and George drove off. I don't know why he hasn't come home yet. I'm really worried. He's been gone about six hours and hasn't called." Sophie heard her Ma choke. "Sophie!" she yelled. "Let me talk to the police!" Christina's nagging anxiety turned into outright panic. "Let me talk to the police NOW!"

The police reported a messy accident scene on a long stretch of Front Street by the Willamette River, in downtown Portland. Drivers and pedestrians on the street witnessed a wild car chase. In broad daylight, they reported hearing the loud popping of what sounded like machine gun fire coming from a black Cadillac chasing a light-green Oldsmobile. Soon, both cars barreled side by side down the street at about sixty miles per hour. Five cars were run off the road. Bullets riddled the side of the Olds and blew out both tires. The car wove all over the road and crashed through a rusty guardrail. It careened down a steep embankment into the swiftly moving river.

Police didn't think anyone could have survived such an accident. They dragged the river, pulled up the car, and found it empty. Tom Elias owned the car that catapulted into the river. His body was never found.

The police and FBI closed the book on Tom. It was deemed impossible that anyone could have survived such a violent accident. Most likely, he was shot and died before his car even hit the water. If not, then surely he drowned in the fast-moving river, swollen and frigid with winter's runoff. But Sophie didn't give up hope that her Pa could still be alive. Christina wondered too.

All indications of Tom's murder pointed to Sam's father, but the police and FBI could not find a shred of evidence to implicate Johnny Tucker.

George and Sophie stayed with Christina for a week. Indescribable grief visited upon them once again, which George understood after the loss of his own father.

Demetri flew out to Oregon with Yiayia Sophia and left her with Christina. Before Sophie's graduation in May, they had a small memorial service for Tom at the Greek church. Afterwards, they threw flowers into the Willamette River.

Yiayia Sophia tossed stems of white stephanotis flowers in the river—one at a time. She turned to Christina. "He learned about love with the help of *Theos* and your Pa. You forgave." She looked back out at the river and saw the bright flowers moving happily along on the surface. She smiled and crossed herself. *Borei na megethynthei i psychi tou.* "May his soul be magnified."

Yiayia Sophia liked George instantly and confided to him, "I know why my Sophie fell in love with you. Because of the nice boy you are and your name is George. I think you smile like our Niko did."

George could understand where Sophie inherited her goodness. In spite of the family's tragedies, he felt like the luckiest man on earth.

He asked Yiayia Sophia and Christina for Sophie's hand in marriage on their graduation day. They were both proud to say yes.

Sophie landed a job teaching kindergarten at Madison Elementary, where she had been a student teacher. George found a job at a local engineering firm. They decided to save their money and get married the next June.

Christina decided to keep her home in Portland for a while but went back to Chicago with Yiayia Sophia to rest and heal. She returned the following April to help her daughter with the wedding. After the wedding she and George would decide about moving back to Chicago for good.

40
Constellations

Forget the former things; do not dwell on the past.
See, I am doing a new thing! Now it springs up; do you not
perceive it? I am making a way in the wilderness
and streams in the wasteland.

— Isaiah 43:18–21

1965

George and Sophie married on a glorious, sunny day at the Greek Orthodox Cathedral in Portland that June. Yiayia Sophia, Thea Toula, Demetri, Anna, Alexander, Johnny, Cousins George and Angie—plus twelve more family members—flew in from Chicago. As George and Sophie took their first steps as a joined couple around the altar, Yiayia Sophia, Christina, and Thea Toula tossed rose petals at their feet.

George's very soul lit up as he held his bride's hand and met her eyes. She was radiant with her swept-back dark hair, blushed-innocent face, elegant white gown, and long veil. Her Athena necklace hung on a delicate chain just below the hollow of her throat.

After the ceremony, George cupped Sophie's face and kissed her lovingly. The church erupted in cheers and applause. Cousin George tugged on his tie and whooped the loudest. Thea Toula beamed. She and Yiayia held hands and leaned into one another.

The reception was held at the Portland Rose Garden at Washington Park under white tents. Twinkling lights were strung throughout. The family had roasted a lamb on a spit in Christina's backyard and brought it to the feast. The tables were spread with mountains of Greek food, including Thea Toula's powdery *kourabiethes* cookies.

After the eating, the music and dancing began. Sophie and George held a handkerchief between them as she led the line dance, *Orea Pou Ine I Nifi Mas* (How Beautiful the Bride Is). Children scurried in between the dancers to pick up money thrown at the couple's feet by the Greek contingent. When the dance ended, they handed Sophie a basket brimming with bills. Sophie and George waved to the guests in appreciation. Soon forks and spoons tinkled against glasses for them to kiss. They happily obliged.

Thea Toula raised her glass and the crowd cheered, "*Opa!*"

George took the hands of his mother, Fiona, and his grandma, Mai, and brought them to the dance floor. They moved in the way of the Navajo to the slow Greek music. He beckoned for Sophie, Christina, Yiayia Sophia, and Thea Toula to join them. When they held hands in a circle, Yiayia studied George's kind face and said, "Look at us—a family. We have more to be grateful for than most." Thea Toula gave George a bear hug and tried to lift him off the floor. They all laughed. Thea was still a force to be reckoned with.

After dinner, Sophie saw the skies turn pink and orange on the horizon. George was engaged in conversation with Demetri. She closed her eyes, imagining Niko sitting on her other side. He would be a young man of eighteen in his tuxedo, bright eyes and mischievous smile, dark hair combed to the side—messed up a little. Just when tears started to come, she felt trembling hands on her shoulders. Sophie opened her eyes and watched a candle flame waver. Looking over her shoulder, she saw Ma. Her face was flushed and her eyelashes wet.

"Ma, is everything okay?"

Christina bent down and whispered in her ear, "Sophie, I...I found something on the gift table." Her voice was quiet—vaguely articulate. "It's a...a box, a beautiful gift box sitting in the middle of an open cardboard box. It wasn't right for me to open it, but I pulled it out and put it over on the far rock wall by the white roses."

"What is it, Ma?"

"Go see."

"Can't you tell me?"

"I want you to see for yourself. I'll stay here to make sure no one bothers you."

"Well…okay." Sophie leaned over to George and whispered his name. He turned and met her eyes. "Ma wants me to see something, and I'd like to look at the roses before the sun goes down."

George smiled. "Okay."

Sophie gathered the layers of her dress and ducked through the back of the tent. "Ma? Come with me."

"You go ahead." She pointed to a far-off wall and said, "It's over there."

As Sophie walked over, the scent of roses rode softly on the warm breeze. The profuse bushes lined up on either side of the cobbled path. Taking care not to let the thorns snag her dress, she walked to the stone wall and rested her hand on a lamppost. Mount Hood rose up sharply like a crown jewel in the distance. The setting sun glistened purples and pinks on the snowy volcanic peak. Lights just began to twinkle on across the city.

She saw a light-blue gift box on the wall by the white roses. White ribbon was neatly squared off under the lid and the bow looped together—a work of art. A small envelope was tucked under the ribbon. She pulled it out and walked over to the lamppost. "Sophie" was written in precise script—*her Pa's writing!* She carefully peeled the envelope open and pulled out a card. Holding it up to the light, she saw it *was* his writing! She grabbed the lamppost. *He's alive!*

> *Dear Sophie,*
>
> *I'm at peace saying the names of those I love over and over. You are the stars, the constellations. God is watching over you and so am I.*

She panted, feeling her heart might shatter when she finally saw what was inside. Slowly, she lifted the lid off. The box was packed with white tissue. It wasn't the kind of tissue that crinkles when touched, but something softer like pieces of cloth. She parted the pieces and saw a shiny-silver round object. Her breathing stopped as she reached inside to pull it out. It was heavier than she expected. The cloth-like tissue spilled out with the object. She cupped her other hand under its triangular base, brought it to the light, and heard the gentle ticking of a clock. The face of the clock was iridescent white and encased behind silver-edged glass. Its delicate silver hour and minute hands pointed to tiny metallic-blue dots where the numbers should be. She brought the clock close and saw that the clusters of dots were miniature constellations: Orion at twelve o'clock, the Big Dipper at one, Aries, Leo, Sagittarius, Lyra, Cassiopeia, Cygnus, Taurus, Delphinus, Corona Borealis, Centaurus. Sophie knew each one. Pa had taught her when she was small. Above twelve o'clock Orion, she saw a tiny window. Recessed inside, a circular disk had a golden sun turning imperceptibly on its way to the silvery moon. She turned the clock around and studied the winding mechanism and clock settings. She unclicked a small latch and opened the back casing on its hinge. Intricate clockwork parts—many delicate gears and springs, all moving in beautiful symphony. Her eyes blurred with sudden tears.

Sophie closed the back and leaned against the lamppost. She brought the clock to her breast and looked up at the first star of the night.

Epilogue

Before Sophie and George started their jobs in August, they went to Chicago for a few weeks. They stayed with Yiayia, and George met the rest of the family. He loved East Side Hamburgers, the colorful family, and the wonderful chaos. Yiayia kept saying, "You're a nice boy, George. You smile like our Niko. Maybe you and Sophie move back here."

George smiled, "Maybe we will someday."

On a Sunday after church, they took Yiayia to visit Niko and Papou's gravesite. Sophie drove slowly through the Jewish and Italian areas of the cemetery and parked on the side of a narrow road in the Greek section. Yiayia pushed her glasses to her forehead to wipe her eyes; they slipped down and dropped to her lap. Sophie sat very still for a second and then reached over to place the glasses into Yiayia's hands. She looked out over the Greek names on the headstones.

"Yiayia, didn't you tell me this is Papou's new neighborhood?"

"Yes, *koukla,*" she said wistfully. "These are all of Papou's friends."

George opened Yiayia's door. He took her hand to help her out. Sophie reached into the back seat to pick up a large basket filled with lunch and a bunch of fragrant stephanotis flowers. They were wrapped in green florist paper. Yiayia hung onto Sophie's other arm as they walked to the big Poulos headstone. Sophie set the basket down and pulled out a quilt. She and George lifted its four corners and set it down evenly. The pungent smell of fresh mowed grass filled their nostrils.

Sophie renewed the flowers at the foot of the headstone and took Yiayia's hands in hers to help her sit down. She kneeled down, lifted the lid of a brass *thimiato* censer, and struck a match to pebbly pieces of incense. They crackled—then glowed. The sacred scent of frankincense filled the air.

Just then, a diminutive sparrow flew down and perched on top of Papou's headstone.

"*Yasou*, my little feathered friend," murmured Yiayia. "How are you?"

The sparrow nodded its head and chirped. Sophie and George stared in amazement.

"You seem to know this bird, Yiayia!" said Sophie.

"*Nai, nai.* This is Papou's sparrow," she said casually. Sophie put her hand to her cheek and smiled.

She stood up and walked over to Niko's grave. Her throat caught as she traced her finger in the grooves of his carved name. *My Niko,* she whispered. That familiar, ragged sensation of sinking into a black abyss clouded her vision. She closed her eyes and the best pictures of him came into her mind. She saw him whooping in the backyard with Noops, his wavy dark hair glistening in the sun, and Teddy's fleas jumping out of his upturned palm on the rooftop.

Sophie turned to Yiayia and said, "Sometimes I just can't stand it. I want my brother back."

Yiayia Sophia looked into her granddaughter's eyes, rubbed her own cheek thoughtfully, and said, "I know, *koukla*. Me too. We all loved him." She patted the blanket. "Come. Come sit down."

The brown-and-tan sparrow flitted onto Niko's headstone and sang a lilting, sweet song.

Το Τέλος

The End

Greek Words

Phonetically Spelled

Adio – *Farewell*

Banyo – *Bathroom*

Bravo – *Bravo*

Catsa hamou – *Sit down*

Diavolos – *Devil*

Doxa ton Theo – *Thank God*

Efkharisto – *Thank you*

Ella tho – *Come, hurry up, Ella cato – Come down*

Filakto – *A symbolic protection for babies*

Kali neekta – *Good night*

Koukla – *Doll*

Kyrie Eleison – *God have mercy*

Mati – *Eye*

Na zisi! – *May he/she live!*

Nai – *Yes*   Oxi – *No*

Omorfos – *Beautiful*

Opa! – *Hooray!*

Paputsias – *Shoes*

Pascha – *Easter*

Pethaki mou – *My little child*, Angelaki mou – *My angel*

Pethia – *Children*, Pethie mou – *My child*, Pethia mou – *My children*

Poe, poe – *Oh my*

Poselene – *What is your name?*

Pulakee mou – *My bird*

Se agapo and Agape mou – *I love you,* Ton agapouso poli – *I love you very much*

Stamata – *Stop*

Stephana – *Wedding crowns*

Then milo Anglika – *I don't speak English*

Theos – *God*

Theotokos – *Jesus's Mother Mary*

Ti kanies – *How are you?* Kala – *Fine,* Me lena – *My name is,* Hero poli – *I'm pleased to meet you*

Xsenos – *Non-Greek person*

Yasou – *Hello, greeting*

FOOD:

Avgolemono Soup – *Made with eggs, rice, chicken, lemons*

Dolmathes – *Meatballs with rice, wrapped in grapes leaves*

Horta – *Cooked greens, often dandelion greens*

Kefaloterie, Mizithra – *Greek cheeses*

Keftethes – *Greek meatballs*

Kota reganata – *Chicken and potatoes baked with olive oil, lemons, oregano*

Kourabiethes – *Butter cookies covered with powdered sugar*

Pasta Flora – *Pastry fruit tart*

Study Guide Questions

1. How did Sophie feel as protector of her little brother, Niko? What was their opinion of the Greek family?

2. What drew Niko to his father? What did he hope to gain?

3. Explore the contrasting personalities and backgrounds of Christina and Tom. What were the joys and sorrows each had experienced? Did they deal with them differently?

4. How did the story of immigration affect you? Do you have ancestors with a similar story?

5. What was Tom's opinion of the Greek family? Reflect upon his reactions to meeting the family, his children's births, and how he assumed the role of fatherhood.

6. Discuss the female characters in *Stand a Little Out of My Sun*. Are there common threads between Sophie, Yiayia Sophia, Toula, Elena Ioannou, and Christina? Do you have a favorite character?

7. Were you surprised that Papou George reached out to Tom when it seemed impossible? Discuss the power of family, Yiayia Sophia's strength, and how she influenced her granddaughter, Sophie.

8. Do you think forgiveness is justified in this case? What situations have you experienced that show forgiveness when it seems undeserved?

9. What are your thoughts about Sophie's healthy relationships with different racial groups? How does the idea of cultural acceptance play out in this story?

10. What did you think about Sophie's perceptions of her Pa at the end of the novel? Discuss the symbolism of the constellation clock and the sparrow who showed up throughout the story.

Acknowledgments

I owe a debt of gratitude to many exceptional people for the completion of this book.

I am deeply thankful to the following: Author Margaret J. Anderson and poet Nancy Chesnutt Matsumoto for their steadfast support, insight, and expertise as this story evolved over the years. Sarah Cypher, of The Threepenny Editor, whose enormous wisdom and honesty helped me shape this story. Jane Bowyer Stewart, my brilliant copyeditor and first violinist with the National Symphony Orchestra in Washington, D.C., who studied my manuscript with a keen eye of discernment. Sharon Castlen, publishing consultant with Integrated Book Marketing, and Anita Jones, book designer with Another Jones Graphics, who have been instrumental in bringing this book to the public. Georgene Karountzos for her invaluable help with Greek pronunciation and the nuances of tradition. Antigone Polite for her guidance with correct phrasing and phonetic spelling in Greek. She made sure scenes did not stray too far from cultural reality. Pat Eshleman and Patti Kimberly, extraordinary women, who read my manuscript with perceptive hearts. Beth Bontrager, whose interest in my novel has been a lightning rod of encouragement.

To my inspirational Greek family, who know how to live and dance.

Heartfelt thanks to my writing group, whose unwavering support helped bring my novel along: Ange Crawford, Betty McCauley, Carolyn McAleer, Ellen Beier, Emily Dashiell, Gabrielle Snyder, Jane Thomas, Jean Copeland, Julie Mathison, Kim Conolly, Kimberly Gifford, Lill Ahrens, Linda Marie Zaerr, Linda Varsell Smith, Margaret J. Anderson, and Nancy Chesnutt Matsumoto.

The Willamette Writers of Oregon and the Society of Children's Book Writers and Illustrators (SCBWI) are to be acknowledged for their superb teaching and professional assistance in all areas of writing and illustration.

About the Author

Angelyn Christy Voss

Stand a Little Out of My Sun draws upon Angelyn's early upbringing on the East Side of Chicago within the folds of a colorful Greek American family. As a writer, teacher, and artist, she touches lives in many ways.

She received her bachelor's and master's degrees from Oregon State University and Western Oregon University, respectively. She has taught English language learners, Reading, and Kindergarten.

Angelyn belongs to Willamette Writers of Oregon, the Society of Children's Book Writers and Illustrators, and Human Dignity and Humiliation Studies—a global transdisciplinary network of educators, writers, artists, and others whose purpose is to promote mutual respect.

Angelyn has studied art at The School of the Art Institute of Chicago as well as continuing her art education at various universities and community colleges. She has attended art workshops in the Northwest and France. Her art has been juried into numerous exhibitions. She is a member of the Watercolor Society of Oregon, the Corvallis Art Guild, and Vistas and Vineyards. She knows the joy of any artistic pursuit is the realization that the adventure and learning never cease.

Stand a Little Out of My Sun has been inspired not only by Angelyn's background, but also by the many children who have touched her life. The happy voices of children resonate in her heart.

Angelyn lives with her husband, George, and her cat, Teddy, in the idyllic university town of Corvallis, Oregon. She has raised three children, has four grandchildren, and is a tap dancer!